CUT ON THE BIAS

Memoir of a Bastard Child of the Empire

Volume I

Susanna Bonaretti

First published by Busybird Publishing 2026

ISBN:
Paperback: 978-1-923501-57-7
Ebook: 978-1-923501-58-4

Cover image: Busybird Publishing

Cover design: Busybird Publishing

Layout and typesetting: Busybird Publishing

Busybird Publishing
2/118 Para Road
Montmorency, Victoria
Australia 3094
www.busybird.com.au

Disclaimer
This is a work of fiction. While certain historical figures are portrayed, their actions and the events surrounding them have been fictionalized for the purposes of this novel. Other names, characters, places, and incidents are products of the author's imagination or are used fictitiously. Any resemblance to actual persons, living or dead, or to actual events or locales is entirely coincidental.

To Robbie

Author's Note

When I began writing Cut on the Bias, it was conceived as a twelve-part mini-series for television. But the characters and their history took hold and the story bloomed into a three-volume memoir by the protagonist—a bastard child of the Empire.

The narrative grew out of my fascination with colonial Australia in the third quarter of the nineteenth century, a society reshaped by its burgeoning migrant population. From the barracks in Paddington to the Special Branch in London and the stately homes of Edwardian aristocracy, the story reaches across half a world and a quarter of a century.

The title refers to the tailor's practice of cutting cloth at an angle to the weave: on the bias. This technique allows a garment to stretch and conform to a body's shape but it also renders it more vulnerable to fraying at the edges. That tension—between structure and vulnerability—runs through the lives of my characters. Their stories are not neatly hemmed; they bear the jagged, fraying edges left by the consequences of their choices.

This is a work of fiction. I have drawn heavily on historical events and personages, and placed my characters within that world. They do not alter history, nor do they influence the future—they live inside it and experience the weight of duty, the pull of desire, and the demand for justice and retribution when Justice fails them.

This book is dedicated to readers who understand that history is a living presence and that fiction set within it can illuminate the human drama and conflicted mores of the time.

Thank you for joining me on this journey and for stepping into this world with me.

—Susanna

PREFACE

by Rebecca Victoria Davies

What follows in these pages is no mere tale—it is my reckoning. I have exposed the unflinching truth of my actions in all their brutality, unsoftened and unadorned. I have withheld nothing. I have excused nothing. I have detailed every minutia as I recalled it.

Yet memory is fickle and time an enemy.

Where I was not present, I have relied upon the voices of others—witnesses, confidants and police reports to which I have been privy. In the rarest of cases, where certainty failed to provide the fullest account, I have taken licence to imagine what might have transpired. These speculative incidents, penned in the third person, are not truths but possibilities—a bridge to carry my story forward.

This work is shaped by my experience. It is in part confession but I ask not for absolution, only that you consider the whole.

Judge me if you must—but know that I have judged myself.

Rebecca Victoria Davies,
June 1936,
Chestermere.

1

Tuesday, 29ᵗʰ August, 1905

A forest in England

Colonist.

One of the more generous names they called me.

Bastard. That, too, was true of me.

Every name I had been given did not change my nature. And it was my nature, not my naming, that brought me to this place. Here, fifteen thousand miles from home, in a forest, in the dead of night, waiting …

The late autumn breeze chilled the air. The moon was high in the sky, casting a ghostly light as it filtered through the canopy, which shifted with every breath of wind.

Wills was about to give the signal. My thoughts turned to the next few minutes. If this ended badly, a life would be forfeited.

I gripped my Webley in one hand and a bullseye lantern in the other. Wills and I were kitted out in our blacks from head to toe, only our eyes visible through the slots in our balaclavas. We hunched behind the briar, waiting.

Wills was the officer in charge.

It was not just Wills and me out here. He'd requested sixteen men, but he'd been given four. They lay at the ready—two on our right flank and two on our left. The night concealed them well.

I looked to Wills. His gaze was fixed on his pocket watch, counting down the seconds. He had returned his compass and map to the case slung across his chest. Even in the gloom I could sense his apprehension—an apprehension that didn't diminish his determination. He was as single-minded as I was—as we all were.

Handsome, moustachioed, just a little taller than I, a little stronger—and sometimes smarter. He and I had a strong bond, having shared almost half our lives since that incident in the Sindh nineteen years earlier. Wills, then Lieutenant Reginald Williams of the Queen's Own Corps of Guides, now Major Williams attached to the Special Branch of the Metropolitan Police, and me, a—

'Ready,' he whispered.

The wait was over.

'Go.'

We rose to our feet and stole through the undergrowth towards our objective, the glow from my lantern picking the way forward.

Onward.

Onward.

There was no sign of her—Laura. She should have been here.

There was no sign of the other four officers.

Wills threw me an uneasy glance.

We continued through the scrub, weaving among the trees and well beyond the coordinates we'd been given.

Nothing moved to our left or right. No one anywhere.

My senses were charged; every muscle, tensed.

Wills drew his revolver and scanned the depth of the forest as I skimmed my light along the undergrowth ahead.

I paused on what appeared to be a pile of leaves a short distance away.

We reached the mound of freshly disturbed detritus. I leaned down and brushed away some of the rotting vegetation and revealed a dirty cloth. I hesitated. It couldn't be—

Wills took the cloth and pulled it back.

'Laura—' I exhaled her name in despair. Her father had paid the ransom and we had failed. We were to secure the girl alive but the Honourable Laura Warburton lay dead before us.

Murdered.

We had allowed it to happen. Again.

I brushed the leaves from her young face. My eyes followed the length of her frame. Her clothes and stockings had been ripped from her body. Her bare thighs were bruised purple. She had been violated and killed.

She was cold but rigor mortis had not set in. Her end could have been prevented if only …

I was overwhelmed by the barbarous act.

Wills gripped my shoulder. I understood the warning: the law will apportion justice.

I shrugged his hand away. I had only contempt for the inadequacy of our laws. Hanging was much too easy for these degenerates. They deserved more. *I'll give them 'justice'*, I silently vowed. The same sort of justice I'd meted out so many times before.

Gunshots shattered the stillness.

'Goddammit!' Wills snapped. 'This way!'

We stumbled towards the reports and encountered the fray in a small clearing. I threw the lantern's light around and spotted two of our detachment, Yabsley and Dolby, crouched behind a fallen tree trunk. Flashes of light from the gun blasts betrayed the positions of the aggressors in a dense stand of trees a short distance ahead.

A shot whistled past my ear.

'Lantern!' Wills yelled.

'Damn!' I killed the light and we rushed to our allies and the cover of the dead tree.

Shots struck the trunk sending splinters of bark flying. The tree was large but its decaying wood offered very little in the way of protection.

Our men returned fire and rapidly reloaded but we were pinned down.

'Where the hell were you? Where the hell are Perkins and Scott?' Wills demanded from beside Yabsley.

'Where the fuck were you? And the others?' Yabsley yelled back as he reloaded his gun. He was more provocative than his partner, Dolby.

'How many are there?'

'I didn't stop to count.' Yabsley turned to shoot wildly into the trees ahead. His arrogance was well-known but this was no time for Wills to put him in his place.

'Must be two, maybe three,' I guessed from what I'd observed and heard.

'A shotgun and hand guns,' confirmed Wills.

Movement in the scrub to our right caught our attention.

A black-clad figure slunk in from the brush, followed by another.

'Hold fire,' Wills commanded. 'It's Perkins and Scott.' He called to them, 'Get back. Take cover!' They immediately withdrew to safety.

'We've got to outflank them.' Wills turned to me. 'Volunteer?'

I looked up and scanned the black sky. I turned to Wills. 'No shooting star.'

The corners of his eyes crinkled and I knew he understood what I meant. I moved behind Yabsley and Dolby in readiness for the command.

Wills called to the two on the right, 'Prepare to cover,' he called. Then to Dolby and Yabsley, 'Cover the left.'

He looked at me. I nodded. He looked at the two to his right. 'Fire!'

Five guns ripped the air—a deafening barrage of sound, smoke, light and hot lead.

The perpetrators returned only a few wild shots.

I broke through the sparse brush to the left.

Wills followed me, pushing through the scrub.

To our right, Perkins and Scott did the same, circling wide to catch the snipers in crossfire.

Yabsley and Dolby continued their now lessened barrage from behind the tree.

The offenders must have been aware of our advance—we could just make them out threading their way through the trees, perhaps 20 yards ahead.

We were gaining on them.

Perkins, ex-army and VC winner, broke into a run, charging the stand of trees, firing and shouting. 'Halt! Surrender in the name of the King!'

The fool!

Wills and I looked on in horror.

Well-aimed blasts from the thicket felled Perkins. His body convulsed. He moaned and his body stilled. Scott was at his side in an instant and he, too, was felled by a gunshot.

Gruff voices from the darkness hooted with delight. 'Come on, boys!' one taunted. 'Come and get us!' With a few parting shots, they withdrew further into the forest.

Wills signalled me to go ahead. He called to Yabsley and Dolby, 'With me! We need them alive!' and darted off to the left.

I pushed on as directed, unseen and unheard. I could just make out two figures as they dashed through the trees, firing backwards as they fled. 'Where's that bastard Dickie?' one yelled to the other.

'Forget 'im!' the other yelled back. 'Them three yokels! Do 'em!'

I swiftly flanked them and glimpsed the murderers scrambling through the undergrowth.

Ducking overhanging branches and weaving through the brambles after them, I caught up to them, unseen. I counted five but only two appeared to be armed.

I couldn't get a clear shot at the two wielding guns. They were several yards ahead of the other three who appeared by their gait to be two older men and a youth. The youth was clutching a small dog, squirming to free itself.

The older men were struggling to keep up with the youth when one stumbled and fell. The other stopped to haul him to his feet.

He saw me. 'Laurence! Coppers!' he yelled to the downed man, pulling his mate's arm. 'Timmy! Here!' he called back to the youth.

I stopped and took aim. He was mine. Before I could demand his surrender, a shotgun blast cut him down. His body slumped onto his fallen friend.

They were shooting their own!

'Leave 'em!' the second shooter snarled.

A short way off, Wills called, 'This way!' to Yabsley and Dolby, chasing the shooters deeper into the forest and away from me.

I approached the two men on the ground, my revolver trained on the living man.

'Francis!' he gasped as he struggled to get free of his dead friend. 'No! Francis!'

The youth watched, crushing his dog to his chest.

Finally freeing himself from under the dead body, the older man lurched to his feet. Seeing the youth, he called, 'Timmy!' and took a step towards him. The boy hunched over his little dog and swayed back and forth, a harsh sob wracking his body.

'Halt!' I commanded.

The man turned to me with a look in his eyes I could not read. Was it anger, horror or revenge? I only felt hatred and loathing. I levelled my revolver at his heart. 'Do it! Come at me, bastard!'

A split second was all it took for him to jerk one step closer and for me to fire one shot. He stopped in his tracks and slumped to the ground, dead.

'No!' The plaintive scream came from the youth. He crumpled to his knees, rocking back and forth, clinging to his dog. Even in the darkness, I could see his tears. I had no pity. There would be no mercy.

I advanced on the boy—he must have been sixteen or seventeen, the same age as Laura. He had to pay for what he did to her—what they did to her.

Images flashed through my mind. Horrible images of rape, murder and reckoning. Images of Mussulmen ... of bushrangers ... of pimps ... of Sarah ... my beautiful Sarah ...

Rage destroyed every shred of compassion in me: *This is justice.*

I was barely a yard away from the youth, my Webley pointed at his head. His eyes closed. He sobbed uncontrollably. The dog whimpered.

I pulled the balaclava from my head. 'Look at me,' I commanded. 'I want you to look at me!'

Hunched down and trembling with fear, his breath hitched with every word. 'Please ...' He stretched out his quivering arm towards me and opened his fist. In his hand was a golden filigree ring. 'Pretty ... Sorry ... The man said I could ... Sorry ...' he cried.

These were not the words of hardened criminal, nor even the words of a young man. These were the words of a child.

My resolve weakened for a moment—but only a moment. This boy was complicit in kidnap, rape and murder. I grabbed the ring out of his sweaty palm.

'Please,' he begged holding the dog away from him. 'Not Mikey ...'

'No, not Mikey. Only you.' My finger tightened against the trigger but as I fired my arm was jerked up. I was pushed away, falling backwards.

'I told you we needed them alive!' Wills' anger was palpable. He pulled off his balaclava, out of breath. 'They got away,' he spat. 'Goddammit! There was a cart waiting.' He turned to the boy. 'You. Get up.'

The boy cowered.

'I said, get up!' Wills pulled him up by his coat and grabbed the dog from his grip, dropping it to the ground.

The boy had soiled himself and wailed as his tear-soaked eyes darted between his two dead accomplices, blood oozing from their wounds. 'Pa ...'

'They're dead, boy, and if we didn't need you alive, you would be, too.' He grabbed the boy's wrists and roughly clamped on heavy iron manacles. The boy flinched. Wills was as unsympathetic as I was but I was driven by revenge. He was driven by justice.

Yabsley caught up with us and inspected the two dead men. He looked at me. 'You can't help yourself, can you, Davies? Fucking murderer.' As usual, any interaction between us was charged with contempt.

Detective Sergeant Yabsley's hatred for me was well-known, deep-rooted and based on his own ineffectiveness, not mine. And it had always been a great pleasure for me to point that out to him. We had come close to blows several times over the past eight years.

'That's enough, Yabsley,' Wills intervened and turned to me. 'I take it you had good reason to shoot them.'

'Same reason as always.'

The dog whimpered, cowering nearby. It didn't give any resistance when I cradled it in my arms.

We led the boy back to the clearing and found Dolby attending to the needs of the wounded Scott, but Perkins was beyond help. Scott's injury was not life threatening. I later discovered that the shot had torn deep through his calf muscle. He would have a limp for the rest of his days—a permanent reminder of that night. He was young, newly-graduated from Sandhurst and full of promise.

Wills took in the carnage and his grim expression conveyed his knowledge that, as leader of the mission, he was responsible for our failure. He leaned towards me. 'This isn't going to end well for us, Rebecca.'

2

Thursday, 31st August, 1905

Southwark, South London, England

The room was small and dark, lit only by randomly scattered candles. Heavy curtains obscured any light from the window and the only furniture was a bed, a washstand and basin. Numerous cushions were tossed about the room on a tattered Turkish rug that covered the old parquetry flooring.

Smoke from the hashish burning in the hookah filled every nook as well as our lungs as we drifted in and out of reality. *Was it day? Was it night? Who knew? Who cared?*

We had made 'love' for hours and I imagined I still had a few more hours left. Nevertheless, Sophie would tell me when time was up. Until then, we enjoyed each other's bodies.

Sophie was young, compliant, energetic and well experienced in meeting her client's fantasies. Mine were of domination and subservience and Sophie was very good at subservience. She had become used to my requirements and my scarred face and body no longer repulsed her. The scars on my body I could conceal with clothing but the twenty-year-old disfigurement that traced from my temple to my jaw, even now faded with time, meant that everyone I met turned away in revulsion or stared and winced at it. But not Sophie; she would even trace her finger along it.

Naked, we lay in each other's arms on the rug, propped up by the cushions, as we passed the hose and drew deeply. I would once again submit Sophie to my prurience before I had to leave.

Of course, I knew this was carnal desire, not love; I had not experienced real love since Sarah all those years ago. Time and distance could never quell the warmth of her smile, the tenderness of her hand upon my cheek and the softness of our first kiss. The only memento of her I still had was her silver locket, which I treasured and wore. I would never give it up.

I closed my eyes and touched my precious locket. My chest tightened as I relived the awful consequences of our actions.

Sophie's hand caressed my cheek. 'Shh, my love, it's all right.' She lightly kissed my cheek and mouth. She knew me well. She brought me back to the here and now.

After the brutality young Laura suffered, after the violent death of my colleague and the deserved deaths of those two cowards, I needed to feel a warm body next to mine even if I had to pay for the pleasure.

This was a habit now—this was how I coped with the violence that had become an everyday part of my miserable life.

I was in a welcome stupor when the door swung open.

'Miss Sophie,' apologised Wills, standing in the doorway, impeccably dressed in his three-piece suit, starched linen collar and silk tie, and topped by King Edward's new accoutrement, the Homberg hat. And I knew that his Webley would be secreted beneath his jacket—he would go nowhere without it. Nor would I venture out without mine.

'Get dressed,' he ordered me. 'Hawthorne demands our presence.'

While Sophie drew the rug over herself as though modesty were ingrained, I could scarcely move; my body was languid and my mind detached from reality.

'Now!' he roared.

***

London of 1905 was a bustling city of six million souls from every inhabited continent and every class, colour and belief. It was the largest and richest city in the world. It was undergoing unprecedented upheaval: women wanting to regain rights lost in the 1832 Reform Act, men wanting fairer wages, the Irish wanting home rule, everyone wanting shorter working hours and, on the continent, revolutionists again stirring up the poor and forgotten. These revolutionists, in particular, were causing problems to the government here with their socialist and communist ideals—ideals that were being touted to the working class as the great social leveller. Ideals that were being used now to justify the rape and murder of the upper classes.

The two-wheeled hansom cab jarred and juddered over the rough road to Whitehall and the New Scotland Yard building. I slouched, hunched and hungover, while Wills sat next to me, stiff and formal. I had pulled on the blacks of two nights ago, a quick wash barely removing the odour of lovemaking and stale hashish. My large Gladstone bag, replete with my Webley, holster, ammunition and other 'tools of trade', was cradled in my lap.

Wills' voice broke into the hubbub of the city. 'How much did that cost you?'

I could only smirk. Wills was now very married and it had been a long time since we had enjoyed the company of women like Sophie together.

'Why does the Home Office provide you with a flat if you don't use it?' he continued.

I remained mute but he persisted. 'You missed the debriefing. It was patently obvious we were given incorrect coordinates. Each of our three teams had a slightly different set. We were too spread out to be effective. Byrne said it was a typographical error.' Wills paused; his lips tightened. 'Hawthorne should have given me the sixteen men I asked for, not four. Then, maybe, we would have intercepted them before they killed the girl.' Wills assumed his usual thinking pose, head bowed, blank stare. 'Something doesn't smell right.'

I agreed. The Special Branch's Department of Special Operations comprised only the best that the Metropolitan Police, the army or the navy could offer. Wills was no fool, and as much as it pained me to admit, neither were the four others on this assignment. Yet we all got it so wrong.

Not possible. Something, or someone, was working against us.

'I had to defend some fairly serious allegations by Yabsley regarding your efficacy in the field,' Wills continued. 'He's convinced Hawthorne that you're the weak link in the chain and Hawthorne is not pleased.'

I snorted with contempt. Both Yabsley and Hawthorne saw me as an aberration, an irritation and a disgrace, and used any excuse to place blame on Wills through me. 'I don't give a rat's arse.'

He gave me a sideways glance and raised an eyebrow. 'You have a special, no, *unique* position with the Metropolitan Police, Davies. Because of me.'

While I was not officially involved with the Metropolitan Police's Special Branch or the Home Office, it was Wills' influence with his former army commander that secured me a position as Wills' 'Assisting Clerk'. This position was unique in every sense: not only was it a contrivance Wills devised to keep me with him at all times, but it was a permanent position warranted by the old Queen and given to me, an antipodean colonial woman—something unheard of in a time when an unmarried working female person of my age had the choice of only two occupations: servant or whore. After nineteen years together, Wills and I had developed a unique symbiosis that had proven successful time and time again. There was no question of my worth to those who mattered and Yabsley and Hawthorne did not matter; they were undoubted misogynists at best.

'You allow your hatred to rule your judgement,' Wills continued— his tone was calmer now that the passion evoked by the memory of the deadly affray had abated. 'That man you shot could have provided valuable information.'

'What of the boy?' I deflected.

'Practically useless. Cried like a babe. Hewitt and I interviewed him after the debriefing yesterday. The only thing we got out of him was that his dog's name was Mikey and the two dead men were his father and uncle and his name was Timmy Saddler.' He gave a derisive snort. 'He said they were playing a game. Undoubtedly an imbecile. I left him with Hewitt to clean him up and give him a meal. He should be in a better state today.' He paused. 'If you hadn't killed …'

I shot him a guilty sideways glance. Yes, I killed an unarmed man who *may* have attacked me, but the man was complicit in an atrocious act upon an innocent. The irony is that, had he lived, he would have been hanged. I was merely facilitating the inevitable.

'The other two got away,' I countered. It was unfair of me to say this to Wills but I needed to regain self-justification. 'And the first man was done in by a blast from a shotgun. Not by me. I trust *that* was in the report.'

There was nothing left to say. I closed my eyes.

'Have you eaten?' Wills asked.

I grinned.

'Food,' he clarified. 'Why do you do this to yourself?'

I knew what he was alluding to and where this conversation was heading but chose to avoid replying.

'The hashish, the whisky, the swizzling, the swiving. It's getting worse, Rebecca.'

I blocked the guilt I should have been feeling. It *was* getting worse. I was drinking more, smoking more and finding comfort in Sophie more often than ever before. I was tired and worn out. Tired of this life, of the lies and deceit, worn out by the constant need to prove myself to men. Maybe now was finally the time to say what I had been considering for a few years now. I took a hesitant breath then uttered, 'I want to leave, Wills.'

Wills fixed an incredulous gaze upon me. I had never before mentioned my desire to quit the service and, consequently, him. After a snigger he was able to muster, 'Well, that will certainly please Hawthorne and Yabsley.'

***

It didn't take long to reach the Victoria Embankment and Westminster Bridge on the Chelsea Reach of the Thames. New Scotland Yard was only fifteen years old and already inadequate for the ever-expanding Metropolitan Police Force. Buzzing with police, government employees, bureaucrats, agents and lackeys, there were plenty of conspiracies and intrigue to keep us all on our feet and alert. The priority of the small force within the Special Branch was the safety and security of the aristocracy, especially now that it was becoming evident that an organised criminal group had carried out two previous abductions and murders, and now Laura's, but for what purpose, we still did not know. Perhaps young Tim could give us vital clues, even if he was mentally deficient.

As we strode through to our destination, up several flights of stairs, various sundry employees greeted Wills and me coolly. Some in the upper echelons held Wills in high regard, but his association with me caused him to be resented and shunned in lesser circles and especially when I was in his company. He seemed to relish stirring the pot of loathing as much as I did. I admired him for that.

We came to an abrupt halt at a closed door that proclaimed '137 – Colonel Sir Giles Hawthorne, Chief Administrator Special Branch DSO'.

The Chief Administrator was respectfully known as Sir Giles but Wills and I called him Hawthorne, and a thorny whore's son he was, too.

Wills took a deep breath, looked at me with a mixture of admonishment and apprehension and swung the door open. We pushed in, jolting Hawthorne's secretary, Fawkner, as he sat at his desk.

'Major Williams and Assisting Clerk Davies for Sir Giles,' Wills announced.

Poor young Edward Fawkner didn't know where to look—his bespectacled eyes darted between the dapper Wills and me, a dishevelled middle-aged woman in black trousers, turtleneck sweater and jacket, intruding upon his tiny domain. 'Er … yes, Major Williams, Sir Giles is expecting you.' He rose from his seat and indicated the sofa. 'Please take a seat, Major and … er … Madam, Sir Giles will be with you momentarily.'

Fawkner could not help furtively glancing at me several more times as he attempted to sit. Not only was I dressed in men's clothing, but my short, white, unkempt hair and the long, ugly scar to my left cheek made his arse almost miss its target. Of course, I revelled in this effect; my features belied any thought of compassion or weakness to my advantage.

The musical ding from the telephone on Fawkner's desk indicated that Sir Giles had completed his telephone call. This was followed by the colonel's harsh, 'Fawkner!' barked through the speaking tube on the wall.

Fawkner jumped to attention, took up the tube and replied into it, 'Yes, Sir Giles.'

'Luncheon meeting with Colonel Humphries at my club. 2 pm,' snapped Sir Giles.

'Today, Sir Giles?'

'Of course today, you fool!'

'Yes, Sir. Ah … Major Williams and Assisting Clerk Davies are here to see you, Sir. Shall I show them in?'

'Just the major.'

'Sir.'

Wills gave me a look that told me he didn't want to do this.

I offered silent commiseration but inwardly I was pleased not to have to confront this pumped-up inconsequence of a man.

'Major Williams, Sir,' Fawkner interrupted as he opened the door to Sir Giles' office. Wills removed his treasured Homberg and entered our so-called superior's inner sanctum.

During the eight years I had been with Wills at the Metropolitan Police, I had never seen the inside of the Chief Administrator's office—not that I had ever wanted to—but the décor of his outer office now intrigued me.

As Fawkner returned to his desk, he kept glancing at me. I stood and examined the numerous framed photographs placed systematically on one wall. They were mostly of exotic wild animals—some alive but more of dead trophies, which appalled me even though I had killed enough of the human animal.

One photograph caught my attention. Positioned in the middle of the arrangement, a large picture showed a group of khaki-uniformed soldiers seated in and standing around campaign chairs. Prominent in the centre chair was the ranking officer, a major. I read the title beneath: '*After the siege of Ladysmith, March 1900*', after which was written the names of the subjects: '*Tr A Brown, Tr J Smith, Cpr T Johnson, Sgt V Goodall, Sgt D Brown, Tr J Middlemass, Tr F Smith, Mjr G Hawthorne, Lt S Trimble, Lc Cpr W Bell, Cpt G Smith*'.

I pointed to the central figure and turned to Fawkner. 'Major Hawthorne. Sir Giles. He was at Ladysmith?'

Fawkner seemed flustered. 'I … I …'

'How long have you been Hawthorne's secretary?'

'Um, two months … Miss … Madam …'

'Do you know anything about these conflicts with the Boers in South Africa?'

Fawkner's brain failed him.

I tapped on the picture and opted for comedic relief. 'A lot of Smiths there.' Something in that photograph struck me as odd. Ladysmith was not something to be proud of. Certainly not something to put up with one's other trophies.

The indiscernible background babble between Wills and Sir Giles exploded with a tirade from Hawthorne. 'I don't give a damn, Williams! This is a foul up of the highest order!'

I could barely hear Wills' calm and steady reply. Whatever he said had no effect. 'I read the reports! That was your last chance, Major! I want that … that invert off this case, out of my department and out of my hair! Do you hear me?'

Further murmurings from Wills only garnered, 'I don't care what royal citations she has! She's a savage just like all damned colonists!'

It was hardly a second before the door flew open and Wills, flushed with anger, strode through and thrust his Homberg on his head. 'Come!' he commanded me.

'Doesn't he want to commend me personally?' I quipped as I collected my bag.

'Shut up.'

I could barely keep up with him as we raced down the corridor. 'What did old thorny whoreson want?'

'Apart from seeing you burn in hell? He wants the boy interviewed again. Now. He wants to know every word that boy heard and every word he utters. And by whatever way I can get it out of him.'

'And what about the savage colonist invert he wants out of his hair?'

'He has no authority over you. And he can go to hell.'

'I hear it's full of roasting inverts and tribades.' Wills' chuckle lightened his mood.

'You said Timmy's a simpleton?' I queried as we entered another corridor. 'How are you going to get any more out of him?'

Wills' frown deepened.

I had an idea. 'Where's his dog?'

'It's … ah … in my office.' The dawning realisation brought a flicker of amusement to his face.

We quickly diverted to Wills' compact office. I noticed Wills had made it quite comfortable for his canine guest: an old cup with fresh water, a sheet of waxed paper that obviously had had food on it and an old piece of sacking on which the dog was now curled asleep.

Wills picked up the dog and abstractedly stroked its tangled white fur. The dog responded by timidly wagging it tail. 'I'm keeping the evidence safe,' he sheepishly confessed.

'Marshmallow.' Wills was fighter of unwavering courage, strength and dedication but in moments like these, he was just like the confection: soft and sweet.

We once again headed for the lockup down several flights of stairs, to the underground holding cells and interview rooms. This was a part of New Scotland Yard about which the general public knew nothing. Here political terrorists, antiroyalists and revolutionists were kept for interrogation until they were charged or released.

***

Wills and I entered the area, the whitewashed stone walls creating a glare under the dazzle of the electric lights.

A police guard unlocked the outer gate and we proceeded to a locked door—one of six along the dead-end passage. Timmy's precious Mikey was nestled in Wills' arms but began writhing with excitement as we neared the cell.

Wills opened the observation panel and gasped. I peered in to see young Tim, sitting in almost complete darkness with one wrist shackled to his chair. He had been brutally beaten; his face was bruised and bloodied. He had been given a clean pair of trousers but his shirt and jacket were the same dirty ones he'd been wearing two days ago, except now they too were splattered with what looked like blood and spittle. I was appalled. 'And Hawthorne called me a savage. You didn't do this?'

'No. He was upset but otherwise fine when I left him with Hewitt.'

It was either Yabsley, Dolby or another of the four officers in the DSO who tortured the boy. They were the only others assigned to this case apart from Hawthorne, and Thorny wouldn't dirty his hands for anything other than to partake of a fat lobster.

At the sound of Wills unbolting the door, Tim roused from his stupor and immediately began to weep. 'No. Please … no …' But as soon as he saw his little dog struggling in Wills' arms, he broke down. 'Mikey! They didn't hurt you!' He reached out to the dog with his unrestrained arm. 'Mikey … Mikey …'

It was a pathetic sight and brought a lump to my throat. Wills had trouble holding on to Mikey until, defeated, he placed the dog in Tim's lap. The unrestrained affection between the two made me turn away. Images of my own dog from thirty years ago brought back painful memories.

'Timmy,' Wills soothed. 'Timmy, listen to me.'

Timmy looked up at Wills through his blackened and swollen eyes, a sickly smile forcing itself through the dried blood on his face.

'Timmy, who hit you? Who did this to you?'

'Don't know …' Timmy's eyes welled. 'Are you going to hurt me, too?'

'No. We just want to talk to you. Do you want something to eat?'

'No. Mikey …'

'He's eaten. Timmy, do you know why you're here?'

He nodded. 'Aye. I stole that pretty lady's ring. The man said I could.'

'Ring?' Wills looked at me.

I fished the filigree ring from my inner pocket.

Wills admonished me with a disdainful glance, obviously not pleased with me withholding evidence. 'Lady Warburton said Laura had a ring.' He turned to Timmy. '*Who* said you could keep this?'

'The big man. Uncle Francis said I had to do what he said.'

'Do you know his name? The big man?'

Timmy's lips twitched into a fleeting, painful smile. 'Croft. My pa called him Crafty Croft.'

'So, there was you, your pa, your uncle Francis, Crafty Croft and who else was there with you, Timmy?'

'Don't know who the ugly man was but he was mean to Mikey and me. Wasn't he, boy? He was mean, wasn't he? Pa said that everything would be all right once we done the job and got the money. That the two men would go away and leave me and Mikey alone. We would be all right after we got the money.'

'Did you get the money?'

'They said Pa and Uncle Francis would get some when we went to the woods.' Tim's face screwed up. He slumped in his chair and lowered his head, drawing in Mikey and nuzzling the matted fur. 'They hurt her,' he sobbed. 'She screamed and screamed and screamed. They wouldn't stop hurting her.' He stopped and began crying. 'Then she stopped screaming.'

Wills and I stood there dumbfounded. We relived the horror along with Timmy.

'What happened then?' Wills quietly urged.

Timmy panted. 'The big man took the ring off the girl and gave it to me as a mento, he said. I didn't want it but Uncle Francis said to take it.'

'Where did all this take place, Timmy?'

'There.'

'So, the girl, Laura, was alive when you went to the woods?'

'Aye, but she didn't want to go. She was scared. I tried to tell her it was just a joke we were playing on her ma and pa.'

'Is that what the big man, Crafty Croft, told you and your pa and uncle—that is was all a big joke?'

'Aye.'

Wills looked at me. Was he as perplexed by this as I was? Why did Crafty Croft involve these three? And supply Timmy with incriminating evidence? We needed to push on. I took up the questioning. 'Timmy, do you remember me?'

Timmy looked at me and shrank back into his chair. 'Aye,' he gasped.

'I'm not going to hurt you, but you've got to answer me true. We want to find Crafty Croft and his mean ugly friend so they can pay for what they did to that poor girl. And for being mean to you and Mikey. Do you want to help us do that, Timmy?'

'Aye.'

'Do you remember anything they said about hurting anyone else? Being mean to another girl?'

'No.'

'Are you sure?' My words came out more forcefully than intended.

Timmy drew back further.

'I'm sorry. I didn't mean to shout. They've already hurt two other girls like Laura. Are you sure they didn't say which ma and pa they were going to play a joke on next? You want us to catch them, don't you? You can stop them if you tell us what they said.'

'I don't know. They said something but I don't know.'

'What did they say? Tell us what you remember.'

Timmy was hesitant, struggling to recall the right words. He clenched the dog tightly to his chest causing the little terrier to squirm. 'Dutch … Abbot … Lady Abbot … Mean man laughed and said she was a grandma.' Tim sagged. He rocked back and forth and hugged his dog. 'I don't know. I don't know! I'm sorry! I want my pa. Pa …'

'Timmy. Timmy …'

Wills eased me away. 'I'll arrange for someone to take him to hospital today.' He indicated that we should leave. We weren't going to get any more from Timmy.

As we wandered back through the corridors, I proffered, 'These two, Crafty Croft and Mean Man, are too base to be the masterminds of the abductions and ransom demands.'

'I agree. They are puppets, but they are not new to abduction and murder—that is certain. We need to find out from Timmy if they mentioned other names.'

The night in the forest ran through my mind. 'I heard one of them call out, "Them three yokels! Do 'em." I'm thinking that if we hadn't shown up, those three Saddlers wouldn't have seen the money, or the light of day.'

'If that is so, and if the Saddlers were gulls to be used as guides, it stands to reason that Croft and his partner are not locals.'

'And if that's the case, did they use locals for the previous two abductions?'

We stopped and looked at each other; we had come to the same realisation.

'I'll get someone to enquire into any sudden deaths of locals around the same time as the two previous victims,' Wills declared.

'There's one more thing,' I added with guilty reluctance. 'I heard one of them call something out as they turned to run. He said, "Where's that bastard Dickie."'

'This is why you must attend the debriefings, Rebecca.' Wills rebuked, barely suppressing his vexation. '"Dickie" could be vitally important. One of our team could have added to that information.'

'Yes. And that's why we need to keep all this to ourselves.'

Wills looked at me with confusion. I continued, 'We have an informer, Wills. A spy. We were given the wrong coordinates on purpose. We were not meant to capture those scum bastards. We weren't supposed to be within cooee of them.'

'If only Timmy's uncle and father had been captured alive.'

'You've said it all before, Wills. It is what it is.'

We reached the aboveground levels of New Scotland Yard and proceeded up to Wills' office to arrange a clearance and a hospital ambulance to take care of Timmy. My legs were beginning to protest the lack of solid sleep during the preceding fifty-plus hours.

Entering Wills' office, it struck me just how small it was compared to Hawthorne's. My Major Williams was not an untidy man—he was organised, well read and with many interests—but this tiny, windowless room was incapable of holding everything in an easily accessible manner. Hawthorne's, on the other hand, was voluminous and practically empty. *This*, I thought, *was the perfect analogy of their respective minds.*

Across the entirety of one small wall, a bookshelf was crammed with books, many of which I had read. Another wall accommodated large filing cabinets crowded with intelligence collected during our eight-year tenure at the Metropolitan Police.

Wills hung his cherished Homberg on the coat hook near the door and took up his usual place behind his desk on a well-worn leather-clad swivel chair squeezed in between the desk and the wall. I, as usual, tossed my Gladstone onto the floor and threw myself onto the battered sofa, avoiding Mikey's sackcloth and dinner setting on the floor and making the pile of files at one end of the sofa jump.

I was damned tired—struggling to stave off exhaustion.

'Look at these,' Wills muttered, rummaging through a series of files and withdrawing a few photographs.

Pulling myself back from the brink of sleep, I pushed out of the embrace of the sofa and edged in behind his desk. He pointed at each of the three photographs and confirmed information I already knew, 'Lady Cecilia D'Arcy, twelve years of age, daughter of the Earl of Meagher. One thousand pounds. Mrs Charles Richardson, twenty-eight, wife of the industrialist. Two thousand pounds. And, now, The Honourable Laura Warburton, eighteen, daughter of Viscount Warburton. The two-thousand-pound ransom he paid has virtually bankrupted him. All abducted and …' Wills looked at me. He could not bring himself to utter the word. '… Brutally murdered. After the ransoms were paid. Wanton depravity.'

'Those two bastards must have criminal records. They must be gazetted somewhere.'

'Yes.'

I stared at the photographs as if by looking at them I could see what the women saw during those terrifying last few hours of their lives. My hand mechanically went to the silver locket hidden beneath my pullover.

Wills noticed and distracted me. 'Those two must have been following orders. They are thugs. Cutthroats.' He withdrew a typewritten report. 'Some of the bank notes from Richardson turned up at the Russian Embassy. Despite the Tsar being the King's nephew, the *chargé d'affaires* has not been forthcoming with any assistance to our enquiries.'

It concerned me that the troubles plaguing Tsar Nicholas, as they had plagued his father, were also being felt in this country. 'The Russians are behind these abductions? The Mensheviks?'

'Or the Bolsheviks. The Foreign Office is keeping a close watch on both.'

'Why would any Englishman betray his country and help those revolutionists?'

'What motivates any of us? Ideals, anger ...'

'Corruption, power, money.'

'As you well know, there's a growing surge of support for socialist reform here. Some trade unions are very aggressive and want what the upper classes have. I don't believe these two brutes are driven by altruism.'

'More like rapacity.'

'Exactly. They are puppets. Their puppeteer ...'

'Socialist?'

'Marxist, anarchist. Anything is possible at this stage. Who has been liaising with the embassy?'

'Hawthorne.'

Wills tidied the reports into a single pile. 'Hawthorne need not know that we are pursuing this line of investigation.'

I understood his caution; the fewer who knew what we were doing the better. I leaned back against the wall, wishing it were a mattress. 'So where do we go from here? Dutch lady abbot grandma isn't much of a lead. Debrett's has over a thousand pages.'

Wills let out a defeated sigh and looked at his pocket watch. 'Lunch.'

I had hoped he would dismiss me so I could go home and sleep, but he ignored my irritated exhalation and removed himself to the door, collecting his Homberg. 'You should have used that breath to blow out one of the ends of the candle of which you're burning both ends.'

I grinned at his convoluted admonition of my indulgences, collected my bag and followed him out of the door.

The corridor and stairs were abuzz with various employees going to or coming from luncheon.

We approached the landing. Normally, I trotted down the stairs but today I could just barely put one foot ahead of the other. As we descended, I caught sight of Fawkner chatting with a young woman at the bottom of the stairs. I recognised her—a typiste in the general office. She was quite pretty; I suppose that's why she caught my eye. As we neared them, I heard them intently discussing an article in the latest edition of Home Chat—a ladies' magazine. Some time ago I had made a mental note to read these gossip pages, as they gave information about the goings-on of the upper classes—mostly misinformation, but it was important to keep abreast of society news. Of course, to date, I hadn't done so, leaving that to others such as Wills' wife, Cornelia.

Fawkner and the young woman didn't see us approach. They appeared to be both shocked and amused by an article in the publication.

'What was she wearing?' Fawkner guffawed.

Miss Pretty Thing read out loud, 'The evening dress was of white *mousseline-de-soie*, daintily trimmed in treillage fashion with pale green velvet.'

We passed them on the stairs as Fawkner declared, 'The Duchess of Bramwell has to be sixty if she's a day!'

'I know,' was the only reply discernible amongst the giggles.

'What's the idea of going around all done up like she's about to be presented?'

'Mr Fawkner!' She chided, laughing. 'Don't be such a puritan. She can do as she likes at Abbottsford Hall.'

I stopped and retraced the few steps back to Miss Pretty Thing. 'What did you say?'

My abrupt tone and steely gaze, with Wills hovering menacingly behind me, put paid to their mirth and they both turned visibly white. Miss Pretty Thing tried to hide the magazine within the folds of her skirt as Fawkner babbled, 'Er … nothing, Miss … Ma'am.'

'Stop blathering, Fawkner. Who were you talking about?'

'No one, Ma'am.'

'Give me that.' I reached for the magazine, which the typiste surrendered with a whimper.

I skimmed the article. 'Dutch lady abbot. The Duchess of Bramwell lives in Abbottsford Hall in Suffolk.' I peered at my now petrified Pretty Thing. 'Does she have grandchildren?'

With great effort, the young woman proffered, 'Yes … Two, I believe.'

Wills and I shared a look. 'Long shot,' he conceded.

'Better than no shot.'

'Regrettably, it is my duty to alert Hawthorne of this,'

'What time is it?'

Wills retrieved his pocket watch. 'Quarter of three.'

'Fancy giving the old bugger dyspepsia?'

'Respect, Davies, respect.' He glanced at the two bewildered onlookers. 'He is your better.'

'My arse.'

3

Thursday, 31ˢᵗ August, 1905

London, England

The exclusive and respectable Marlborough Club in Pall Mall was 'a convenient and agreeable place of meeting for a Society of Gentlemen', as they so vehemently touted. It was also Hawthorne's home-away-from-his-nagging-wife, and it was just about three by the time we reached it.

Getting past the concierge was a matter of Wills showing his credentials and demanding to see Sir Giles on a matter of national urgency and that I was … well, important to the case, and leaving him open-mouthed in our wake.

I could see the dining room at the end of the long, wood-panelled and plushily carpeted corridor, and that its etched glass doors were closed. However, the almost deserted dining room was busy with a few waiters clearing tables of the food debris spattered about by quasi-inebriated old farts who had removed themselves to the reading room to complete the task of intoxication to the point of unconsciousness. Gentlemen, indeed.

I shouldn't criticise, I thought. I was just as bad but, at the very least, I did it in private.

Within the vast room I almost gagged on the miasma of pipe and cigar smoke. The waiters who noticed us showed their displeasure by gawping at us as we made our way through.

In a secluded booth along the wall some distance away, I caught sight of a balding head and heard Hawthorne's unmistakeable discordant voice. He was answered by, I presumed, Colonel Humphries—the luncheon guest that he had announced to Fawkner earlier that day.

They tossed down port and sucked on cigars, jovially recounting stories, parts of which carried across the room to us.

'And then, the silly fool,' Hawthorne roared, 'disguises himself as a woman and slips out of the farm house with the rest of the women!'

Humphries chortled, adding, 'In petticoats, no less! Those damned Boers couldn't find hide nor hair of him!'

'Captain of the dickies!' Hawthorne rejoined, and the more he laughed, the louder he became.

Wills raised an eyebrow at me and we slowed our pace, unobserved by Hawthorne and his guest. Something in the conversation piqued my interest, and Wills' too, by his expression.

Hawthorne took a long draught of his port. 'Do you know what's become of old Smithy? We lost touch a few years back after he was cashiered.'

'No idea, old man,' replied Humphries, drawing on his cigar.

Hawthorne observed almost offhandedly, 'You seem in much better spirits, Neville.'

Humphries paused mid-exhalation. 'Yes, the doctor has me on a new regimen.'

'And the wife? How is she coping?'

'Well. Well enough. All is good. How's the investigation coming along?'

'Hm?'

'The abductions. Anything new?'

'No,' Hawthorne scoffed. 'Nothing, I'm afraid. The boy's quite stupid and my men aren't much smarter.'

'Perhaps you should reinterrogate him. With a little more persuasion, he might remember something.'

Why was Hawthorne discussing this with Colonel Humphries? Who was Colonel Humphries?

'Major Williams is attending to that as we speak.'

'Major Williams?' Humphries drawled. 'Would it not be better to have those other two reinterrogate him. Dolby and, ah … ?'

'Yabsley,' Hawthorne proffered. 'Rather grim, I'm afraid. Poor young chap didn't fare too well under their earlier, er, persuasiveness. Didn't get much out of him, either. As I said, quite stupid.'

'Hmm, yes. The sooner he's hanged, the better.'

'I doubt the Crown will put him on trial. He has the mind of a child.'

'Of course.'

Wills elbowed me and whispered, 'Follow my lead.' We strode up to their table, catching both by surprise.

'What the dickens are you doing here, Williams?' demanded Hawthorne.

'I beg your pardon—'

'And with that … that …'

'Woman, Sir Giles. I'm a woman.'

'You're a disgrace!'

'That makes two of us.' I said, letting the words hang between us.

Colonel Humphries, clearly embarrassed by the exchange, glanced at his pocket watch and stood abruptly. 'I must be off. You will keep me appraised? Do reconsider my recommendation regarding the, ah, matter we discussed.'

Hawthorne, clearly flustered, stood and shook his hand. 'Of course, old boy, of course. I am most grateful for your guidance, as always.'

As soon as Humphries left, Hawthorne snarled at Wills, 'I hope you have a bloody good reason to burst in like this.'

'Sir Giles, again, with apologies, I—we—have interviewed young Timmy, er, Timothy Saddler and he cannot tell us anything we don't already know …'

Well, that was a lie, I thought. What's Wills up to?

He continued, with feigned deference, 'I will be arranging for him to be taken to a hospital where he can be treated for the injuries he's sustained. Ah, are you aware of the young boy's injuries?'

Hawthorne, visibly nonplussed, stammered, 'Well … no … I, I haven't read any report.'

'Well, Sir Giles, I thought is best you know that we had reinterviewed the boy and my report will be on your desk tomorrow. Again, please pardon our intrusion.'

With that, Wills gave a slight bow, turned on his heels and marched out the door with me following close behind. What scheme was Wills devising?

As we boarded the hansom, Wills instructed the driver, 'Louisa Mansions, Borough Road, Newington.'

Thank God, I thought, *home*, but I was very curious to know why Wills had made a complete about-face.

He saw my expression. 'Did you find it bizarre that Hawthorne should confide in this Colonel Humphries?'

'Very. Who is he?'

'When Hawthorne's had a few, he babbles on about the war with the Boers and how this Colonel fellow was his commanding officer. Humphries, to my knowledge, has nothing to do with the Metropolitan Police or the Home Office, but I know who can confirm it.'

'Quinn.'

'Yes.'

Alexander Quinn, the head of the Metropolitan Police Special Branch, personally appointed Major Reginald Williams and his assisting clerk, me, to the position in Hawthorne's department, much to Hawthorne's displeasure. Alexander Quinn had final say over our deployment, also much to Hawthorne's displeasure. Wills' commanding officer back in '85, Major General Stokes, had introduced Wills and me to Quinn and highly recommended us for our field work in the Sindh and India back then.

My eyes fluttered shut and, what seemed to be the next moment, the cabbie pulled up at the mansion block in Newington. Mine was a small flat within, located on the third floor and also provided courtesy of Alexander Quinn and the Home Office.

'Tomorrow afternoon. One o'clock,' Wills confirmed as I stumbled out of the hansom. 'Rest. I want you refreshed. And eat. No booze.'

'Of course.'

Gladstone in hand and desperate for sleep, food and bath, I trudged up the front steps to the letter boxes, retrieving two letters, which were two more than usual. One was from my wines and spirits merchant—most likely an invoice—and the other a very welcome distraction. It was postmarked GPO Sydney, and the sender, printed in raised script on the top left-hand corner, was 'Patrick Morrison, Esq, MLA, 63, Oxford-street, Paddington, New South Wales, Australia'.

My lethargy gone, I tore the envelope open and read the contents as I mounted the stairs to my third-floor flat.

>*My dearest Becky,*
>
>*It was with extreme pleasure that I received your letter of the fifth inst., but you really ought to write me more often.*

You will be as delighted as I was to know that Michael's Emily was delivered of a fine baby girl—my first grandchild! I convinced them both that Isabella Rebecca Morrison was the perfect name for such a perfect child. I hope that you are pleased that she is named in your honour.

When will you return home? I miss you terribly. There isn't a day I don't think of you and the rascally things we got up to. Paddington has changed; Sydney has changed. You would not recognise the place now. I doubt you would recognise me! Not the skinny lad you delighted in teasing …'

My throat tightened. I had to stop reading. The stairs seemed never-ending.

Once inside my small residence, I placed my bag on a chair and the letter on the table. Rummaging through the pantry and ice safe, I found some cheese, salted biscuits and a can of cooked meat, but Patrick's entreaty continued to run through my thoughts. I did want to go home but so much had changed—not just Paddington and Patrick, but I, too, had changed.

And what I had done in Sydney, and the consequences that followed me to Melbourne, meant I never could go back.

I picked at the cheese and biscuits and couldn't bother to find the can opener. The absinthe was calling me from the sideboard but I decided to heed Wills' remonstration and, instead, headed for the bathroom. My flat may have been small but it was relatively new and had all the modern conveniences: running hot and cold water, a radiator in the bedroom and living room, electric lighting throughout, one electricity outlet for my bread toaster, a separate room for my bathtub and a flushing water closet.

The bathtub filled quickly as I removed my clothing and slid into the warmth that enveloped and comforted me. Sarah's silver locket clung to my skin and I never felt closer to her than when I heard from Patrick and home.

So many years had flown by since I last saw Patrick—gave him that final reassuring hug and promised I would return. So many promises broken. So many lies.

I closed my eyes, touched my locket and began formulating my reply …

> *My darling Patrick,*
>
> *It is always with much joy that I receive your letters and this one, bringing news of your first grandchild, has filled me with a longing to be there with you to share your happiness and to finally meet your lovely wife and two sons. You must be so terribly proud.*
>
> *I, too, wonder where the time has gone since I left you to discover my mother's family in Wales. At the very least, my darling Patrick, you have achieved great things. Who would have guessed that the son of an immigrant hotelier would now be a member of parliament? Certainly not I. I am so proud of you.*
>
> *Have you ever wondered, Patrick, how different our lives would have been had I not left all those years go? Had I been a different person? Had we married? For I did love you, Patrick, and still do.*
>
> *I tire so easily these days. Life at the manor has become dreary and the hubbub of London is now mere humdrum. I feel my lucky star is on its return orbit and my life is circumscribed. As much as I adore the children in my care, I have made the decision to take my leave and, perhaps, come home once young Daisy returns to school in the spring …*

My muscles relaxed as I floated in the warm water. My mind was a confusion of thoughts, images and sounds … I was falling into a deep sleep. I saw a warm summer day and my dog, Napoleon, running along the dusty road towards the barracks. The scene shepherded me deeper into slumber …

4

Tuesday, 13th January, 1874

Paddington, New South Wales

'Napoleon! Where are you going?' He must have caught sight of a rabbit and veered off into the undergrowth along the Old South Head Road. 'Napoleon!' I could see the scrub moving but I couldn't see my silly dog. We were late as it was; I didn't have time to play hide-and-seek. 'Napoleon! Come back here at once!'

Following him across the drainage channel and into the waist-high grass, I let out an expletive, 'Damn!' Had Mr Morrison heard, he would have had me in my room and without my supper.

As though to mock me, a distant pair of laughing jackasses chimed in with their distinctive ridiculing calls.

'Napoleon!'

Then, as quickly as my recalcitrant dog had loped into the bush, he loped back out and onto the road. He stood there grinning at me like the Cheshire Cat, wagging his tail nonchalantly.

I struggled back out of the grass and shook my finger at him. 'Bad dog! You're a bad dog, Napoleon. Don't stand there with that look on your face. We're late.'

I was so intent on chiding my beloved dog that I didn't see the young woman approach.

'I beg your pardon, young man. Would you be able to direct me, please?'

'*Young man?*' The impudence! I swiveled to give this woman a piece of my mind. 'How …'

The woman's gaze darted to my shirt. 'Oh, I do beg your pardon! I thought … Your short hair … your trousers … I thought …'

Her words floated about my head but missed my ears. She was beautiful. Not even the apparent horror she felt in mistaking me for a lad marred her exquisite features. Napoleon approved, too, tail wagging eagerly.

I gathered my wits. 'Ah, pardon, you said … ?'

She smiled.

My heart pounded.

'I'm looking for the Morrison Family Hotel. Is it far from here?'

'Morrison … ?' the name sounded familiar. 'Morrison family … ! Of course! I live there! No, not far. We're on our way home now, Napoleon and I. That's Napoleon.'

'Nice to meet you, Napoleon.' She directed her conversation to him. 'My name's Sarah. Sarah Harper.' She turned to me. 'Would you like to show me the way?'

'To where?'

Sarah's expression radiated warmth; I was truly dumbfounded for the first time in my life. 'To the Morrison Family Hotel.'

'Yes.'

'Is it this way?'

'Yes.'

She took the first steps towards home. I kept pace with her as we ambled along, past the toll gate and along the barracks' great stone wall, the urgency of my return completely forgotten.

'And what's your name?' Sarah asked.

'Ah …'

'Or should I ask Napoleon?'

'Rebecca. Rebecca Davies.'

'Nice to meet you. May I call you Rebecca? You may call me Sarah. We seem to be of the same vintage.'

'I'll be eighteen in a few months.' The next question popped out of my mouth before my brain could stop it. 'How old are you?'

Sarah laughed with such gentleness I could have swooned then and there. 'I am twenty years of age and that's a most impertinent question,' she chided, but in a most agreeable way.

It was only then that I noticed she was carrying a covered basket.

'Are you delivering wares to Morrison's?'

'I'm delivering lunch to my husband.'

My heart sank. 'Husband? You're married?'

'When one has the former, it's usually the consequence of the latter.'

'Oh.'

'You seem disappointed.'

'No. It's just … I thought … um … I thought we could be friends, is all.'

'We can still be friends, surely.'

'Yes. Of course. I'd like that.' I pushed my disappointment away. 'Do you live close?'

'Just down the road. In Darlinghurst.'

'Darlinghurst is nice. With the new hospital and all.'

Sarah didn't reply. We walked on, Napoleon trotting ahead, scouting for rabbits and rats, garnering a pat from a passerby now and then, me trying to work out what sort of fool I had made of myself, and Sarah strolling on, sometimes giving me a sideways glance.

Something glistened around Sarah's neck and caught my eye; I broke my awkward silence. 'That's a lovely pendant you have there, Sarah.'

'It's a locket. A wedding gift from my parents. It has a photograph of my husband John on one side and me on the other.'

Several carts carrying goods to and from the village of Paddington passed us servicing the village which now boasted some thirty or forty shops along the Old South Head Road. Morrison's Family Hotel was one of those, established some twenty years earlier to cater to the soldiers stationed at the Victoria Barracks—those same barracks we had just passed as we began the steady incline to the top of the hill.

The soldiers there were mostly good natured—at least, those who patronised Mr Morrison's public house were, where I served at the bar in the evenings. And business was good—good enough for Mr Morrison to buy the adjacent plot and extend the building to cater for more travellers. The new hospital in Darlinghurst and the gaol there also furnished us with guests who could not afford the higher rates in town.

'What does your husband do?' I enquired as honestly as I could, even though I felt quite jealous of him.

'He's a carpenter. I believe he's working on your hotel.'

At that moment, a skinny, redheaded youth appeared some fifty yards ahead and called out, 'Rebecca Victoria Davies, you're in big trouble!' Napoleon commenced to bark up a frenzy as he galloped towards the youth.

The youth ran down and met Napoleon halfway, stopped to ruffle Napoleon's ears as the dog excitedly jumped about, and then ran on down to me. 'Where have you been? Pa's beside himself.'

'Good. Then there's two of him to do the work.' I was annoyed that he should interrupt my very private conversation with Sarah.

'Who's this?' he asked. His enthusiastic grin betrayed his anticipation in being acquainted with a beautiful young woman.

'Mrs Sarah Harper, may I introduce Patrick, the *Bothersome*, Morrison, son of the owner of the hotel.'

'How do you do?' was Patrick's formal and snooty reply as he bowed and held out his hand. He was barely two years my senior but such a child! Of course, we always had lots of fun together.

'How do you do?' replied Sarah graciously as she took his hand.

'Becky, you'd better get up there. You should have been back an hour ago. The tables need setting and the dishes need washing. And put on a skirt! You know how Pa feels about you dressing like me.'

With extreme reluctance I took my leave of Sarah. As Patrick and I trudged the remaining few yards to the hotel, Sarah called after me. 'Perhaps I'll see you tomorrow?'

I turned back, elated by the thought, and gave her a wave. I went on with high spirits and the energy to face Mr Morrison's wrath.

***

The facade of Morrison's Family Hotel was made of bricks rendered to look like sandstone blocks. It was an imposing structure, three storeys high and as wide as the block of land it sat on. A narrow laneway allowed for passage between it and the lower building on one side. On the other side, on the lot Mr Morrison had just purchased, there stood a wooden structure—or I should say, lean-to—in the process of being demolished to make way for the extension.

Patrick raced ahead and disappeared into that lot, while I, led by Napoleon, made my way along the passageway between the two brick buildings and into the open courtyard at the back where one could access the stables and coach house. These were also accessible from the back lane—the gate was rarely closed, let alone locked.

My little room—the one to which I was relegated when I was deemed inappropriate—was on the top floor and overlooked this courtyard and, even though my 'imprisonment' may have been ordained, I was easily able to leave by the stairs that lead down through the back verandas on each floor. Mr Morrison was particularly proud of this feature: an alternative escape route should fire take hold.

On the ground floor, the hotel's kitchen also opened out into the courtyard and that's where I headed—to my work and likely a severe reprimand.

Patrick had been right. There, in the kitchen, holding a clutch of rolled-up papers, stood Mr Morrison, his flaming red hair a few shades greyer than his son's, in deep discussion with an older man I had seen only twice before. Mr Morrison glanced up at me. I froze, dreading what was to come. Mr Morrison stopped speaking, folded his arms and glared at me.

'Just how long does it take you to return two books to the library?' he demanded in his thick Yorkshire accent.

I opened my mouth to offer an explanation—

'No. None of your excuses. You stopped to look at more books, didn't you? How many books do you need? You have a hundred upstairs if you have one.'

'But I was looking for a book on China—'

'No excuses, young lady. This should have been cleared up an hour ago.'

He was right, of course. The kitchen was a mess.

'But Napoleon ran into the—'

'And Napoleon should not be in the kitchen.' He looked sternly at Napoleon and pointed to the door. 'Out!'

Napoleon slunk out the door, turned and laid himself across the threshold with a grunt and a mournful look.

'And you,' Mr Morrison turned to me and pointed to the internal stairs that led to my living quarters. 'Upstairs, skirt on, finish your work.'

'Yes, Sir.' Completely deflated, I turned towards the stairs.

'And Rebecca,' his tone changed to his usual, affectionate one, 'a parcel came for you this morning.'

I couldn't stop my squeal of delight in receiving this news.

He promptly felled my excitement. 'No. The books must wait until you've finished your work. Now away with you!'

I ran upstairs. New books! All the way from England. I could never fathom why Mr Morrison indulged me so. These new tomes arrived like clockwork, once a month, from the same bookshop in London, from ever since I could remember. The subject matter was diverse and always in keeping with my age at the time. History, geography, mathematics, philosophy; the most recent volumes were by the ancient Roman writers Suetonius and Pliny the Younger, but my favourite writer, so far, apart from Emily Brontë, was Lewis Carroll.

With the thought of new books as a reward, despite wearing a cumbersome skirt and petticoat, I took on the kitchen with vigour. Thank goodness I forsook the bustle and boned bodice; how did women work encumbered so?

My thoughts unbidden turned to Sarah.

'Why are you smiling like that?' Patrick sauntered into the kitchen from the dining room with a pile of table cloths.

'Do you know any other way to smile?' I replied, not looking up from my task of scrubbing the last of the pans.

Patrick dumped the linen in the basket and approached me. 'You won't talk to me like that when we're married, Becky,' he teased and prodded my side with his finger.

Of course, that made me jump and, of course, that started a water fight. Patrick became soaked with dishwater but that didn't deter him from tickling me mercilessly. How I wish I had worn that boned bodice! We ended up on the floor, giggling, wrestling, tickling, struggling to be free until, exhausted by the sheer effort of laughing, we collapsed side by side, and lay there, on our backs, catching our breath.

Patrick faced me and most seriously asked, 'You will marry me one day, won't you, Becky?'

The question caught me off guard. I loved Patrick, but like a brother. I did not want to hurt him. 'No!' I replied resolutely, then teasingly added, 'You only want me for my inheritance!'

He took the bait and resumed his tickle-attack.

5

Wednesday, 18th February, 1874

Paddington, New South Wales

The summer days wore on—some were very hot, others pleasantly cooler, but all of them were humid. Even quietly sitting and reading a book in the shade made me sweat—or perspire as Mr Morrison always corrected. The occasional thunderstorm came and went, frightening the horses and Napoleon, and the demolition work next door was complete. The new build progressed steadily.

During that time, I learned that the older man who had been with Mr Morrison in the kitchen that day was Mr Brendan Rourke—the builder contracted to erect the new extension. He was Irish, from Belfast, and had built up quite a business in the twelve years since he immigrated, taking on apprentices and young men who had found themselves in trouble either financially or with the police. He was a good Catholic man as was Mr Morrison and, I suppose, that's why they worked so well together.

I often saw Sarah delivering the midday sustenance to her husband. We sometimes sat together in the shade of a tree on her way home or, at other times I would waylay her just as she gave the food to John. She seemed not to want to interrupt John with our chatter and always led me away, saying she had to hurry home.

When we conversed, she told me very little about herself, other than that she was born in Parramatta and her parents had land holdings there. She and John moved to Sydney town to find work, which, she said, was difficult to find back home.

"

Whenever it was available, Sarah took in dressmaking or needlework to supplement John's income. Other than these details, she would divulge nothing about herself or her husband. She always seemed to direct the conversation anywhere but there.

I also noted that Sarah wore the same dress every day she came to bring John his lunch. I thought it a little strange for a dressmaker, but then it didn't really matter because she was always clean and well presented; Sarah would have looked splendid in sackcloth.

She was ever happy to see me, or so I believed, and I was always elated to see her. I can now admit that what I felt for Sarah was something I had never felt before. Something overwhelming—more than friendship, more than fondness—something that lifted me whenever I thought of her. *Was this love?*

One sultry day, a thunderstorm caught Sarah as she was about to return home. Dark thunderclouds roiled in from the west, pushing the clear blue skies out to sea. Sarah would never make it back to Darlinghurst in time to avoid the imminent downpour, so I suggested she come up to my room to wait it out. I was on my free time so Sarah, Napoleon and I raced up the back stairs as fat raindrops plopped around us. We made it to my room on the third floor just as the rain fell in sheets and thunder rumbled through the heavens.

Shaking off the rain and laughing, Sarah took in my cosy little room. 'This is lovely,' she said.

I never thought of it as lovely. It was the attic. But it was cosy and comfortable and had everything I could possibly need or want.

I had lived in this room all my life and it contained all my possessions and my life's experiences, expectations and dreams. Most of those dreams came from my treasured collection of books, which I had carefully catalogued and cross-checked so I could find what I wanted with ease and expedience. Each had my own personal bookplate pasted onto the front flyleaf. These bookplates had been a surprise inclusion in one of the parcels I had received a few years back. The illustration was of a Masked Owl on a perch next to a stack of books upon which rested an ancient oil lamp, the whole boldly affirming 'Ex Libris Rebecca V Davies'. The owl, of course, represented sagacity and the books and lamp alluded to the acquiring of knowledge deep into the night. I now had five hundred and eighty-three tomes and they ranged from the readers of my school years to a wonderful, new Chambers's English Dictionary. The bookshelf filled an entire wall.

'Where does that door take you?' Sarah asked indicating the door opposite the one we had just entered.

'To the corridor. The other staffs' rooms. But this is the door I use most. I can come and go as I please without disturbing anyone. Or if I want to sneak out,' I added with a wink.

'Aha,' Sarah acknowledged, raising an eyebrow. She resumed her inspection of my sanctuary, stopping at the large north-facing window and absorbing the panorama that swept across the skyline beyond the buildings. 'What a wonderful view!'

'That's Port Jackson,' I explained. 'And there's Rushcutters Bay and the gentry of Rushcutter Valley live there. And from the front rooms you can see Botany Bay.'

Sarah twirled around. 'You have everything.'

'Everything I need.'

'And so many books! Have you read them all?'

'Yes. Some twice. Do you have books?'

She hesitated. 'Yes, of course I have books.' She laughed. 'You have more than the free public library! How did you acquire so many?'

'Mr Morrison has them sent from London every month for me. But a lot of them were my mother's.'

'Your mother?' Sarah asked quietly. 'Tell me about your mother.'

I wondered what caused her sudden subdued tone but that was a question for another time. 'She was born in Wales, Cardiff, and became a governess. The wife of some army major stationed there employed her to teach their three children. When he was posted here to the barracks in fifty-four, he brought his family, and my mother, with him.'

'And you?' Sarah queried. 'You wouldn't have been born then.'

'No, I was born in fifty-six.'

'A currency lass, like me.'

Normally, I would have objected to being called a currency lass, or a colonist or a colonial, but coming from Sarah it wasn't an insult. 'Yes, I suppose so,' I continued. 'Mother said that education was the most important thing to have and from that, everything follows.'

'That's what they claim …' Her response was tinged with regret.

'Anyway, I love reading. I want to be a teacher like my mother. Maybe in China or someplace exotic. I want to see all the places I've read about.'

Sarah eyes crinkled at my enthusiasm. 'What happened to your mother? Your father?'

'Mother passed away from consumption. Five years ago.'

'Oh, I'm so sorry, Rebecca.'

'It's going to happen to us all.' I shrugged. 'I just hope that I don't suffer the way she did. What about you, Sarah? Your parents?'

'They're both well. And your father?'

I hesitated; I was a little ashamed but I really couldn't be blamed for it. 'My father? I don't know who he was.' But I hastily added, 'Mother was not an immoral woman. She was good and honest and she loved and cared for me and did everything possible for me—'

'Rebecca, I can see that she loved you. I can see, also, that Patrick and Mr Morrison are very fond of you. Do you think Mr Morris—'

'My father? No! Do I have red hair? Do I look even remotely like Patrick? I hope not!'

Sarah laughed—oh, how I loved her laugh—how I loved that I could make her laugh.

I quietened my diatribe and continued. 'She never told anyone who my father was. Once, she said she promised him that she would never tell. She told me that she loved him deeply and he loved her but they could never be together. That saddened her but she said I was the culmination of their love and I was very much wanted and adored by my father.' I paused and then added, 'Of course, that doesn't alter the fact that I'm a bastard.'

Sarah almost choked on that last epithet. 'Rebecca!'

'I was born in this very room, you know. In this very bed. Don't be alarmed—the bedclothes have been changed since then.'

Sarah laughed, unguarded and bright. It made something flutter in me.

'Come, sit.' I took Sarah's hand to lead her to the bed. The touch of her soft hand moved me. I regained my senses. 'Come … come.'

We sat side-by-side on the edge of the bed. Was I mistaken or did Sarah purposely sit close to me, her leg touching mine? I pushed the question away and relished the sensation of her warmth and her hand in mine.

'Mother said that at the moment of my birth a shooting star streaked across the night sky. She saw it through this very window. She said that was my lucky star—a good omen of a long and happy life and that it would protect me. I truly believe that my soul came to me on that shooting star.'

Sarah drew back but still kept hold of my hand. 'Does that mean that your soul will be taken when it reappears?'

'I never thought of it like that. You may be right—my soul may be reclaimed upon its return.'

Just at that moment, a bolt of lightning flashed followed almost immediately by a boom of thunder. Sarah and I jumped. Napoleon scrambled under the bed.

Then we both burst into laughter.

'Maybe that was God trying to tell me something,' I proffered.

'Rebecca! You mustn't blaspheme.'

I was charmed by her religious directness. 'Anyway, I think Mother had a lucky star as well.'

'How so? She died young, didn't she?'

'Yes, but she was cared for. When the major found out she was with child—me—he dismissed her. Couldn't have that sort of scandal. Mr Morrison took her in. Mrs Morrison had just passed away leaving Mr Morrison alone with a new hotel and two-year-old Patrick. Mother looked after the baby like he was her own and Mr Morrison looked after Mother. Once I was born, it was like we were a family.'

'But you address him as "Mr Morrison".'

'I can't call him Pa because he's not, but he is as dear to me as a father could be. And as strict! Patrick's like my big brother.'

'More like your fiancé. He's very sweet on you.'

'I won't be marrying Patrick. I love him but not like that.' My eyes dropped to Sarah's hand nestled in mine upon my lap. My thumb stroked her tender skin.

'I must go,' Sarah announced rising abruptly. 'The storm seems to have passed. Thank you for showing me your room.'

'I would love to see your home, also,' I said in hope.

Sarah offered no reply, just an unreadable expression, and left. I watched her descend the rain-soaked stairs.

6

Friday, 27th March, 1874

Paddington, New South Wales

At the end of March, autumn had well and truly set in. One cool day, I was sweeping the footpath outside the front door of the hotel, Napoleon dozing in the afternoon sun, when Sarah emerged from the building site next door and hurried past me.

'Sarah!' I called as she sped by. I hurried and caught up to her. 'Sarah?' Her pace didn't falter. I took hold of her elbow. 'Sarah, what's the matter? What is it?'

She stopped to look at me and trembled an awkward smile. 'Oh, Rebecca, please forgive me. I really can't stop to natter today. Forgive me.' She delicately prised her arm from my grip and with an apologetic look to both me and Napoleon, sped on down the hill towards Darlinghurst.

What had I done? I could think of nothing that would have caused offence. I turned to resume my sweeping but caught sight of John, Sarah's husband, standing at the edge of the building works scowling at me. What had transpired between him and Sarah? What had she said to make him so sullen? I had not expressed to Sarah how I felt about her and I certainly had not enacted what I fantasised, for fear of losing her friendship.

Napoleon noticed him, too, and barked once as though he were chiding John.

As we approached the front door, John turned and disappeared into the near-complete building.

***

That night, after the public bar closed and we'd fed and watered the hotel guests, the family and staff sat together, as usual, at the supper table. Mr Morrison took prime position at the head, young Patrick on one side of him and me next to Patrick. The other four positions were occupied by the hotel's permanent staff: the housekeeper Mrs Potter, Edith the chambermaid, the groom Ernest, and Mrs Archer, the cook whose grizzled hair belied her youth. The position opposite Mr Morrison was empty; it had been the late Mrs Morrison's, Patrick's mother, who had passed away eighteen years before and then my own mother's, five years gone.

Mrs Potter was a lean, angular woman, attractive in a mannish way, who ran the staff with a precise set of rules and tolerated no backchat from Patrick or me, in particular. Mrs Archer, I suspected, existed to be Mrs Potter's opposite in every respect. Where the housekeeper was sharp and severe, the cook was ever-cheerful and soft-edged, cuddly and quite attractive. Her whole body shook like a boiling kettle whenever she laughed and she laughed often. The best attributes I could ascribe to Edith was that she was a Mrs Potter in the making. Young and restrained, her terse replies seemed to hide secrets. The groom Ernest was a childless widower and about the same age as Mr Morrison. He had no other family—this was his family. At this table, only Patrick and I were native-born Australians.

The conversation was always lively and convivial; Mr Morrison had a very good relationship with his staff, his family and generally most people—a trait also endowed to Patrick. Tonight, after the strange incident with Sarah and John, I sat quiet and introspective, playing with my dinner.

Patrick noticed. 'All right. Who's kidnapped Rebecca? The one sitting here is definitely an imposter!'

'You are awfully quiet, young lady,' Mr Morrisson added. 'Has something upset you?'

'Mr Morrison, what do you know about the carpenter, John?' I blurted, caught off-guard by their questioning.

Mr Morrison raised an eyebrow. 'John? Not much. Why do you ask? Has he done something to you?'

'No.'

'He's strange,' offered Patrick. 'The way he treats his wife.'

My body tensed. 'What do you mean?' Thoughts of Sarah being mistreated shook me.

'I don't know. Sarah does everything to please him but he just treats her like … I don't know … Unrespectful.'

I was so surprised I couldn't ridicule Patrick for his misuse of the word.

I silently resolved to find out more about John.

'What books did you receive yesterday, Becky?'

'Huh?'

'Huh?' Patrick aped. 'Most eloquent, Becky. Books. What did you get?'

'Oh. A travel book on China and the Far East, *Old Kensington* by Anne Thackeray Ritchie, *Nancy* by Rhoda Broughton, and Mrs Beaton's *Book of Household Management*.'

'Hah! That last one should be a boon to you. Does it explain how to do women's work in men's clothing?'

'Patrick …' Mr Morrison warned.

'Sorry, Pa,' he said, shooting a sassy grin my way.

***

The next day was a Saturday, which was always a busy day at the hotel—guests coming in to spend the weekend visiting their loved ones either in hospital or in gaol, end-of-working-week spendthrifts drinking their earnings away at the pub, or couples taking an evening meal in the hotel's renowned dining room, thanks to Mrs Archer's excellent cuisine—but I was determined to see Sarah before she arrived with John's lunch.

I rushed through my duties, threw off my apron and headed for the kitchen door then stopped abruptly—an apple! I'd bring her an apple! Grabbing one from the bowl, I raced out the door—followed closely behind by Napoleon—along the passageway, and down the Old South Head Road, hoping to catch Sarah on her way up.

I saw her just before I reached the toll gate. 'Sarah!'

Upon seeing my rapid approach, she bowed her head and continued on her way towards me. Unusually, she wore a scarf draped over her head, wrapped about her neck and covering most of her face.

I skidded to a stop, panting, and Napoleon and I joined her on her trek back up the hill. 'I brought you an apple.' I placed it in her basket.

'I can't stop and talk to you today. I have too much to do,' she whispered.

This confounded me. She was earlier than usual and I had raced through my chores so I could talk to her. And she wouldn't look at me. 'Sarah,' I enquired, 'what's the matter? What have I done to offend you?'

'Rebecca, please leave. I can't … I don't want to speak to you.'

'Stop right there, Mrs Sarah Harper and look me in the eye when you say that!' My anger was fuelled by confusion. I took her by both arms and turned her towards me. 'Tell me!'

'Don't!' She shrugged me off and continued on her way defiantly.

I was completely bewildered and stood there frozen, watching her walk away.

A moment later, I was by her side again, keeping pace. She glanced around her scarf at me. 'Please don't, Rebecca. Please go away.'

'Not until you tell me what I've done.'

Sarah bowed her head and her pace slowed to a stop. 'Don't …' her plea was a mere breath.

She would not meet my eyes. Carefully, I turned her to face me and, with a hand under her chin, I lifted her head. Her beautiful face was contorted by dread. I eased back her scarf.

'Sarah!' I gasped. Her cheek and eye were a grotesque and swollen purple mass.

She recoiled, pulling the scarf back over her face. 'I tripped and fell onto the corner of the table. I'm all right. Thank you for your concern. Now please leave me alone.' And she scuttled off.

I didn't believe a word she'd said, but I also couldn't believe the alternative. How could anyone hurt such a wonderful person? What on earth could she possibly have done to deserve that? She was so soft-spoken and loving. My chest tightened at the thought of her being maltreated; I felt helpless.

I willed my leaden legs to move and followed Sarah as she made it to the building works. Head down, her response to the greetings of the various masons, bricklayers and plumbers was an indiscernible nod or a hushed good morning.

Rourke, the builder, greeted Sarah with his usual cheeriness as she passed. 'Ah, the lovely Mrs Harper. Good day to you,' he said in his musical Irish accent.

Sarah avoided looking at him and replied almost inaudibly, 'Mr Rourke. John's lunch.'

'Of course, my dear lady. We're just about to break now.'

She passed through to where her husband was working on laying floorboards. Moving to where I would be unseen by John or Sarah, I watched and listened.

John downed his hammer and chisel and met her. 'About time. Are you all right?'

Sarah didn't respond as John peered under the scarf at her bruise. 'You should mind yourself. Did you tell him?'

She shook her head. 'He wouldn't listen. He made me promise—'

John grabbed her arm. 'What? What did you promise?'

With this, Rourke turned and glared at John.

'It's all right, Mr Rourke,' John assured him apologetically. 'It's all right,' and turned back to Sarah. 'What did you promise McDonald?' he hissed.

'He wants it by Friday … Five … John, he wouldn't … you're hurting me—'

'Then you can go and un-promise him.' He grabbed the contents of the basket, as well as the apple meant for Sarah, and turned his back on her.

She stumbled her way back through the building and onto the street, head bent low and fists clenched. I was barely able to resist the urge to run to her and console her—or to storm in and whack that son of a bitch with his own hammer.

As Sarah left, Rourke approached John. 'What was that about, boyo? Money?' he guessed. 'What happened to the money I advanced you, Johnno?'

I didn't care for what 'Johnno' had done with the money; I cared for what Johnno had done to Sarah.

Sarah had practically run from John but, instead of turning to go back down the hill, she turned the other way and continued up the road and around the bend. Napoleon and I pursued and found her in a paddock, sitting on a tree stump, weeping.

'Sarah …' I whispered as we approached.

She looked up at me, her beautiful eyes swollen and red, tears glistening in the sunlight. 'What am I to do?' she sobbed.

My heart broke to see her so anguished. I knelt beside her and folded my arms around her. She didn't resist, but leaned into me and rested her head on my shoulder. My embrace tightened and her sobs lessened. 'I don't know what to do, Rebecca.'

'Tell me. I'll help you.'

She let out a plaintive gasp of defeat.

'Why don't you leave?' I implored.

'We did leave but the troubles simply came with us.'

'I mean leave him. John.'

She shook her head. 'And go where? Do what? I have no money.'

'I'll take care of you. You can live with me at the hotel.'

Her face softened. 'If only …'

'*We* could leave. Go abroad. China. I have this book—' I was desperate to help her.

'I can't. John needs me. He does love me. It's just when he …'

'Do you love him?'

She hesitated.

'*I* love you, Sarah.'

'I know you do, Rebecca, but it can never be.'

'Why not?'

Her eyes held pain and regret. Could she see the longing in mine? A desperation to be with her?

I reached up and gently cupped her face in my hands. 'I would never hurt you,' I sighed and drew near. My lips met hers. She didn't resist. A warmth overcame me; my body relaxed and I surrendered to the glorious sensation. She *did* love me the way I loved her.

She drew back. 'No … I can't … I must go.'

Her sudden rejection confused me. She rose and ran from me the same way she had run from her husband.

'I'll bring you the book on China,' I called as I watched her retreat.

7

Saturday Evening, 28th March, 1874

Paddington, New South Wales

That evening, the hotel guests and patrons were enjoying the company of their grouped compatriots in the public bar. Patrick drew the beers while I collected the empties from the tables scattered about the commodious room. Sometimes we swapped roles.

Mr Morrison took care of the 'exclusive clientele', as he called them, but in reality they were merely his old cronies from Mother England with whom he loved to chinwag.

As usual, fresh oysters from the fish market at sixpence per dozen were on the public bar's scant bill of fare and, with a pint of beer, were always popular and sold out no matter how many Mr Morrison bought in.

My serving livery fitted my mood perfectly: black; black skirt and bodice with white cuffs, collar and apron.

After the revelations of that afternoon, I was not in the mood for joviality or the usual raucous banter between the soldiers, Patrick and me. Patrick had noticed and didn't make any comment, but I became aware that he kept a close watch on me.

During the course of the afternoon, I had made numerous excuses to go to the building site just to peer at John and to wonder how he could do what he'd done. I envisaged dashing *his* head against a table until it was a mush of blood and bone. I would be as callous as he had been. On one or two occasions, he had seen me staring at him and sneered.

The patrons making the loudest noise tonight—and every night—were the six soldiers from the barracks. The loudest was Corporal Roberts, a ruddy-complexioned monolith of a man from Ulster and the only regimental soldier amongst the lot of infantry volunteers who now occupied the barracks. He had been with the 18th Royal Irish Regiment but decided to stay when the regiment was ordered back to England some four years past.

It had been quite busy all evening and I longed to see how Sarah was but, with so many patrons coming and going, my absence would not only be missed but frowned upon by Mr Morrison. So, I carried on with my duties and, empty tray in hand, headed for the Roberts cacophony.

Roberts was well into his cups but still *compos mentis* as he heralded my arrival with a loud and discordant alternative rendition of 'Oh! Susanna': 'Oh! Rebecca, don't you cry for me, I've come from old Vic Barracks with a crooked broken knee.'

I wasn't in the mood to join the deafening laughter that followed, instead loading my tray with the dozen or so empty mugs. 'Six more, Corporal?'

'Yes, my sweetest of sweets, and oysters.'

'Sorry. All gone.'

I turned to fill his order from the bar and caught sight of someone in the furthest corner, in semidarkness. It was John, slung carelessly into his chair, slowly drinking his ale and staring at me. I wished I were a man so that I could have beaten him senseless then and there.

'What'll it be? Becky?' Patrick followed my gaze to John. 'Oh. He's drunk.'

'If he thinks he scares me, he's mistaken.'

'You'd best leave them alone. No good interfering between a man and his wife.'

'He hit her!'

'Maybe she did something to deserve it.'

'Patrick! Since when is it all right for a man to strike a woman?'

'No, I didn't mean … Becky …'

'Six beers for the Corporal!' I ordered, slamming the tray onto the bench and upturning some of the empty mugs.

Duly chastised, Patrick withdrew and concentrated on filling the order as I regained control of my temper. I didn't hear or see John's approach and froze when he stood so close behind me that he pushed me against the bar. 'You dirty little tom,' he slurred into my ear. 'I saw you. Go near her again and I'll … I'll kill the both of you.'

His foul breath was hot on my face.

'You don't scare me, you bastard.' I shouldered him away from me.

He staggered a few steps back and guffawed. 'You …' he slurred. 'You calling me a bastard!'

That drew both Patrick's and Corporal Roberts' attention.

'Watch your mouth, mate!' Patrick warned from behind the bar.

The corporal bounded towards John, grabbed him by the shoulder and spun him around. 'You got a problem with her, boyo, you come see me, right?'

John snarled and pushed the corporal's hand off. He shot me a menacing look then lurched towards the door.

I hardly had a moment to compose myself before the front doors were flung open and six hard-faced men pressed their way in. John attempted to push his way through them but was buffeted from one to the other. Eventually he found the door and stumbled out as they jeered at him.

All eyes were now on those six strangers as they stood inspecting the room and its occupants, who were in turn inspecting them.

In front was a wiry, scar-faced man of about thirty years and not much taller than I. His malevolent smirk did nothing to endear him. Nor did the company he kept, all attired in a similar fashion: bell-bottomed pants in varying shades of dirty, no waistcoats, very short black paget jackets—some few buttoned up, others missing all buttons—and shirts with no collars. Each man also wore a distinctive gaudy neckerchief around his bare neck. High-heeled boots gave them a little added height but certainly no class.

Mr Morrison watched on with evident concern.

I looked to Corporal Roberts who was eyeing them warily. 'Who are they?' I whispered.

'The Rocks Push,' was his equally quiet reply. The corporal looked to his fellow soldiers who stood up, ready, as Corporal Roberts approached the apparent leader of the group. 'Now, lads, this is a respectable place. No trouble.'

The leader raised his head to peer up into the corporal's eyes and grinned, baring his crooked, yellowed teeth. 'Tether your horse, Captain, it was him what assaulted us.'

His cohorts expelled mocking grunts.

'What are you doing here in Paddington, Hickson? Are you rats deserting the Suez Canal?'

'That's unkind, Major. We're cut real deep, aye, boys?'

'This isn't the kind of grog shop you're used to. We won't put up with any trouble. Hear me?'

'We just want some refreshment is all, Colonel, Sir. Disposing of garbage has made us real thirsty, like.' The private joke brought scornful laughs from the group standing with him. 'Them Forty Thieves is now but twenty.'

'Forty Thieves?' I asked Patrick.

'A rival larrikin gang in Surry Hills,' he confided.

Corporal Roberts put on his sternest face. 'No trouble. Got it?'

Hickson stood to attention, clicked his heels and saluted. 'Aye, aye, Admiral!'

With a final warning glance, Corporal Roberts returned to his table and the six soldiers resumed their seats, keeping a watch on the Push while Hickson approached the bar. His cluster of reprobates peeled off and took up the table that John Harper had just vacated. I wondered what they were all about. I had heard of the larrikin gangs of Sydney, of course, but had never encountered any before.

Hickson fronted the bar near me—he stank of sweat and horse manure as most honest carters would at that time of day, but his demeanour certainly was not that of an honest carter.

'Six of your finest whisky, barman,' he demanded of Patrick.

'Six shillings,' Patrick responded, without stirring to get the glasses.

'And they call me a thief!' He tossed the coins onto the bar.

'You said the finest,' Patrick retorted, scraping up the coins and moving off to fill the order.

Hickson turned to me and looked me up and down. 'You all right, Miss?' he asked.

'Right enough, thank you,' I responded coolly. This man was dead-ugly and his breath matched his body odour. I didn't like his impertinence. He was an inconsequence looking for aggrandizement by deliberate pettifogging until it escalated into a fight and then trouncing the victims—something he couldn't do without the support of his flunkeys.

'You're a comely lass,' he continued. 'We could use someone like you.'

I could see Patrick observing the scene and my dear friend had a look I had never previously seen—one of cold loathing.

'What's your name, lass?'

'Rebecca. Rebecca Davies,' I threw back at him with equal insolence. 'And yours?'

'Jeremiah Hickson, at your service, Miss Davies.' His mocking tone made me cringe.

Patrick returned with six glasses of John Walker's Old Highland Whisky on a small tray. 'Six of the best,' he grunted, and pushed the tray towards Hickson.

The grin Hickson gave Patrick was more of a threat than a thank you. He picked up the tray, looked at me and winked. 'If ever you want a real man, lass, look me up. Harrington Place. The Rocks.' He joined his minions at the corner table.

Corporal Roberts approached once more. 'You shouldn't front those larrikins, Rebecca. They're trouble.'

I turned to him, confused. 'He said he could use someone like me. What did he mean?'

'As a lure. To entice drunks and sailors into the Suez Canal and rob them. It's a bad spot, Harrington Place. Keep well clear of it. And them.'

***

Eleven o'clock finally chimed. 'Last drinks, gentlemen,' Mr Morrison called. 'Closing time. Drink up.'

I was exhausted and, despite my fatigue, I was desperate to see if Sarah was safe. There would be a price to pay in the morning because of lack of sleep but I was willing to pay it to make sure no harm had come to her.

I made my excuses to Mr Morrison and left by the back door, intending to go to my room and change into trousers. Outside, my faithful Napoleon rose from his nap and greeted me with a wagging tail.

My attention was drawn in the other direction to the back of the worksite. In the darkness, the street's gaslight picked out two men hunched over a prostrate figure on the floor of the unfinished building.

Napoleon growled low.

'Shh!' I ordered, and he fell silent.

One of the men was Mr Rourke and the other must have been one of his workers. They were attempting to raise the figure on the floor.

'Up you get, lad. Come on, time to go home,' Mr Rourke urged as he and his worker pulled up the drunkard. 'Wake up, Johnno. Your wife's probably worried sick about you.'

They pulled John up to standing but instead of being thankful he grumbled and fought to free himself from their assistance.

'Get away from me!'

'All right, laddie, we're only trying to help.'

'Let go!'

John elbowed out of Mr Rourke's grasp and stumbled. He righted himself and staggered through the almost complete building to the road.

'He's an ungrateful lushy-cove, that one,' the youngster with Mr Rourke commented.

'Aye, that may well be, but he's fighting many a demon, poor fella.'

'Poor fella' indeed, I thought. John Harper had brought it all upon himself and blamed the world for it. I decided to follow the 'poor fella' home, uncomfortable as I was in my skirts.

I kept to the shadows and was unseen by him or passersby, few as they were. Napoleon kept close to me, skulking along, his dingo-like instincts for the hunt showing through.

As Harper became steadier on his feet, he became more aggressive, shouting to anyone and the world. 'Fuck you, you son of a mongrel bitch! Fuck you too, you cunt! Bloody swiving molly! Piss on you all … God! Why have you done this to me?'

I almost pitied him but he was giving himself enough pity that it left no room for mine.

I was so intent on pursuing Harper that I didn't hear the approach. A hand on my shoulder jerked me backwards.

'What the hell are you doing?' Patrick uttered in the loudest of whispers.

'Go away.'

'You want to die? Worse still, do you want Sarah to die? I heard what he said to you.'

'He's drunk and full of rage. God knows what he'll do to her.'

'He'll probably collapse unconscious in bed. Come home now or I'll tell Pa.'

'Patrick—'

'No. Don't get involved. She will suffer if you do. We'll find a way to help her. If she wants our help.'

He was right. Harper's threat was real. I didn't care what happened to me, but I didn't want to be the cause of any more harm to Sarah. 'All right, but you will help me find a way of helping her, right?'

'Yes. Now come home.'

I prayed to God that He would look after her and keep her safe from her abusive drunkard of a husband.

***

Unaware that Rebecca had been following him, John lurched from one foot to the other, stumbling and weaving down the dimly lit Old South Head Road towards his home in Palmer Lane, a narrow back street of Darlinghurst. He continued with his barrage of expletives and curses, mostly garbled and unintelligible.

The 'home' he and Sarah shared was the upper floor of a ramshackle building that had been a large stable when it was constructed about forty years earlier. The ground floor had housed horses but the owner of the property now used it as a storage house for unused and unwanted furniture.

The upper floor Sarah and John occupied—the former loft used to store bales of hay—had been converted to very primitive and basic accommodation. The whole structure was destined for demolition soon. The very low rent reflected this.

This was the only building that fronted the lane. The rest of the houses along that unlit narrow laneway were far newer, fronting onto Palmer Street.

Rusty nails and chicken wire held together the rickety flight of wooden stairs that led up to their home. Arriving at the bottom of the stairs, John braced himself on the balustrade, waiting for the world to stop spinning.

'Highland prick bastard …' he mumbled, hauling himself up one step at a time. Misplacing a foot, he fell onto the rough hardwood treads. 'Fuck … Fuck, fuck, FUCK!' He righted himself and mounted the stairs on all fours. 'Mine … She's mine!' he mumbled.

***

Inside the hovel she called home, Sarah stood peering through the window down at John and watching his intoxicated progress. Her breath became shallow and her brow wrinkled with concern. Wringing her hands, she took up her position at the stove, stirring the thin stew she had been able to put together with their meagre provisions.

Their home comprised one room. The floorboards were uneven, some rotten in places, some missing. The most dangerous areas were covered with sheets of embossed tin, salvaged from other derelict buildings set for demolition. There was no ceiling; bare rafters and posts held up the corrugated iron roof.

One end of the room was curtained off. This bedroom of sorts was made up of an old double bed with clean but tatty bedclothes and a small chest of three drawers topped with a chipped washbasin.

In the middle of the room stood a small wooden table and two mismatched chairs. A place was set for John. Shelving along one wall served as the pantry. One corner harboured a large frayed basket that held the tools of their auxiliary income—Sarah's sewing.

The cast iron wood stove that Sarah was now standing at was twice her age. She stirred the stew, dreading the moment John would enter.

She really had tried hard to convince Mr McDonald. She tried to please John, to be a good wife, to support him … to love him.

She tried.

The door burst open and swung hard against the wall, startling her. John clumped in, barely able to keep his balance, and made his way to Sarah. She shrunk back as he reached over her to the shelf and pulled out a half empty bottle of rum.

'John, should you be—'

He turned to her and raised his hand. 'Don't tell me what to do!'

Sarah recoiled and John reconsidered his response. Instead, he stumbled to the nearest chair, flung himself into it and guzzled from the bottle.

She turned to the stove and ladled out a portion of stew, very aware of his intense scrutiny.

'Did you speak to that Scotch bastard?' His words were slurred but the menace behind them was clear.

She couldn't speak, she couldn't move, she couldn't breathe; she knew what was to come.

'I asked you a question. Did you speak to him?'

'He said Friday, five o'clock,' she whispered and closed her eyes, every muscle taut with anxiety.

He flew out of his chair, grabbed her and spun her around to face him.

'WHAT DID I TELL YOU?' He slapped her face hard. 'NOT FRIDAY!' He slapped her again and again sending her reeling. Her head hit the corner of the table and she fell to the floor, clutching the bleeding gash to her brow.

John staggered to her and dropped to his knees, enfolding her in his arms. 'Sarah … Sarah … I'm sorry. Sarah … Why do you disobey me? You make me do this …'

8

Sunday, 29th March, 1874

Paddington, New South Wales

I couldn't sleep that night worrying over what John may have done to Sarah. Patrick had insisted that John was too drunk to make it back and probably had slept under a bush somewhere.

This hadn't allayed my fears and I rose very weary the next morning. I was not savouring the normal Sunday morning chores of helping Cook prepare breakfast for our guests and then attending Mass with Mr Morrison, Patrick and the rest of our staff members.

I knew that Sarah worshipped at the Sacred Heart in Darlinghurst where we used to go, but since the newly built St Francis church here in Paddington was inaugurated, Mr Morrison insisted we join its congregation to show our support. I was desperate to know that Sarah was well and suggested we attend Mass at the Sacred Heart, but to no avail.

I could see Patrick was unhappy with my suggestion but kept his tongue still—until we were on our way to church. He took my arm and slowed his pace. 'What are you hoping to do, Becky?' he began when the group was a few paces ahead of us. 'Didn't you hear what John threatened to do if you kept company with Sarah? What's the matter with you? I know you have a special friendship with her, but it will pass. It's just a girlish infatuation—'

I pulled my arm out of his grip. 'Oh! And you know all about "girlish infatuations", do you?'

'I don't want anything to happen to you—'

'And I don't want anything to happen to Sarah.'

'Becky—'

'You said you would help me save her from that brute. I want to go and see that she's safe!'

Mr Morrison's attention was drawn to our persistent kerfuffle. 'You two arguing on a Sunday?'

'No, Pa. We're chatting.'

'Come along, then. No more chatting.'

Patrick must have seen the determination on my face because he gave a defeated huff. 'All right. After Mass, we'll go together.'

'You don't have to come.'

'You're not going alone—'

'Patrick! Rebecca! Stop that "chatting" now!'

***

Mass was tedious, as was our new Reverend Father and his hellfire and brimstone sermon, especially since all that my heart held at that moment was murderous intent. I rushed off at the end, barely genuflecting and splashing holy water in a rough semblance of the sign of the cross.

Patrick was on my heels. 'Wait. Wait!' He grabbed my arm again.

'Stop doing that!' I protested.

'You can't just charge up there like Wellington at Waterloo.'

He caught me off guard; his simile did have some truth to it. 'What do you suggest then, Mr Know-all?'

'I suggest *I* go and see if Sarah's unharmed—which she will be— with the excuse that Pa wanted to know something about the panelling or something in the new place. Does that sound feasible?'

'No. Harper's not smart but he's not stupid, either.'

'Well, the only other choice is home. You're not going and I'll make sure you don't, even if I have to tell Pa.'

'Tell me what, Patrick?'

Patrick and I jumped. We were so intent on arguing we hadn't heard Mr Morrison approach.

'Pa … Nothing,' Patrick stammered. 'Becky, ah, wants to wear her trousers for the rest of the day.'

Mr Morrison frowned. 'Is that so, young lady?'

'I told her it wouldn't please you,' Patrick replied.

'Hm,' was Mr Morrison's sceptical response as his glance darted between me and his son. 'Come along. Time to help Cook prepare luncheon.'

Patrick and I exchanged irritated glares and followed the troupe back to the hotel.

***

The time couldn't come fast enough. I wished I hadn't let Patrick dissuade me from going directly to Sarah's. Finally, luncheon was over and Patrick and I were on our break until dinner. I changed into my trousers and donned a plain shirt, jacket and boots, topping it off with an old cabbage tree hat just in case it rained.

I knew Sarah lived in Darlinghurst but not where. Using all the charm I could muster, I interrogated the staff and managed to wheedle the Harpers' address from Ernest, who remembered Mr Rourke mentioning it in conversation. It was in Palmer Lane on the first floor of the only building with an outside staircase leading up to it.

Armed with that information, Patrick met me and Napoleon at the bottom of the back stairs and we hurried off together, down the back lane and towards Palmer Street and on to Palmer Lane. I knew Patrick cared about me and perhaps I had used that affection to embroil him in my quest to save Sarah. Patrick was a fair and just young man— qualities he inherited from his father. He would make some young woman a wonderful husband, but that young woman wouldn't be me.

The streets were busy with families and courting couples on their Sunday afternoon promenades, coming and going from Moore Park and its sports and entertainments, even though it was a little chilly. The foolhardier took to the dangers of the Lachlan Swamps for their adventures or trysts.

When we reached the entrance to Palmer Lane, Patrick stopped. 'You wait here,' he instructed me earnestly. 'I will go up and see that she's all right. You wait here. Promise me.'

I understood Patrick's concern. If Harper saw me, it would bring devastation upon Sarah. With much reluctance, I nodded my agreement.

Patrick turned into the lane and, halfway up, glanced over his shoulder, possibly to look to me for encouragement but more likely to ensure I hadn't moved.

I had.

I'd taken tentative steps into the lane and was aghast to see that the only building—if it could be called that—with a staircase leading to the upper floor was an old, almost derelict barn.

The clapboard building had obviously been a stable and a relic from the olden days of the tyrannical Governor Darling, after whom the location had been named. The upper floor Sarah and Harper occupied would have been the former loft. The only way to rectify the whole structure would have been to demolish it.

Patrick gestured wildly for me to retreat. I returned to Palmer Street and stood backed up against a paling fence, nervously fidgeting with Napoleon's ears, my eyes darting up and down the street scouring for any movement. I was in a bad position should Harper appear around the corner. How would I explain my presence? Certainly nothing to do with the wainscoting Patrick had schemed.

After a few long minutes, Patrick returned. 'I knocked several times,' he offered. 'No one answered. Maybe they've gone to visit her parents. You said they live in Parramatta?'

'Maybe.' But I didn't believe it.

'I looked through the window. I couldn't see anyone in there. No movement.' After a moment, he added almost with reluctance, 'Nothing much in there. A table, an old stove, a couple of chairs. Not enough to cater to one guest, let alone two.' He saw my concern and assured, 'It'll be fine, Becky, you'll see. Let's get back before Pa notices.'

We turned to go, except for Napoleon who stood statue-like, staring towards the stairs.

'Napoleon,' I called. 'Heel, boy.' He gave one sharp bark, turned and followed Patrick and me.

'You know, for a carpenter, it should be easy for him to fix those stairs,' Patrick commented. 'They're downright dangerous.'

***

I spent another restless night, tossing and turning, worrying about Sarah, wondering what I could possibly do to protect her, where we could go.

My eighteenth birthday was coming soon and I was aware that my darling mother had left a small sum of money in Mr Morrison's care until I came of age. Maybe that would be enough to take me and Sarah away from these problems. We could start a new life together, perhaps in Queensland or Victoria. I had read that the discovery of gold there meant there had been a huge influx of people from around the world and one in which we could easily find anonymity and refuge.

These were my hopes and plans as I rose that Monday morning.

The hotel extension was almost complete, so very soon Sarah would no longer deliver Harper's midday meal to him. The threats Harper made on Saturday night weren't going stop me. I wanted to see Sarah, to be with her and steal as much time with her as I could before she no longer came. I wanted to tell her of my plans. To go away together. But more than that, I wanted to make sure Harper had not harmed her.

We were busier than usual on this Monday but I wasn't bothered. I slipped out the kitchen door, into the back courtyard and through the passageway to the front of the hotel. Napoleon, my shadow and protector, followed me.

From the footpath, I peered down the road towards Darlinghurst for a glimpse of Sarah. She was nowhere to be seen. I glanced inside the building to see if she had already arrived. All the workers were still at their labours.

The time of her usual appearance came and went. My insides felt like they were being squeezed. Where was she?

Damn the consequences, I thought.

I marched into the new extension where Mr Rourke was inspecting the finishing touches with two of his workers. Napoleon stood by my side and peered into the distance, his hackles raised. In the corner of the room, in shadow, we could see Harper sweeping shavings and offcuts into a pile.

Mr Rourke greeted me. 'Young Miss Rebecca, how can I be of assistance to you this lovely day?'

'Has Mrs Harper been today? With Mr Harper's lunch.'

'No, my sweet, Johnno's brought his own today.'

I gasped for breath. The worst images flashed through my mind. 'Ah … are you sure?'

'As sure as any culchie with two eyes and half a brain can be sure, Missy.'

Napoleon growled. I looked up to see Harper staring at me with such hatred and intensity, it made me shiver.

At that moment, I loathed him. I wanted to say things—do things—

'Lunch break, boys,' Mr Rourke's general announcement broke the tension. He turned to me. 'If you'll excuse me, Miss, I have an errand to run.'

Suddenly, it was just Harper, Napoleon and me.

Harper took a few steps towards us, his eyes never leaving mine, and picked up his tiffin box. He glowered at me, moved a few steps closer, and offered his meal. 'Want to share?'

Napoleon growled.

I knew what Harper meant. 'No,' I said decisively.

'And neither do I. Keep away!'

Napoleon lunged forwards, snapping and barking.

Harper struck out with his foot. 'Mongrel!' he snarled and sent Napoleon flying with a kick to his abdomen. 'Keep that animal away from me.'

'You're the animal!' I yelled as I consoled my whimpering Napoleon.

'Next time, I'll kill it!'

'You don't deserve Sarah.'

'And you'll never have her!' He grabbed his belongings and marched outside leaving me with Napoleon, cowering with his tail between his legs.

I resolved then and there that he would pay for hurting Napoleon. And Sarah. He was bigger than me but not smarter. But first I needed to know that Sarah was safe.

I watched Napoleon anxiously for a few moments. He seemed sore but not too damaged. After I took him up to my room, I changed into my workman's outfit. I was determined to see her. I collected the book on China that I had promised her. I carefully wrapped it in brown paper, tied it with string and headed off.

Harper would be on site until about five, so I had a few hours. I would explain and apologise to Mr Morrison and Patrick later; it was easier to do that afterwards than to get permission beforehand.

It didn't take me long to get to Palmer Lane, running most of the way. When I reached the bottom of the staircase, I saw Patrick was right—they were unstable. Why wouldn't Harper take the time to repair them?

I climbed them carefully and, reaching the top, looked around. This place was as deserted on a working day as it was on the day of rest; no one around. It must be eerily dark and foreboding at night.

I turned to the closed door and knocked.

No answer.

I knocked again a little louder.

Still no answer.

I went to the window and peered in. It was dark and there was no movement. 'Sarah,' I called softly. 'Sarah, it's me, Rebecca. I have something for you. Sarah—'

I heard the bolt of the door slide and the door opened slightly. I turned to it and spoke softly through the crack. 'Sarah, it's me—'

'Rebecca, please go away.'

'I have something for you.'

'I really can't see you.'

'Please let me in. I'll only be a minute. I promise.'

'Rebecca ...'

I could hear by her tone that her resolve was waning. 'I promise,' I repeated.

The door creaked open just enough for me to sidle in.

The room was shrouded in dimness and desperation—I was taken aback by the sheer poverty of possessions the Harpers displayed. She was always so cheerful and buoyant when we were in each other's company and had never made any reference to her wretched circumstance. I wanted more than ever to take her away from all of this. My mother's bequest would see us start a new life somewhere. Anywhere but here.

Sarah stood in the semi-darkness of the room, her form silhouetted against its gloom. I shook off the feeling of despair and took a few steps towards her. 'I brought this for you.'

As I drew nearer, my breath caught. Her forehead was bruised and swollen and a raw gash cut the ridge of her brow.

'What happened?' I uttered, barely able to breathe. 'And don't you dare tell me you tripped and fell and hit your head on the table.'

'That is what happened,' she said, her voice laced with irony. 'I did fall and hit my head on the table.'

'Who made you fall?' I demanded.

She hesitated. 'You said you had something for me?' she asked, her voice soft.

I knew who had caused her to fall and let it go—for now. I proffered the paper-wrapped parcel.

She took it and slowly unwrapped it with trembling fingers.

'Oh, my dear Rebecca, the book on China. Thank you.' She carefully placed the book on the table—the same table she claimed had debased her.

'You can read all about China and decide where you'd like to go.'

Her wistful gaze fell upon me—I saw the anguish there.

'I'll be getting my small inheritance soon and I want to take you as far away from here as we can go.'

She collapsed into a chair; her eyes shimmering with hopelessness. 'That would be impossible.'

'Nothing's impossible. Nothing.' I was at her knees, clasping her hands in her lap. 'We are young. We are strong. We will have funds and a plan. Nothing can stop us—you'll see.'

'Rebecca—'

'Nothing will harm you ever again. I promise. Believe me. Trust me. Please.'

She closed her eyes and bowed her head as though the weight of her conscience was too much to carry. Her hands clung to mine tightly. I despaired seeing her so distressed. I delicately raised her bruised face and our eyes met.

'I love you.' My declaration was a soft exhaled breath.

Her eyes searched mine and I saw longing. I rose to my feet and tenderly coaxed her into my embrace. She yielded willingly and wrapped her arms about me, melting into my sanctuary. At once I felt at peace, that I had rescued her, that she would be safe with me. I kissed her damaged face, each kiss willing away the pain she was suffering. I kissed her hair, her eyes, her neck—each kiss a blessing, a vow.

Her eyes ventured once more into mine and her lips parted, inviting me to prolong the ecstasy. My heart pounded. I accepted her tacit invitation and our lips met. All my fear and apprehension coalesced into rapture. I found my soul in her. Her embrace tightened and the need in her kiss deepened. I tasted her sweetness and sorrow, her hope and her promise. Her heart was beating in time with mine—I never wanted this moment to end.

But all too soon, Sarah broke away, breathless as I.

Long moments passed before she disentangled herself from my arms.

'You must go,' she whispered.

The words jarred me back to reality. I desperately wanted to stay but she was right. My absence would have been noticed.

'Mr Morrison will annihilate me,' I joked and drifted to the door. 'Read the book,' I urged. 'And we'll leave all this behind. Soon. Very soon. I love you.'

***

I sprinted back to the hotel, up the stairs to my room, changed into my afternoon livery and made sure Napoleon was happy.

The kitchen was still abuzz with Patrick and Edith cleaning up after luncheon and Cook baking the teatime delicacies.

Patrick, who was washing the dishes at the sink, eyed me as I strode in. I calculated that arrogance was better than subservience.

'Where have you been?' I demanded of him feigning annoyance.

'What?' he exclaimed. 'Where have *I* been?'

'Yes, I've been looking for you everywhere.'

Patrick shook his head. 'Just tell Pa when he asks that you were in your room not feeling well,' he advised. 'You have your you-know-whats.'

Any other time I would have ridiculed Patrick's modesty but worry for Sarah kept my playful spirit at bay.

9

Friday, 3rd April, 1874

Paddington, New South Wales

I did everything possible to avoid seeing Harper; I kept away from him and he kept away from me.

By Friday, the week had been a monotonous tedium of hotel duties broken only by the excitement of the secret moments I stole from work to be with Sarah. Harper had told her to stay at home lest Mr Rourke question him about her 'accidental fall'. Was it his guilt, shame or remorse that protected her? It mattered not to me for he would soon regret his actions when Sarah was no longer part of his miserable life.

Her injuries were slowly healing, the swelling had abated and the angry deep-purple bruising was fading to mauve, green and yellow. The other victim of Harper's vindictiveness, Napoleon, was on the mend as well. He would join us, of course, when we left for a better life.

The new extensions to Morrison's Family Hotel were now complete and ready for the grand opening Saturday afternoon and the celebrations Saturday night. The new rooms and amenities had doubled the number of guests we could accommodate and, consequently, Mr Morrison had taken pity on us and put on two more maids—one chamber and one kitchen—and a footman who would double as a factotum, like Patrick and me.

With the building work completed to the excellent standard prescribed, Mr Morrison paid the final instalment to Mr Rourke in the hotel's office situated off the public bar.

Both Patrick and I were preparing for the usual Friday night swill near the open office door.

'There you go, Gareth, young son. Sign here,' Mr Rourke said, addressing one of his men. 'Caleb, here's yours. Johnno.'

I heard the tearing open of envelopes and one of the young men saying, 'Thank you, Mr Rourke, thank you.'

'Don't thank me, Gareth. Just continue doing the job like you have and there'll be a little extra in each packet for you both.'

The other also was very appreciative. 'Thanks, Mr Rourke.'

The only dissenting voice was Harper's. 'Where's the rest of it?'

'I'll see you both on Monday,' Mr Rourke dismissed the other two. As they left through the bar and passed Patrick and me, Mr Rourke continued, 'Johnno, the job's finished. You knew the advance was only until now. Son, I've put a little extra in there for you as well.'

'A very little extra. This isn't going to be enough.' Anger was mixing with desperation in Harper's voice. 'I need more.'

'I've got a new job starting on Monday, John. You're the best carpenter I have and I don't want to lose you. Once we get that underway, you'll have more—'

'Monday's too late. I must have it tonight. You can advance me, Mr Rourke.'

'You know I can't do that—'

'Well, fuck you, then.' Harper snapped and stormed out of Mr Morrison's office.

Patrick and I stood there flabbergasted by his outburst. I was barely able to jump out of his way as Harper barrelled towards me.

We watched him push past a few patrons wandering in through the front door.

My thoughts immediately turned to Sarah and prayed that she would be all right. I took a determined step to follow him only to be pulled back by Patrick.

'Becky!' he warned. 'Don't do it! *She'll* suffer!'

Patrick was right, of course. Now was not the time to confront Harper. It was Mr Rourke he was angry at. He had no reason to harm Sarah. To his knowledge, I had kept away from her.

The night wore on and I saw no more of John Harper but I heard from Corporal Roberts that he had seen Harper walk into the Greenwood Tree Hotel shortly after he left here.

***

The Greenwood Tree Hotel was one of the first opened in the area, catering to the largely Irish population employed to build the now twenty-six-year-old Victoria Barracks. It was a little run down but well-patronised by the old swills.

Five o'clock was early to start drinking but it was now close to six. The public bar currently accommodated only the oldest of its most faithful patrons, many of whom were no longer fit for work, each smoking a newfangled machine-made cigarette or sucking on their meerschaums or handmade clay pipes. The one exception was a dark and miserable figure slouched alone at a table in a corner: John Harper. A number of empty pots scattered on the beer-soaked table attested to his state of inebriation.

There he sat in complete self-pity, counting his dwindling wages.

The barman removed the empty tankards. 'Shouldn't you be making your way home, son?' he asked in a conciliatory tone.

John tossed a coin in the barman's direction. 'Another pint.'

The barman shook his head but collected the coin with the empties.

In time, the bar filled with its regulars and its regulars filled themselves with Irish whiskey and Guinness and, before long, the place was abuzz with jolly brogue banter, songs from the old country and patriotic calls of 'Erin go Bragh'.

John had drunk away almost half of his wages. Each pennyworth of ale that soaked his stomach dulled his propriety and brought forth his bitterness towards the world and how it treated him. The ale didn't make him forget, it made him care nought for the world and, right now, he hated everyone and everything in it.

A trio of merrymakers pushed their way through the crowd towards John's empty chairs and plonked their drinks onto the table. 'Oy, matey, are you minding if we set ourselves at this table?' one asked.

John's sneer barely acknowledged them as he collected the meagre remainder of his wages, stuffed the coins into his pocket and pushed his way through the crowded room and out through the front door. Once outside, it was obvious that it was the crowd that had been holding him upright and he stumbled and fell.

A couple of old Irish workers picked him up and set him on his way. 'There you go, son.'

His slurred 'fuck you' was barely discernible.

The autumn night was dark and chilly and it was nothing short of a miracle that John was able to find his way home, winding down the low hill towards Darlinghurst. He was drunk but not so insensible to forget it was Friday night—the night he was to meet his long-outstanding obligation. He didn't care. They could all go to hell.

Stopping by the water pump near the toll gates, John drenched his head under the flow. It awakened him but his thoughts were still befuddled. His brain didn't communicate with his legs and the road rose and fell unpredictably. He managed to thread the correct streets and mostly stay out of the path of hansoms, sulkies and wagons on the roads, and pedestrians and other inebriates on the footpaths.

As he turned into Palmer Lane and saw the staircase to his upper floor home, his shoulders slumped in relief; the expected was not there.

With one hand on the banister and one unsteady foot on the first step, a male's voice murmured effeminately, close to his ear, 'You missed our appointment, Johnny.'

Every muscle is John's body jolted. Even in his drunken stupor, he knew who it was. He knew what was to come. Wide-eyed, he turned to face the disembodied voice.

'Mr McDonald ...' he stammered.

'John ...' McDonald admonished, pursing his lips. The coquettishness of the reply contradicted the speaker's physicality. He was a plump, ruddy-complexioned man of about fifty years of age, dressed in the latest of English fashion. His brown herring-bone tweed top-frock hung open on his shoulders revealing a cobalt-blue sack coat over a red silk-brocade vest and a floppy polka-dotted puff tie. His trousers were slim-legged and much too narrow for his fleshy legs and paunch. His manner, as with his clothes, was flamboyant and exaggerated.

'Mr McDonald ... I didn't—' John faltered as he caught sight of a large, burly monolith of a man standing a few feet behind the fop. Just as McDonald was the epitome of fashion, Oxley, his companion, was the antithesis, clad in the baggy, ill-fitting, mismatched clobber of a dockworker.

'Didn't what, darling boy?' McDonald asked, drawing John's attention back to him. 'Didn't know it was me? Didn't know it was Friday? Didn't know it was past five of the clock? Didn't know today was the day you promised to pay the piper? You've had a merry tune, my boy.'

'Mr McDonald … I need more time. My boss didn't pay me what was due.'

'Is that another of your little excuses, Johnny? Like those you told me last week? And the week before that? Was it a lie that you would pay me back today?'

'No! No … My wife, Sarah … she shouldn't have—'

'But she did.' McDonald feigned a regretful sigh. 'What are we to do, my dear?'

'Look,' John desperately spat out, clinging onto the banister to steady himself. 'Look, Mr McDonald, what if we pay you … in kind?'

McDonald pursed his lips seductively. 'What do you have in mind, my sweet boy?'

'My wife … my wife could … satisfy your … you could have her … for your—'

'For my what, dear boy? Pretend wife? Concubine? For my pleasure? Hmm?' McDonald's chubby belly was now in contact with John's as McDonald continued. 'I'd be more persuaded if you offered yourself to be my pretend wife. Or concubine. Perhaps we *can* come to some arrangement.'

'No! No,' John reeled back. 'I'll pay you back, Mr McDonald, I promise, I'll pay you back!'

Stepping away, McDonald glanced towards his malevolent shadow, Oxley.

'You've made that promise before, John. Twice before, in fact. You don't seem to understand what a promise is. Or a debt.'

'I'll pay you on Friday, Mr McDonald. I promise.'

'John, I regret doing this, I really do. You are such a comely young man, but you need to understand that a debt must be repaid and a promise must be kept.'

'Please … no …'

'This is so you remember to keep your appointment next Friday.'

McDonald stepped aside and Oxley stepped forward.

'NO!'

Oxley grabbed John by the coat and pulled him away from the stairs.

'Not the head,' instructed McDonald as he averted his attention to brush away some minute dust particle from his shoulder.

At once, Oxley's huge hand steadied his drunken target. The first punch caught John in the ribs, only Oxley's grip prevented him staggering backwards. The second, delivered to his stomach, winded him. John doubled over in pain and dropped to the ground gasping for life, like a fish out of water. The business-like brutality of Oxley's mnemonic continued. Oxley booted John's curled-up form in the back, buttocks and legs until McDonald reached over and placed a gentle hand on Oxley's shoulder.

'That should suffice, Mr Oxley.' He addressed John. 'Please remember your appointment, John. Otherwise, Mr Oxley will be most disappointed. And you would not want to disappoint Mr Oxley once again, would you, John?'

As McDonald and Oxley disappeared into the darkened laneway, a figure stood on the stair's unsteady landing looking down on the scene. Sarah watched her husband as he lay beaten and bruised, writhing in pain. Her hand touched the bruising to her own face. For long moments she stared at him, blankly, unmoved.

John struggled to his knees and vomited, the foamy yellow contents of his stomach coating parts of his clothing. He collapsed, hugging his battered ribs.

'Sarah ...' he moaned. 'Sarah ...'

Sarah carefully and mindlessly made her way down the shaky stairs to John and, with much difficulty, they clambered up each unstable step to the landing. John whimpered with the effort.

Inside their home, she helped her husband to their bed, carefully lowering him onto it. She proceeded to remove his vomit-stained coat and shirt but he shoved her away. 'Leave me!' he growled. 'I don't need you. You could have helped,' he slurred. 'You could have helped ...'

'How? I give you everything I earn, everything—' Sarah's pent-up frustration gave voice.

'You could earn more if you didn't spend all your time with that ... that ... unnatural bitch tom.' John struggled to a sitting position. 'What do you two get up to, eh?'

Sarah held her tongue. He may have been drunk and damaged but she knew the extent of his violent capabilities in that state.

'Nothing. We talk—'

'Yeah, talk. Sucking each other's cunnies—'

'No!' she screamed, appalled by his crudeness. 'We just talk!'

John grunted and pushed himself off the bed, his rage obliterating the pain in his ribs. He advanced.

She retreated.

'We'd be better off if you offered your cunny down at the barracks, instead. But who'd shag you? Look at you, you scrawny piece of scrag. Who'd pay a farthing to tup you?'

'Stop! You don't know what you're saying!'

He stopped and stood wavering, staring at her. His face screwed up. Sarah knew an explosion was building.

'WHERE ARE WE GOING TO GET THE MONEY?' he screamed.

She shrank back. 'John … I can ask … I'll ask Mr Morrison. He's a good man. He'll help us—'

He lunged at her, grabbing her throat and shaking her. 'You'll stay away from there! Do you understand? Do you?'

Barely able to breathe, she gasped, 'Yes …'

He discarded her with a rough push.

'You keep away,' he growled, exhausted by the effort. His rage diminished, he dropped himself into a chair next to the table.

She was horrified to see that she had left Rebecca's book on it. She had neglected to hide it! Waiting for John's return, she had been reading it by lamplight when the altercation with Mr McDonald had drawn her away.

He saw it. 'What's this?' He picked it up. 'Since when do you own a book?' He opened it and saw the flyleaf. The words reignited his rage. 'Who gave you this?'

'John—' she pleaded.

'It was her, wasn't it? It was that bitch, wasn't it? She was here. In my home! You let her into my home!' John surged to his feet, unsteady, book in hand. 'You won't ever learn, will you, you stupid trollop. This is what I think of her.' John ripped the book apart, sending shreds of paper in every direction. 'And this is what I think of you.'

He grabbed her by the arm and hair and pulled her close to him, bending her backwards. She cried in pain but he didn't relent, his face in hers, his voice low and menacing. 'If I ever catch you with her again, I will kill the both of you.'

10

Saturday, 4th April, 1874

Paddington, New South Wales

I rose early Saturday morning. Sleep had eluded me, lost in concern for Sarah. I couldn't go to her because of the preparations for the grand opening of Mr Morrison's hotel extensions, which only served to worsen my anxiety.

Combined with that apprehension, my eighteenth birthday was only a few weeks away and I'd lain awake calculating how far my inheritance would take us and formulating ways and means of getting there with Sarah—to China, the Americas, Mother England, anywhere.

Mr Morrison had invited half the population of Paddington including its new mayor Benjamin Cocks Esquire, our Reverend Father Hellfire and Brimstone, the builder Mr Rourke, Corporal Roberts and his coterie of course, all the hotel's current guests, and all of us—his family and staff.

It had taken us all of the week and most of this day but, by five o'clock, the bunting was hung, the tables laid out with the most exotic morsels Cook could concoct, the band from the barracks all tuned up and eager to impress, and the best beer, wines and spirits our young colony produced, all in abundant supply.

It felt as though all of Paddington fit into Mr Morrison's new premises and he was pleased. I should have been happy for him but my thoughts were elsewhere.

***

Sarah had lain awake until long after John finally succumbed to his inebriation and slumped unconscious beside her in their marital bed.

So many images swirled through her head as she listened to him snore. She eventually gave in to her restlessness and left the bed to watch the sun rise, but seeing the pages of Rebecca's cherished book, torn and strewn about the floor, undid her. Her tears fell unrestrained.

With a heavy heart she collected all the scraps. She would explain to Rebecca … what? How could she explain this? What could she possibly say that wouldn't bring herself shame?

She looked around the barren room and a leaden melancholy overwhelmed her. Is this what her life had become? A struggle and fight against poverty? Would there ever be a way out? Seeing John in peaceful slumber made her wish for the days when they were first married. What had changed him?

***

It was late morning when Sarah rekindled the stove and put on the kettle for tea and a little porridge. She dressed silently and sat down to her breakfast alone.

She was tired and her head throbbed and her neck ached but worse still was the torment in her heart. She knew she couldn't continue the charade of loving John, of believing that he would change or hoping that everything would work out for them.

She watched her husband; he would be of no use to anyone today. He would most likely sleep all day and well into the night. That's what he did after every bout of heavy intoxication. And when he woke, he would be remorseful and apologetic as always, but, even so, he would blame Sarah for each of his outbursts.

Sarah spent the day brooding while she maintained their little hovel and prepared the evening meal, such as it was.

The sun was now low in the western sky and it would be dark soon. Every now and then she would go to John who lay there still, breathing deeply.

If only, she thought. She loved being with Rebecca. She loved Rebecca.

She decided.

Taking her shawl quietly from the top drawer of the chest, she left, closing the door carefully behind her. She fled down the stairs and away.

***

'Hey, Becky, why so glum?' Patrick shouted into my ear. His words were barely audible over the revellers' cacophony. 'Pa knows how to do a turn, eh? Want to dance?'

All the tables and chairs in the public bar had been stowed away and the crowd filled this room and the commodious new extension to capacity. The barracks band was banging out a lively polka—one of my favourites—but I was not in the mood.

'No, Patrick, not now. I'm tired.'

'Come on. You'll feel better when you do.' He pulled me towards the mass of sweaty bodies bumping into each other as they swirled around the floor in pairs.

Patrick grasped me around the waist and practically carried me into the throng of whirling dervishes. I clung on to him for dear life as he galloped one way and then the other, laughing with each bump and jostle of our neighbours. For a brief moment, I forgot my cares and laughed … until I caught a glimpse of Sarah near the door, craning her neck as she scanned the room.

'Sarah,' I gasped.

I disentangled myself from Patrick's embrace with a vague apology and pushed through the crowd to the door.

She had disappeared. I made my way through the busy anteroom, searching each face, until I reached the back courtyard. I found her in the shadow of the stairs that led up to my room. Even in the dim light cast through the windows of the hotel, I could see she was as jittery as a rabbit, twitching and surveying every corner of the yard. She relaxed a little once I reached her.

Several merrymakers staggered by, three sheets to the wind, oblivious of us.

I was so happy to see her until I saw the bruising on her neck. Reaching out, I touched the finger marks, my anger barely in check. '*He* did this?'

'I'm leaving John,' she said.

It took a moment to absorb what she'd uttered.

'Did you hear me, Rebecca? I've left him.'

So many thoughts fought for prominence. 'I heard you but … I haven't received my mother's …' I hadn't planned on this happening now. 'Does he know? Have you told him—?'

'No. You said I could stay here.'

'Of course. Of course.' Suddenly, I realised that Sarah would be with me. The joy that overcame me could have lit a thousand lamps. 'Sarah!' I flung my arms about her and pulled her tightly to me. The racket of the band, the din of the crowd all faded to non-existence. The warmth of our embrace soothed every fibre in my body. I breathed in Sarah's essence.

The clatter of shattering glass jolted us apart.

A disembodied voice in the distance admonished another. 'You sod! Look what you've done.'

It brought us back to reality—we giggled.

'Where are your things?' I asked, not seeing any luggage.

'I have everything I need—my parents' locket.'

I reached for the locket around Sarah's neck and carefully opened it. She had removed Harper's photograph.

'He's gone from my life.'

'You won't regret this. I'll be of age Sunday fortnight and be able to retrieve my inheritance the Monday after.' I took her by the hand. 'Come to my room. Mr Morrison won't miss me. And it'll be a little quieter there.'

We reached the top floor and I closed the door behind us, slipping the bolt to ensure our privacy. I lit the kerosene lamps.

Napoleon roused from his nap and met Sarah with an enthusiastic wag of his tail. She bent down and ruffled his head. 'Napoleon. Sorry to wake you, boy. Is he all right?'

'Yes, he's a brave little soldier.'

'It's a wonder he can sleep at all with all that noise,' she observed.

'The volunteer band may not be good, but they're loud,' I quipped. 'Come sit and tell me what happened. Those bruises on your neck.'

Sarah sat next to me on the bed, and removed her shawl. She bowed her head and shut her eyes then took a deep breath and sat rigidly upright.

'You might as well know,' she began with quiet determination. 'John has difficulty controlling his temper, especially when he's drunk.' Her words were uttered softly, almost with regret. 'In Parramatta, he borrowed a lot of money to pay a debt. We left because of that debt.' She shook her head in disbelief. 'He's becoming like his father. He drinks his wages away, then borrows money to pay the bills. When he can't pay those because he drinks, he borrows more. And when he borrows more, he drinks that away as well. It's a cycle that never stops turning.' She took a moment to order her thoughts. 'John's mother bore the brunt of his father's drunkenness. He beat her so badly once that she lost an eye. She left him and her two boys and has not been heard of since. Last night, John almost strangled me. Because he couldn't pay back a debt. I don't want to die, Rebecca.'

I took Sarah's hands into mine. I had never known physical abuse or brutality. I don't know how I would react if someone treated me the way Harper had treated Sarah. *Thou shalt not kill*, but what if he did the unthinkable to Sarah?

I caressed her face, stroking away the tension. She relaxed and rested her head on my shoulder.

Napoleon growled.

'Hush boy,' I ordered and realised he was looking at the door. 'Napoleon …'

The dog pounced to his feet and barked ferociously, hackles raised, ready to attack.

A mighty crash and the door burst open, splinters flying everywhere and showering Napoleon.

The dog unleashed his fury.

Sarah and I jumped to our feet, my heart thumping in my chest. I pulled Sarah close to me. She was gasping for air.

The aggressor filled the doorway.

Harper.

His fists were clenched; his look, murderous.

'Get out!' I roared desperately, searching for something— anything—to repel him.

Sarah shrank into a corner.

Napoleon continued his violent barrage, baring his fangs and snapping at Harper.

'I want my woman!' Harper growled and advanced, his face an ugly contortion of hatred.

Napoleon attacked, snagging Harper's trouser leg in his jaws.

Harper kicked the dog with such violence that he released his grip with a pathetic yelp. Harper kicked him again and sent him careening across the room.

I rushed Harper, attacking with my fists. He was too big, too strong.

He slammed his fist into the side of my head.

I reeled back and fell to the floor, the pain intense. My ears rang and my vision blurred.

Harper advanced on Sarah.

I grabbed at his leg.

He turned on me. 'You're dead, you fucking bitch!'

He gripped me by my dress bodice, pulled me up and drew back a fist.

Sarah grabbed his arm. 'No, John! Don't!'

His glancing strike stung my cheek. His grasp kept me upright. I was dazed, clinging onto consciousness.

He turned on Sarah, seized her by her throat and flung her against the end of my bed. Her head struck the wrought iron frame. She lay stunned, struggling to get up.

Napoleon, limping, attacked again. His fangs sank into Harper's thigh.

Harper screamed and hurled me away.

I hit the floor hard. The pain was excruciating. I struggled to get up but couldn't. I could only watch.

The dog tore at Harper's thigh, twisting and pulling.

Harper punched Napoleon's head again and again.

Napoleon let go but Harper did not relent. He punched and kicked Napoleon until blood oozed from my beloved dog's head and he lay motionless on the floor.

Then he turned to me. 'I told you what I'd do,' he rasped. 'I told you to stay away.'

I tried to move. Harper pulled me up once more and pushed me against the wall. I could barely raise my arms. We were face-to-face.

His breath was hot and reeked of alcohol.

He raised his clenched hand. 'I am going to kill you.' His words were guttural, spat through clenched teeth.

I didn't see her.

'John!' Sarah screamed, desperately pulling at his arm. 'Don't hurt her! I'll come with you! Don't hurt her!'

Harper didn't avert his gaze from my face. 'Oh, you'll come with me, my love.' He elbowed her away.

He was a wild animal, snarling, nose flaring, eyes mad with fury.

I wasn't going to die so easily. I rallied my arms and thrust my thumbs into his eyes with all the strength I had left. He easily shook them off and headbutted me. Scintillas of light filled my sight. His fist pounded into my chest and abdomen, winding me. He punched the side of my face. Blood dribbled from my mouth. He released me and I dropped to the floor. I curled up in agony, my arms wrapped around me. Pain racked my whole being.

But he wasn't finished with me.

He kicked me again. Again.

I could hear Sarah screaming for him to stop. He wouldn't.

I tried to protect my head, my body, my life. The excruciating pain had reached its peak. I could no longer feel anything. Sarah's screams faded.

Sarah …

One by one, my senses deserted me.

Then all was black.

***

'Becky … Becky … Oh God! Becky …'

I could feel someone's hand on my face but I couldn't see anything and could just barely hear … then nothing.

***

Someone was lifting me. The pain in my chest stifled my breathing. My head felt like it was about to explode. My eyes wouldn't open. I groaned.

Mr Morrison told someone to be careful.

'Sarah …'

***

When I awoke, smells of carbolic acid, urine and vomit filled my senses. It was difficult to open my eyelids; they were painful and swollen. I could just make out that it was daytime and I was lying down and surrounded by indistinct forms.

'Sarah?' I uttered in a hoarse whisper.

'Becky …' came the gentle reply.

'Patrick?' Then the intensity of the pain in my chest caught me. 'Oh, God!'

'Sh. Lie still. Doctor said you have three fractured ribs. You've been badly beaten.'

I closed my eyes to the overwhelming pain then the awful memories came flooding back. 'Sarah,' I begged. 'Where's Sarah? Is she all right?'

'Becky … Sarah's—'

'Rebecca …' I peered through slits in my eyelids towards Mr Morrison's gentle interruption. 'You need to rest. The doctor is here.'

Barely able to move and through blurred vision, I took in the scene around me. Patrick and his father were on either side and two nuns and a doctor stood at the foot of the bed. 'Where am I?'

'St Vincent's hospital,' Mr Morrison replied softly.

'And Sarah? Where's Sarah? Is she here?' Panic caused the soreness in my ribs to intensify. I groaned.

'You must rest, Miss Davies,' a deep male voice interjected. 'Sister.'

One of the nuns pushed a syringe into my mouth and squirted a bitter liquid. 'Swallow,' she ordered. I gasped, spluttered and swallowed involuntarily.

'It will help you sleep,' the doctor added. 'Come, Mr Morrison, Master Morrison. The sisters will take good care of her.'

It was only moments before my eyes closed and I was free of pain once more.

11

Saturday, 11ᵗʰ April, 1874

Paddington, New South Wales

During the six days they held me captive at the new hospital under the soporific effect of laudanum, I had only one dream that I remember. It was vivid and terrifying: Harper's malevolent face was pushed up close to mine and his voice was harsh and threatening as he whispered, 'I told you I would kill you both but you didn't believe me.' I could smell his rum-soaked breath hot on my face. That awful image replayed itself every time I regained consciousness.

There were times when I awoke and all was darkness. I was thirsty and hungry and alone with my pain and distress for Sarah. I would call for her but only a nun would come. Other times, during the day, Patrick was there and took care of me with the kind of love I knew I could never reciprocate.

Through all this, no one would tell me about Sarah.

Time heals all wounds, so goes the old idiom, but only those of the body.

My chest still hurt but I could move now without the debilitating pain of before and the swelling to my face had lessened, which meant I could now see even though I had bouts of dizziness and ghastly headaches. I was finally released from the custody of the Sisters of Charity and given into the care of Mr Morrison with the recommendation that I be kept in a calm and quiet state of mind. But calmness and quietude for me were lost to fear and worry for Sarah. I was determined to know that Sarah was well and with her parents in Parramatta.

The short buggy ride home over the uneven Old South Head road caused me to feel my injuries despite the medicine the nuns had administered on my departure. That same medication made me drowsy and unable to form coherent sentences. My brain was working but my mouth was not.

When we arrived at the courtyard of the hotel, Mr Morrison helped me out of the carriage and Patrick led me to the back stairs. I clasped the banister at the bottom step and willed myself up, but my feet were leaden dead weights and any energy in my limbs had been exhausted by inactivity.

'Hold on, Becky,' Patrick murmured as he scooped me up in his arms and carried me up the three flights. I clung to his neck in a painful stupor.

Mr Morrison preceded us and, upon reaching the top landing, opened the door to my room and we went in. I realised where we were and the memories flooded back. An anguished cry escaped me as Patrick placed me on my bed. I was overcome with anger, regret, grief. My ribs stabbed with each strangled sob. I peered at the floor where Napoleon had lain.

'Napoleon?' I whispered.

'We buried him in the courtyard, under the banksia,' Patrick quietly replied.

I expelled a heavy sigh and wiped away the tears of sorrow for the dog who gave his life to protect mine.

My thoughts turned to Sarah.

'Becky ...' Instinctively, Patrick tried consoling me.

I took his arm. Panic fuelled my question. 'And Sarah. Where's Sarah? Is she safe?'

Patrick couldn't meet my eyes. He looked to his father. My glance darted between them; I felt my heart race. I stopped breathing.

Mr Morrison sat on the end of the bed and cradled my legs. He spoke softly, gently, 'Rebecca, my darling Rebecca ... Sarah's dead.'

Every muscle in my body spasmed and an unbidden guttural cry filled my lungs.

I turned to Patrick and curled up. His arms wrapped me in his firm embrace as I wept.

So many emotions swirled and pulled at me: remorse that she had suffered because of me; grief that she had died because of him; anger that I was unable to save her; hatred for the man who took her from me; regret that we had not run away sooner.

But the most overpowering emotion was vengeance.

It overpowered remorse, drowned grief in a tide of retribution, anger and hatred burned in its fire, and regret withered in its intensity.

He would pay.

I don't know how long I stayed that way, curled up against Patrick, insensible to my surroundings, reliving the hell John Harper had brought upon us. At some point someone administered me more opiates and gradually my mind allowed the embers of vengeance to settle beneath the ashes, with a promise of rekindling.

When I awoke, it was nightfall and I was covered with a blanket.

'Here, drink this,' Patrick said, approaching with a cup of tea. 'It's fresh and hot.'

I gingerly sat up and took the cup.

Patrick pulled a chair close. 'I'm so sorry, Becky,' he said with subdued compassion. 'I know what she meant to you.'

The tea was a welcome restorative. After a few minutes, I regained control of my roiling thoughts. There had to be payment for taking a life. At the very least, I knew that justice would prevail and that bastard would hang for killing Sarah.

'Tell me he's in gaol.'

Patrick looked away.

'Patrick?'

'No.'

I did not understand. 'No?'

'The police superintendent said there was nothing they could charge him with.'

Words briefly escaped me. 'Sarah's dead. He killed her. He threatened to kill us both. And he did his damnedest to kill me. I will testify to that and more.'

'Becky, Pa and I tried, but the police determined that Sarah's death was an accident. Pa even went to see the Inspector General of Police, John McLerie.'

I could not process what Patrick was telling me. It contradicted every truth I had suffered. I shook my head, struggling to understand.

'She was found at the bottom of the stairs in Palmer Lane,' he continued. 'The staircase had come away. You know how rickety it was.

Harper said a scream and a crash woke him from a deep sleep early Sunday morning. He went to see what it was and found Sarah at the bottom of the stairs, motionless.'

'No … no …' I was in utter disbelief.

'Pa and I both know it's complete and total horseshit but there is no proof of what he did to you and Sarah. And Napoleon.'

'Who, then, did do this to me—and Napoleon?' I demanded.

'A burglar!' Patrick said, unconvinced by the absurdity of what he was saying. 'The police said you most likely disturbed a housebreaker when you came up. Harper swore that he and Sarah never left their place Saturday night.'

'He was here! Harper came here to take her back. She left him when he tried to strangle her. He must have followed her. Sarah came here! You saw her.'

'I didn't see her, Becky. You and I were dancing and you pulled away and left. I didn't know where you went or who you went with. The place was crowded and completely insane. But I do believe you. I do believe she was here.'

'Someone must have seen Sarah arrive. Heard the noise. Harper broke the door in.'

'The police made enquiries and no one came forward. No one saw or heard anything that night. Remember that almost everybody was here and it was quite raucous. And free grog. Most of the mob were swizzled. Palmer Lane is deserted at the best of times. You saw what it was like when we went. And if they took the back streets and dunny lanes … And he has an alibi.'

'An alibi? Whoever gave it is a liar.'

'His father.'

'Harper's father? He lives in Parramatta! How could—?'

'I know. But the police followed up and old Harper confirmed that he had visited his son that night in Darlinghurst and Sarah was with them all night.'

'That's an utter and complete lie!' I couldn't believe what Patrick was telling me. I stared at him, my head pounding. I couldn't believe the ineptitude of the police.

'Pa and I worked out how he did it. After the police interviewed Harper on Sunday morning, he took the train to Parramatta and told his father what he'd done and they concocted this story. It took the police two days before they went to Parramatta and spoke to the old piece of scum. He confirmed what his son claimed. They swallowed every word of it.'

I was becoming mired in desperation. Harper was getting away with murder. 'Napoleon mauled Harper's thigh. Did they ask him about that?'

'I didn't know that, Becky.'

'I'll tell them. And I'll tell them Harper's old man's a liar. Take me to the police.' I threw the rug off and attempted to climb out of bed. Patrick carefully pushed me back down.

'It won't make a difference, Becky. The police super has closed the case.'

'No!'

Harper had won.

'No! He has to hang for what he's done!'

'I want him to hang as well but, other than your word, there's no proof that he did it. I know how you felt about Sarah and how much you hated Harper. The police will see your evidence as spite. We have no actual proof that he was here and did this to you. Or Napoleon … or Sarah.'

'She was here. Sarah was here and Harper did do this to us.'

'I believe you, Becky. I believe you.' He went to my tallboy and removed a folded cloth from the top drawer. 'I found this when I cleaned up your room.' He handed me Sarah's shawl. 'I know she was here. I do believe you.'

I took it reverently and buried my face in its folds. 'Sarah …' I remembered the first time I saw her; the brief times we spent together; the promises I made. I'd let her down. I'd failed to protect her. She died because of me. 'Oh, Patrick, how could anyone do what he did?'

'Because he is what you said he is. A drunkard and a bastard. And he's got away scot-free.'

I felt like I was drowning in a sea of hopelessness; my reason for living had died with the woman I loved. 'Where is she now?'

'At St Patrick's Roman Catholic cemetery. Her parents took her back to Parramatta. They didn't want Harper to have anything further to do with her or her funeral. He came to see you, you know. At the hospital.'

My evident confusion spurred him on.

'On Thursday,' he continued, 'when I came to see you, there he was, like nothing had happened, standing over you. I don't know what he said to you but when he saw me, he left. I followed him out and warned him off. I told him he wasn't welcome at the hotel, either. In his usual charming manner, he told me to … well you can imagine what he told me.'

It wasn't a dream. 'He told me he was going to kill me.'

***

Mr Morrison was very considerate and allowed me all the time my body needed to mend itself; my heart and soul, however, would never mend. I wore Sarah's shawl and kept it beside me on my bed, always with me.

Patrick attended to my every need and kept close; he must have feared Harper would try to fulfil his promise.

I felt detached from the material endeavours that surrounded me. I read but absorbed nothing; I slept but fitfully; I missed Napoleon's antics. I missed Sarah.

***

'And who's going to be an old maid the day after tomorrow?' Patrick's cheerful goading spread a little sunshine on my gloom and raised a chortle from Mr Morrison as the three of us had a late breakfast together.

I was not looking forward to the celebration that Mr Morrison and Mrs Archer had been planning for months. My eighteenth birthday anniversary was to have opened the door to a new life for me and Sarah.

My yearning to see Sarah overcame me. 'I'm going to Parramatta,' I announced to no one in particular.

'I don't think that's a good idea,' Mr Morrison counselled. 'You don't know who'll be there.'

'I want to pay my respects.'

'Not by yourself.'

I looked to Patrick.

'I'll go with her, Pa,' he offered.

'I don't like it.'

'Harper's working in Botany now,' Patrick reassured. 'And, if he's not there, he'd be dead drunk in Darlinghurst. Why would he visit Sarah, anyway?'

Mr Morrison frowned. Clearly, he was not happy with this proposal and took his time to deliberate. 'All right, Son. But take the revolver with you.'

Patrick and I exchanged horrified looks.

'You don't know what feral dogs you might come across,' Mr Morrison concluded.

***

It was the middle of autumn and the weather was cool and threatening rain. Much to Patrick's dismay, I dressed in my trousers, collared shirt and jacket, as much to keep warm as to not feel restricted should the worst happen. Mr Morrison's old revolver was wrapped in a cloth that Patrick carried in the satchel slung across his shoulder.

We took the omnibus to the new Redfern Station close to Devonshire Street. There, I found a flower stall and purchased a large spray of red and white carnations. Carnations to represent love—my love for her—red for courage, passion and respect and white for purity and innocence—hers. I had wanted red roses but none were to be had.

The train journey took us through the stations at Newtown, Ashfield, Burwood, Homebush, Parramatta Junction then on to Parramatta Station. At each stop, I apprehensively scanned the passengers on the platform awaiting to embark.

Alighting at Parramatta Station, we were only a few blocks away from St Patrick's Roman Catholic Church and its cemetery … and Sarah.

It didn't take us long to locate her resting place. Her parents had erected a beautiful sandstone marker. Beneath the Calvary cross, the chiselled words brought renewed hopelessness and grief, but the last lines astonished me:

In Memory of our Beloved Daughter

Sarah Kathleen Harper

nee O'Dwyer

Born 16th July 1853

Died 5th April 1874

Weep not for me or my brief life;

I was a loving daughter and a dutiful wife;

My life was taken by a worthless sot

And God will punish whom the Law did not.

There was no doubt that Sarah's parents knew Sarah had died by Harper's hand and that they were, as we were, helpless in bringing that murderous bastard to justice.

Patrick put a reassuring arm around my shoulders. More to Sarah than to him, I whispered, 'Harper will pay. I swear this on my mother's grave—he will pay with his life.'

'Becky …' Patrick's words were more a warning that a comfort. 'Becky, he'll drink himself to death before long.'

I put the carnations at the foot of the headstone, made the sign of the cross and bowed my head in a silent prayer for Sarah's eternal peace … and for God to give me strength. Patrick did the same and, after a few minutes' silence, we left the cemetery. I did not know at the time that I would never visit Sarah again.

***

The next day, the eve of my eighteenth birthday, the heavens roared with thunderstorms and drenching rain. The gloom of the day clung to me like a cloak of foreboding. Visiting Sarah made her death real. My own mother's death hadn't even affected me this way. There had been no feeling of injustice in my mother's passing; it had been God's will. Sarah's? Was it God's will or the act of a man driven by his demons? I'd made Sarah promises that I had not kept but this last promise that I swore to her, I would keep very soon.

After supper and the day's work was finalised, I excused myself, bade everyone a good night and went to my room by the internal stairs.

Once there, I changed into my trousers and jacket and put on my mackintosh and cabbage tree—it was still raining an aggravating heavy drizzle but the violent storms had passed.

I went down via the external stairs to avoid being seen. I carefully opened the stable door and made sure the groom, Ernest, was still inside the hotel (most likely playing whist with the rest of the staff) and selected my favourite pony, Whiskey.

With an apology for waking him, I led him by his halter out through the door and out the back gate where I easily jumped onto his back. We walked off down the laneway in the persistent drizzling rain. I was a reasonably good horsewoman and had ridden bareback many times. Whiskey was docile and compliant so we would have no difficulty reaching my destination in good time and without incident.

We took the Old South Head road towards the city right up to George Street and then down towards Circular Quay. There was little pedestrian traffic this night and those who passed hurried along to get out of the rain. The carriages and omnibuses, too, appeared to be scurrying for shelter.

Reaching the end of George Street and the infamous Rocks, I looked for the street signs and found what I was seeking: Harrington Place.

I turned Whiskey on to it. It was dark, the street lighting was poor, and the only movement I saw was from the shadows of doorways—the burning red tip of a cigarette, the wispy smoke from a pipe decimated by the rain, a shiny water-soaked rat scampering from one pile of rubbish to another.

Corporal Roberts' words echoed in my head: It's a bad spot, Harrington Place. Keep well clear of it. And them.

Whiskey walked on until we came across a dishevelled old woman huddled in an entranceway.

Retrieving sixpence from my pocket, I offered it to her. 'Do you know where I can find Jeramiah Hickson? The Push?'

The old woman looked up at me with suspicion. 'What would you be wanting with him?' she croaked.

'Where can I find him?' I pushed the coin closer.

'Wharf three. The shed,' she said and snatched the coin from my hand.

'Thank you.'

I soon found what I sought. The old wooden shed next to the wharf was dimly lit from inside and, under the sizzling sound of the rain, I could hear the disorderly carryings-on of several men.

I slid off Whiskey and knocked on the door.

The voices fell silent. After a moment, the door opened slightly and a husky, genderless voice demanded, 'What do you want?'

'Jeremiah Hickson. I was told he was here.'

'And who are you, dearie?'

I didn't want to announce myself. 'Tell him it's the girl from Morrison's Hotel in Paddington. He probably won't remember me—'

'Course I remember you! The comely lass.' Hickson gushed as he pushed the interrogator out of the way. 'Come in, come in.' His invitation lacked any sincerity and made me cringe.

'No ... thank you.'

'All right, you're the one what's getting soaked. What can I do for you this fine evening?'

This was it. There was no going back once I made my declaration.

'Ain't going to wait all night, me lovely.' He began to close the door on me.

I pushed it open. 'I need your help.'

'Of course, sweetness, but I ain't no charity.'

'I can pay.' The words escaped me before I could reconsider the enormity of my contract.

'Up front.'

'I'll have the money on Monday.'

'Then I'll help you on Tuesday.' He looked me up and down and his lecherous thoughts amplified onto his ugly face. 'What is it that you want from me, my timid little titter?'

12

Sunday, 19ᵗʰ April, 1874

Paddington, New South Wales

The much anticipated night had finally arrived—much anticipated, that is, by Mr Morrison and Patrick, but not by me. My dream had been that Sarah would be with me to celebrate the event and to plan our future together. But this night, in the midst of twenty or so jovial people, a pall of betrayal enshrouded any thought of gaiety. I tried my best to show gratitude for every wish of long and healthy life offered; I tried to not seem unappreciative.

My mother, bless her memory, had made sure that I would be provided for and that my eighteenth birthday would be my 'coming of age' as she deemed. With Mr Morrison's guidance, she intended that I would become mature enough to lead my own life and control my own finances. She had entrusted Patrick's father with looking after my small inheritance until then and it was this that I now avidly anticipated.

The table in our private dining room was extended to accommodate all of the staff as well as my dear friends from the barracks, Corporal Roberts and his company of merry men.

The meal was splendid. Cook had prepared all my favourites—fricandeau of veal, stewed cucumbers with white sauce, potato ribbons and stuffed onions—lifting me out of my gloom. I allowed myself to feel special. I enjoyed the light-hearted chatting and amiable reminiscing. No one spoke of Sarah nor what had happened to me.

Patrick, as usual, was seated beside me and every now and then glanced my way, apparently checking to see how I was coping.

At some point, Cook and Patrick disappeared only to return moments later carrying a large iced cake with a burning candle atop it. The assembled crowd gave a mighty cheer.

My cheeks flushed with embarrassment that such a fuss was being made. The cake was a beautiful confection decorated with sugar roses and leaves.

Patrick carefully set the cake down in front of me. Cook resumed her place with an air of triumph.

Mr Morrison stood with a glass in his hand and tapped it with his knife. 'Quiet. Quiet, please.'

Everyone's attention turned to him.

'Thank you,' he continued, then addressed me directly. 'Rebecca Victoria Davies, today you have completed eighteen years on God's earth—'

The crowd cheered and stomped their feet and those who weren't encumbered with a glass of frothy beer clapped their hands.

Mr Morrison raised his hands, signalling for the crowd to settle down. 'The day you were born, when I first heard you cry, I remember thinking, "this one's trouble".'

This brought on another round of hooting and laughter, subdued once again by Mr Morrison. 'But, despite your propensity for wearing trousers and beating Patrick to a pulp at fisticuffs, you have grown into a fine young lady.'

I felt so deceitful when the crowd agreed and cheered; if they only knew what was in my heart and what I had planned.

'Your dear mother, Anwen, may God rest her soul, asked me to read these words—her words—to you tonight.' He retrieved a folded sheet of paper from his pocket. Those in the room who knew my mother held her in the highest regard. She was educated, well spoken and gentle. She would do anything to help anyone. Six years since her passing, I still missed her.

Mr Morrison read slowly and with compassion into the silence. As he read, I heard my mother's lilting Welsh voice speak directly to me.

'My darling daughter Rebecca, how I wish I could be there to celebrate this important milestone with you, but it is not God's will. Today, you leave your childhood behind and step tentatively into womanhood. If only I could be there to guide you through the dark, twisting alleyways of self-doubt into the broad, sun-filled boulevards of love and devotion. There is nothing more precious than respect and love; respect that is earned and love that is given. In the scant twelve years I have known you, my dearest Rebecca, I know that in whatever you choose to do, you will choose to do it for the right reasons and with honesty, integrity and love. Your lucky star will guide and protect you, and I will watch over you forever. May God bless you with a long and happy life. Your loving Mother.'

I thought that I had no more tears left, yet I found them falling once again. Were they for the grief of losing my mother; for the love that she and Sarah gave me; or for the hypocrisy that was to unfold?

Whatever my reasons, I found that the room had hushed save for a detached sniffle or two. Patrick wiped his eyes and blew his nose on his handkerchief and even Corporal Roberts, big and burly as he was, swiped his sleeve across his nose.

Finally, Mr Morrison took his glass up and addressed me. 'Make a wish and blow out the candle, dear.'

I did as requested. The wish I made that day ruled the rest of my life. I wished that God would give me the strength and courage to deliver justice to those who harm women or children. Or dogs.

The festivities continued late into the night.

One by one, the guests and staff, hunger sated and thirst slaked, made their way home or to their quarters after delivering me their final wishes and farewells.

Mrs Archer, Edith and the two new maids quickly cleared the table leaving Patrick and me to close up.

Once Patrick slipped the final bolt in place, he quietly approached me as I turned down the paraffin lamps.

'Rebecca Victoria Davies, will you marry me?' His earnest voice was little more than a whisper.

I could not hide my surprise and perhaps he read it. He flushed a bright pink.

'Of course, you don't have to answer me now. Think about it. Good night.'

He hurried out, leaving me bobbing in the wake of his words. We had joked about marriage many times but this was a genuine proposal. If I had ever wanted to be married and have children, it certainly would have been to Patrick, for I knew no other more sincere, caring or supportive young man in the whole colony. Had I misled him? How could I decline his offer without hurting his feelings and damaging his pride?

***

As promised, Mr Morrison took me to the Bank of New South Wales the very first thing the next day, a Monday, and formalised the transfer of my mother's bequest to me. It was a tidy sum—more than I had expected. Mr Morrison was an astute businessman and, while I certainly wasn't the richest eighteen-year-old in the colony, my inheritance would have made a handsome dowry.

Once the transfer was completed, we took care of a few errands in town and then made our way home where, outwardly, nothing had changed.

Patrick was his usual ebullient self, even though I knew he was smarting from my tacit rejection, and Mr Morrison still treated me like his own daughter, even though I knew he was concerned that I would squander the small fortune. And I pretended that all was well, even though the plans I had devised meant that everything would imminently change forever.

After the luncheon ritual was complete, I took my afternoon break. I urged Whiskey along faster than his normal unhurried pace and made it to the bank just before closing time.

At our next stop, I would commit to an act, if I went ahead with it, that I would never be able to undo.

My face and heart hardened with resolve. It had to be done and I was the only one to do it. I heeled Whiskey and headed for the wharves.

13

Tuesday, 21ˢᵗ April, 1874

Paddington, New South Wales

Due to the heavy rain, it was unlikely that there would be any activity at the many building sites around the city and surrounding areas. The roads were drenched and muddy, as were the few patrons who ventured out in such inclement weather to share a beer with their mates. Consequently, there was not very much to do in the bar that evening.

The night wore on and each time I looked at our longcase clock in the foyer, the passing of an hour seemed to take twice as long as the one before.

Closing time finally arrived and the rain had abated but still persisted with sporadic outbursts of drizzle. After completing the last of my chores, I said my good nights and headed up to my room. Rather than changing into my night dress, I donned my shirt and trousers, and wrapped Sarah's shawl about my neck. I lay down on my bed, eyes fixed firmly on my little mantle clock. It was quarter of twelve. 'Only a few hours left,' I found myself whispering.

I felt nothing but righteousness.

***

I stood at the foot of the long ladder that stood in place of the shattered stairs—they lay discarded in pieces on the ground nearby. These were the accomplices in a cowardly act of murder. The rain desisted and the sallow moon peeked from its hiding place low in the western sky. I peered up to see the door ajar and a feeble light flickering through the window. Faint shadows glanced against the uncurtained window. I tied Whiskey's halter lead to the forsaken stairs and took my first tentative step up the unsteady ladder. Was it I who was shaking or the ladder? With each step my apprehension grew.

I made it to the landing and avoided looking through the window. My heartbeat quickened and my breathing shallowed. I tightened the shawl around my shoulders. Steeling myself against what I imagined I would find when I opened the door, I pushed it open enough to edge in unobserved and merged into the shadow of the furthest corner.

The room that Sarah had kept so clean and neat a few short weeks ago was now an untidy, unkempt confusion of empty rum bottles, discarded clothing and unwashed kitchen utensils, which the one fat tallow candle, burning slowly near the bed, pitilessly highlighted.

The curtain that divided the bedroom from the rest of the chaos hung pushed to the side.

Strewn haphazardly across that bed was the unconscious, dishevelled form of John Harper, a bottle of rum clenched in his fist. I could not loathe anybody more than I loathed him.

The intermittent rain resumed with persistence. It hissed on the corrugated iron roof and seeped through its several rust holes, plopping onto the floorboards. The only other sound was Harper's snoring; he was in a deep, alcohol-induced sleep.

The rain had prevented him from working so his days must have been occupied by drinking away the wages he earned from Rourke. Had he paid his debt to the usurer? A moot point. Soon all debts would be paid—in full.

Harper hadn't heard me, nor had he heard the four men who had preceded me and who now surrounded his bed.

I knew what was to come. I stood and watched unmoved, my mind perceiving but not reacting.

'Wake up, princess,' the gruff mocking voice wheezed into Harper's ear. 'Wake up, your highness.'

A hand prodded Harper's shoulder. He grumbled and flung off the offending hand. 'Go away!' he slurred, rolling towards the wall. But the hand was insistent and soon joined by another that jerked him out of his incoherence.

'Rise and shine, your majesty.'

Harper suddenly became aware of the obnoxious face, practically nose to nose, sneering malevolence. He recoiled, pushing himself upright to see three others standing behind the owner of the ugly face. 'Who are you?' The shock of seeing these loathsome intruders seemed to jar him awake.

'Let me introduce ourselves. That's Ratface, Shingles and Tuppenny. And I'm Jeremiah Hickson,' was the rough reply.

'What do you want? I don't have any money.'

'We know that, sunshine. Money ain't what we want.'

'I don't have anything worth stealing,' he volunteered as he pushed himself against the bedhead, his face betraying his confusion and fear.

'An apology.'

'Wha—?'

'You heard, petal. We want you to say you're sorry. An apology.'

Harper's breathing became erratic. A glimmer of recognition appeared in his eyes. 'You're … you're the Larrikin mob from Morrison's pub—'

Hickson grabbed Harper by his shirt and pulled him off the bed. 'Got it in one, darling. Now for that apology.'

Hickson pushed Harper towards the table while Ratface, the shabbiest of the four, cleared the unwashed cup and plate and placed a sheet of paper and pencil.

John was clearly regaining his sensibilities and began to rail at the intrusion. He struggled with Hickson but his arms were grabbed by Shingles and Tuppenny, both larger than Hickson, who thrust Harper into the awaiting chair and held him there, unable to move.

'Let me go!' he ordered, his voice assertive yet quavering.

'Soon,' promised Hickson, pushing the piece of paper and pencil towards Harper. 'Now let's make this simple. Write, "I'm sorry for everything".'

'Tell them to let go of my arms!'

Hickson nodded and Tuppenny released Harper's arm. Seizing the opportunity to break free, Harper sprang from the chair and pushed Shingles away. He took a few steps before all four louts slammed into him. A heavy punch by Hickson to Harper's diaphragm instantly subdued him and he was thrust back into his chair, doubled up, struggling to breathe.

Hickson bent over him. 'Don't make this harder than it need be, Johnno,' he threatened. 'It'll be done soon and we'll be gone. Now write.'

Harper, still gasping for breath, picked up the pencil and scrawled as Hickson slowly dictated.

'"I'm sorry for everything." Good boy. Now sign it.'

Ratface, peering over Harper's shoulder, queried, 'Ain't "everythink" with a "k"?'

'Shut up, idiot.' Hickson picked up the sheet of paper and admired it. 'Good. Good.' He placed it in the centre of the table.

Harper's eyes darted from one to another, his breath as shallow as the puddles of dripping raindrops that plopped nearby. His hands shook and his mouth was as dry as the Simpson. He roused his courage. 'You got what you wanted, now go.'

'Not quite done yet, laddie,' Hickson teased, then glanced at his men.

Shingles produced a long coil of rope and tossed one end over a rafter; it was tied into a noose.

'No! NO!' Harper shouted, and sprang to his feet, darting towards the door. Hickson caught him by the legs and in a heartbeat, Ratface and Tuppenny were on top of him as he thrashed about in a desperate struggle to free himself. They hauled him up to his feet.

It was then that Harper caught sight of me.

'YOU!' he screamed.

He writhed, kicked and thrashed but their hold was unbreakable.

His energy depleted, he stopped struggling. 'No, please don't,' he wailed as they dragged him towards the awaiting rope. 'Please, please,' he cried, tears streaming down his face. 'What did I do to you? Please don't do this. You!' he shrieked at me, 'You won't—'

Hickson took hold of the noose and managed to push it over Harper's head. 'This won't hurt a bit …' he assured. 'It'll hurt a lot!'

That brought peals of laughter from his gang.

'No … no … NO …'

The rope tightened around Harper's neck. Shingles pulled the other end taut. Harper was lifted by his neck, his feet just barely touching the floor in a macabre ballet dance.

The three men holding him let go.

Harper desperately grabbed at the rope around his neck that was slowly strangling him, trying to loosen it. The three men joined the fourth and pulled down on the rope in unison.

Harper was lifted several feet into the air, thrashing his legs, twisting and turning, unable to breathe, unable to speak, unable to beg for mercy. Mercy was something he would never get from me; it was something he never gave Sarah.

I watched, detached from empathy, untouched by remorse and satisfied that justice was being served.

Hickson and his boys found immense amusement in the horrendous sight, whooping and slapping each others' backs in merriment.

'He's a fine dancer, ain't he?' mocked Ratface.

Harper's struggles became involuntary twitches as the tightening noose squeezed the life from him.

His body finally stopped moving and hung limply.

Hickson wrapped the end of the rope around a post and securely tied it.

'Top'd and twisted,' Hickson declared with satisfaction as he placed the chair near Harper's feet then kicked it over. 'Job's done, Missy,' he advised casually as though he had just swept the floor. 'Come on, boys.'

Hickson saw Ratface rifle through the chest of drawers. 'Oy! What are you doing?'

'Just seeing if there's anything worth having,' was the frank reply.

'Leave it, idiot. Suicides don't steal from themselves.'

They filed out of the hovel and all was silent save for the hiss of the rain on the corrugated iron roof, the plopping of the drops on the floorboards, and the creaking of the rope as it stretched under the weight of John Harper's dead form.

I can't recall how long I stood transfixed by the sight of the corpse and by the enormity of what I had set in motion, but what I saw in the dim, flickering candlelight suddenly made my stomach turn. I retched. Was my conscience conquering my lack of compassion? Was I justified in taking a life, in meting retribution? Vengeance?

Regaining my composure, I stepped cautiously out of the dimness and forced myself to look at the scene before me: John Harper, his unseeing eyes bulging through his eyelids, his swollen tongue protruding from his blue lips, suspended from the ceiling rafter, slowly turning like a carousel in a fairground. His corpse was limp and had lost control of its bodily functions; urine and excrement soiled his trousers and the floor beneath him.

I stared at him for a long time, conflicted by what I had put in motion. My arms tightened around me and pulled the shawl closer.

Had he not been the John Harper who had murdered Sarah, killed my dog and tried his damnedest to kill me, I could have found sympathy for this man and would have prayed that God take his soul in peaceful rest. But he *was* John Harper and he had escaped the law's justice and this, his end, was what he deserved. I did the righteous thing but I would surely pay dearly for it.

'I will see you in Hell, John Harper,' I cursed, for that's where he and I would spend eternity.

I willed my anger to dissipate and looked about the room that until a few weeks prior, Sarah had filled with her light and presence. Despite the havoc of Harper's living habits, I could still see Sarah there. I imagined what horror her last few hours must have been, the fear and pain she had suffered. The last vestiges of sympathy or remorse I may have had for the bastard were consumed by the coldness of my heart.

I wanted something more to remember her by. I turned to the chest of drawers and opened the top one carefully. It was as disordered as the rest of the room and held only Harper's few items of outer and underwear. The middle drawer was empty save for an old tin can with some shirt studs in it.

The bottom drawer was filled with an old woollen, moth-eaten blanket. I found nothing of Sarah's. Not a comb, not a glove, not a pair of shoes or stockings. The bastard had rid himself of his wife and all that reminded him of her.

I pulled the blanket aside and heard the clunk of metal against the side of the drawer. Lifting the blanket, I discovered an old revolver and a small canvas bag with a dozen or so cartridges in it. The gun was loaded. It puzzled me: Sarah would have known of its existence. Why had she not used it to protect herself?

Speculation was useless.

I slipped the gun and the canvas bag into my coat pockets and closed the drawer. Among the debris that littered the floor was Harper's rumpled coat. A glint caught my attention. Stooping down, I grasped the silvery metal that peeked from an inside pocket and pulled free a silver chain and locket. Sarah's locket. I imagined that this was not a keepsake but that it would have been the next item pawned to satisfy his alcoholism.

I opened the locket. Sarah's image looked back at me, serene, youthful, unchanging. I closed my eyes and once again felt the touch of her hand, heard the joy in her laughter, savoured the tenderness of our first kiss. This silver locket, a gift from her parents, was Sarah. I fastened it around my neck—she would be with me always.

Taking one last look about the room, I felt complete—the final promise I'd made to Sarah had been kept.

It was a long way back to my bed. Both Whiskey and I were exhausted by the long day and night. In a few hours, the sun would rise bringing a new day for most in the colony of New South Wales. But not for one.

***

'Did you hear the news?' Patrick panted as he ran into the dining room. We had just sat down for our luncheon break. He sat in his usual place next to me, spreading his napkin across his lap and helping himself to the food. 'John Harper is dead.'

A gasp of horror echoed though the room.

'Yes,' he continued. 'Brendan Rourke went to his place to collect him when he didn't show up for work this morning and found him hanging from the roof beam. Suicide. There was a note that said he was sorry.'

'His conscience must have got to him,' offered Mr Morrison unsympathetically.

'Should have done it months ago,' I said flatly. 'Then Sarah would still be alive.'

Patrick broke the silence that had followed my words. 'Corporal Roberts told me that there were muddy footprints on the floor. He could have had visitors.'

'Or they could have been Rourke's,' I suggested. 'Are the police going to investigate or assume suicide just like they assumed Sarah's death was an accident?'

Patrick screwed up his face at my cold directness. 'Why would they think otherwise?' He addressed his father. 'Rourke's in a state of apoplexy. Not only has he lost one of the few carpenters left in Sydney, but he's lost the hefty advance he gave Harper when he started the new job. Harper left nothing of any value except the few tools he hadn't yet pawned.'

Patrick shot me a suspicious glance. I knew what he was thinking but I wasn't about to say another word. I resumed eating my meal.

For the remainder of the day, I kept to myself and completed my chores quickly, then retired to my room for my afternoon break after I had spoken to Mr Morrison in private. I wasn't there half an hour when a frantic knock on my door took my attention away from the list I was making.

'Come in, Patrick.'

Patrick closed the door behind him and sat on my bed.

'Just say it,' I urged when the silence had stretched long enough.

'Pa just told me you're going away. Why? Where to?' He sounded hurt.

I felt for him, but not enough to forestall my plans. 'I need to get away from everything that reminds me of what happened. To allow my body to heal. To forget.'

'But this is your home. You've never been away. You've only ever gone as far as Manly and … and—'

'Parramatta?'

'You want to get away from me? From Pa?'

'No, I don't want to get away from you or your father but, unless you both come with me,' I joked, 'there's no other way. I can't stay. I don't want to stay.'

'Harper's gone. He's no longer a threat. *Why* must you leave?'

A pang of guilt squeezed my heart. I couldn't meet his eyes. And I couldn't tell him; that would make him complicit in my crime. Paying to have Harper killed was a felony for which, if caught, I would surely hang, regardless of my motivations. I had to leave and become invisible, lest the truth be discovered.

'I need to find some peace, Patrick, and I won't find it here. Once I have achieved that, I will return. I promise.'

'Marry me.'

Those words were thrown at me as a distressed appeal rather than a threatening demand. I was desperate to tell him and yet desperate to keep him ignorant of my actions, in case he should forsake me for them.

'Patrick, you're like a brother to me. I love you but not like that.'

'It doesn't matter. You'll come to love me like that.'

His pleas only worsened my guilt. I was betraying him. But more so, I would be betraying myself if I gave in.

'I can't love you. Not the way you want. It was Sarah who captured my heart in a way no man ever could … or will—'

'I'll come with you,' he blurted in despair, rejecting my honesty.

'And leave your father to manage the hotel that will one day be yours?'

Defeated, he finally accepted my words and his shoulders slumped.

'When are you leaving?' he asked as last.

'After I've sorted out my room.'

'This room is yours. I'll keep it for you … forever, if necessary.'

I was genuinely grateful and while I doubted that I would ever return, one could never foretell the direction one's life's path would take.

'Where are you going to go?' Patrick asked.

'Wales,' I lied. 'Cardiff—to see where my mother was born and where she lived until she came here.'

'Well, at least she left you with enough to take care of the passage and then some.'

'Yes,' I lied again, for I had used most of my inheritance to pay for services rendered by the Push.

Patrick stood up and came over to where I sat. 'You will come back, won't you Becky? You are the only girl in this whole colony that I would ask to marry.' He took my hand and guided me from my chair and into his arms, tenderly folding them around me.

I returned his gentle embrace and replied in all honesty, 'And you are the only boy I would ever consider marrying if my nature were different.'

***

A frantic ten days later, I was ready to travel. I had packed everything I needed in two new red leather valises. For my own safety, I dressed in male clothing but had also packed ample feminine attire with my extra shirts and trousers. With much reluctance, I left all my precious books behind, save two.

I wore Sarah's locket about my neck and Sarah's shawl wrapped my shoulders beneath my coat. Harper's revolver was safely packed in one of my valises.

The buzz that surrounded Harper's death had subsided and the police, according to Corporal Roberts, were to submit their report to the Coroner who would most likely return a finding of suicide, driven to it by the grief over the death of his beloved wife.

At last, I was ready to go. I stood in the middle of the room that had been my world since I drew breath eighteen years ago. I looked around and could see my mother reading to me, Sarah sitting beside me on my bed laughing at my silliness, Napoleon, as a puppy, gambolling about. Happy memories, filled with love … then darkness. I heard Sarah's screams, Napoleon's yelps, Harper's violent threats …

Patrick broke my trance. 'The buggy's ready. Are you sure you don't want me to see you off at the docks?'

'I'm sure. I don't want tears in public.'

'It's all right for you to cry,' he consoled.

'Not me! You!' I joked.

At this, he prodded me in the ribs. I flinched—they were still quite painful.

'Oh, sorry!' he promptly apologised.

I was going to miss him.

With a contrite look, he picked up my valises and we left. 'You will write, won't you?'

'Every day.'

I was finding it easier and easier to lie. In truth, I was not going to the docks but to the Cobb office in the town. I was not going to the Mother Country but to Melbourne and the goldfields. I would not write to Patrick, nor anyone else.

14

Friday, 1ˢᵗ September, 1905

London, England

After a restful sleep I woke to a pleasant autumn day. The bath had cleansed my mind as well as my body and although my dear Patrick's letter brought back some terrible memories, it also made me feel homesick.

Once I was released from this assignment, I vowed to myself, I would write to him and tell him the truth about the past thirty-one years of my life, sparing no detail. I did so want to see him again. Mr Morrison, his father, had passed away some years ago and the Morrison Family Hotel was now Patrick's. He had done exceptionally well by all accounts.

But the job at hand was the breaking up of this ring of anarchists or communists abducting our heiresses.

It was 8 am and I expected Wills to collect me at one. With renewed vigour, I washed and dressed in my customary Special Branch clobber: black calf-length split skirt, knee-high riding boots, white shirt with stiffened linen collar and cuffs, a black tie and a loose black cropped jacket under which I concealed my holstered Webley in a bespoke harness that nestled under my bosom against my stomach. Inside my right boot I carried a switch-bladed stiletto—all issued by the Metropolitan Police to their Special Branch officers. In effect, I was as much a spy and assassin as Wills and the eight men in our covert section.

My Gladstone accompanied me wherever I went and contained the remaining tools of trade: my blacks, a battery-operated flashlight, manacles and other devices I would need to subdue or eliminate threats.

I ran my fingers through my short-cropped white hair smoothing it down before containing it in my woollen cloth cap. While I may have been comely in my youth—maybe boyish—now, in my middle-age, the most generous term given me is 'mannish', and the least, 'repulsive'. I was as plain as poor Jane Eyre, as Charlotte Brontë so insistently described her. Adding to my physical defects were my facial scars, evidence of the brutality inflicted upon me some twenty years prior. The small scar over my right brow had faded to be almost imperceptible but the much larger one to my left cheek, tracing from temple to jaw and now faded to a jagged white line, was a reminder that the slash from that wretched Mussulman's dagger had just missed my eye. The pain had gone, but the memory was raw. For this reason, I rarely looked in a mirror. While I was not ashamed of the mementos, I was well aware of how I appeared to those who laid eyes on me for the first time.

Checking the watch strapped to my wrist, I collected my overcoat and kit bag, and, satisfied that all in the room was as it should be, locked my front door behind me.

Exactly on time, a hansom pulled up and I joined Wills as we settled in for the short journey to New Scotland Yard.

'I had a letter from Patrick.' We rarely bothered with greetings.

'Oh? And what tale have you spun in your reply?'

'That I'll be leaving the service of Mr and Mrs Quinn as soon as the children go to boarding school.'

'As long as the children *have* been sorted and *are* in school. You're not leaving until then, old girl.' As an afterthought, he added, 'You don't really want to leave me, do you?'

'No. Just the service of Mr and Mrs Quinn.'

Ours was a special relationship—one that *Mrs* Major Reginald Williams did not understand nor appreciate. She was sure that Wills and I were more than colleagues, even though Wills went to great pains to explain to her that I would be more interested in bedding her than him. This, of course, disgusted her and made her dislike me even more, if that were possible. But it suited me—I could keep her at arm's length.

We sat in silence the rest of the way—it was indiscrete to discuss our 'work' in public. Only upon reaching the inner sanctum of Wills' compact office could he appraise me of his recent endeavours.

'We've been taken off the case,' he unconcernedly informed me as he hung his Homberg on the coat rack.

'What do you mean?' His casual announcement stopped me mid-step.

Wills settled into his old swivel chair. 'Hawthorne's put Yabsley in charge and we're to take leave.'

'Yabsley? That's as good as putting a lunatic in charge of Bedlam.'

'That's harsh, Rebecca,' he admonished. 'I went to see Alexander Quinn after I dropped you off yesterday and reported what we overheard at the Marlborough. As we suspected, that Colonel Humphries fellow has nothing to do the Metropolitan Police nor the Home Office. The only connection he and Hawthorne have is that they fought together in South Africa. Quinn was intrigued as to why Hawthorne was conferring with Humphries on a confidential case.'

'Why take us off the case?'

Wills' face gleamed with self-satisfaction beneath his neatly trimmed and waxed moustache. 'Hawthorne approached Quinn yesterday evening and requested that you and I be removed because of the foul up in securing the girl's safe return.'

'That's nothing for you to gloat over.' I was annoyed that we were to lose the case to incompetence.

'The report Hawthorne gave Quinn,' Wills continued, 'did not correspond with the one I gave him. Hawthorne glossed over some very salient facts, such as the confusion over the coordinates. Quinn is no fool. This morning, he summoned me and we discussed at length our suspicions that the next victim will be the Duchess of Bramwell. He's not willing to risk another woman's life through lack of action, so you and I are going on a lovely holiday in Suffolk.'

'When do we leave?'

'As soon as we've packed and finalised the paperwork here.'

'What about Hawthorne? Who's looking into his activities?'

'Quinn. The most important thing now is to foil another murder and to apprehend the perpetrators.'

I was very pleased that Hawthorne had not thwarted us yet again and that we might at last bring the fiends to justice.

'What about Timmy?' I enquired, genuinely concerned for his wellbeing—even though I was ready to dispatch him when I first laid eyes upon him. He was a dupe and I knew firsthand what it was to be desperate for money and gulled into doing something criminal.

Wills hesitated. 'The boy's dead.'

I struggled to process his utterance. 'Dead? How?'

'Yabsley was to have interviewed him after we left.'

'He killed the boy?' The beating meted out to Timmy was bad enough but to return and then finish him off was more than I could tolerate. 'The lunatic bastard!' I snapped. 'He'll pay!'

'As much as you …' Wills searched for the right word, '*dislike* Yabsley I don't believe he did this, but that's for another day.'

Wills' assessment of character was usually right. As much as I detested Yabsley, I gave way to reason and eased my rage back into its box. 'What about his dog?' I eventually asked.

'The gaoler was told to get rid of it.'

I recoiled from the thought of the dog being destroyed. Wills swiftly continued, 'But I managed to find Mikey and took him home to Cornelia before I collected you.'

Before I could call him a marshmallow, Wills added immediately. 'For Reggie, you understand. A seven-year-old needs a dog.'

He shuffled some papers on his desk, glanced up at me, then rose to his feet. 'Right then. Quinn wants to see the both of us before we're officially suspended. Ready?'

***

The Special Branch of the Metropolitan Police had been formed a little more than two decades earlier as a unit dedicated to countering terror attacks carried out by the militant Irish Fenians. The DSO— Department of Special Operations—was the secret section within the special branch that dealt with matters so sensitive that they were directed to be kept secret from the general public.

While Colonel Sir Giles Hawthorne was the acknowledged head of the DSO, matters of particular urgency or sensitivity were handled personally by the Special Branch's head, Mr Alexander Quinn, an erudite and energetic man who always made time for Major Williams.

Whether his favour was due to the several citations and medals Wills had earned during his military career or Wills' connection with Major General Stokes, it was a mystery to many why Wills was not in Hawthorne's position. Wills readily admitted in private he preferred the field work (as did I), disliked the paperwork, and felt he was of more benefit to the empire being involved in protecting the aristocracy and the monarch.

Quinn's demeanour was always subdued and gentlemanly, as was his appearance. A little under six feet tall and balding, he was nevertheless handsome and ruggedly built. Like all ex-military men, he sported no facial hair, save a generous moustache. And like Wills, he was fashionably-dressed.

Quinn greeted Wills and me cordially. Our meeting was brief and our orders succinct: proceed to Abbottsford Hall, protect the Duchess of Bramwell and capture *alive* any person who threatens her life. He directed that last order at me.

We had only a day to prepare for our indeterminable stay and to get to the country seat of the Norlands—one of the oldest families in England. The modus operandi of these insurgents seemed to be to abduct one frail female, hold her to ransom—in ever-increasing amounts—and then despatch the victim once the ransom was paid but not before subjecting her to indignities too vile to name.

Hawthorne had a contingency of eight well-trained men but seemed to flounder in making decisions based on evidence and probabilities; every one he had made so far had led to dead ends. He had blamed the inaccuracy of the evidence, the inability of certain men to carry out their assigned tasks and, finally, Wills for fouling up the coordinates and allowing the perpetrators to escape.

Something was definitely amiss in the Chief Administrator's office.

After our meeting with the Head of the Special Branch, Quinn immediately contacted the Home Secretary, Aretas Akers-Douglas, who contacted the Prime Minister and a meeting was arranged between Quinn and the Duke of Bramwell, Charles Dunmore Norland. Quinn was to meet us at Abbottsford Hall without announcing our real agenda to his subordinates.

15

Sunday, 3rd September, 1905

Abbottsford Hall, Suffolk, England

After the three hour, monotonously hypnotic train journey, it was another fifteen minute coach ride to Abbottsford Hall. Wills and I hardly exchanged a word, as was our wont.

The duke's brougham carriage was snug but not warm without the foot warmers the coachman had obviously forgotten to provide. Wills re-donned his great coat, obscuring his immaculate dark brown three-piece suit. He occupied his time reading through volumes of reports and making notes, while my thoughts led me through the incidents that brought us to this moment. More than once they veered away and into the distant recesses of my past and I realised how similar my circumstances had been to young Timmy's.

I had been the same age as Timmy and while perhaps not as naïve, I certainly had been duped into committing a dreadful crime by the need for money to survive. I toyed with the silver locket through my shirt as I gazed at the distant landscape.

'You're quieter than normal,' Wills observed, neatening the files on his lap. 'Penny for your thoughts,' he bid.

I shot him a stern glare.

'Oh, all right, threepence, then,' he offered with a gentle chuckle.

While Wills was officially my 'superior officer' and mentor, his attitude towards me showed that he considered me his equal in every way. He reminded me of Patrick who was two years my senior. Wills was five years my junior and we made a cohesive, symbiotic team.

'Thinking of Paddington again? Of Sarah?' he probed. 'London's your home now, Bec.'

'I'm tired. That letter from Patrick brought home just how much I've missed of his life in Sydney.'

'That's his life; this is yours.'

'He's a respected member of parliament and I'm a … a … Just what am I, Wills?'

'You're an agent of the king, and your job is to protect him and his realm.'

I couldn't help expressing my thoughts and fears. 'Maybe Hawthorne and Yabsley are right.'

'What utter horseshit.'

'I was ready to blow Timmy's brains out without a second thought.'

'Pull yourself together, Davies. We have a very difficult task at hand. I don't want you being maudlin and feeling sorry for yourself.'

He was right, I was drowning in self-pity.

'Besides,' he added in a genial manner, 'what would you do with yourself if you gave this game away? You don't have a husband to support your … peccadillos. What would you take as employment? Nurse? Governess? Teacher? I'd be happy to write you a character: "To whom it may concern. Miss Rebecca Victoria Davies, proficient spy and assassin, deadly shot with pistol or rifle, lethal wielding a garrotte or stiletto, excels in stealth, subterfuge and cunning." Yes, highly sought-after qualifications in the art of looking after children.'

He was right again; I was no good for anything useful in the normal world.

'Now pull yourself out of this funk. I won't hear any more of that rubbish.' He returned to his pile of papers then looked sheepishly up at me. 'And you would miss me, wouldn't you?'

I chuckled. 'As much as you would miss me.'

He gave me a broad smile and again resumed his reading.

I knew he truly cared for me—in a platonic way. He was a gentleman and had never tried anything with me—except that time, all those years ago, when we were both so drunk. What a fiasco that had been—one that we had vowed never to mention again. Once we had returned to England, Wills had settled down and finally proposed to his longtime sweetheart, Cornelia Coltrane, and has been happily married ever since. They had only one child—a much-loved seven-year-old son, Reginald Junior. Of course, being who and what I was, Mrs Williams never requested my presence at the family residence.

I returned to gaze out the coach window, seeing nothing but blurry impressions of trees flashing by. My thoughts turned once more to Timmy and how he and his father and uncle had been used. Images of my own flight from Paddington came flooding back—that damned letter from Patrick.

16

Saturday, 2nd May, 1874

Beechworth, Victoria

The red and yellow coach-and-five trundled along the stony bush road to Beechworth, made slushy by puddles from the recent late autumn rain. The driver was a middle-aged American who deftly handled a separate rein for each of the five horses. He had graciously and unexpectedly introduced himself at the beginning of the journey as Lucas Taylor from San Francisco and each of his passengers replied in kind. From that time on, he addressed each of us by name.

I had presented at the Cobb office in Sydney as *Robert* Davies, attired as I was in male costume. I purposely lowered the pitch of my voice to carry the charade more effectively. Being a young man, I was expected to sit atop the coach and leave the more comfortable arrangement of inside seating to women, children and the elderly.

This, I discovered, would be to my benefit, for the inside of the coach was dark and cramped with thinly padded wooden seats. On this leg of the journey, four women, two children and an elderly man were crammed inside and jostled together with each bump and knock from the rutted road. I was pleased to be sitting on the carriage roof with the luggage arranged and strapped down around me. Huddled under my mackintosh and hat, I felt quite safe and cosy. My ribs were still sore but I had bound my chest tightly so that the jarring from the rough road caused me only minor discomfort at times.

Next to Taylor sat a young man, Godfrey Saunders, who had introduced himself as a clerk and who had paid a small 'gratuity' to be allowed to sit on the box seat. Had I the wherewithal, I might have done my best to outbid Godfrey Saunders, but I was content enough where I was.

Up here, apart from some light rain, the air was fresh and the conversation interesting. Taylor was garrulous and kept up an incessant string of chatter with Saunders and me, even though I was not in any mood to be talkative.

We travelled at a steady trotting pace and every fifteen to thirty miles or so, we changed horses for a fresh team. Each team was perfectly matched in colour and made a fine showing. Compared to train travel, where it was available, this mode was slow going, but what little money I had left meant I had to economise and the railways were out of the question.

Our next change station was going to be just outside of Beechworth, nestled in the May Day Hills and along the Reedy Creek, which was as far as my money was allowing me to go. This township had grown considerably with the discovery of gold some twenty years before and now it had settled into a stable country town determined to have a railway connection. I had to find some sort of employment there so I could continue my journey to Melbourne, and anonymity, some hundred and eighty miles away.

'What are your plans in Melbourne?' Taylor enquired of Saunders over the clatter and rumble of hooves and wheels.

'I'm to oversee our branch office in Elizabeth Street,' Saunders replied.

'Married?'

'Not yet. My fiancée will join me once I've settled in and found a house.'

'Ah, family. I have a boy in Bendigo just about his age,' Taylor said referring to me. 'And you, Robert,' he said over his shoulder, 'you're leaving us in Beechworth. What are your plans?'

'Look for a job to pay for the rest of my fare to Melbourne,' I replied reluctantly.

'Not gold prospecting, then?' Taylor laughed. 'Make a quick buck?'

'No. I wouldn't know how.'

'Easy come, easy go,' Saunders chimed in. 'An honest day's work for an honest day's pay is the best way. There's really no other choice.'

Saunders' rhetoric spurred me. 'There's always a choice, Mr Saunders.'

'I think you're wrong, boy,' Saunders asserted, half-turning in his seat to face me. 'God has your path all laid out in front of you. Just like this coach to Melbourne.'

I was becoming a little annoyed by Saunders' supercilious tone. 'Sometimes we have to choose something that may seem wrong to others.'

Saunders guffawed with contempt. 'Exactly what I'm telling you. Your path is predetermined by God. There's no choice. Whatever you do, God has chosen for you. You can't go against God's will.'

'I disagree. God always gives you two choices. His will is the choice you make, not the other way around.'

Taylor chuckled to himself.

Saunders persisted, 'Are you saying, then, that God wills you to be bad?'

'No, you're saying that. I'm saying that you choose to be bad or good. You choose to be drunk or sober. You choose to hurt someone or love someone. Nobody makes you do anything except you—you have a choice; you make the decision. And it's the coward's way out to blame someone else for the choices you've made.'

'It sounds like you're speaking from experience there, son,' Taylor remarked.

Immediately, I felt that I had said too much. Saunders, however, was relentless. 'No. I believe that our lives are predetermined by God and nothing you do will change that divine plan.'

'You believe what you like, Mr Saunders, and I will follow my path, making a choice at each fork in the road.'

The rear wheel hit a rather nasty bump and sent us all six inches into the air with squeals and gasps from the women and children, and a cry of pain from me.

'Apologies, ladies!' Taylor called, then looked back to see if I was unharmed. 'Your ribs okay there, son?'

I had mentioned my injury at the start of the journey, without, of course, going into details. 'Yeah, I'm all right,' I lied—my chest was smarting from the jolt.

'You say you need a job?' Taylor continued. 'Maybe I can help you, son. The German who runs the change station is always in need of help. I'll put in a good word for you.'

'Thank you, Mr Taylor.'

'You're most welcome.'

The few remaining miles to Beechworth were relatively smooth and uneventful and it was getting close to sunset. The thick bush thinned out to pastureland and fenced paddocks and, in the distance, we could see the curling smoke from homestead chimneys. The distinctive scent of the eucalypt trees and the sounds of the bush birds filled the evening air, calling their last farewells to each other. I was weary from the long distance travelled that day and looking forward to a plate of warm food and a bed.

Taylor reached beneath his seat into the compartment of the fore boot and retrieved the bugle. As he had done approaching each station, he pursed his lips to the mouthpiece and blew a huge lungful of air through the instrument, emitting an ear-piercing blare. The horses, rather than being frightened by it, seemed to be comforted by it, perhaps knowing that rest was not far off.

Within a few minutes, we had reached our destination—the change station on the periphery of Beechworth. It was a collection of stone and clapboard buildings, a few paddocks and a small cluster of fruit trees peeping from behind the main, double-storey building, which, I surmised, was the inn. This and the other buildings were not new but appeared well looked after. Inviting aromas of cooking food emanated from what must have been the kitchen. Another building close to the capacious stables most likely was the stable hands' or groom's quarters. A chicken coop and paddock housed chickens, a few goats, cows and sheep, and would have provided the family and guests with ample eggs, milk, cream, butter and cheese.

Taylor applied the brakes and reined in his five. 'Whoa, whoa there, boys!'

We came to a stop between the stables and the inn.

From the stables, two young men ran out to greet the coach and take hold of two of the three lead horses, settling them.

At the same time, two women darted out from the inn towards the coach. They looked quite similar; one was older and the other most likely her daughter. Both were dressed neatly and cleanly in clothing that suited hardworking women.

'*Frau* Schwartzman!' called Taylor in an amiable tone.

'*Herr* Taylor,' the older woman called back, equally affably. '*Herzlich willkommen!*'

The coach emptied itself of its passengers as I climbed down from the top. I peered about me in the dim evening light and took in the freshness of the area while I stretched, easing my aching ribs.

Taylor made the introductions. 'Ladies and gentlemen … and children … this is your hostess for the night, Mrs Schwartzman and her daughter, Hilda. You won't find two lovelier ladies in all of Victoria. Or better food.'

Mrs Schwartzman openly flushed at the compliment and in a dense German accent replied, 'Mr Taylor, you make me blush. But thank you and *herzlich willkommen* everybody. Hilda will take you inside and register you. Hot supper and warm bed is ready for you all.'

While I waited to see if Taylor could secure me a position with this company, I caught a glimpse of the two young stable hands as they unhitched the horses. They were sniggering to each other, darting their glances between me and Hilda. My attention diverted to Mrs Schwartzman's daughter who, while ushering the other passengers into the inn, kept glancing towards me, putting her 'comether' upon me. The youths seemed to find it quite amusing that Hilda should be paying me so much attention—attention I did not seek nor desire.

'Son!' Taylor called to me, catching my attention and gesturing for me to join him and Mrs Schwartzman. 'Missus, this young lad here, Robert Davies, is in need of employment and I reckon you could do with a spare pair of willing hands right now.'

Mrs Schwartzman appeared troubled by this suggestion. 'Mr Taylor,' she faltered, 'Mr Schwartzman does all the hiring and he is in Melbourne presently with our son, Gerhardt.'

'Another reason to put young Robert on until the lord and master returns. Then he can decide to keep Robbie on or not. I'm sure he'll do an excellent job, even though he don't look like much, eh?' He turned to me. 'Eh, Rob? You'd do a good job, wouldn't you?'

'Yes, Sir. I worked in a hotel in Sydney all my life.'

'*All* of your life, you say?' Taylor repeated with a touch of good-natured sarcasm. 'What do you say, Missus? Why not give the youngster a try? If he don't oblige then you can throw him on the next coach through here. Or under it. He won't be no trouble.'

'I really don't know—'

'He's a good lad. And he's smart, too.'

A long moment passed while Mrs Schwartzman considered her options. Something seemed to concern her more than putting on a worker without her husband's approval; her apprehensive expression suggested something deeper. Perhaps the looking-over that Hilda had given me and the amusement it caused the two stable hands was the cause. It was obvious that her two stable hands were struggling to manage the five horses and unloading the overnight baggage of the guests.

Finally, she decided. 'All right, Mr Taylor, I will give Robert a position here but only until Mr Schwartzman and Gerhardt return in two days' time.'

'Thank you, Missus. You won't regret it, I'm sure. Say thank you, Rob.'

I obliged with a truly grateful, 'Thank you,' even though this whole situation didn't feel quite right.

'Robert, since you will be a worker and not a guest, take your valises to the stablemen's quarters,' Mrs Schwartzman directed. 'Wolfgang and Daniel will show you which bed you can have. You can have supper with the guests tonight but, tomorrow, you will eat with the staff. Mr Schwartzman will discuss wages with you when he returns. Is that suitable?'

I gratefully agreed.

I took my two cases to the stable hands' cottage. There, I removed my mackintosh and hat and carefully folded Sarah's shawl and locked it in one of the valises. Both valises stood side-by-side against a wall with my hat and folded mackintosh covering them, awaiting the assignment of a bed.

In the warm and inviting dining room, my travelling companions had settled into little groups at various tables and were being served plentiful plates of stewed meat, vegetables and hot crusty bread. Tea and coffee were on offer for those of the temperate persuasion and beer and ale for the others.

Mrs Schwartzman attended to Taylor, who sat alone at a table, while Hilda looked after the other guests. I searched for a spare table and must have appeared quite lost—Taylor spied me and invited me to join him, which I gladly accepted.

Once again, Hilda caught my eye but this time she was paying particular attention to Godfrey Saunders, quite overtly and scandalously flirting with him. Every now and then, she would glance over to me to see if I was watching but I tried my best to ignore her.

Taylor noticed it all and between large mouthfuls of stew commented, 'Don't pay no heed to Hilda, son. Her pa keeps her on a short lead and she tends to play around a bit when he's away.'

'I won't, Mr Taylor,' I replied, breaking some bread and preparing to enjoy my meal. 'I need this job more than I need any dalliance.'

'Dalliance,' Taylor chuckled. 'That's a mighty big word for such a young feller. You know how to spell it?'

'Yes.'

'I knew you were a smart one. What's for you in Melbourne when you get there?' He scooped some more stew into his mouth.

I paused as I reflected on the reason for my flight. 'Nothing,' I eventually replied, attempting to sound indifferent. 'I suppose this is my "grand tour".'

'Well, you take care, Robert my boy. It's a mean and nasty world out there and there are many who would take advantage of someone like you.'

'Thank you,' I earnestly replied. 'I will. I don't intend to let anyone take advantage of me … or those I care for.'

Taylor gave me a look that was both warm and fatherly; we ate the rest of our meal in companionable silence.

When supper was finished, the other guests sat and chatted or played games while I returned to the stable hands' quarters. There, Wolfgang and Daniel were sprucing themselves up for a night on the town, it being Saturday.

Wolfgang was the taller and of obvious north European heritage, being fair-haired and blue-eyed like I was. He spoke with a slight Germanic accent and it was quite probable that his position here was due to his parentage.

Daniel, on the other hand, was a tawny-skinned, dark-eyed and dark-haired lad and spoke with a distinct colonial twang—a mixture of Cockney, brogue and Cornish—as did all us currency lads and lasses.

They were of that age between adolescence and adulthood where they looked like adults but behaved like children, and that's what all that sniggering was about.

Preening themselves in the small common mirror on the opposite wall, Wolfgang addressed me through its reflection. 'You can camp it there,' he said indicating a vacant bed. 'Coming to town with us? Do the block?'

'Lots of girls,' Daniel chimed in, before sniggering immaturely.

'No,' I replied. 'It's been a long day. But thanks.'

'Maybe girls don't interest you?' Wolfgang's suggestive remark caused Daniel to snort and elbow Wolfgang with a knowing wink.

'Come on,' Daniel urged Wolfgang.

'Don't wait up,' Wolfgang advised as they both rollicked out by the only door to the quarters.

At the time, I did not know whether they suspected me of not being male or whether they were suggesting that as a male, I was also a molly. I was too tired to try to work it out and, at that point, I really didn't care. I just needed this job to earn some wages to get to Melbourne.

Keep your head down and keep out of trouble, I thought to myself as I placed a valise on the bed and unlocked it. I took up Sarah's shawl and buried my face in it. It was only four weeks since that dreadful night. I thought of Sarah every day and prayed for her soul every night, asking for her forgiveness for all my broken promises at the end of each prayer.

I shook off my despair and replaced Sarah's shawl, relocked the valise and stowed it under my bed. I tossed my mackintosh and hat onto the bed and hefted the other case onto it. Opening it, I rummaged to find my night dress—a long shirt—to change into. I uncovered Harper's ancient revolver and the terrible images of that night rushed back.

He'd paid.

I buried the gun in the folds of my shirts and closed the case. Removing my jacket, I placed it neatly on the end of my bed and then removed my shirt. Sarah's silver locket was around my neck and the bandages were still tight and firmly in place, wrapped around my chest from armpit to waist. I was a little concerned that the physical work in store for me tomorrow would cause some grief but the thought of getting to Melbourne helped to firm my resolve.

'Why didn't you go with Wolfie and Daniel?' Hilda's low and husky query startled me. I faced her and modestly held my night shirt up to my chest.

She approached me, her nonchalant air and coyness belying innocent intent. 'What happened?' she asked referring to my bindings.

'Ah … a horse threw me.'

Hilda chuckled. 'That's very honest of you, Robert. Most boys would say they had been in a fight and won.'

She was now a soft breath away from me. About the same size as Sarah, a few inches shorter than I, her hair was light brown where Sarah's had been a lustrous dark auburn. Hilda's eyes were hazel, Sarah's a deep brown that I'd fallen into. How different the two women were; how I missed Sarah.

Hilda must have wondered what I was thinking as she glanced from my eyes to my mouth. 'Penny for your thoughts,' she whispered, her breath caressing my bare throat.

I shook my head—I didn't know how to respond to her overt flirtation.

'We have time,' she promised as she took a small step back and spied the locket at my neck. She took it between her fingers. 'Pretty. Your sweetheart's?'

'Yes,' I answered as I prised it from her fingers and pulled on my night shirt.

'Lucky girl,' Hilda retorted, draping herself across my bed. 'Mr Taylor said you're smart. I suppose you read a lot. My father has lots of books. Maybe you'd like to read some of them? They're mostly in German. But I could teach you.'

'I won't be here that long.'

Hilda launched herself upright once more and sidled up to me. 'Maybe you would stay if there was a good reason …?' She caressed my face with the back of her hand.

I wanted to push her away but would that jeopardise my employment? If I yielded to Hilda's wanton needs, that, too, could see me expelled.

I did nothing. Without provocation or invitation, Hilda captured my mouth with her lips.

She was not Sarah and while I needed comforting, I would not betray Sarah so soon and with someone so brash. Taking Hilda by the arms, I eased her away from me. 'I think you'd better go.'

Hilda turned to leave but glanced back. 'The library's always open for you, Robert.'

***

We were up before dawn the next morning and out in the hitching yard after a quick breakfast of hot sweetened milk and bread. I didn't know what time Wolfgang and Daniel had returned the night before, but I had been fast asleep when they did. Now we were all three hitching five chestnuts to the rails; the two stronger and larger polers in the back row and the three smaller pacers in the front. The centre horse was the leader and the most valuable to the driver, instrumental in steering the coach.

As we worked, Wolfgang said, 'Looks like you know what you're doing, Robert. Dan and I had a bet. I won.'

Daniel snarled a grunt of disappointment.

Wolfgang continued, 'We saw Hilda come in after we left last night.'

'She don't waste no time that one. She's fast. Did she *show you around?*' Daniel probed.

'A word of warning, Robert, if her papa finds out—'

'You're dead,' Daniel concluded.

'She doesn't interest me.'

Daniel sniggered in his usual, annoying way. 'We figured as much.'

We had completed the harnessing when Taylor approached, paying particular attention to the centre lead horse but showing kindness and affection for all the horses in his care. 'How's it coming along, boys?'

'All ready, Mr Taylor,' Wolfgang answered. Taylor was followed by a straggle of passengers, most of whom were still half asleep.

'Time to load up,' Taylor instructed Wolfgang. 'Maybe not you, Robbie. Best you give them ribs a chance to heal.'

'You can muck out the stables before church,' Wolfgang ordered, as he and Daniel stacked the passengers' overnight baggage onto the hind boot and the passengers arranged themselves in the coach.

The rakes, shovels and barrow were stowed just inside the stable doors in the tack room. Grabbing one of each, I went into the first of the empty stalls and began the arduous but necessary task of removing the horses' night soil and replacing the straw with a clean covering. There were twenty stalls in all, twelve of which were still occupied and whose tenants Daniel would remove to the paddock once the coach had departed.

The sun was just breaking over the horizon and it was going to be a beautifully sunny autumn day. Laughing jackasses and lorikeets called and screeched their morning overtures. The coach was ready to depart but for one passenger: Godfrey Saunders.

'Mr Saunders,' Taylor called, his voice echoing through the tree-fringed courtyard, 'we're set to go, if you please.'

The announcement brought me, rake in hand, to the stable door. Saunders, accompanied by Hilda, emerged from the inn. Their close proximity to each other exhibited that theirs had been more than a business relationship. Even from my standpoint, I could see an intimacy between the two.

'Thank you, Mr Saunders,' Taylor prompted.

At his words, Hilda scowled in defiance and Saunders ashamedly straightened to attention. 'Righto, Mr Taylor,' he called. 'Just finalising … my … my account with Miss Schwartzman,' he stuttered.

The man scurried past Taylor who stood, hands on hips, in silent admonition. He shook his head at Hilda who turned and left in a huff, nose in the air. The two men climbed onto the box seat and, as Taylor settled in and took up the reins, Mrs Schwartzman hurried from the kitchen annex to see off her itinerant guests.

'Take care, *Herr* Taylor,' she farewelled.

'See you on my return, *Frau* Schwartzman.' He tipped his hat and with a click of his tongue and a gentle flick of the whip, the coach resumed its rattling, bone-shaking journey to Melbourne.

With the departure of the coach, Wolfgang and Daniel began moving the spare horses from the stables into the paddock. I felt somewhat abandoned watching the coach depart.

'Robert,' Mrs Schwartzman called. 'Robert, I want you to help me be ready for the next *Kutsche*. Come. *Kommen*,' and retreated into the inn.

I stowed my mucking out equipment and made my way towards the inn when, from the north, four horsemen clip-clopped towards the hostelry.

The events that unfolded from that day would irrevocably reshape my existence in ways so profound that there would be no turning back.

The horses and their riders were bedraggled and scruffy and, given the time of day, I surmised they had either camped nearby or travelled most of the night. The four riders were unshaven and wore their wide-brimmed hats low over their eyes. As they neared, I saw that two of them displayed a holstered sidearm just visible within their opened oilskin dusters. All had rifles strapped to their saddles or to their carpetbags and bed rolls. They may have been stockmen on their way to a new job, but they certainly appeared to me to have lived a hard life on the road.

Pulling up ten yards or so from the inn's doorway, they looked about, surveying the lay of the land.

'This'll do,' the leader announced as he dismounted, removing his carpetbag and sleeping roll. The rest followed suit.

I would soon learn that the leader was Johnson, about late middle-age with a snarly, leathery face that did not invite sympathy. He wasn't terribly tall but certainly taller than two of his compatriots, Tanner and Pitt. The younger of these two, Pitt, was baby-faced and in his mid-twenties. He sported a sparse blondish beard and hair that spiked from beneath his hat like straw. Tanner was wiry and about the same age as Johnson and his feral, wild-eyed look and toothy, crooked grin would have rattled the bravest heart.

The last man was Percy—tall, brawny, swarthy and stern but not displaying any arrogance or malevolence, only wariness. While he was as dishevelled as the other three, his attire was altogether of a better quality.

I suddenly remembered that I had been called into the inn to assist Mrs Schwartzman.

Hilda had repositioned herself behind the registration counter and was busily doing nothing but daydreaming and doodling when I hurried by to the waiting Mrs Schwartzman in the adjacent dining room, where she was busy clearing up the breakfast dishes.

'Sorry, Missus, some riders took my attention.'

She deftly picked up the unsteady tower of soiled dishes and cups and instructed over her shoulder, 'Wash down the tables, then sweep the floor. Then come to the kitchen.' Her words trailed behind her as she rushed out.

Bucket and sponge in hand, I started the first task when, through the doorway, I saw three of the unkempt wayfarers stroll in. The best dressed of them—the swarthy man, Percy—was not with them. They scrutinised every corner of the room as well as Hilda and me.

Hilda looked up and jolted to attention. 'Ah … yes … good morning … gentlemen,' she stuttered.

Johnson leaned his elbow on the desk. 'Morning, Miss. Me and me lads need a couple of rooms for a couple of nights.'

Hilda hesitated.

'Is there a problem?' Johnson enquired. 'You don't seem to be run off your feet.'

'Ah, no. No problem. Sorry. How many? Three?'

'Four. And four horses.'

Hilda pushed the registration book to Johnson who inked the pen and began writing. 'Here on business?' she asked, clearly attempting to be cordial.

'Yeah.'

'To do with the mines?'

'Yeah.' Johnson's response caused Tanner, the wild-eyed and ugliest of the trio to giggle, which in turn earned Johnson's silent reproach.

'Where are you headed?' Hilda persisted.

'Myrtleford. Want to come with me?' Pitt, the baby-faced and youngest of the group replied, apparently seeing a chance to obtain some 'extra service'.

This earned him a deathly glare from Johnson.

Pitt immediately took a step back, eyes downcast.

'Are you assayers?' she asked. 'You don't look like assayers.'

Tanner stifled a laugh.

'How much, Miss?' Johnson cut in, ignoring her question.

'Ah … a shilling for each bed and sixpence for each horse. Two nights—twelve shillings, please. Breakfast's included but not dinner or supper.'

'You got someone to look to the horses?'

'Er …' Hilda stalled, craning her neck to see if she could summon Wolfgang or Daniel through the open doorway.

'What about him?' Johnson said, indicating me.

***

Wolfgang and Daniel were in the back paddock seeing to the horses as I approached the tall man standing at the entrance to the stables holding the reins of four horses.

'I'll take those for you, mister.'

The man I came to know as Percy handed me the straps and it was only then, up close and peering at him, that my expression betrayed my thoughts.

'What?' His brow wrinkled with annoyance.

'Nothing. Sorry.'

'Take care of these animals. Feed and water. And a rub down.'

'Sure,' I said, taking the reins from him. 'You're staying here a couple of nights?'

'Yeah. Do you have a problem with that?'

'No.' My response was quick but then my words caught in the void between my brain and my mouth. Percy's mouth, hardened by my unwelcomed stare, softened.

'You're wondering if I'm a blackfella.'

I was embarrassed by his perception.

'Half,' he disclosed. 'My father was a white fella. You?'

I looked at him nonplussed; I was white, blond and blue-eyed. Then his big toothy grin revealed that he was larking.

'I don't even know who my father was,' I confessed, matching his grin. 'So I suppose I could be.'

He chuckled. 'Well, this is a fine establishment. I don't know if I want to stay in a place that lets a boong and a bastard in!' He held out his hand. 'Percy.'

I took it and shook hard. 'Robert.'

'Robert the stable lackey. Been working here long?'

'First day. Saving to go to Melbourne.'

'Someone waiting for you there? Fiancée? Wife?'

'No! I just turned eighteen!'

'Don't get hitched too soon,' he earnestly advised. 'As much as you love them, they can be a millstone, wife and kids.'

'You're married?'

'Yeah. Wife and kids in Bathurst.' He paused, his eyes distant. 'This will be my last … job.'

From near the inn came a loud, 'Hey! Perce!' interrupting our cordiality.

'What do you want?' Percy called back.

'Get your black arse over here!' The man approached us—he had a face that would scare the freckles off a highlander—and looked me over. 'You like the white fella, eh, Perce? Taste better than blackfellas?'

'Shut up, Tanner.' With an apologetic glance back to me, Percy led Tanner back into the inn.

I turned my attention from that curious transaction to the four horses in hand and realised that, although they were tired and dirty, they were actually of high quality; one was even a thoroughbred. I thought it unusual for four men of that calibre to have four steeds of *this* calibre.

Leading the horses towards one of the newly mucked out stalls, I saw that one of the saddles still had the bags and rifle tied on.

***

When I reached the inn with the rifle, carpetbag and sleeping roll, I found Hilda arguing with Johnson. 'You didn't say one of you was a … a—'

'Boong?' Johnson offered.

Tanner sniffed. 'Is that what the smell is?'

'Shut up, Tanner.' Johnson turned to Hilda. 'His money not good enough for you?'

'It's just … my father doesn't want blacks in here. Or Chinese.'

'I can understand Chinks—' Johnson conceded.

'Maybe he can sleep in the stables,' Hilda suggested.

That wasn't the Christian thing to do. I had to say something. 'He's not an animal, Hilda.' I gave the carpetbag to Percy. 'You left this.'

'Robert! This is none of your concern.'

'I'll wager that even your German bible says that humans were made in God's image. Who's to say He wasn't black?'

'That's sacrilege!'

'Or a woman, for that matter,' I added for good measure.

'I assure you, Miss, I won't be any trouble to you,' Percy addressed Hilda directly and respectfully. 'I left my nulla-nulla and spears in my humpy back in Bathurst.' The last sentence was issued with a touch of playful irony.

Hilda seemed to waver; she didn't know what to do. I could see her brain ticking over, considering whether they would be gone before her father returned. 'Two days,' she warned Johnson. 'Only two days.'

She turned to me. 'I do this for you, Robert Davies. You owe me.'

The threat was implicit. I only hoped that before the time came to service my debt, I'd have enough saved to leave for Melbourne.

'You can stay. But use the back door,' she added to Percy—a final indignation.

***

Once Wolfgang and Daniel had paddocked the coach horses, they'd told Mrs Schwartzman they were off to church and disappeared for the rest of the day.

I took the opportunity to have a thorough wash in uninterrupted privacy. The little lavatory attached to the quarters was lockable and didn't have any windows so I was confident I could carry out my ablutions undisturbed.

With my valise in hand, I locked myself in and stripped off, removing the bindings from my chest. I lit the large tallow candle and began. The bracing, icy water felt good as I cleansed my body. I quickly dried off and rebound my chest if only to hide my breasts, for the discomfort of my mending ribs had lessened somewhat. A fresh shirt and half-stockings made me feel new; I would wash the discards later. I was now ready for the rest of the day.

I, too, attended my own private *missa solitaria*—a mass with no congregation or, in my case, no priest—in my quarters. I was given a few more chores to complete and, apart from subtle discomfort to my ribs, I didn't mind at all—it gave me the opportunity to show I was a willing worker … and it kept Hilda at bay.

After resting for most of the day, the four horsemen took to the saddle again and rode off to the west, towards Wangaratta, and returned just as the sun was shedding its last rays.

17

Monday, 4ᵗʰ May, 1874

Beechworth, Victoria

The next morning, Wolfgang and Daniel, having returned late the night before once more, were still soundly sleeping when I arose. The clear pre-dawn air was crisp and the frosty grass beneath my feet crunched as I wandered through the fenced field, the sharp fragrance of the eucalypts clearing my mind. The sun's faint rays pushed low through the surrounding bush, casting long west-bound shadows over all. This was the time of day I felt most at peace with the world, with me, and with what I had done.

A coach was expected late in the afternoon and all was in readiness for it. By midday, the three of us had mucked out the stables, fed and watered all the horses including the four belonging to the 'assayers', polished up the tack and were ready for a break and a light repast. Wolfgang and Daniel headed off for the kitchen; I would join them later after doing my laundry and headed for the quarters to collect the discarded clothing I'd left the day before.

'We have a laundress, you know.'

Hilda startled me—she certainly was stealthy. 'Don't you ever knock?'

'Why? What do boys do when no one's watching?' Her smirk told me she knew very well.

'What do you want, Hilda? I'm busy.'

'Do you miss your sweetheart?' she asked, stalking towards me.

'Yes,' was my wary reply.

'Maybe I can help with that.'

'I don't want your help. I don't need your help.'

'You owe me.'

I hadn't expected this so soon. 'So what do you want?' I threw back.

'You know what I want,' she whispered, backing me into a corner.

'If your pa finds out—'

'Are you going to tell him?' Her warm breath against my throat sent an involuntary shiver through my body.

'You might be the one who's sorry,' I warned.

'Try me.' Her voice trailed off as she pressed her body and mouth against mine.

Despite my efforts, my body mutinied and responded to her insistence. Aware that she would be seeking a reaction from my nether regions, I raised my thigh and pressed against her to keep her away and avoid discovery. My mouth and hands acted on unrestrained impulse and seized her. She tasted of warm coffee and honey, of want and desire. Our tongues fought for supremacy; my hands searched out and stroked every part of her body. Heat spread from my groin to my neck, overpowering me.

Within a few short seconds, we were breathless. Hilda reached for my belt; I caught her hands. 'No,' I said, not only to her but to myself.

'I want to see. I want to touch,' she pleaded, trying to free herself from my grip.

'No. I'll give you what you want but not that way.'

Hilda tilted her head, confused.

'The bed,' I directed and guided her to it. She lay down, her gaze never leaving mine. I climbed onto the bed and lay close beside her, propped on my elbow. She was soft and warm with the fragrance of lilies about her. If it were not for her insistent promiscuity, I could become fond of her. I caressed her blushing cheek. Her hand wandered down my side and to my trousers.

'You must not touch me,' I whispered as I urged her hand away. 'I will do the touching.'

My hand ventured down the length of her body and found its path beneath her skirts and along the inside of her thigh. I lost myself in Hilda's eyes imagining them to be Sarah's and that this was the culmination of my love for her—a love we never had the chance to consummate.

Sarah …

Her breath quickened and deepened as my fingers reached the moist velvety entrance to her desire. I could feel she was aroused and stimulated her tenderly. She closed her eyes and arched her back; soft moans escaped with each breath. My fingers probed her deep recesses and stroked her gently. Each ministration pushed deeper, faster, more fervently, matched by the rhythm of her breathing until she stopped altogether. Every muscle in her body spasmed in a contraction I felt around my invasive hand. My own body tensed and throbbed.

She finally took a long shuddering breath and her body collapsed, her energies depleted, releasing me. I withdrew. My eyes lingered on her face; a knot of remorse tightening in my chest. I longed for Sarah; how I wished she were Sarah.

'Oh, Robert,' she sighed. 'I've never felt that before.'

I turned away before she noticed the sorrow in my eyes.

'My debt is paid,' I threw at her, barely able to conceal my anger. Anger at myself for succumbing to my carnal urges with someone I cared little for; for betraying Sarah.

The rumble of a horse and cart roused us, followed by Mrs Schwartzman's frantic calls. 'Hilda! Hilda! *Dein Vater ist zu Hause!*'

Hilda sprang off the bed and adjusted her skirts. 'He wasn't supposed to be back until tomorrow,' she mumbled, clearly irritated. She hurried out, leaving me in a state of confusion.

Through the window, I could see the approach of a heavily laden cart, still some fifty yards away, pulled by a solitary, overworked Clydesdale, driven by an older, potbellied man and a youth, whom I assumed to be Hilda's father and brother.

Hilda ran to her mother's side and I heard Mrs Schwarzman, seeing from where Hilda had come, ask, '*Was hast du da drinnen gemacht?*'

'Nothing, Mama, *Nichts*.'

'*Du weißt, was dein Vater tun wird, wenn er es findet,*' she warned her daughter.

'There wasn't anyone in there, Mama.'

Mrs Schwartzman sighed. '*Was soll ich nur mit dir machen?*'

At this point, Wolfgang and Daniel finally emerged, munching on the last bites of their meal. I thought it best not to appear shy so I walked out and joined the greeting party. My emergence took

Hilda's mother by surprise; her lips tightened in a distinct sign of both disappointment and disapproval. She uttered nothing as the cart trundled to a stop close to her.

Mrs Schwartzman showed herself happy to see her husband and son, but in a restrained way that strangely lacked excitement. '*Herman, es ist so schön, dich zu Hause zu haben. Hat dir Melbourne gefallen, Gerhardt?*'

Gerhardt was the same age as Patrick, I guessed. 'Yes, Mama, it's a big city,' he replied with controlled enthusiasm.

'*Ich habe dich erst morgen erwartet, Liebster,*' she said to her husband.

Schwartzman's tone was as gruff as his exterior. 'We had to push on and beat the weather before it flooded the river. *Und sprich Englisch, Ursula,*' he grumbled, then addressed his son in the same imperious manner. 'Get down. Start.'

He only then noticed his daughter and his bearish behaviour changed appreciably. '*Schatzi!*' he called as he climbed down from the cart and engulfed his daughter in a smothering hug.

Hilda, struggling to breathe, gasped, 'Papa, did you bring me something from Melbourne?'

He let go. 'All in good time,' he reassured her. 'All in good time.' Looking around he appeared to sour again. 'What do you want?' he barked at his workers. 'An invitation?'

They jumped into action, joining Gerhardt in unloading the provisions from the cart.

Would I be introduced? I waited. Gerhardt had been watching me all this time, his face unreadable.

Schwartzman finally saw me. 'Who is that?' he asked his wife.

'Oh, that is Robert Davies,' Mrs Schwartzman most reluctantly and almost apologetically replied. 'He needed a job … Mr Taylor … He's a good worker.'

'No, we don't need anyone more.'

'Mr Taylor recommended him. It is only for a short time. He needs to earn his fare to Melbourne.'

Schwartzman shook his head in adamant disapproval, then glanced at Gerhardt. 'Not the sort of boy I want around Gerhardt.'

'I am sure you are mistaken, Herman,' she said, plainly mortified by the notion.

'He's not like that, Papa,' Hilda interjected. 'He has a sweetheart. In Sydney. He is not like that.'

Like what?

Schwartzman was clearly in a quandary. 'Hmm. Boy,' he addressed me. 'Any trouble and you are out. Understand?'

'No trouble, Sir,' I reassured the old despot. I was not about to jeopardise my employment there.

He emitted a grunt. 'Go help Wolfy and Daniel.'

Mrs Schwartzman linked her arm in his and led him towards the inn. 'You must be starving.' Then she addressed her son with a backward glance, 'Gerhardt. *Kommen.*'

'These go in the kitchen and these in the front room,' Gerhardt instructed, abandoning the unloading of the cart and sprinting after his parents. He, too, gave me a look that made me shudder but for a different reason from that of his father. It was then that I realised what Gerhardt was all about.

What was it with this family? I felt trapped.

'You'd better take your lunch in the kitchen …' Hilda threw back at me as she joined the procession to the inn. Then in a lower tone she added suggestively, '… if you're still hungry.'

I was—for food—but the overlord had decreed I assist with unloading the goods so 'Wolfy' loaded me up with a stack of cardboard boxes and I followed the family into the reception room of the inn as directed.

Inside, in the area set aside as the dining room, I could see that all the tables were vacant save one which accommodated Johnson, Pitt and Tanner. They had helped themselves to the limited-in-variety but plentiful-in-supply offerings on the buffet table and were devouring their selections in a slovenly manner.

Schwartzman surveyed the room and, seeing the three, asked of his wife, 'Business good?'

'Yes, *Liebster*, these … gentlemen are assayers but will be leaving us today,' Mrs Schwartzman replied, her voice patently tight with anxiety. Was she relieved that Percy was not present?

Schwartzman turned the registration book towards him and grunted with approval as he scanned the pages. 'When is the coach due?'

'Half past four,' Hilda replied. 'Everything is ready for them. Robert is a good worker, Papa.'

'We'll see, *Schatzi*. We'll see.'

'Missus,' I interrupted, 'where do you want these?'

'In the corner, behind the counter,' Schwartzman grunted before she could reply.

Gerhardt had made his way to the buffet table and dished up a portion for himself, well aware that he was being watched by three pairs of eyes. He took himself to the table furthest away from them and ate. This clearly amused the trio—Tanner, in particular.

'And now there's two of 'em,' he commented louder than he should have, which brought about a derisive grunt from Johnson and a confused grimace from Pitt. Tanner leaned towards Pitt to explain, 'He's a mollycoddle just like the other one there.'

Much to Mrs Schwartzman's evident alarm—she stiffened, wide-eyed and aghast—Percy descended the stairs from the rooms above and approached the desk with a letter in hand. Addressing Hilda, he requested, 'Do you have a penny stamp, Miss? I have a letter to post.'

Schwartzman's face reddened and he took his wife by the arm, pulling her into a corner.

'Why is that black in my hotel?'

Mrs Schwartzman, flushed, reverted to her native tongue. '*Liebling, er ist ein guter Mann. Er ist sauber—*'

'English!'

'He is very clean, Herman. And polite. He and his friends will be gone today. Please. Remember what the constable said.'

'Why do I leave you in charge? And you give me a useless son! I can't take my eye off him for a minute! Argh!'

He retreated to the courtyard in a fury that left the woman visibly shaken and embarrassed under the attention of the rest of the room.

The anger this man displayed and his mistreatment of his wife brought back painful memories and I felt empathy for her, but the situation was something she and her family had to overcome—I was not about to involve myself. My future was in Melbourne.

'Ahem, Miss,' Percy continued as though nothing had happened. 'A stamp?'

His indifference to what had just happened made me presume that Percy was used to being treated as an inferior being and a social pariah. For him, too, I felt empathy.

I straightened the cartons and resumed earning my wages.

***

It was midafternoon, a coachload was expected in a few hours and the 'assayers' would be leaving us soon. Wolfgang and Daniel were still sorting, stacking and storing the provisions we had unloaded from the cart and I was assigned to the stables and the preparation of the fresh horses for the coach.

Gerhardt caught my attention when he strolled in from the courtyard and over to the tack room. I was aware of his gaze on me, following me, assessing me. He looked outside with a wary eye then stalked slowly to the stall where I was rubbing down one of the dappled greys.

'Hilda told me all about you,' he said, his voice low and suggestive.

'Oh?' I asked impassively.

'She said you are from Sydney and you have a sweetheart.'

'Did she also tell you that I don't want any trouble?'

He laughed. 'You're already in that, my friend, if my father finds out.'

I moved around to the other side of the horse and brushed the offside, leaving Gerhardt in the vacuum of my indifference.

He followed me around. 'I don't believe it,' he continued, and then waited for a reaction. 'I don't believe you fucked my sister,' he clarified.

My only reaction was a sideward glance.

'I know what you are,' he blurted.

I couldn't help but gasp. *How did he know?*

'And what's that?' I managed, maintaining as neutral a tone as possible even though my heart was pounding.

'Let's just say you like to receive as well as give.'

I stopped brushing the horse, clapped the two brushes together and tossed them aside. I was in a defiant mood and I wasn't about to let this milksop better me.

'Just what lies did your sister tell you?'

'She's anybody's, you should know that.' He sidled up close to me and whispered, 'Dan and Wolfy won't have her so she's leeched on to you. But you're like me, aren't you, Robert Davies?' He put his hand on my shoulder and slid it down to my hip.

'Get your hand off me!' I hit his hand away. 'Don't fool yourself, Gerhardt. I'm nothing like you.'

I pushed the back end of the horse away from me so I could get out of the stall and left the little molly there. I remember thinking that I'd left two horse's arses in the stall that day.

Upon emerging, I found Percy standing a few paces away.

'Is he troubling you?' Percy asked, obviously having overheard the exchange. He joined me as I stormed past and into the neutrality of the courtyard.

'I've dealt with worse than him.' My response was abrupt and charged by the anger I felt; anger that Hilda had told her brother; anger that he assumed he knew me; anger that my life had become so complicated; but I wasn't angry with Percy. I calmed myself. 'I suppose you heard?'

All he did was raise an eyebrow.

'I'm not like that,' I reassured him.

'It doesn't matter to me if you are, Robert. You seem a decent fellow. Even if you are not the manliest of men.' He chuckled. 'Don't let those who don't know you rattle you, boy. You just be the best you can be and that's all anyone can expect of you.' His advice came across as his own personal philosophy. He laid a reassuring hand on my shoulder. 'Now, to business. We'll be heading off just before the coach comes. Have our horses ready to go by then, all right?'

'All right.'

'By the way, where's the post office? I have a letter for my wife.'

'I could take it for you.' I knew not where the Post Office was, but the task should be simple enough.

'Thank you,' he said, handing me the stamped envelope, which I dutifully put in my jacket pocket.

'Hey! You! Boy!' came Schwartzman's coarse and abrupt bark. 'I don't pay you to stand around and talk all day. Get back to work!'

I wondered just how long I had to put up with this before I had enough cash to get to Melbourne.

Over the proceeding hours I helped Wolfgang move the last of the stock into the storeroom, thankfully, out of the surveillance of both Hilda and Gerhardt.

One or two weeks of this and I'd be gone, I reassured myself.

The time came to saddle Percy and his mates' horses—my job as Wolfgang and Daniel were readying five for the coach.

I entered the first stall and saddled and bridled Percy's mount, checking that the girth was not too tight and the channel and gullet sat in the right position. Content with that, I moved to the next stall, to the third and, finally the fourth, completing the tacking up of each horse swiftly.

I left the stall, ready to remove each horse, when I was yanked backwards into an empty pen and hurled, chest first, hard against the rough wooden stall lining, my ribs taking the brunt of the impact. One of my arms was twisted up my back and my body held in place by a forearm pressed against my neck.

'Get off me, you bastard!' I yelled at Gerhardt.

'You gave it to Hilda,' he rasped into my ear. 'Now it's my turn.' He thrust his body against mine. I writhed and twisted but couldn't break free. He released my arm only to pull up my jacket and tear away my suspenders. He reached in front and tore open the fly to my trousers.

I panicked. My arms flailed but couldn't reach behind me nor push myself away from the wall. He yanked down my breeches and underpants.

'You want it! You know you want it!' he spat in my ear.

Rage overcame desperation. I could feel his erect penis pushing against my buttocks.

'I'll kill you!' I screamed. Fear and panic gripped me but he wouldn't stop. 'No! Let me go, you bloody mongrel! Let me go!' I yelled, tears forming in my eyes.

Suddenly, Gerhardt released me.

I stumbled free and dragged up the front of my trousers and spun around to see Schwartzman, seething, snarling at Gerhardt. Gerhardt was lying in the straw, where he'd clearly been flung across the stall.

'Get out! Get your belongings and get out of here!' Schwartzman snarled at me.

'Papa …' Gerhardt feebly pleaded as he pulled his clothes together.

'You, shut up!'

I pulled my trousers into place. 'It wasn't my fault. He attacked me!'

'I told you to get out!'

'You owe me wages,' I whimpered, suddenly feeling desperate and powerless.

'There's nothing owing!'

'Two days,' I said, sounding more pathetic than demanding.

'You're lucky I haven't broken your face. Now get out of my sight. Now!'

There was no reasoning with this vile human. I angrily wiped the tears from my face and stumbled out of the stall and into the forecourt, righting my dishevelled clothing as I staggered for the stable hands' quarters.

By the time I'd reached the door, the ramifications of what had just happened hit me. No money, no friends, nowhere to go and I had almost been violated in the most brutal of ways. My legs gave way and I fell back against the wall and slid to the floor, the tears starting up again.

I didn't see the shadow loom over me but I heard its rough voice. 'That ain't no way for a man to behave.'

I looked up to see Johnson's hard face sneering at me.

'What's it to you?' I barked back, angrily wiping my face and getting to my feet.

'I heard what the old Hun bastard said. Maybe I can help.' I stared at him, daring him to continue. 'You need money. Where are you headed?'

'Melbourne.'

'There's five quid in it for you.'

'That's a lot of money,' I dismissed with a snarl of contempt.

'Do you want it or not?'

I considered my options. None. Maybe Godfrey Saunders had been right.

'Yeah,' I said. 'I want it.'

Johnson left me and joined Tanner, Pitt and Percy waiting nearby. 'We're set.'

'Who'd you find?' Tanner quizzed with an evil smirk on his twisted features.

'The molly boy.'

'The owner's son?'

'Nah, the other one. Him. Robert.' This brought a round of cackles from both Tanner and the younger Pitt. Percy, on the other hand, appeared alarmed and watched me with concern.

***

Johnson had taken me aside and informed me of my role in the task at hand. With renewed optimism—and as much trepidation—I spent what was left of the afternoon in the quarters packing my few belongings. I relived the journey that brought me to this time and place and pondered each and every decision I had made. Without exception, I would not have made a different choice if I had the time over. *Was my involvement in Johnson's 'venture' God's will or mine? Could I live with the outcome? What was the adage about being hanged for a sheep as a lamb?*

A gentle knock on the door caught my attention and the door slowly opened.

'May I come in?' Hilda asked quietly, peering around the door.

'What do you want, Hilda?' was my terse and unwelcoming reply.

'Mama told me what happened,' she said closing the door behind her. 'I just want to say I'm sorry, Robert. I didn't mean to—'

'Why did you tell your brother?'

'I … I just wanted to see if—'

'I liked boys or girls? I like girls, Hilda, girls.'

'I didn't know he'd do that.'

'What? You didn't know your brother would rape me or your father would fire me? I needed this employment, Hilda. You knew that. I didn't get paid and I have nowhere to go. Because of you. Do you always set out to ruin lives?'

'I am so sorry, Robert. Please forgive me.' She did sound truly sorry but I was not in a forgiving mood.

I picked up my jacket, mackintosh and hat and my two red leather valises and pushed past her to leave. At the door, I stopped. 'Life's not a game, Hilda. People get hurt. People die.'

18

Tuesday, 5th May, 1874

The road between Beechworth and Wangaratta, Victoria

I left Hilda in the stable hands' quarters to ruminate my last statement. While I had been packing up my hopes and belongings, Percy returned from Beechworth town with an aged hack and an even more aged saddle for me to ride. As I strapped my two valises onto the horse's flanks, Johnson, Tanner and Pitt joined us on the horses I had tacked up earlier.

We left along the western road just as we heard the bugle announcing the arrival of the late afternoon coach a short distance behind us. I wondered what those travellers would make of the family I'd left behind.

We travelled well into the night, westward towards Wangaratta, taking bush tracks instead of the main road. Finally, exhausted, we made camp at a small billabong obscured from the road by tall gums. Throughout the whole journey here, no one had said a word to me and what they had spoken had been conveyed in hushed tones.

Even Percy kept his thoughts to himself and occasionally shot me an unreadable glance—part apology, part remorse. I had agreed to the plan and I was prepared to carry out my part in it. I needed the money. *All will go well*, I reassured myself. *No one will be hurt*. Johnson had told me so.

It was an icy night and the campfire and my mackintosh went some ways towards keeping me warm, but I was still cold and hungry—I hadn't eaten since lunch. Johnson and his boys had come prepared with a pack of cold food but I was too proud to beg for some, so I sat huddled in my mack against an old gum and watched the group squatted by the fire.

Percy looked over to me and rose to his feet with his share of the food. 'You want some?' he asked.

I cast a glance towards Johnson and the other three.

'Don't mind them,' Percy insisted. 'This is from my share. Take it.'

'Thank you, Percy,' I said, accepting the offering. I didn't waste a crumb and soon dozed off.

***

The next sensation I had was my feet being kicked.

'Get up,' Percy urged. 'We're moving out.' He tossed me a small parcel of food wrapped in cloth. 'Eat.'

It was daybreak—the sky was cloudless and promised sunshine. I roused myself as Johnson, Tanner and Pitt were dousing the campfire by urinating on it.

We saddled up and headed for the predetermined place about ten miles west of Beechworth.

***

They left me perched on the top of one side of a low rocky alluvial valley, keeping a lookout. The valley was only relatively short—about five hundred yards—and the compacted sandy road running through it connected the lower plains on either side of the rocky outcrop that extended several miles in either direction. This rutted, boulder-strewn part of the road was the most direct way between the two townships of Wangaratta and Beechworth—about twenty-four miles apart.

I left my poor old hack at the foot of the rise in the shade of the scrubby gums that dotted the stony area, discreetly tethered to one of them. I could not see Percy and Johnson, nor his mates, from my position but I guessed they could see me.

So I sat and waited and watched the road, the warm sun on my face—at least, it wasn't raining.

After an interminable length of time, I saw some movement at the far end of the valley, to the east. Time to earn my five pounds!

I scrambled down the blind side of the rise and, as instructed, tossed myself onto the ground and rolled about, soiling my clothes, face and hands before lying there, holding my leg and moaning.

It wasn't five minutes before the leader of the convoy came into view. I was staggered to see that this was not the small gang of bushmen that Johnson had told me had robbed them, but a large company of troopers escorting a wagon. The escort and the size of it could only mean they were transporting gold. This wasn't a reckoning—this was a gold robbery! And *not* the easy five quid Johnson had promised.

I was dead scared. These twenty or so troopers were not a small gang of mismatched miscreants but a well-trained body of soldiers who knew how to kill.

The leader was a sergeant and, upon seeing me, raised his hand and called, 'Halt!' He scanned the valley walls apprehensively. 'Weapons at the ready!' he ordered and drew his pistol while I writhed about. My heart quickened.

The sergeant warily urged his mount forwards, his gun trained on me. 'You there,' he called, stopping some ten yards away. 'Hands where I can see them.'

I complied, showing that I was unarmed.

'What's the matter with you?'

My mouth and throat were dry with fear but I managed to continue. 'A big brownie … My horse skittered … I think I've broken my leg …'

The sergeant suspiciously glared at me then looked around once more and saw my horse a short distance off. With consternation and some evident reluctance, he called back to his men. 'Hold there. Stay alert.' Then he dismounted and strode the few paces towards me.

'Let's look at your leg, laddie,' he said as he holstered his gun and bent down to inspect my leg. The instant he touched my leg, I groaned, feigning extreme pain.

The sergeant looked at me with concern. 'I can put you in the wagon and take you as far as Wangaratta.'

'Thank you,' I whispered, my heart pounding, fearful of what was about to happen.

The sergeant stood. 'Bring the wagon up!' he ordered.

The soldiers complied quickly, clearly wary of the situation.

The wagon was only fifteen yards away from me and the entire convoy completely within the valley when a single shot rang out. The sergeant collapsed to the ground beside me, blood streaming from a gaping wound to his head.

He was dead.

'A trap!' one trooper called out.

In an instant, a barrage of gunfire burst upon the valley from all sides, overwhelming the troopers.

One rode up and levelled his gun at me. 'You bastard!' he roared, but before he could fire, he too was shot and fell from his horse.

This was a massacre!

One by one, the troopers were cut down by the concealed gunmen. Horses, too, were not spared—when the wagon driver attempted to race away, one of the four horses was felled. The driver slumped over the reins, moaning in agony. Another shot ended his life.

I watched in horror; the shooting didn't stop until all the solders had fallen. A few of the horses bolted.

Then all fell silent.

Slowly, I staggered to my feet and took in the carnage. The barbarity of what had happened shocked me—

A shot rang out. It whizzed past my head! Then another! They were shooting at me! I dropped to the ground, partially obscured by the Sergeant's body, and curled up, making myself as small a target as possible. Another two shots rang out just missing me, hitting the dead Sergeant. I slumped, pretending I had been hit, hoping they would stop firing.

It worked.

Lying there, coiled into a tight ball, breathing as shallowly as possible and seeing through the narrowest of slits, I prayed to God and asked His forgiveness for all my grievous sins. I wasn't afraid to die. I was afraid that I would not go to heaven and be with Sarah, but to hell to endure eternity with John Harper.

I lay there motionless as the crunch of footsteps come closer. My heart hammered against my chest so hard I was sure it could be heard. Not far away, I could hear the crazed glee of Tanner, gloating as he plundered the bodies of their valuables and weapons.

The footsteps stopped just behind me and I heard the click of a single-action revolver—its hammer primed.

The seconds that passed felt like hours as I lay there waiting for the *coup de grace.*

'Get on with it, Perce!' Johnson's unmistakable voice yelled. 'We ain't got all day!'

'Yes, Boss,' Percy replied as he came around to face me.

'Got a live one here, Boss!' Tanner yelped, his mad enthusiasm apparent in his voice.

The wounded trooper, lying helpless on the ground, begged, 'Please … I've got a wife—'

A shot rang out.

'Widow,' Tanner derided with a cackle. 'Hey, Perce,' he called. 'How's the little molly boy? Need any help there?'

Percy looked down at me; I could see remorse in his eyes.

His mouth gaped open when I involuntarily blinked. I didn't move.

Percy hesitated then called back, 'He's a goner.'

'I'll be blowed! Took me four shots!' Tanner complained.

Pitt chimed in, 'You need more practice, mate!'

They laughed that same vicious, dissolute laugh that Jeremiah Hickson had laughed when I'd paid him his blood money. Percy laughed as well but it was not the same. I could feel his loathing for Tanner and Pitt.

Percy must have caught a glimpse of the chain of Sarah's silver locket protruding from my shirt collar. He pulled it out and yanked it off me. Rummaging through my pockets, he called out to his companions, 'This little bugger's poorer than a church mouse. He really did need that fiver.'

Standing, he reached over me and rifled through the sergeant's pockets, collecting sundry items, coin and pistol.

'Get a move on!' Johnson called out.

Percy gave me one final, unreadable look then strode towards his cohorts.

They unhitched the dead horse from the wagon, leaving three to pull the load. Johnson irreverently pushed the dead driver out of his seat and replaced him. Pitt jumped up and sat next to him until Tanner got in and pushed Pitt into the back. Percy jumped into the tray—he would have been relegated there, anyway.

'Change of plans,' I overheard Johnson say. 'Tarrawingee. Dixon's. That little strumpet at the change station took too much interest in where we were going.' With the crack of a whip and a 'Geehar!' the wagon trundled off.

***

Time froze.

Nothing moved. An unnatural silence engulfed me.

I don't know how long I lay there paralysed by fear, suffocated by dread. Disbelief washed over me. Disbelief gave way to reality. The metallic smell of blood seeped into my lungs. Distant sounds were deafening; a doleful whinny, a buzzing insect; my heartbeat.

I fought the numbness and fear and staggered to my feet. I struggled to make sense of what I saw: a field of silent, motionless bodies. Here lay the shattered lives of husbands, fathers, sons and brothers and I was the instrument of their murder. The weight of this realisation became unbearable. My stomach tightened. I wanted to scream, to vomit … to unsee. I could offer these men no solace, no favour, only a prayer.

The suffocating guilt slowly surrendered to my plight. I was part of this butchery. I could go for help but if Johnson were captured, he would surely implicate me and I would hang alongside him.

No one was going to help me. I was on my own. I could simply lie down and wait to die … or I could save myself. I had to leave these men and pray they would be found soon.

But where to go? I had no money, no food and the angle of the sun told me that it was around midday. The skies were greying over with foreboding clouds to the south and it would be night soon.

If I couldn't vindicate the murder of these men, I would extract payment in my own way.

Godfrey Saunders was wrong: I did have a choice, and I made it.

All the horses that had escaped injury or death had run off except one, the sergeant's.

My horse still stood where I'd tethered it.

Unstrapping my two valises, I opened one and took out Harper's old revolver. He had not looked after it and I chided myself for not oiling and testing it after I stole it from him. I put the gun in my belt and hoped that the cartridges in the chamber and those in my handkerchief would fire. Thrusting the handkerchief into my pocket, I felt something there: Sarah's silver locket. Percy …

I shook Percy's kindness from my thoughts and, donning my mackintosh and hat, I unfastened the reins from the tree branch and slapped my old horse on, hoping he would find his way home to Beechworth. The police would eventually discover its owner by its branding and that would link it to Percy, not to me.

The sergeant's mount was compliant as I secured my valises to it; I assured myself that I was only borrowing his steed.

***

The sergeant had chosen his mount well—he was a strong bay gelding with good speed and very obedient to my urgings.

I was able to follow the route the wagon had taken, veering off along a wide bush track, but soon it would not be possible to see. It was apparent they were heading towards Wangaratta—the original destination of the gold. This puzzled me. But the gloomy night was catching up to me and scudding clouds obscured the moon's potential brightness.

My thoughts flipped from what lay ahead to what would have transpired in Wangaratta. The authorities, awaiting their shipment of gold, would have been concerned that it hadn't arrived. They would be mounting a search party soon and I had to get off the main road. I knew that Johnson had changed their destination to Tarrawingee because Pitt had let slip to Hilda that they had been headed for Myrtleford. But I had no idea where Tarrawingee was. I had to persist following the wagon tracks for as long as I could see them.

It began to rain. Only a drizzly shower at first and then it grew a little heavier. I could still see the road ahead but the persistent raindrops were steadily obliterating the tracks. Luck was on my side—I reached a junction in the road with a sign post. Three signs pointed west, east and south. According to the markers, to the west lay Wangaratta 14 miles, and Tarrawingee 5.5 miles; Beechworth 10 miles east and Everton 3.5 miles along a bush track south.

I spurred my horse towards Tarrawingee—the town Johnson had nominated. Tired and hungry, I felt fatigue weighing down my arms and I was feeling lightheaded. I needed food, as did the horse. The sergeant's water bottle had long emptied and I'd since quenched my thirst by capturing the cold rain in my cupped hands. My thighs and back ached with each jolt in the saddle and reminded me that my body needed to rest.

The rough road to the village was bordered by a spattering of fruit trees—wild apples. It was late in the season but some of the tart fruit was still on branches and in the tall grass beneath. Grateful for this happenstance, I stopped and plucked some from the canopy while the horse crunched his share from the ground. These fruit were small and sour but a very welcomed alleviation of my hunger.

***

The tiny village was dark and quiet when I reached it. I guessed it was about seven o'clock and the rain kept everyone indoors except for one late-night patron leaving the Star Hotel—one of the village's two public houses. I accosted him mid-stride and he wasn't in any mood to dally, immediately directing me to Dixon's—an old homestead a few miles south along the Dry Creek Road. He seemed surprised that I should want to go there.

My determination drove me on.

The rain had eased and my clothes clung to me, proving the ineffectiveness of my mackintosh. Up ahead, a simple sign on the gate proclaiming '*DIXON – KEEP OUT*' came into sight. The gate and its supporting post were all there was—the softwood rail fence it had been attached to was almost non-existent, evidently destroyed by white ants long ago. Only a few ghostly sentinels stood at random intervals to mark the border.

In the distance, through the misty drizzle, I could just make out the homestead on a low rise, with a smoking chimneystack and a feeble light glowing from a window. Dismounting, I led the bay along the fence line, quiet and unseen, and towards the back of the hut where the scrub had been allowed to impinge on the paddock and stables. Crossing the fence line through a wide gap, I cautiously picked my way towards the hut. Every step, every sound, every shadow could bring disaster. My mouth was parched and every nerve in my body tingled with apprehension. One misstep and I would be the hunted, not the hunter.

I reached the cover of untamed bushes and tied the bay where he wouldn't be seen by the hut's occupants.

A whickering from the stables put me on full alert; I froze waiting for destiny to descend.

Nothing.

Carefully, I pulled Harper's gun from my belt and moved slowly, quietly towards the hut. The sounds of boisterous, alcohol-fuelled laughter wafted over to me on the sodden night air. Tanner's piercing gibber confirmed I had the right place.

***

The hut, like the fence, was a rotting carcass of rough-hewn timber warped with age and neglect. Desiccated daubing had fallen from joints leaving gaps in the slabs. I edged up to the wall, my head throbbing, my heart pounding. Through a gap, I saw them. If any of them saw me, I would be dead.

Inside, the shack was lit by a kerosene lamp and a blazing fire in the open fireplace, over which was suspended a steaming cast-iron cauldron. The rich, warm smell of whatever was cooking floated through the fissure to my nostrils; my mouth flooded with saliva. I pulled myself away from my hunger and took in the rest of the room.

The table in the middle of the space was a crude confection of roughly hewn planks attached to trestle legs at each end. The chairs were of odd sorts, homemade of whatever material had been at hand.

Several large stone jars of home-distilled liquor lay on the table and floor, their contents in partially consumed mugs and cups and splashed on the table. Among this chaos of victuals, were several large metal strongboxes, their locks smashed apart and discarded and their lids thrown open. Piles of bank notes, gold sovereigns, coins and gold bullion, separated into neat piles, stood along the centre plank of the table like a regiment of soldiers at attention awaiting deployment.

This was what so many lives had been sacrificed for.

Six men occupied the shanty.

Johnson, Tanner and Pitt, in varying stages of intoxication, were sprawled in three of the rickety chairs, while Percy stood by the fireplace, nursing his cup. He was the only one of the murderous guild who didn't appear to be slewed. This is what he'd meant when he'd said that this would be his last job. Any sympathy I held for him was drowned beneath the weight of his crime.

Two other men were at the table: one elderly, thin and stooped, the other far heftier and younger. I surmised that these were Dixons, possibly father and son, but their specific identities were of no consequence. It did matter that there were six, not four.

'You know what I'm going to do tomorrow?' boomed Tanner senselessly, slamming his cup on the table. 'I'm going to go back to the Hun's daughter and tup her till her ears fall off!'

'If you can get it up,' laughed Pitt. 'You're so drunk your prick's gone into hiding!'

This brought on another round of raucous laughter—from all except Percy.

'Well, boys,' Johnson said once the laughter subsided. 'A nice haul. Dixon, Junior,' he handed the old man a few bank notes, 'here's your twenty for the use of your place. Tanner, Pitt, Percy—an equal cut each, give or take a farthing. I'll sort out the bullion tomorrow.'

With little hesitation and much voracity, Tanner and Pitt scraped their respective hoard towards them and filled their pockets while Percy ambled to the table and collected his.

I heard all of this as I stood paralysed outside the door, gun in my hand and heart in my throat. *They tried to kill me … they owe me … this could all go terribly wrong.* Each thought tumbled into the next.

I took a deep breath of resolve and, with a silent prayer for God's deliverance, one way or the other, I told myself it was now or never.

Now!

I flung the door wide open and stood at the entrance of my hell. I'd taken everyone by surprise and they sat there stupefied. I aimed my gun directly at Johnson, who sat with his back to me barely four feet away. He turned his head to see me.

'You forgot my share,' I said, trying desperately not to show how terrified I was.

Tanner and Pitt made a shaky effort to get to their feet.

'Don't …' I warned.

'Steady, boys,' Johnson played along, and indicated them to sit down. Turning slightly in his chair to meet me eye to eye, he grinned. 'Careful, son, that ancient thing could be loaded.' He glared at Percy.

'I just want my money.' No matter how tightly I held onto that gun, and with both hands, it still trembled.

'You'll get your money. Just put that thing down. No one has to get hurt,' Johnson promised.

'Yeah,' I scoffed. 'You tried to kill me. Just give me my money and I'll go.'

'How many rounds you got?' Johnson drawled. 'Five? Six? Let's see, one, two, three …' he counted. 'I hope you're a quick, dead shot, boy, because I reckon you'll only squeeze off one before—'

'And that one will be yours, you bastard. Give me my money!'

'Fair enough, Boss,' Percy quietly interjected. 'He did his part. Give him his fiver.'

'A share,' I said looking straight at Johnson.

'Eh?' Percy queried.

'You heard. I want an equal share.' I was going for broke and I didn't care. These murderers had planned to kill me all along. I was dead in their eyes, anyway.

Tanner and Pitt laughed.

Johnson's grin was more a snarl. 'You got balls. I'll say that, boy.'

'Just give me my share, you prick!'

This brought on a round of mirth from Pitt. 'Looks like you do need more practice, Tanner,' he mocked.

Tanner glared at me.

'Boss, no need for any more bloodshed,' Percy said, once again trying to calm everyone down. 'We got plenty. Give the boy a hundred.'

'What's to say he won't snitch to the coppers?' Tanner protested.

'I was your decoy, you imbecile. I helped you murder those twenty troopers. I'll hang as high as you lot if I snitch.'

'Come on, Boss,' Percy urged, then addressed me. 'A hundred, all right?'

My options were limited and a hundred was far better than five. 'A hundred.'

'A hundred. Out of your share, Percy,' Johnson said with a sneer.

Percy hesitated as though he was searching for a response that wouldn't come. 'Um … I'm good with that, Boss,' he said and peeled off some bank notes from his share.

He took a few steps towards me, stretching out his arm. I snatched the notes out of his hand and stuffed them into my pocket.

'I don't want to see you anywhere near me, you understand, my fancy-boy?' Johnson warned. 'If I do, I will tear your eyes out and make you eat them and then I will beat you senseless and only then will I kill you. Now piss off!'

'Go, Robert,' Percy solemnly advised.

With that, I took one last look at the astonished, contemptuous faces staring at me with homicidal eyes, and slowly backed out of the door, slamming it behind me. I turned and ran as fast as I could. Reaching the dead sergeant's horse, I jumped on and spurred him on, praying he wouldn't stumble on the sodden tufts of grass.

By God's mercy, the rain that could have hindered my progress had stopped but my tracks would now be visible.

I urged that horse harder than I should have through the scrub and back to the road. I was beyond caution, beyond sense. But the beast obeyed with little reluctance and didn't stumble or falter. He was sure-footed and had a long stride, the sodden, muddy earth giving him very little impediment. We dashed back along the track from Dixon's to Tarrawingee. I kept glancing behind me, my eyes straining in the darkness, certain they were in pursuit.

The rainclouds that had obscured the moon began to break and stars glistened in the dark patches of naked sky. The moon revealed itself and its light shimmered in puddles, casting a soft ethereal glow over the sodden earth.

We finally reached the junction to the road between Beechworth and Wangaratta.

Which way? I hadn't thought that far ahead. Glancing back again, no movement, no sign of them.

I reined the horse left: Wangaratta. Fourteen miles away. It had a railway station, Beechworth didn't, and now I had money. If—*when* I reached there, I would board the train to Melbourne. To anonymity. No one would find me. Not even Johnson.

We slowed to a trot; the horse was tiring and I had far outreached my endurance—we couldn't go much further. I had to find a place for us to rest, somewhere off the road.

I saw what seemed to be a track down a narrow break in the thinning bush and guided the horse down it. We slowed to a walk.

It was cold. An eerie darkness pressed in from all sides but the heavens. Had the moon not been full or obscured by clouds, we would have been lost.

The bush track led us south and narrowed until it petered out. Ducking low-hanging branches, we pushed through and came to a small clearing that had recently been used. *Must have been a trapper's rest camp,* I thought. It didn't matter what it was; the horse and I were completely spent and, away from the road, this was as good a place as any to rest. I was soaked to the skin but a fire was out of the question— even if I'd had the means to light one, it would've given us away.

I dismounted and tied the bay nearby where there was some good growth of grass for him—he must have been as ravenous as I was. A large old red gum beckoned me and I eased myself into the concave curve of its trunk. It cradled me like an old upholstered armchair. My damp mackintosh covered me like a tent. I was shivering with cold and fear, not knowing if they would come after me and praying that they would not find me if they had. I was in God's hands. My eyes closed in silent prayer and, somewhere between the words and the silence, exhaustion claimed me and I fell into a deep sleep before I could say 'Amen'.

***

I don't know how long I slept if, indeed, I slept at all, but I was jarred awake by the sound of a twig snapping underfoot. Terrified, my body jerked in response and a gloved hand clamped over my mouth and pinned my head against the tree.

'Shhh …' came a voice.

My eyes darted towards the sound and the man crouched beside me.

Percy.

'Hush,' he hissed. 'Pitt's close.'

I nodded my understanding. He removed his hand from my mouth. My mind was awash with questions, my eyes searching the gloom for Pitt. He was not a maniac like Tanner but still a murderer who did as he was told without question.

'Johnson wants the money back,' Percy whispered, 'and your balls. Give me the money and I'll say you got away. I don't want to hurt you, Robbie.'

Before I could utter a word, Pitt lurched from the pre-dawn gloom of the bush, gun in hand and a malevolent grin on his face. 'Kissy, kissy, Percy?' he mocked. His speech was slurred; he was still inebriated.

Percy stood abruptly and faced Pitt. 'No need to harm the boy—Just take the money and let him go.'

'Without the money, he'll snitch. Besides, Perce, you're not the boss. And I don't take orders from black mongrels.' Pitt was unsteady on his feet as he waved his gun about menacingly.

'Think about it, Pitt, another death on your—'

A shot rang out, then another and Percy slumped to the ground, dead.

'It don't matter a whit to me,' Pitt muttered. He then looked at me as I sat stupefied by the cold-blooded ease with which this man could end a life. He took a staggering step towards me. 'That's one …' he uttered and raised his arm to fire.

Two shots rang out: one narrowly missed me and lodged in the tree trunk, the other slammed into Pitt's thigh.

Pitt looked at me, stunned and incredulous. 'You bastard. You shot me.'

I jumped to my feet and levelled my gun at Pitt.

Pitt took shaky aim.

'Don't …' I warned—I didn't want to shoot him.

He fired, missing again.

I fired. I fired again and again and again and again until the chamber of my gun was emptied. Every single bullet found its target.

Pitt slid to the ground, gaping wounds draining his life's blood into the damp earth.

I stood frozen, petrified by what I had done, by what had happened and by what might have been.

I approached him slowly, my empty gun pointed at him useless as it was. He didn't move or make a sound. His eyes were glassy and distant.

A sudden wave of fear swept over me—where were the others? Percy had said Pitt was close. Were the others close enough to hear the gunshots? I scanned every direction of the surrounding bushland through the murk of the pre-dawn, listening for any sound or movement beyond the roar of blood pulsing in my ears.

Nothing.

I stood there for what seemed to be an eternity. *They came alone,* I finally told myself.

I went to Percy and knelt beside him. He was dead. I made the sign of the cross and said a silent prayer for God to take his soul and give him eternal, peaceful rest. This man was a murderer but he did try to save my life and I was truly indebted to him. There was nothing I could do for him now. Nothing I could do for either of them.

I returned to Pitt and crouched beside him. I prised the revolver from his hand and rummaged through his pockets, doing to him as he had done to those troopers. I relieved him of his share of the booty, a pen knife and his cartridge pouch, stuffing each into the large pockets of my mack. I retrieved his fob watch and was barely able to see the time in the dimness: 6:38. The sun would rise soon.

Feeling the rest of his pockets revealed nothing more. My hands felt sticky; they were coated with his blood. I had taken his life. The thought sent a violent shudder of repulsion through me. I wiped my bloodied hands on his jacket but it didn't clean the feeling; I doubled over and retched.

This felt different from Harper's reckoning … or, perhaps, it felt the same … I cannot say. I was the instrument that had taken both lives. I forced my gaze on Pitt. I'd done to him what he had been about to do to me. I was not sorry. He and Harper deserved to die; both had tried to kill me. Both had failed.

I returned to Percy and searched through his pockets, removing his share of the plunder and all his personal items, including a neatly tied packet of letters postmarked 'Bathurst'. I bundled the meagre collection into his handkerchief—perhaps there was something I could do for him.

Percy's gun was still in his grip—I had an idea. Returning to Pitt, I placed Harper's old weapon in Pitt's hand. It was a ruse that may or may not work but it meant that, at the very least, I was now in possession of a much newer weapon and cartridges. I no longer would have to gamble that Harper's old abused gun would not misfire nor would the cartridges explode on ignition.

Rustling from the undergrowth made my pulse leap again and I took cover by the tree that had cradled me. Pitt's gun was at the ready when Percy's handsome mount, the thoroughbred, trampled his way in towards its slain master. There was no other movement from the surrounding bush.

The horse seemed to understand that its master was dead and stood there, head bowed, nuzzling Percy.

I carefully made my way to it, hoping it would remember me and the rubdown and feed I had given it. 'Easy, boy,' I coaxed. 'I won't hurt you. Easy.'

Keeping the sergeant's horse would link me to the massacre. Leaving it here would link them, so I took hold of the thoroughbred's reins and led it to the sergeant's and transferred my valises from it to the thoroughbred.

The rising dawn sent the first long shards of filtered light through the dense bush.

One last look.

'I'm sorry, Percy,' I said—whether I meant it, I wasn't sure. He saved me—twice—but he hadn't told me that I was to be killed along with the troopers.

I climbed on his horse and never looked back.

19

Wednesday, 6th May, 1874

Wangaratta, Victoria

We followed the road to Wangaratta. Would the bodies of Percy and Pitt be discovered? When and by whom? Johnson and Tanner? How long would they wait before looking for them? The sun was low on the eastern horizon, inching its way relentlessly upwards. It would take about two or three hours to reach our destination at this pace but I didn't want to tire the horse too soon in case … I kept Pitt's pistol fully loaded and at the ready should anyone come upon me without warning.

Percy's thoroughbred would have had feed in Dixon's barn the previous night but I was desperately hungry and we were both dead tired. The skies were all clear, the threat of more rain fading and my clothes were slowly drying out.

*****

In the morning light I could make out a large township in the distance: Wangaratta. At the Cobb office, I had heard that it boasted a new railway station linking it to Wodonga to the north and my destination, Melbourne, to the south. The fairly large population meant there was a good selection of hotels and a certain amount of anonymity for me.

We were on the main road, approaching the town. The usual bustle of a thriving settlement met us. Carts rumbled by, their drivers indifferent to my existence.

'Make way!' came the shout from the leader of a small company of troopers galloping towards us. They thundered past, hooves churning the waterlogged road and kicking up mud.

I knew where they were heading.

We entered the township at around ten o'clock. It was alive with activity—mounted stockmen wove between the slower carts and drays, while tradesmen and craftsmen alike were hard at work in their workshops and stores.

Small groups of people assembled here and there, urgent and conspiratorial. Their topic of conversation was evident.

I steered the thoroughbred along the town's outskirts and headed south through the streets where the smells and sounds of the industrious population invaded my senses. As I passed cottages, the scent of cooking drifted out to meet me—fresh bread, frying bacon, woodsmoke—I nearly swooned. Hunger gnawed relentlessly and my stomach clenched tighter with every breath of that warm, homely air.

I stopped at the first stable I came across and spoke to the old stable owner. I did not want to engage in any conversation that spoke of the robbery and I asked him to agist my horse for a month. He agreed and I paid him with gold sovereigns I had taken. The stable owner was much impressed by the horse and would not have any trouble selling him and his tack when I didn't return in a month's time. I asked the owner where I could find a good cheap establishment to bathe and he directed me to a small inn not far from the stables. I also asked him which was the best hotel in the town proper.

Leaving the horse with the stable owner, I hauled my red valises to the Prospectors Inn, and registered as Patrick Morrison. The accommodation was basic, rustic, but had everything I needed: a warm bath and—more importantly—privacy.

The washroom was an annex to the kitchen at the rear of the inn. I locked the washroom door after the hotelier's wife and servant filled the shallow tub with steaming hot water. Stripping off in its privacy, I immersed my aching body into the bath's warm embrace. But I didn't dare linger. There was no time for comfort. Hunger clawed at my insides, but fear clawed harder.

Clean, refreshed and with much reluctance, I left the tub, dried off and unpacked fresh clothing from my valise. My soiled clothes would have to wait to be washed. I needed to go.

I eased the door open and slipped out into the courtyard, praying no one noticed that the young man who entered the shack, emerged as a young woman.

***

'Ahem.'

The gentle clearing of my throat alerted the desk clerk of my existence. 'Good morning, Miss, and welcome to the Royal Victoria Hotel. How may I help?' he graciously queried.

On the other side of his counter was Rebecca Davies, not Robert. I was clad in my Sunday best with a newly purchased bonnet to cover my short hair. I smiled at the clean-shaven young man, who was dressed in a black suit, white shirt with a stiff winged collar and black tie.

'I would like a room, please. With a bath if at all possible.'

'Of course, Miss. The Royal Victoria can accommodate any request. How long will you be with us?'

I looked about me and took in the richness of this new establishment, recommended to me—rather, to Robert—by the stable owner. 'When is the next train to Melbourne?'

'The day after tomorrow. That is, Friday, Miss. In the morning.'

It was a little later than I had hoped but, rather than submit myself to another Cobb coach ride—this time on the inside—I decided to wait for the train. 'Then I'll be with you until Friday, the day after tomorrow, thank you.'

The clerk appeared to hesitate. 'Erm, Miss, that will be, erm …'

I understood his dilemma and put him at ease. 'How much will that be?'

'Thank you, Miss. That is always the most difficult part of my job. That will be one guinea. Meals can be provided in the dining room at an extra charge.'

That was a little more than I'd anticipated but something I should have expected seeing that this particular hotel appeared to have been built with no expense spared—it even had its own theatre, or so the sign proclaimed.

But the thought of a hot meal in the dining room overcame me.

'I've been travelling all day,' I said, mustering a glimmer of hope.

'Might the kitchen staff be able to accommodate me with something hot to eat?'

'Certainly, Miss, nothing is too much trouble. In fact, the dining room is open now.'

I withdrew the coin purse from my newly acquired reticule and counted out the one pound and one shilling. The young man turned the register around to me and handed me the pen. I filled in my name: 'S Davies, Sydney'.

'Travelling alone, Miss … er, Davies?'

'Yes.'

'Quite dangerous, if I may say so. Just yesterday a gold escort was bailed up on its way from Beechworth. Twenty good men lost their lives. Slaughtered. All for gold.' He paused, his voice heavy. 'I knew many of them,'

The stranger's words hit me hard. The guilt I had pushed away surged through me. All my justifications meant nothing. The deaths I was party to—the families left behind—all came rushing at me. My eyes filled with remorse and guilt.

'Are you all right, Miss?' the clerk earnestly enquired.

'Yes … yes … I'm sorry. I'm so, so sorry.'

'Please don't fret so, Miss. It won't be long before those callous murderers are brought to justice. They will hang.'

'Do … do they know who did it?'

'Not yet. Troopers and black trackers are looking for them right now. They'll be found, despite the rain.'

'Yes,' I agreed, numb.

The clerk handed me a key and rang the bell on the table. At the sound, a younger man stepped up and took my two red valises.

'Room seventeen,' the clerk instructed the porter then turned to me. 'Do enjoy your stay, Miss Davies. And please don't fret.'

I hesitated, shook the despair and anguish out of my head. 'May I ask a favour of you?' I asked quietly. 'Could you arrange a train ticket to Melbourne, please? I am quite weary and would dearly like to rest after I have taken a meal.'

'Certainly, Miss. First class?'

'If you would. Thank you.'

With these transactions finalised and with a heavy weariness pressing my soul, I followed the porter to my room.

***

They were on the same road I had taken and overlooking the same vista I had the day before: the township of Wangaratta.

'Reckon the little molly is there, Boss?' Tanner asked.

Johnson didn't reply but his steely, piercing gaze confirmed that he did.

20

Sunday, 3rd September, 1905

Abbottsford Hall, Suffolk, England

'Ah! It appears we have arrived,' Wills observed, glancing out of the coach's window.

Abbottsford Hall, the seat of the tenth Duke and Duchess of Bramwell, sat in the middle of splendidly tended gardens in an immense acreage with its own forest and river. These had provided the current duke's ancestors private hunting and fishing grounds, which had also been enjoyed by various monarchs over the centuries. The current duke, however, was no shooter or angler. He preferred his books to guns and making a killing on the stock market to making a killing in the field. Despite the many subtle hints over the years from the king's equerry, the duke remained steadfast in denying access to his lands and appeasing the monarch's thirst for blood sport. He always had a ready, plausible excuse on hand and delivered it with just enough charm to avoid offence.

The hall itself was an immense and imposing pile—a veritable palace. I was impressed by the majesty and grandeur of the holding and understood why the duchess was to be the next victim: the ransom demand would be enormous. Perhaps the previous three abductions had been mere rehearsals. If our information and deductions were correct, this would be the biggest haul yet.

'Full, undivided attention, Davies,' Wills pressed.

I detached myself from the memories Sarah's locket held and brought myself back to the present and the mission at hand.

The coach drove to the stairs leading up to the main entrance—something we had not expected as we were, in effect, servants and would normally have used the tradesman's entrance at the rear. The butler and three footmen were there to meet us—another surprise.

'Welcome to Abbottsford Hall,' greeted the butler as he opened the carriage door for us. 'The footmen will take your luggage.'

We alighted from the coach and one of the three attempted to relieve me of my Gladstone.

'I'll keep this with me, thank you,' I insisted, glowering at the unfortunate servant.

'Very well, Madam,' the butler graciously replied with a slight bow and led us up the stone stairs, through the imposing portal, inside to the vast vestibule and up the impressive staircase, followed closely by the three footmen carrying our few cases.

Wills glanced at me and noticed my stern expression. He leaned in and whispered, 'Don't frighten the duchess, Davies.' Then he gave me one of his mischievous grins.

'Major Williams and Miss Davies, Your Grace,' the butler announced with dignified formality.

The duke's study in the large eighteenth century country house was opulent and displayed all the characteristics of an ancient family's background, breeding and wealth. The duke, as I would soon discover, was an elegant and handsome man of sixty-five years—lean, stylish and softly spoken, but his gentlemanly mannerisms belied the incisive and shrewd mind of a businessman. The Duchess of Bramwell, Mary, was the second daughter of the twelfth Earl of Chestermere, equally as elegant, quietly spoken and stylish, abreast of the fashions of the day no matter how absurd. The duke and duchess had been married for thirty-six years.

With them in the study was Alexander Quinn, who had arrived earlier that day by private motor car.

Wills and I stepped into the study, leaving the butler at the door.

'Ah!' Alexander Quinn said as he approached Wills with his arm outstretched. 'A good journey, I hope.'

'Yes, Mr Quinn,' Wills replied, taking the offered hand and shaking it warmly.

The other two occupants of the room, evidently the Duke and Duchess of Bramwell, cast a critical eye over us from afar. I could not immediately discern if they objected to us and our intrusion or welcomed it.

'Let me present you,' continued Quinn leading Wills to the duke with me following a step behind.

The butler, still standing at the door, enquired, 'Will that be all, Sir?'

'Ask Florence to bring tea for our guests, would you? Thank you, Thomson,' the duchess interceded, her expression softening as she regarded me, immediately making me feel welcomed.

'Right away, Ma'am,' Thomson replied and closed the door behind him.

'Your Graces,' Quinn beamed like a proud father, 'may I present to you Major Reginald Williams of the Queen's Own Corps of Guides and the Metropolitan Police's Special Branch.'

Wills stood to attention and bowed his head sharply. 'Your Graces.'

'And his Assisting Clerk, Miss Rebecca Davies,' Quinn continued.

My bow was somewhat less snappy and more casual. 'Your Graces.'

The duke seemed impressed, tilting his head and nodding appreciatively. 'Major Williams. The Queen's Guides, you say?'

'Yes, Sir.'

He gave an approving 'Hmm,' and then addressed me. After pausing to take in my facial disfigurement, he continued, 'Miss Davies. You come with quite a reputation, I must say.'

'I trust a good one, Sir?' I enquired. 'And Davies is sufficient. Sir.' That last bit caused an audible gasp from Quinn but earned a twinkle of amusement from both the duke and duchess.

'Is that an Afrikaans inflection you have there … Davies?' the duke asked.

'Australian, Sir.'

'Ah, yes. Wool, wheat, beef, irrepressible subjects. A rich, young country.'

'Sir, if I may,' interrupted Quinn. 'I'd like to fill in the major on our discussions?'

'Of course, Quinn, go ahead.' Taking a seat, he added, 'Please, make yourselves comfortable.'

Wills and I occupied an upholstered antique sofa with Quinn and the peers taking up one of the several matching chairs each.

'Chippendale?' I asked the duchess.

She nodded. 'The sixth duke's acquisition. A very shrewd man.'

'Williams,' began Quinn, 'you have been installed in a suite on the same floor as the duke and duchess. Being on the same floor means you will have easy access to the duchess at night should the need present itself. But it may also incur questions from the other servants as to why you haven't been relegated to the upper floors, since you are not a peer nor related.

'Davies, because you will accompany the duchess during her waking hours, you have been assigned a room on the floor above. The story we have concocted is that you, Davies, have been engaged as the duchess' personal secretary and, as such, are required to be at her side every minute of the day, barring meal times, unless otherwise invited by Her Grace.

'Williams, as you will be active only at night and sleeping during the day, your purpose here is that you are conducting an audit of the duke's entailed estates and will be working within the confines of your suite. That should explain your daily absences.

'All servants, except two trusted chambermaids, the duchess' maid and the duke's valet, have been expressly debarred from being on your floor, Williams, on the pain of instant dismissal and without a character, if they disobey.

'Only the butler, Thomson, whom you've met, and the housekeeper, Mrs Plummer, know of your identity and real purpose here. Both Thomson and Mrs Plummer have been in the employ of His Grace for more than forty years and are completely trustworthy.

'Oh, and another thing, the duchess' niece, the Countess of Chestermere, will arrive the day after tomorrow to conclude some business with the duke. Her Ladyship will be in a suite on the same floor as you, Williams. Of course, her maid will also have access.

'To keep everything as normal as possible, the duchess' planned weekend will proceed as scheduled on Saturday. The fifteen guests will be allocated rooms on the upper floors—'

'Fifteen guests?' Wills interrupted, a little alarmed. 'Would it not be better to postpone the event until this matter is concluded?'

'It is imperative that long-standing arrangements are not suddenly altered,' Quinn explained. 'This house may already be under observation—possibly from within. Hence the necessity that only those I've already mentioned be appraised of the situation.'

He paused, clearly awaiting our concession to this extraordinary circumstance, then proceeded, 'Thomson has arranged for the agency to provide three extra footmen and two extra chambermaids and they are expected Friday. They, too, will be restricted. Any questions?'

Wills and I looked at each other; Wills responded on our behalf, 'No, Sir, I believe your rundown and the brief you have already given us is all we need.'

A gentle rapping on the door diverted our attention.

'Enter,' said the duke.

Thomson opened the door for the maid, a young woman of pale complexion and rosy cheeks, who entered wielding a very large silver platter with silver teapots, creamer and sugar bowl filled with lumps of white sugar, delicate cups and saucers and silver teaspoons.

She skilfully manoeuvred her way to the low table in the middle of the room and dexterously placed the tray on it without so much as a clink of teacups.

'Please serve our guests, Florence,' the duchess instructed. 'Miss Davies, how do you take your tea?'

'Black, thank you.'

Florence carefully poured a good measure into a cup and brought it to me.

'Madam—' She looked up at me for the first time and caught sight of my facial mutilation. 'Oh!' Her hand jolted in shock, sending the tea cup off balance and some of its contents into my lap, much to her additional horror and dismay. 'Oh, Madam, I am so terribly sorry …'

Thomson ran to her aid as she tried desperately to soak the hot liquid from my skirt with her white apron.

'Don't fuss,' I said trying to suppress my irritation. 'I've had worse things happen to me.'

Thomson waved poor Florence off. 'Go!' Then finished mopping up with several napkins from the tray.

Florence raced from the room, hiding her tears.

***

'Oh, Mrs Plummer,' wailed Florence as she burst into the housekeeper's sitting room and threw herself into the only armchair. 'I'm going to be sacked!'

'What? Again?' was the nonchalant reply from Mrs Plummer, not even looking up from the ledger book she was checking.

'I'm done for!' she said, wiping the tears from her eyes.

Mrs Plummer put down her pencil and looked up at Florence sprawled gracelessly across the chair. 'What happened this time?'

'I've just had the awfulest discombobulation. There was I, serving tea as proper as you please, when I look up and see this … this … woman—'

'Lady,' the housekeeper corrected.

'She weren't no lady, Mrs Plummer. Not like what normally visits Her Grace and His Grace. She was like … like … well, I mean to say, her hair was real short, shorter than a badger's eyebrow, and her face all cut up. She looked daggers at me and gave me the trembles then I spilt tea all over her. And the rug.'

'Oh, Florrie, what am I to do with you?'

'Her face. It was like she's been through the wars. Or a window! And I've been told about women like her by Lady Westmorland's maid when they went to Berlin.'

'And what women would they be then?'

'Well, I mean to say, you know … men haters.'

Mrs Plummer heaved a long sigh and stood up. 'Florence, that *woman* is here at the behest of His Grace to take care of Her Grace's needs. Both she and Major Williams. You are to treat her with respect and refer to her as Miss Davies, no matter what you may or may not think she is or what she looks like.'

'She's real scary, Mrs Plummer,' Florence whined, standing.

'Have you been listening, Florence? How are you to treat her?'

'With respect, Mrs Plummer.'

'Good. We have an understanding. Now back to work before I discombobulate you.'

Florence slouched out, closing the door behind her.

'*Discombobulation* indeed,' Mrs Plummer muttered. 'Where does she pick up these Americanisms?'

***

In London, Sir Giles Hawthorne was enjoying a quiet evening alone at the Marlborough Club—away from his wife and mother-in-law—reading the evening Times and sipping his favourite port, when Colonel Humphries appeared in front of him.

'Giles! I didn't expect to see you here this evening.'

'Neville. My wife … you understand. Won't you join me?' invited Hawthorne, folding away his newspaper.

'Thank you,' Humphries accepted as he made himself comfortable in the large upholstered chair next to Sir Giles. 'I heard what happened last week to that poor unfortunate … er, Timothy? Rotten luck, old boy.'

'Yes, that damned heavy-handed fool Yabsley went too far.'

'What now? Any indication as to who the abductors were?'

'None, I'm afraid. We got nothing but the ramblings of a confused imbecile's mind.'

'Hmph,' Humphries grunted as he withdrew his silver cigarette case and offered one to Hawthorne.

'At least one good thing has come of all this,' Hawthorne said, clearly pleased, as he took a cigarette and put it to his mouth.

'Oh?' Humphries raised an eyebrow and produced his new Matchless Cigar Lighter and lit both cigarettes.

'I say, old man, that's an interesting gadget,' Hawthorne said, taking the lighter from Humphries and admiring it. 'Where did you get it?'

'From the United States. You were saying? One good thing?'

'Yes. Quinn—upon my recommendation, mind you—finally suspended Major Williams and that vile excuse of womanhood, his so called 'Assisting Clerk', for fouling up the operation in the forest. We had those abductors in the palm of our hand.'

'They're no longer on the case?'

'No, thank God. Quinn listened to me for once.'

'Have they been assigned to another case?'

'I believe Quinn ordered them to take leave, as I suggested. Not that I give a damn,' Hawthorne replied handing back the lighter and taking a draw on his cigarette.

'Do you know where they are now?'

Hawthorne felt a tickle of irritation and narrowed his eyes. 'You seem awfully interested in those two, Humphries.'

'My interest is only out of concern for you, dear boy,' Humphries offered. 'The further away from you and the case, the better, I say.'

'Quite. I have no idea where they've gone. On suspension until further notice is all I need to know. And good riddance, too.' He took a long, satisfied draw on his cigarette.

'Yes. Good riddance.'

There was a pause. Hawthorne took up his newspaper, clearly believing the conversation—rather, the inquest—had concluded.

Humphries regrouped his thoughts and offered in that well-oiled, offhand tone of his, 'You know, dear boy, your quandary has been dogging my thoughts …'

'My quandary?'

'Yes. Not being able to find the perpetrators of these heinous acts.'

'Not a quandary. All I need is a police force with an ounce of intellect. The buffoons I currently have are nothing more than fopdoodles and cumberworlds.'

'Quite so, but have you thought that the more hostile trade unions may be behind these monstrous crimes? Since they were legitimised—'

'How so?' asked Hawthorne, placing the broadsheet on his lap and intrigued. 'What have you heard?'

'Well … perhaps it's nothing … mere speculation—'

'Out with it!'

'My man tells me he overheard three of the labourers on one of the East End building sites talking about a kidnapping and how much their union would benefit from the ransom. I can't attest to the veracity of what my man heard but I can say that if it came to pass—another abduction, that is—it would be a black mark against anyone who didn't follow this through and a gold mark for the man who did and prevented another murder.'

Hawthorne's eyes lit up. This presented an excellent opportunity to gain a mark of merit—and respect—from the head of the Special Branch and a long overdue promotion.

'Which unions are you talking about?' he demanded.

'Well, I don't quite know, but the building site engages workers from the National Association of Builders' Labourers, the National Amalgamated Labourers' Union, and the Amalgamated Society of Carpenters and Joiners to name a few.'

'Send your man to me, so I can have a word.'

'I'm dreadfully sorry, old man, but he had to leave for Ireland. His mother, you know. I will get word to him by telegraph if you like.'

Hawthorne was visibly frustrated by not being able to interview Humphries' 'man' himself but was grateful for what seemed to be, finally, a positive lead to catching the murderers.

21

Monday, 4ᵗʰ September, 1905

Abbottsford Hall, Suffolk, England

The next day at Abbottsford Hall was a lesson in household management. It was a large and complex household, easily and deftly managed by the duchess who deftly delegated to Thomson and Mrs Plummer. They, in turn, managed their charges with utmost proficiency and economy. The household staff comprised about fifteen individuals—valets, footmen, and maids of every description—while another fifteen or so were employed outdoors as groundsmen, gardeners, stable hands, and handymen and boys all under the supervision of the steward, Truscott, who, in turn, answered to the duke. In addition to these permanent workers, when social events were in the offing, as was the case that Saturday, extra staff were taken on to help and guests, more often than not, brought their own retinue of servants.

As arranged, Thomson had provided a complete list of permanent employees, which had been passed on to Detective Constable Scott. Despite the debilitating injury to his leg, Scott had valiantly volunteered to remain in London and on duty. So long as he had his crutches, he asserted, he could work and help bring these miscreants to justice. His assignment was to investigate each employee and report his findings to Wills. His review of the extra three footmen and two chambermaids was going to be more difficult, as the agency would send whomever was available at that moment. All in all, Wills and I had a difficult task and had to be extra vigilant and cautious.

Lady Chestermere, the duchess' niece, would be accompanied by her maid, her chauffeur and her business secretary, all of whom were held in the highest regard by Mrs Plummer and Thomson and, indeed, the duchess herself.

Those accompanying the fifteen guests due Saturday, however, were an unknown quality and quantity. *One problem at a time*, I thought.

The duchess took me on a 'Cooks' tour' of the extensive grounds, introducing me as Miss Davies, her personal secretary, to those in charge of specific functional areas. The stables were of particular interest to me as, while I endured riding in a hansom or a coach, I enjoyed sitting astride a good mount and giving the horse its head. This was becoming more difficult to do within the confines of a city like London. There was nothing like racing across the countryside on a brisk autumn morning with the wind surging through your hair, short as mine was.

The stables were vast and accommodated all of the estate's equine inhabitants, from Hackneys to Shires, all in excellent condition and well-tended by the head groom and his assistants.

Strolling down the spotless centre aisle, the duchess must have seen my eyes light up when they set upon a magnificent seventeen-hand thoroughbred.

'Peleus,' the duchess announced. 'The Duke's favourite. He's won Ascot, you see. Beat the King's horse by a head. He's a wonderful animal,' she confirmed, scratching his inquisitive nose. 'And that's Tommy, his companion. They are inseparable.' In the stall next to Peleus, watching us intently, was a smaller chestnut gelding, also a handsome specimen of horseflesh, being enthusiastically brushed by a lad of about nine or ten who was likewise watching us intently.

'He don't run half as hard as when Tommy's with him,' the lad declared.

'And that's Henry,' the duchess introduced, ignoring his lack of manners. 'Henry, this is Miss Davies, my secretary—'

The duchess barely finished her introductions when Henry's hand shot through between the rails for a shake. 'Pleased to meet you, Miss … Gaw! What happened to your face?'

His naïveté was disarming—enough to make the duchess blink in amused disbelief—but I took his hand and shook it. 'An unfortunate accident,' I replied.

'It must have hurt some.'

'Quite some,' I confirmed.

'Don't matter but. Peleus likes you. He usually bites them that he don't, so you must be all right.' He resumed brushing Tommy. 'I'm going to be a jockey. The duke said I could race Peleus when I'm old enough. I ride him now but just a walk or a trot in the yard.' At that, he returned to concentrating on his task, virtually dismissing us. I admired the young fellow.

That the duchess permitted the lad's impudence gave me insight into this noblewoman's persona. She was not, as Fawkner and Miss Pretty Thing would have it, an empty-headed slave to fashion, but a woman of tolerance and, indeed, grace.

We walked on. 'Do you ride?' she asked casually.

'Yes, Your Grace.'

'Very good. The countess is quite the horsewoman and we'll be on the bridlepath every morning she is with us. Bright and early,' she added with a warning glint in her eye.

Her comment only worked to raise my concerns over how obscure the trail was and whether it presented the perfect opportunity for an abduction. I would need to speak to Wills about this. It would be better if the duchess stayed in the company of more people, rather than fewer.

The duchess, accompanied by Mrs Plummer, then showed me through the truly palatial house, from top to bottom, finishing the expedition in the large kitchens where I met Mrs Russell, the cook. By a quirk of coincidence, she reminded me of Mrs Archer, Mr Morrison's cook all those years ago. Like Mrs Archer had been, Mrs Russell was in her middle-age, quite attractive and lean, but was obviously foreign-born and spoke with a Nordic inflection.

There, in the servant's hall, Florence and I once again crossed paths.

'I believe you've met Florence?' Mrs Plummer asked me. 'And I believe she owes you a proper apology.'

'That's not necessary, Mrs Plummer. I doubt Florence will be serving me tea again any time soon.'

***

I had left the duchess to take her evening meal with the duke in the dining room, assured that they were safely surrounded by their servants. Wills and I discussed our progress in his suite of rooms opposite the duchess'. He thought it best to go along with the plan to ride each morning, as any change to normality could raise suspicions. 'If the duchess and countess usually ride,' he advised, 'then they must continue doing so.'

'Oh, and I borrowed a copy of Debrett's from the duke,' he added as an afterthought. 'It's on your desk. I thought you'd like some background on the countess since she and the duchess are likely to spend all their free time together. The entry is marked with a slip of paper.'

My room on the third floor was almost as big as my flat in Newington and included a small study area with a desk, a sofa and a low table on which stood a very generous platterful of cold meats, cheeses, bread and various condiments. There was also a private bathroom and water closet, and an enormous double bed.

I made up a thick sandwich and went to the desk to write up my report, eat my sandwich and go to bed. Debrett's was there, just as Wills had indicated and, munching on my snack, I opened the book at the mark and easily found the entry:

> *'CHESTERMERE, COUNTESS OF (Delaney)*
> *– Katherine Agnes Stuart Delaney (Countess of*
> *Chestermere); b. 1865 ...'*

I read through the whole, full-page entry and was impressed by her achievements and lineage. She was forty, unmarried and a countess in her own right, having succeeded her mother, Agnes, upon the elder's death in 1879. Agnes had also been a countess in her own right, with the title having a Special Remainder and going to the eldest child, male or female. The Duchess of Bramwell, Mary, Agnes' younger sister, married the Duke of Bramwell while Agnes married a commoner—a Scotsman. It was interesting to note that Katherine, the current Countess of Chestermere, was one of only two 'in her own right' countesses, who were not dowagers or widows, listed in Debrett's. She was the fourteenth to hold the title.

Impressive, I mused. *All that and not married—what is wrong with her?*

22

Tuesday, 5ᵗʰ September, 1905

Abbottsford Hall, Suffolk, England

After a good night's sleep—the bed was remarkably comfortable—I arose early, bathed and dressed, ready for the day ahead and the arrival of the Countess of Chestermere and her entourage, despite the inevitable headaches that would entail. I was not looking forward to the interminable, inconsequential chatter that seemed to be the only occupation of women of high social status and wealth. While the duchess was undoubtedly charming and had made me feel very welcomed, she still had that air of aloofness that brought into focus my very lowly status. I was well aware of my lack of social standing, lack of breeding and obvious physical defects, but I'd be damned if I allowed others to make me feel less worthy than they.

A final glance in the mirror confirmed I was scrubbed, macassared and combed, and my necktie was straight. *As good as it gets*, I thought and collected my daily report for Wills and my 'secretary's notebook', before heading downstairs.

I came across Wills in the corridor on the duchess' floor, striding along and reading a ledger book as officiously as possible.

'Oh, it's you,' he said looking up. He lowered the ledger and the pretence. 'What time is it?'

I looked at my wrist watch. 'Seven.'

'There's a fluster of activity in there.'

'The arrival of her niece, I expect.' I handed him an envelope. 'My report.'

'Thank you. With any sort of luck, Scott should have something on

Croft and his accomplice by now. I'll telephone him before I hit the sack.' Wills took a step towards the stairs before pausing and turning to whisper, 'Listen, regarding the niece,' he began with a smirk, 'I read she's near forty and unmarried. Possibly ugly. More so than you. Treat her with respect and no gloating over it. Countess or not.' He flashed that all-knowing grin of his, the one that told me he was having fun at my expense.

'Bugger off.'

'Good night,' he said chuckling, and walked away.

I watched his back with a feeling of foreboding then turned to the duchess' door. Before I could knock, it swung open and the duchess flounced out, beaming and leaving her maid in the room in midmotion of installing the last of the hairpins to the duchess' hair.

'Good morning, Davies. Beautiful day, isn't it?' She breezed past me.

A few loping strides and I had caught her up. 'Good morning, Your Grace.'

We passed two chambermaids at the linen closet who promptly stood aside and curtseyed.

'Good morning Bertha. Good morning, Candice.'

'Good morning, Your Grace,' they said in unison, their voices fading behind us as we raced down the stairs. The Duchess of Bramwell could have won at Ascot herself, without a horse, at the rate she was travelling.

She swept into the morning room, and I followed, like a leaf caught in a fast-running stream.

'Good morning, Bramwell,' she chirped to her husband as she hurried to the buffet and helped herself to an assortment of breakfast foods. 'What a glorious day!'

'Good morning, dearest,' replied the duke, looking up from his freshly pressed, salmon-pink Financial Times. 'My, my, if I had to guess, I would say that you're expecting someone rather special today.'

Her reply was an expression that beamed excitement and joy as she took her selection to the table. Thomson was instantly at her side pouring hot coffee.

'Good morning, Thomson,' she acknowledged, before taking a sip.

'Your Grace,' he replied with a slight bow and then replenished the duke's cup at the other end of the table.

I took myself to a corner of the room near a window overlooking the gardens at the rear of the building. Amid the profusion of floral colour and lawns stood a magnificent, white, wrought-iron gazebo. Three gardeners were tending the grounds, mowing the lawns and trimming the rose bushes in readiness for Saturday. One was cutting long-stemmed roses and handing them to Florence, who in turn added them to the already large collection in her basket.

'And when may I have her all to myself?' asked the duchess.

The duke gave a genial laugh and put down his paper. 'We should have all the documents and contracts signed and sealed by teatime, dear, if Hollingsworth doesn't dither over the small print.' It was only then he noticed me at the window. 'Good morning, Davies.'

''Morning, Sir.'

'You will have your work cut out for you today keeping pace with the duchess and her niece and their relentless chatter.'

My expectations sank; it would be as I thought: *tedium ad nauseum*.

'Now, Bram, we don't chatter, we discuss. By the way, Davies,' Mary continued, 'I've arranged a nice beast for you tomorrow.'

'Riding? Is that wise, dear? With all the goings-on? Perhaps it would be better—'

'Pish. You know very well how I feel about this supposed abduction.' She calmly rearranged the food on her plate. 'I've said it before—I don't need to be coddled like a child.'

'It's for your protection, my dear. I could not bear the thought of you being harmed in any way. Besides, it's only for a week or so, isn't that right, Davies?'

'Yes, Your Grace. Perhaps more, depending on circumstance.'

It surprised me that the duchess did not take the threat to her life more seriously. On the other hand, perhaps Wills and I were mistaken; perhaps we were wasting our time on a wild goose chase and the abductors were ready to pounce elsewhere. Another woman's life may be in jeopardy.

'Now, come, Mary. What if the threat is real? What if this little jaunt puts you in danger? And Katherine? And Davies? Remember that Davies is risking her life to keep yours safe. I strongly urge you not go riding until this is concluded. And certainly not through the woods.'

She sighed. 'Very well. I concede to your infinite wisdom. We will take the river path,' she replied, her tone laced with mischief.

The duke frowned, plainly disappointed by her meagre concession. 'Truscott tells me that poachers have been at the Catfish lodge. Left an awful mess. I really think you should reconsider.'

That piece of inconsequence aroused my interest; I would need to investigate further.

'Poachers poach, dear, they do not abduct,' countered the duchess. 'Besides, as you said, they are long gone.'

The duke harrumphed and shook his head in defeat. He looked at me. 'You do ride, Davies?'

'I—'

'Of course she rides,' the duchess jumped in. 'She's Australian.'

'Ah, yes. Damned fine horsemen, Australians.'

'Language, Bramwell!'

'Forgive my errant tongue, my dear. Horsewomen, too, I would imagine. Is that where you met Major Williams? Australia?'

'No, Sir. The Sindh.'

'You don't say. I was there in eighty. The end of the second Afghan war. Dreadful business. You?'

'Eighty-five, Sir.'

'In heaven's name, what would a young Christian woman be doing there at that dangerous time?'

I hesitated to reply, the memories still raw. Not even Wills brought up our time there unless I initiated the conversation.

The duchess perceived my hesitation and addressed the duke. 'Er … did I tell you that Katherine acquired a motor car?'

'A motor car? Damned noisy contraptions! Forgive my errant tongue, dear.'

'It's a fine British make—Rolls-Royce, I believe—and she's driven it all the way back from Glasgow.'

'Terrifying all the horses and villagers along the way, no doubt. What say you, Davies? Motor cars.'

I was somewhat reluctant to offer an opinion but had to respond. 'It's the way of the future, Sir.'

'Hmph!'

'I will drag you into the twentieth century if it's the last thing I do, dearest,' the duchess said, closing out the conversation.

***

Colonel Neville Humphries had made his way to the Marlborough Club in Pall Mall early that morning, partly to avail himself of the fine breakfast offered there and partly to await an important telephone call. It came as he was finishing his coffee in the reading room. The porter brought forth the telephone set.

'Pardon me, Colonel Humphries. A telephone call for you, Sir.' He placed the unit on the table and plugged in the cord at the wall.

The porter retreated and busied himself clearing a nearby table of its abandoned breakfast remnants.

Humphries picked up the receiver. 'Colonel Humphries here.' He listened intently to the scratchy voice on the line, his demeanour slowly changing from attentive to concerned to incensed. 'Keep me informed,' he finally barked. 'But not here. Not at the club.' He replaced the handset and sat in stern and concentrated contemplation then picked up the receiver.

'Yes, put me through to 715, London Wall.' He nervously tapped his finger on the upholstered easy chair's armrest as he waited impatiently. 'Gregory? Gregory, I've had word our train may have come off the rails … No, it will still proceed but we need a deviation. This is what I want you to do …'

***

After breakfast, the duchess and I relocated to her study, which overlooked the long front driveway. She and Mrs Plummer removed to her desk to pore over the account book and the entries of purchases and payments, while I peered out the window, making mental notes of the activities of various servants.

'Mr Graves?' queried the duchess in a snippy tone. 'Are we still dealing with that awful man?'

'Yes, Your Grace,' apologised Mrs Plummer. 'Regrettably, Mr Woods was unable to supply the provisions for the weekend in time.'

A small dust cloud near the front gate caught my attention and, barely a moment later, Emma, the duchess' lady's maid, hurried into the room. 'Your Grace! Lady Katherine!'

The duchess and Mrs Plummer, in unison, rose to their feet, abandoning the account audit, and hastened out the door with Emma at their heels.

A second glance out the window confirmed that a motor car was approaching quite fast. I gathered my wits and my notebook and followed the excitement out the door, down the stairs and to the grand entrance door. Thomson and three footmen were already lined up and standing at attention on the gravelly ground as the duchess descended the imposing stone staircase and joined them, eagerly awaiting the arrival of the Countess of Chestermere and her entourage. Mrs Plummer and Emma stationed themselves on the first and second steps respectively while I remained at the top of the stairs, partially obscured within the shadows, my notebook wrapped in my arms and my Webley nestled against my chest, beneath my jacket.

The shiny, new, green and brass Rolls-Royce motor car pulled up near the greeting party, close to Thomson. The crunch of the gravel under the car's tyres was actually louder than the purr of its engine. This was not the noisy contraption the duke had expected. It was a massive automobile with an open compartment for the driver and a footman, or the like, beside him. The passengers' compartment was fully enclosed with large windows all around and it appeared to be capable of seating four comfortably. The roof was fitted with side grilles to keep the cases, trunks and luggage in place, and these appeared to be doing a capital job at the present.

I could see two people occupying the front seat: the driver, a young man neatly dressed in a grey suit, cap, goggles and gloves, and beside him a young woman, also with goggles and gloves, dressed in a duster coat and a wide-brimmed sun hat, which abjectly failed in keeping her frizzy red hair contained. I assumed these to be the chauffer and the lady's maid.

The passenger compartment, therefore, must have held the countess and her business secretary. The countess was hard to make out, past the duster coat and large veiled hat she wore. From my vantage point, the business secretary was almost completely obscured.

With great purpose and aplomb, Thomson opened the passenger door with a bow, his actions contrasting the fervent activity of the chauffeur and the business secretary, who sprang from their seats to assist the lady's maid to alight. Even though the chauffeur reached his objective first, the secretary shouldered him out of the way and held out his hand for the maid. The business secretary was very well dressed, clean-shaven and around the same age as the chauffeur and both of similar, well-proportioned build.

My attention returned to the sedate Thomson, who extended his hand to the countess and assisted her out of the compartment. By this time, her maid had reached the countess and swiftly assisted in removing her dust coat revealing not the dumpy, frumpish form I had imagined but a striking figure straight from a fashion plate: broad-shouldered and narrow-waisted with a fine carriage.

In a trice, the duchess was upon the countess just as the veils were drawn back, revealing a genuinely affectionate smile—all I could see of her face from my elevated position. Mary warmly embraced her niece and kissed her on both cheeks; there was no doubt as to the closeness of the two women.

Mary held the countess at arm's length and admired her. 'Katherine, my sweetling, how wonderful you look.'

'Thank you, Aunt. And you look so well.'

'Pish!' she replied, then added ambiguously, 'There is so much to tell you, my dear.' Her attention was diverted by the business secretary who had joined the countess and the maid. 'George. How nice to see you again.'

George gave a sharp nod. 'Your Grace.'

'How is your mother?'

'Exceptionally well, Ma'am. But she refuses to retire even though Lady Katherine has set aside a lovely cottage for her.'

'Retire?' Mary scoffed. 'Your mother is barely my age! Pish, young man. We have many good years left in us yet.'

George became visibly flustered. 'I … I beg your pardon, Ma'am, I didn't—'

Mary's eyes sparkled with mischief. She moved to the maid. 'Turner, I see you are doing an excellent job keeping Lady Katherine in form.'

'Thank you, Your Grace,' Turner replied with a curtsey and a broad Scottish brogue. 'Her Ladyship is mostly amenable tae my suggestions. Mostly.'

In the background, Thomson directed the flurry of activity, overseeing the footmen and a disgruntled chauffeur, unloading the valises and trunks.

'Come, dear,' Mary said, hooking her arm into Lady Katherine's and leading her up the staircase, leaving an embarrassed George to be consoled by Turner. Sidling up behind George, the chauffer leant in and teased in a distinct Mancunian accent, 'You can remove your foot from your mouth now, *Mister* McPherson.'

'Jimmy Isham!' Turned reproached. 'Shame on ye! He is yer better.'

'Hah! He's still the housekeeper's son,' Jimmy shot back as he returned to unloading the car.

Turner put a hand on George's shoulder. 'Dinnae pay him any mind, George.'

Mrs Plummer and Emma, both beaming, curtseyed in unison as Lady Katherine and the duchess approached.

Lady Katherine acknowledged each with a gracious nod. 'Mrs Plummer. Emma.'

Mrs Plummer spoke for both. 'Welcome to Abbottsford Hall, my lady.'

'Mrs McPherson sends you her regards and trusts you are well.'

'Very well, my lady. And not ready to retire, either,' she said, giving George a pointed glance. 'Everything is in readiness for you in your usual suite, my lady.'

The duchess and Lady Katherine led the procession up the stairs.

'I must say, Aunt, the groundsmen have done a wonderful job.'

'Yes. It's been a truly exceptional summer and they have excelled themselves,' the duchess confirmed as they ascended the staircase at an unhurried pace. 'They tidied every cottage on the estate as well. We even had poachers for the first time in years in one of the fishermen's huts. They left an awful mess, or so Bram informed me this morning. By the way, did you attend the concert by that Ravel chap?'

Only when they had reached the top of the stairs did I catch sight of Lady Katherine's face. I must have audibly gasped; her resemblance to Sarah shook me. The delicate complexion, soft, intelligent brown eyes, lustrous dark hair … unsettled me to my bones. Despite their opposing stations in life, both women possessed a quality that stood them apart from the ordinary: they commanded attention without asking for it—I could not help but stare. A feeling overcame me—one which I hadn't felt for thirty years—sharp, familiar and unwelcome. A feeling I had buried deep and never wanted to feel again.

Lady Katherine caught sight of me in the shadows, her step faltered and her face registered mild shock.

Mary noticed. 'Oh. My day shadow. I'll explain all presently, my dear.' And she placated her niece with a pat on her hand and an easy charm, and continued their stroll through the vestibule.

I followed several yards behind, my mind numb. *Pull yourself together, Davies!* I thought, admonishing myself. *The duchess is the business at hand.*

***

We arrived at the suite of rooms prepared for the countess—we being the duchess, Lady Katherine, Mrs Plummer, the maid, Turner, and I. The remainder had peeled off to return to their various tasks and assignments.

Lady Katherine glanced around her rooms and was very pleased to see the large vase brimming with roses. 'Oh, Mrs Plummer, they're beautiful. And so fragrant.'

'Late bloomers, my lady. I know how you love roses so.'

'Thank you, Aunt. This has always been my favourite room.'

'Well, you rest now. Luncheon is at one and Mr Hollingsworth will be here at three. Mrs Plummer will send up some refreshments.'

The housekeeper bobbed a courtesy and left to carry out her task.

Having regained my composure and purpose, I stood by the doorway, observing. Turner kept glaring at me as she unpacked one of the small cases she had brought up with her.

Her defiance amused me. *This woman is going to give me grief*, I thought. *She won't win.* I maintained my stern demeanour.

The countess was likewise not giving her aunt her full attention, every now and then shooting me a furtive glance. I knew my visage was discomforting to most, but her interest seemed more than appalled curiosity.

'Katherine … ? Katherine, did you hear me?'

'Aunt,' Lady Katherine said, jolted from her musings. 'I beg your pardon, you were saying?'

What had the countess been thinking before she was brought out of her reverie?

'Never mind, dear. Freshen up. Luncheon is at one in the morning room.' As she passed me, the duchess paused then turned slightly towards her niece. 'Oh, and this is Davies, my secretary. Apparently, I need one.' She then cast me a sharp, unmistakably cautionary look before we both left Lady Katherine to her preparations.

***

The morning room, situated on the ground floor of the sprawling estate, had two internal access points—one at each end. A pair of French doors opened out onto the eastern lawns, allowing generous light to pour in during the morning hours. At present, they stood open, letting in the gentle early-afternoon breeze.

Although my instructions were to allow the duchess privacy during meals, my duty was clear: to ensure her safety at all times during daylight hours. I was not precluded from attending her from *outside* a room. Accordingly, I settled myself on a padded cast-iron garden bench positioned just beside the open French doors, close enough to attend if needed, but discreet enough not to intrude—and privy to any conversation within.

The duchess had decided that just the three of them would luncheon in the morning room—aunt, uncle and niece. Only Thomson would serve to ensure privacy.

'Jimmy reached speeds of fifty miles an hour on some of the better roads. Quite unnerving, yet thrilling,' Lady Katherine admitted with a faint note of achievement in her voice.

'Hmph.' The duke was not impressed.

'Shall we acquire one, Charlie?'

I imagined the duke giving his wife a withering look, which promptly would have earned knowing glances of mischief between the two women.

'Aunt,' began Katherine with hesitant inquisitiveness, 'why did you engage a secretary?'

'Ah, my day shadow. The Special Branch Department sent her along to preserve my life.' This was all conveyed in an offhand manner, as if it were of no particular import to the duchess.

An item of cutlery clattered—a fork dropped in shock?

'Special Branch? I don't—'

'Mary, this is not a trifling matter,' the duke interjected. 'Please don't treat it as such. Katherine, there have been several horrible murders over the past six months—all abducted for ransom.'

'I have heard rumours.'

'The details were suppressed by the court. There is evidence that points to your aunt being the next victim.'

'Aunt!'

'Pish! Katherine, I will tell you as I've told your Uncle Charles, it's all theory and conjecture. The idea is utterly laughable. No criminal type from an anarchist movement is about to abduct me.'

'And that woman … ?'

'Her bodyguard,' the duke offered.

'Is *that* all the Special Branch has to offer as protection?' Katherine's sharpened tone indicated her disgust and outrage.

'Oh, there's two of them,' Mary added gleefully. 'The other is quite a nice chap, really. Pity he's married, Katherine.'

'I'm appalled! Uncle, shouldn't you take her away somewhere? Keep her safe?'

'Oh, no, dear,' the duchess cut in. 'The Special Branch wants me here so they can capture these scoundrels and bring them to justice.'

'By using you as *bait*?'

'Katherine, sweetling, do try not to get into a flutter. Nothing will come of it. You'll see. Besides, each of my two Special Branch people has a most impressive curriculum vitae. I have faith they will keep me safe should something untoward happen. But it won't. Have you tried the sherry? It's from the Jerez region in Spain.'

An awkward truce fell upon the room as each fell silent.

'Katherine …' Mary began hesitantly, 'that woman, my day shadow—'

The bustle of movement quietened further.

'Her name is Rebecca Davies and … I saw how she looked at you. Katherine, sweetling. I love you as my own child … I don't want to see you hurt again.'

Katherine laughed unconvincingly. 'Aunt! That was more than twenty years ago. I had forgotten all about it.'

'Well, good. There are two very eligible gentlemen I think you should meet. They'll be here on Saturday. One is a peer's son from an old Aberdeen family and the other a wealthy American entrepreneur.'

'Aunt, I thank you, but I'll be going on to my estate well before the weekend.'

'To an empty house?'

'This is beginning to sound like one of the many conversations we've already had.'

'And we'll continue having it until one of us raises her hand in defeat.'

'Uncle—' Katherine implored.

'No, don't seek assistance from your uncle. He long ago learned the wisdom of silence in this matter.'

Katherine gave a long sigh of resignation. 'If this is about marriage …'

'What other?' the duchess replied. 'Yes, your situation is most comfortable, but are you happy?'

'I am settled.'

'Yes, but happiness is entirely another thing.'

'I assure you, I am immeasurably content.'

Mary's manner became quite serious. 'By what measure? Guineas? Acres? Or perhaps factories and farms? If so, then I concede you should be extremely happy. No, my dear, the measure of happiness is having no regrets. You're not as young as you once were and as beauty fades, doors close. And children—'

'Those are definitely the last thing on my mind.'

'The line will be broken—'

'The title will pass to your son, Arthur. We've been through all this before, Aunt.'

The duke, who must have predicted that this conversation would end the same way as others had, interjected with perfect timing, 'How fast did you say you were going?'

Only now did I understand the warning in the duchess' glance when I first set eyes on her niece.

23

Thursday, 7ᵗʰ May, 1874

Wangaratta, Victoria

My room in the Royal Victoria had luxury appointments—having my own private bathroom was an untold indulgence I gratefully appreciated, but my night was sleepless. Now that I had sated my fatigue and hunger, the course of awful events and atrocious acts that had led me there played through my mind relentlessly. Images of Percy's murder, the disbelief on Pitt's face when I shot him, the needless slaughter of so many good men, the molten hatred of that German tyrant for me, my detestable treatment of Hilda, Harper's limp body hanging by the rope around his neck … and Sarah. If only I had not loved Sarah.

The morning sun slowly lit up my room and, as its intensity grew, so did my resolve: I would not be the cause of harm to anyone ever again. My kind of love was poisonous and, if this meant I could not love as my heart desired, I would not love at all.

***

Johnson and Tanner had camped in the scrub just outside of Wangaratta on Wednesday night, convinced that their prey, Robert Davies, had come this far and was heading for Melbourne by the fastest means possible: train. Their plan, cooked up that night along with a rabbit they had shot, was to find the little bastard and, not only to relieve him of the cash he had stolen from Pitt and Percy, but also of his life. Johnson decided to start searching all the hotels, boarding houses, doss houses and bordellos in the area at first light; he was here and they were determined to find him.

The township of Wangaratta was slowly shaking off its sleepiness as the two unkempt riders walked through the town's outskirts and surveyed each of the buildings sparsely scattered along the road. As the buildings became more concentrated, Johnson and Tanner stopped at each that offered accommodation or travellers' respite, enquiring the whereabouts of their 'missing little brother, Robert'.

Each of the first dozen or so establishments had turned up nothing, but Johnson was resolute and adamant that the little snake was here, somewhere.

***

I spent the day barricaded in my room, ringing for the chambermaid and porter to bring me the local papers as they were published, along with meals I hardly touched. I scoured the newspapers for any news of the robbery and the efforts of the police, but found nothing. Other than the information the desk clerk had provided, there was nothing new. Just silence. Too much silence. Silence before the storm.

The chambermaid assisted me by taking Robert's clothing to the laundry and purchasing some extra items of clothing I required. I handsomely rewarded them for their service. Perhaps too handsomely.

Emptying the pockets of my jacket, I came across Percy's letter to his wife—forgotten in the maelstrom of events that carried me here. It stopped me cold. This, at least, I could make right.

On the porter's next visit, I gave him a small, paper-wrapped parcel that contained Percy's letter, his personal effects and his full share of the stolen money, together with a note I had written to his wife. I told her the truth wrapped in lies: Percy had died in a tragic accident while saving a friend's life and these were his things, his savings. I signed it only as 'Robert' with no return address.

The day dragged on. Shadows shifted across my room and darkened my thoughts.

That evening, I sat alone with my abandoned dinner, wondering where Johnson was. I flinched at every knock on a door, every shout from the street below. I lurked behind the curtains, scanning the dimming street for any ghost of the man.

Where was Johnson?

Would he give up? Percy's warning echoed ominously in my mind: *Johnson wants the money back. And your balls.*

He wanted my life, not just the money. Pitt's cold-blooded murder of Percy was proof of how ruthless these bushrangers were.

I brooded on this as I imagined what might be unfolding elsewhere: Johnson scouring the town's streets, questioning stable hands and innkeepers, his temper flaring each time a lead went cold. I could see him menacing some trembling hotel clerk. He would not tire. He would not stop. I was sure of that.

And if someone had seen me leave the Prospector's Inn that morning—or had spoken too freely—then he could be closer than I dared to believe.

***

It was coming onto dusk and Johnson had spoken to almost every owner of each of the places a youth on the run could hide out, when, on the southern edge of town, they came upon a stable and accompanying paddock.

Tanner pulled up his horse. 'Ain't that Percy's nag over there? The bay?'

Johnson peered at the magnificent animal and, without acknowledging Tanner's comment, turned his mount towards the stable. 'You there!' he called to the man near the entrance. 'The bay thoroughbred in the paddock—who owns it?'

The stable owner looked at Johnson suspiciously. 'Why do you ask?'

Johnson quickly framed an excuse. 'My little brother has one just like it. He's run away from home and his ma and pa are worried. He's a little slow-witted.'

'Slow-witted, you say? The fellow who's agisted that bay certainly isn't an imbecile.'

'Yeah, yeah. So you know who owns it?'

'The bay? Let me think …'

Johnson was becoming impatient with this old bugger but persisted through gritted teeth. 'I'll describe him to you, all right, mister? Just tell me if you seen this bloke. He's about five-seven or eight, skinny, blond hair and peach-fuzz face.'

'Yeah,' added Tanner, 'and a bit of a milksop.'

The stable owner stroked his chin. 'Family, you say?'

'Yeah, our ma and pa are real worried,' Tanner jumped in.

'You two are brothers?'

'Look, you old codger,' Johnson snarled. 'That's his horse over there. Just tell us where the little bugger is and there won't be no trouble.' Johnson pulled back his oilskin coat and put his hand on the pistol on his belt. 'You understand?'

The stable owner gave Johnson a look of wry amusement. 'No need for that, son. The young fellow who left the horse asked for cheap lodgings and I told him the nearest one was the Prospectors Inn up the road and two streets to the left. He took his two valises and left.'

'When was this?'

'Yesterday morning.'

Without another word, they turned their horses and headed off back down the road.

By the time they reached the Prospectors Inn, night was resolutely enveloping the town. Johnson, sure that they had cornered their quarry, told Tanner to wait outside with the horses and to keep their carpetbags safe—and to shoot the little bugger should he try to escape.

Johnson trudged in and scanned the reception room and its few occupants. Failing to see his quarry, he approached the man at the desk. 'You got a Robert Davies here. What room?'

'What?' the man asked.

Johnson snatched the register and spun it towards him.

'Hey!' the man objected.

Johnson ran his finger down the names.

Johnson lent over the desk and grabbed the man by his waistcoat. 'Listen, you son of a bitch! A boy, five-seven, blond, carrying two red valises came here yesterday morning. Where is he?'

The man's face drained of colour and panic tightened his breath. 'A boy … yes … a boy like you described did come in yesterday … but his name was … was—'

'Did he have two red valises?'

'Yes.'

'Where is he?'

'G ... gone ... He must have left before dawn ... No one saw—'

Johnson jerked the man closer. 'If you're telling me bullshit ...'

'No ... no ... He's gone. His room's empty. I swear ...'

Johnson pushed the man back and stopped to think. 'I want a room for the night—his room,' he demanded. 'And you'd better not call the coppers.'

'No ... no, Sir ...'

24

Friday, 8ᵗʰ May, 1874

Wangaratta, Victoria

I would miss the Royal Victoria Hotel. The staff had been particularly hospitable, the premises maintained to an excellent standard and the food tasty and plentiful—all the qualities Mr Morrison strived for in his hotel in Paddington. How I missed Mr Morrison, Corporal Roberts and, in particular, Patrick.

Enough sentiment! I silently chided myself. *You made your choices.* I heaved a deep regretful sigh and took one final look around my room. Nothing left behind. It was only 7 a.m. and my valises had been collected by the porter and stacked with others on the trolley, ready to be wheeled to the railway station. I had parcelled together the stolen banknotes with most of the gold sovereigns and hidden them in one of my valises. Carrying such a large amount on my person would only encumber me and invite suspicion and risk. I kept only a modest sum of coins and sovereigns in my reticule for immediate use.

One final check of my reflection in the mirror and what stared back was a forlorn, weary shell of Rebecca Davies: long, dark-blue skirt, matching bodice, white undershirt tied at the neck, three-quarter length, olive-green coat and my newly purchased bonnet tied in place. Robert—my mask, my other self—was securely packed away in one of my valises. Pitt's revolver was safely nestled in the new canvas satchel I'd had the chambermaid purchase for me the day before.

If they were coming, I was prepared.

Everything was in readiness for my six and a quarter hour train journey to the Melbourne Terminus in Flinders Street and a new start. A new life—if God allowed it.

There was excited activity in the hotel reception area as many of the guests were also catching the train, due to arrive from Wodonga at seven forty-five and leave for Melbourne at seven-fifty promptly.

My eyes flitted from face to face in the throng that swirled around me, my senses alerted. Had Johnson made it this far? I watched the porter wheel the trolley, laden with trunks and valises of many types, out the front door. My two were in amongst that jumble and each of them tagged with the Royal Victoria's label indicating their station destination: 'RD, Melbourne Terminus'.

I had already settled my account but something compelled me to ask the busy desk clerk to recommend a hotel in Melbourne. My turn came at the counter and the young man who had tended me upon my arrival, greeted me warmly. 'Miss Davies. Good morning. I trust your stay with us was to your satisfaction.'

'Very much so, thank you. And please convey my thanks to the chambermaid and porter,' I replied. My voice sounded strange even to me: strained, raspy. 'I know you are extremely busy, but could you recommend a quality hotel in Melbourne?'

'Certainly, Miss,' he said as he reached under the counter and retrieved a calling card. 'The Menzies Hotel in Bourke Street is highly recommended. If you prefer, I can send a reservation on your behalf by electric telegraph?'

'Thank you. That would be ideal. One week, please.'

'My pleasure, Miss,' he said as he handed me the card. 'I'm sorry to see you go … if I may be so bold to say.'

I gave him an apologetic nod. This just added to my remorse; he was a nice young man and, had circumstances—and I—been different …

I tightened my grip on the satchel.

It was time to go.

***

Johnson and Tanner strode towards the Prospectors Inn stables, carrying their heavy carpetbags and sleeping rolls, no less unkempt or soiled than they had been the day before. Fixing their belongings to their saddled horses, Johnson turned to Tanner. 'If that jackanapes was here yesterday and Percy's horse is agisted, then he would have wanted to get to Melbourne the fastest way.'

'Coach?' Tanner queried.

'Rail.'

'But that costs money.'

Johnson swung his ire at Tanner, eyes narrowed. 'He's got money, you idiot—our money!'

'Yeah, right, Boss. Lots of money.'

Johnson spat near Tanner's boots, gave his stupid flunky a sneer and swung himself into the saddle. 'Let's go have a chat with the station master.'

***

At precisely half past seven, those of us leaving by train were ushered onto an omnibus, provided by the hotel, for the short journey to the newly built Wangaratta train station. Our luggage had preceded us there—the porters would load it onto the train.

At the station, we were invited to proceed to the waiting room and for the ladies to avail themselves of the seating provided therein.

I followed the group of fellow travellers towards the waiting room, each step measured, every muscle tense.

Then I saw them.

Just beyond the edge of my bonnet's brim, the two faces froze me in place. Faces I knew far too well.

Johnson and Tanner.

They were only yards away, holding the reins of their horses, approaching the station master.

My breath caught, my heart raced, and I stopped mid-step unable to move.

They hadn't seen me yet.

'Are you all right, Miss?' a male voice from behind me asked, jolting me back to my body.

I turned slightly and lowered my head, my heart pounding.

'Yes … yes. I beg your pardon,' I apologised. I was blocking access to the waiting room.

I joined the rest of my party there and sat in controlled panic. Attempting to keep my head down, but also to observe what passed, I saw Johnson through the window, standing over the station master. The man shook his head and turned his back on the two inquisitors.

As if sensing my presence, Johnson looked my way.

My breath came hard and fast. I opened my canvas satchel slipping my hand inside to clutch Pitt's revolver. I prayed to God that this would not lead to further bloodshed.

Johnson gave his horse's reins to Tanner then strode purposefully towards the waiting room.

Towards me.

My grip on the revolver tightened. I tilted my head down, letting the bonnet obscure my face. My pulse thundered in my ears.

The gentleman who had been concerned about my well-being had sat beside me and was keeping a watchful eye on me. He appeared to notice my apprehension over the approach of this dirty, unshaven ruffian and offered his reassurance.

'Miss, do not concern yourself. No need to fear. If you will permit me,' he kindly reassured me and took hold of my free hand.

I looked up at him and saw the benevolent face of an elderly gentleman. He was a lifeline.

Johnson stepped into the waiting room to the unwelcoming stares and glares of those waiting with me. The conversations faltered; the mood shifted. I held my breath, clutching onto the elderly gentleman's hand as Johnson's eyes menacingly raked over each of us. He took a step in my direction; my gentleman friend whispered words of support and gently squeezed my hand. I swallowed my anxiety and rested my head on his shoulder forcing myself to breathe.

Johnson took another step forward, then stopped.

He gave one final look around the room and left with a condescending grunt, re-joining Tanner just as the shrill whistle of the train from Wodonga broke the silence and pulled into the station.

One by one, the awaiting passengers stood and prepared to embark the train, commenting to each other about the vile character of the interloper.

I turned to my protector, my mouth so dry with fear that I had difficulty saying my words. 'I … I can't thank you enough, Sir. That man—'

'No need to explain, dear girl,' he said with quiet reassurance, giving my hand a final squeeze. 'Travel these days is very dangerous for anyone, let alone a young woman such as yourself. You may not have heard about the recent murders of the troopers from Beechworth. Senseless waste of human life.'

I managed a feeble nod. If only he knew …

I merged into the line of passengers boarding the first-class carriage, found my allocated seat next to the window and sat, hands trembling as I adjusted my skirts. Further down the platform, I could see our luggage being loaded into the baggage compartment. My valises were near the bottom of the stack, in plain view.

Johnson and Tanner remounted their horses and watched the goings-on with intense scrutiny. I saw Tanner point to the trolley and say something. Had he recognised my valises?

Johnson snapped his attention to the trolley and spurred his horse towards it, pulling up a hair's breadth from one of the porters. He jumped from his mount, grasped the label attached to one of the handles and tore it off.

'He's on board!' He threw his reins to Tanner and jumped aboard the train.

I panicked.

I looked around, desperate. If I stayed, Johnson would surely find me. If I fled, Tanner would pursue me. Either way, someone would get hurt, someone could die—all three of us were armed.

Behind me, the ticket collector entered our carriage. 'Tickets, please!'

Johnson had pushed through the second-class carriage and was now at the door of mine.

'Ticket, please, Miss,' the collector requested. I fumbled in my pocket, my fingers clumsy with fear, and retrieved it. 'Thank you, Miss,' he said as he checked and punched the slip.

Johnson was now inside my carriage and less than six feet away.

His eyes swept the compartment like a savage fighting dog pulling at his lead, craving blood.

'Ticket, please, Sir,' the ticket collector demanded of Johnson.

'Get out of my way,' Johnson growled, attempting to push his way through.

The beefy ticket collector stood his ground. 'If you don't have a ticket, please get off the train. Sir.'

Johnson stood up to the ticket collector, almost nose to nose, breath rasping with rage.

For a terrifying heartbeat, no one moved.

Then, chairs creaked. Several gentlemen, including my saviour, stood in their seats in tacit support of the railway employee.

All was still, silent.

Johnson could see he was outnumbered, despite his weapon. He scanned the remaining passengers and must have concluded that Robert Davies was not present.

He gave a derisive sneer and a huff and turned, pushing one gentleman aside.

'Fuck youse all,' he sneered, much to the apparent horror of the ladies present, who gasped and lifted handkerchiefs or gloved hands to their faces.

I did the same, hiding my face and willing my breath to come.

He was gone. I finally took a breath and collapsed into my seat, barely able to subdue the trembling.

Around me, appalled passengers broke into shocked, indignant voices speaking of the 'coarse and cowardly blackguard lowlife'. Little did they know how close they had come to true danger.

Peering around my bonnet through my window, I watched Johnson get off the train. Tanner brought forth his horse and he mounted. He said something to Tanner—I couldn't hear his utterance over the hiss of the engine.

'All aboard!'

The whistle shrieked and we were on our way, rolling past Johnson and Tanner whose stares clung to me like evil curses.

***

It was going to be a long journey. Along the way, some passengers alighted while others embarked at the sixteen stops to Melbourne. I was not in a convivial mood and found myself staring out of the window, enveloped by my own thoughts and internal conversations. I wondered what was in store for me there, in Melbourne, the place I thought would be my refuge.

25

Friday, 8ᵗʰ May, 1874

Melbourne, Victoria

The efficiency of the Royal Victoria's desk clerk in Wangaratta astounded me. Not only had he sent an electric telegraph to reserve a room for me at Melbourne's Menzies Hotel, but he had also arranged for a hansom to collect me and my luggage at the terminus that afternoon, to take me directly to the hotel, only a few streets away.

There was a small problem, however, when only one of my valises was presented to me: the one without the money.

Had Johnson taken it? I was sure I had seen it loaded into the baggage car. I did my best to remain composed and asked the porter to check once more. 'There should be another,' I insisted politely. 'It is the same as this one.'

The porter disappeared into the storage room and, after a few anxious, breathless minutes, returned triumphantly holding my case aloft.

Notwithstanding this minor setback, I was most grateful for the Wangaratta desk clerk's organisation and made a mental note to send him my thanks once I was in a better frame of mind.

The Menzies Hotel was a magnificent three-storey stone building with a columned arcade and pavilion towers on each corner. It occupied the north-west block on the corner of Bourke and William Streets, like a palace transplanted from Mother England. As I entered the opulent reception room, I was struck by the lavish décor and the richness of the furnishings. The carpets were lush and deep and every step upon them was like walking on a layer of cotton bolls. Heavy chandeliers hung from the ceiling and dripped with sparkling rainbow-hued crystal icicles. The walls were gleaming dark-lacquered panels of fine timber.

It was not a quiet place to find rest; indeed, it reflected the bustle of Melbourne itself—what little I had thus far seen of it. The air was thick with the scent of tobacco, leather and strong coffee wafting from the café in one of the many rooms leading off. Elegantly dressed gentlemen in frockcoats and spats clustered in little groups discussing business or whatever elegantly dressed gentlemen discussed. Porters rushed hither and thither, their purposes known only to themselves, while ladies attempted to keep agitated children distracted.

A large notice board next to one of the windows to Bourke Street announced the schedule of auctions to be held that day in one of the several sale rooms here: sheep from the Western District, gold lots from Ballarat, plots of land in Albury and Bendigo and beyond.

This was not just a place for transient travellers to stay—this was a hub for commercial dealings. It was clear that the Menzies attracted the most affluent of Melbourne—a city that now rivalled London in its wealth, thanks to the discovery of gold some twenty years prior. And the hotel reflected this. Even the hotel's owner, Mr Archibald Menzies, had made his fortune in the gold fields. It seemed ironic— and cruelly so—that it was gold that allowed me to stay here.

I was personally checked in by the manager of the hotel and I wondered if this was all due to the clerk in Wangaratta. Mr Romsford, the manager, was impeccably mannered and attired in a formal morning suit and possessed of a thoroughly pukka English accent. With little ado, I was promptly shown to my room by a concierge who was also perfectly groomed and uniformed, the epaulets of which bore the Menzies tartan. My room was on the top floor, facing northward and overlooking busy Bourke Street. It was only a few blocks away from the Yarra River and Prince's Bridge at the end of Swanston Street to the south.

The décor in my room was equally as sumptuous as the reception hall: walnut panelling lined the walls and a French bedstead ornamented the bedroom like a throne. This was first-class luxury, but I did not fully appreciate it. It did little to pull me out of my funk—it pressed down on me like an immoveable weight. I should have felt safe and delighted but my thoughts relentlessly hovered over the events that had led me here. They clung to me like soot and no amount of luxury could wash it off.

I hung my green overcoat in the immense wardrobe with my meagre belongings, and placed my underwear in one of the drawers in the dressing table—the only items left in one valise were my trousers and shirts, mackintosh and hat—and a thick wad of bank notes and a bag full of gold sovereigns. I stared at the small fortune, mesmerised. It stared back at me, rightfully accusing me of being a thief and murderess.

I should give myself up and accept the consequences of my actions, I told myself. But, if I were not hanged for my part of the gold robbery, I would surely be hanged for my part in Harper's murder. For murder it was and I had been the instigator.

Giving up the bank notes and gold to the police would only raise questions that I would not wish to answer. Spending the bank notes would certainly lead the police directly to me; as I was well aware from my years at Morrison's Hotel, the notes had serial numbers and those would have been registered by the issuing bank and circulated to the authorities. While the gold sovereigns were untraceable, and I had what amounted to more than several years' wages, they would soon run out if I continued with the profligacy of my current style of living. I needed to find a ladies' boarding house and I needed to find a paying occupation. I certainly could not maintain this standard of lavishness in the long term.

My head reeled and I struggled to stop self-pity from continuing to appropriate my thoughts. Hunger pangs reminded me that I hadn't eaten since breakfast. It was three o'clock, so I decided to proceed to the coffee house located on the ground floor.

As I descended the grand staircase, I noticed an elegantly dressed young woman in conversation with the desk clerk and couldn't help overhearing.

' … Miss Dubois, you know the house rules,' the desk clerk said firmly but politely.

'Mr Hemmingsworth is expecting me.' Miss Dubois' voice was smooth, cultured and without a hint of annoyance.

'No doubt. But we do not allow unescorted … er, ladies into gentlemen's rooms. You know that.'

'Please, Hobson—'

It was quite obvious that these two had sparred over this matter before.

'Perhaps you'd care to take a coffee while you await Mr Hemmingsworth … ?' I heard Hobson suggest as I made my way into the coffee house.

It was filled with ladies and gentlemen enjoying light refreshments and I was disappointed that there seemed to be no available tables. A matronly waitress addressed me from behind. 'Table for one, Miss?' she kindly asked.

I nodded an acknowledge.

'This way, Miss,' she said, leading me towards a small table against the wall, not far from the door. She handed me a bill of fare.

As I settled in to peruse the menu, Miss Dubois appeared in the doorway, much to the disapproval of my waitress. 'I'm afraid, Miss Dubois, there are no vacant tables at present,' she informed the lady rather brusquely.

I watched Miss Dubois crane her neck to see if the waitress, indeed, was telling the truth. Miss Dubois was elegant in both dress and speech, beautiful of face and shapely of frame, and about ten years my senior. She intrigued me. Before I could overthink the gesture, I caught the waitress' attention. 'Miss … Miss, I am happy to share my table.'

'There,' said Miss Dubois triumphantly. 'A willing confederate.'

The waitress appeared most displeased but she showed Miss Dubois to my table. 'She obviously doesn't know what you are,' she hissed to the lady in a barely audible voice, to which Miss Dubois responded with a serene expression indicating she had heard it all before.

I don't know what prompted me to invite the lady to join me— loneliness, desperation, comfort? It was done now.

'Thank you, my dear,' Miss Dubois graciously said to me as she slid into the chair opposite, removing her gloves. 'Madeleine. Madeleine Dubois.' She extended her hand.

I took it and shook it politely. 'Rebecca Davies.'

The waitress approached and waited for our order.

I offered the menu to Madeleine.

'No, thank you, dear girl. I believe our lovely waitress knows what I usually order.' She looked up to the scowling face.

The waitress huffed then turned her attention to me with a marked change of attitude. 'And what would Miss like?'

'Oh, ah, coffee, and perhaps a portion of cheese pudding, please.'

'Right away, Miss,' and with a swirl of her skirts, she left us, but not before sparing a final disparaging glare for Madeleine.

We sat in awkward silence for a few moments while I took in Madeleine's exquisite features. I didn't know what to say. Thankfully, Madeleine broke the impasse.

'Are you visiting Melbourne?'

'Yes.'

'On business?' The question flummoxed me. My quizzical look brought an explanation. 'The Menzies has many commercial rooms. You may have noticed. Thousands of pounds worth of property, fleece, wheat and gold change hands here every day.'

'Oh. Yes. Of course. Is that what brings you here?' I said without even thinking.

'Yes. I suppose one could say that. And you, are you here with your parents?'

'No. I'm travelling alone.'

She raised an eyebrow in obvious surprise. 'How old are you? Fifteen? Sixteen?'

'Eighteen,' I answered a little more tersely than necessary.

'Still quite young to travel unescorted. From where do you hail?'

'Sydney.'

'And what brings you here, to this wonderful city?'

A younger waitress interrupted us, bringing my coffee and pudding and another coffee for Madeleine. Madeleine sugared her coffee and, after stirring it thoroughly, looked up at me. 'You are running away.'

She couldn't fail to observe my look of horror.

'Perhaps from an unsatisfactory marriage arrangement?'

I didn't deny her assumptions.

'No need to fear,' she continued conspiratorially. 'I will keep your whereabouts secret, Rebecca. Marriage is so constrictive. For women, that is. Men, on the other hand, can continue enjoying their premarital proclivities, so long as they have the wherewithal to support their indulgences. Thank God for that, I say,' she added with a laugh.

It was then that I understood the nature of her 'business'. I looked at her and wondered what had made her choose such a profession. She had grace and beauty and could have had the choice of any number of suitable beaux.

'Are you staying long?' she enquired, sipping her coffee.

'A week. I've booked in a week.'

'Perhaps I could show you the city sights, if you have the time?'

I was caught between delight and apprehension. I didn't want to insult the generosity of the elegant woman who had offered her time, but she was a stranger to me. And I had become very wary of strangers and of their generous offers. I wondered what had fired her interest in me.

My emotions did not evade Madeleine's attention. 'What's the matter, my sweet girl? I thought you would welcome the diversion.' She had perceived me to be a girl fleeing something unpleasant: a marriage. I had allowed her that impression. I gratefully accepted her generosity and chose to believe in the sincerity of her offer.

'Yes. Yes, I'd like that.'

'Excellent. What room?' My questioning look prompted her to add, 'So I can leave you a message.'

'Of course.' I looked at the tag on my room key. 'Two thirty-two.'

'Oh, that's a lovely room. You've chosen well.'

Our matronly waitress returned and addressed Madeleine curtly. 'Your gentleman "friend" is waiting for you.'

Madeleine turned in her seat to see Mr Hemmingsworth standing at the door. She greeted the stout, well-dressed sexagenarian affectionately, then addressed me. 'I'll leave a message for you.'

I watched her interaction with the portly gentleman and marvelled at how well she comported herself against the public's very obvious disapproval of her profession. As they left, arm in arm, Madeleine glanced over her shoulder and gave me a languid wave with an expression that sparkled with mischief.

I no longer felt alone.

***

After finishing my coffee and pudding in a far better mood, I returned to my room. It wasn't long after that there came a sharp knock on the door. I hesitated, my heart quickening. *No, they can't be here,* I reassured myself before crossing the room to answer cautiously.

It was a porter who informed me that Miss Dubois was in the foyer and requested I join her.

I was surprised by the invitation, as I'd thought she would be otherwise occupied for the evening and night. What could she want of me?

My curiosity preceded me down the staircase. I saw Madeleine before she saw me and I couldn't help but admire her poise as she drew glances, subtle and lingering, from nearly every man who passed her.

A radiant expression lit her face when her eyes met mine.

'Rebecca, wonderful news. Mr Hemmingsworth's wife has unexpectedly arrived from Geelong.'

I was mildly shocked. '*Wonderful* news?'

'Yes. My gentleman friend had arranged an evening at the theatre for us and supper afterwards.'

'Oh, I'm sorry your plans have been spoilt.'

'Not at all. Mrs Hemmingsworth abhors the theatre.' She produced two theatre tickets. 'And she abhors wasting money on expensive restaurants even more so.'

I hesitated, glancing down at one of the only two frocks I possessed, neither of which was remotely suitable for such an occasion.

'I … I don't have … I didn't bring the proper evening attire to attend such events.'

'Is that all? Don't concern yourself. Come with me.'

There was no refusing her without offence, so I acquiesced and followed her out the door and into a cab.

It was a short hansom ride to her apartment above a haberdashery shop at eighty-seven Collins Street. I was quietly excited yet, as we travelled, I became aware of my vulnerability in a vast city that was wholly unfamiliar to me. I had left my protection—Pitt's revolver— in my room and put my trust in a woman whose profession went against all of my upbringing and my church. And yet, I went willingly. Bewitched. Beguiled. I was caught in Madeleine's charm although a part of me whispered that I may come to regret it.

Her abode was small, or so it seemed, as it was brimful of beautiful furniture, oriental vases, shawls draping the settees and Persian rugs cluttering the floor. I was captivated; I had never seen such richness and luxury in a private residence. Madeleine was pleased that I was impressed and told me to turn around. My breath caught in my throat when I took in the full-size portrait of Madeleine standing at the ocean's edge, looking wistfully at the breaking waves—completely naked!

'Do you like it?' she asked, obviously amused by my reaction.

'Ah …' I did not know what to say.

'One of my clients painted it. It's a copy of Andromeda by Poynter.'

'Is that really you?' I naively asked.

'In the flesh. Come.' She took my hand and led me along a short corridor. I found it hard to tear my eyes away from the painting. Within the bedroom, two large mahogany armoires filled an entire wall. A matching dressing table with a full-length mirror, a wash basin and stand, and a large bed with a superb bedhead each took their place along the other walls.

With a grand gesture, she flung open the doors to both armoires. 'Tea gowns, day dresses, walking dresses, outdoor dresses, indoor dresses and, of course, the reason we're here, evening dresses,' she declared. 'Which would you like to wear?'

I could not believe the trove of riches this young woman had. 'How did you acquire so many wonderful things?'

'I have some very generous, and very rich, patrons and this is how they thank me for treating them in ways their wives will not.' She raised an eyebrow expressively. 'What do you think of this?' She took an evening dress from the rail and sized it up against my body. 'It should fit you perfectly.'

It was a lush golden jacquard woven, silk dress with ruching on the front skirt panel, and a wide, shallow neckline abundantly trimmed with rows of lace that revealed the tops of my shoulders and more of my chest than I should have dared to show.

'Try it on,' Madeleine enthusiastically urged, helping me out of my coat.

***

I felt like a princess when we entered the Theatre Royal. Even though my short hair posed a problem—no lady cut her hair short unless she had been ill—Madeleine hid it under a jaunty, narrow-brimmed hat trimmed with feathers—much *à la mode*.

We arrived by hansom promptly at seven and were ushered to the dress circle. The heads of whomever she passed turned to Madeleine, most of the men fascinated and some acknowledging her with a slight nod, others with a sly look. Some ladies also admired her but mostly they either ignored her or looked upon her with expressions of mild contempt. Madeleine was unruffled and acknowledged only those who acknowledged her—I supposed it was a courtesy of her profession to be discreet.

At half past seven, the programme began with a farce and was followed by an original play specially written for the brilliant American actress May Howard.

My prior preoccupations and fears dissolved during those hours of excellent entertainments and we left the theatre in a light-hearted and jovial mood for a little supper at a nearby restaurant.

I was giddy with excitement and wanted to ask Madeleine a million questions. This was the first time I had been in the exalted company of dress circle attendees and the first time I had been to the theatre at night. I walked close beside her, matching her measured pace, down the street towards our destination. Along the way, we passed several narrow, darkened laneways of which Madeleine seemed to be wary; villains ready to pounce on us, I imagined.

We had almost reached our objective when a rough, hoarse voice called out from the shadows. 'Maddie.'

Madeleine froze, the warmth drained from her face and her hand instinctively reached for mine. The owner of the voice emerged from the alley's shadow and into the pale wash of gaslight. We turned to face her accoster. He was a brute of a man, no taller than me, thickset with a pockmarked, jowly face that broached no easy conversation. His straggly greasy hair was barely held in place by the bowler hat wedged low on his brow. His clothing, though clean, stretched over his corpulent torso.

Behind him lurked malevolence itself—a taller, gaunt man enshrouded by a long dark overcoat. A dirty cloth cap was pulled down low, casting a shadow that obscured most of his face. In one hand, held loosely by his side, a long, thin blade glinted in the dim light, threatening punishment.

'Maddie, you haven't been to see me,' the jowly man croaked.

'I told you I'd be there tomorrow,' Madeleine explained in a voice tight with anxiety

'And who's this? A new recruit?' he slavered, looking me up and down.

'No. A friend. Only a friend.'

The man gave a disdainful huff. 'Tomorrow. Don't forget. You know what happens when you forget.' We watched them slink back into the shadows of the laneway; they reminded me of the rain-sodden rats in the Suez Canal.

'Who was that?' I asked, afraid for Madeleine.

'Nobody. Come, let's have supper.' She was visibly shaken. Though she straightened her shoulders and attempted breezy conversation, her effervescence had all but gone. She tried to make light of the incident but it was clear the encounter with that horrid man had affected her.

Throughout our meal, she became increasingly distracted and seemed only partially involved in our conversation.

I could not help myself. 'What did that man want, Madeleine?'

She gave me a quick, weary glance of reassurance.

'Don't concern yourself, my sweet child. You can't do anything to help. Finish your jelly and I'll take you to your hotel.'

'Will I see you tomorrow?'

Madeleine appeared to contemplate her reply for a moment then replied warmly, 'No. Sunday. We can cruise up the Yarra River in the paddle steamer.'

***

I didn't get to bed until two o'clock that morning and had very little sleep. Confused images tumbled incessantly through my mind: Madeleine laughing, the antics of the farcical actors, the horrid implied threats from that disgusting man, the American actress May Howard, Madeleine's agitation and fear ... why did that hideous man frighten her so much?

Suddenly it all became clear—the way he spoke to her, the way she recoiled, her trepidation—he wasn't a stranger. She knew him but nor was he a punter. He *owned* her. He controlled Madeleine and women like her—he was a pander, a procurer, a flesh-monger. And that menace that hovered in the shadows, that was the flesh-monger's protection, his dog. Revulsion twisted my stomach as the realisation set in. Her world was not all glamour and glittering charm; there was a seedy, sordid side to it as well. Sleep became impossible.

26

Saturday, 9th May, 1874

Melbourne, Victoria

Madeleine said she would see me on Sunday as Saturday nights were always busy for her so, given my lack of sleep, I decided to stay in bed a little longer than usual and made a lazy day of it.

***

The train from Wodonga pulled into the Melbourne Terminus right on time, at 1:58 pm bringing visitors from New South Wales who had transferred from Albury, as well as Victorians boarding along the route. Alighting along with these passengers from the first-class carriage were two rough-looking men carrying several heavy carpetbags and sleeping rolls: Johnson and Tanner. They first made their way to the Left-luggage Office and emerged a few minutes later without two of their bags before heading to the cabbie's stand. There, they impatiently waited to hire the next available hansom, their eyes furtively darting about for any sign of constables.

When their turn came, Johnson pulled out a crumpled, bloodied business card. 'Menzies Hotel,' he instructed the driver.

The driver looked at each of the two slovenly, unshaven ruffians. 'The Menzies? Are you sure?'

'Yeah, we're sure,' Johnson grunted, and threw his bags into the cab as they both got in.

***

By half past two I was washed and dressed and had decided to spend the rest of the day, after a very late breakfast at the coffee shop, at the Melbourne Public Library in Swanston Street. I was missing my favourite pastime and was particularly interested in reading more from Charles Darwin's book *On the Origin of Species*. I would ask Madeleine to help me find a suitable boarding house tomorrow. Today, I would spend with Mr Darwin.

***

The controlled clamour of the sophisticated crowd in the elegant foyer of the Menzies Hotel subsided when Johnson and Tanner swaggered in. Guests, visitors and staff alike recoiled, scowling and turning their backs to the intrusion of the two men—grimy, unwashed and completely out of place in their company.

They made their way through the parting crowd to the reception desk where Hobson had momentarily turned his back to sort the mail that had just been delivered.

The hotel's manager, Mr Romsford, was engaged at the other end of the long counter, attentively assisting another guest with the refinement expected from a man in his position.

'You there!' Johnson's bark of impatience caught Hobson off guard.

'Yes, s—' Hobson began, turning from his task. He stopped midsentence when his eyes fell upon the repugnant countenances of Johnson and Tanner. 'Sir, may I help you?'

'You have a young man, a boy, here. Goes by the name of Robert Davies. What room is he in?'

Hobson's indifference was thinly veiled by polite suspicion. 'I'm awfully sorry, Sir, but I cannot give out that sort of information.'

Johnson palmed three gold sovereigns onto the desk. 'What about now?'

'I'm truly sorry, Sir, but we only sell rooms here, not information.' He seemed more offended than surprised by the bribe and half-turned to resume his task.

'We'll have a room, then.'

Tanner snapped his attention to Johnson. 'Wha … ?'

Johnson ignored him and insisted. 'A room.' He withdrew some notes from the inside pocket of his jacket and threw several ten pound notes onto the counter. 'That should be enough for a few nights, right?'

'Hobson?' The interjection by Mr Romsford startled the clerk but also gave him a reprieve. 'Do you need assistance?'

'These *gentlemen*,' he explained, 'would like a room. I don't believe we can accommodate them.'

Mr Romsford moved down the counter and studied the pair with professional detachment.

'What's the problem, here?' growled Johnson. 'Isn't my money good enough for you? You don't think I can pay? I got plenty. Enough gold to buy this shithole and half of Melbourne while I'm at it,' he boasted.

'Sir,' soothed Mr Romsford, 'that is not our inference. May I ask, are you prospectors?'

'Eh?' questioned Tanner.

'What's it to you?' Johnson queried, irritation colouring the question.

'We understand the difficulties endured by men such as yourselves,' explained the manager. 'Mr Menzies, the owner of this fine establishment, was himself a prospector and his bounty brought this into being.'

Realisation dawned on Johnson's face. 'Yeah, we're prospectors.'

Tanner screwed up his nose with unvoiced confusion.

'I am sure we can accommodate persons of Mr Menzies' ilk, can we not Hobson?'

'Whatever you say, Mr Romsford,' Hobson returned, nonetheless glaring at Johnson.

'An apology won't go amiss, right?' Johnson insisted, addressing Mr Romsford.

'Of course, Sir,' Mr Romsford acquiesced. 'Hobson?'

'I do beg your pardon, *gentlemen*. I was out of line. Please accept my humblest apology.' The words rushed out of his mouth, scarcely touched by abjection.

'Yeah,' Johnson said, the only acknowledgement he was about to give.

With much evident reluctance, Hobson slid a blank registration card towards Johnson. 'Please complete your details, Sir.' He turned to the board of keys and removed one.

Johnson filled out the form as required, albeit with false information, and slid it back to Hobson, who, reading it, slid the selected key across the desk to Johnson. 'Room two thirty-four, Mr Flinders ... and Mr Spencer.' Hobson's tone was neutral but his frown clearly betrayed his disbelief.

Tanner shot Johnson a half-witted smirk, which earned him a surly scowl in return.

Hobson rang for the porter but Johnson declined. 'We can carry our own bags. What floor?'

'Second floor and to the right.'

'And send up something to eat.'

'Yeah,' added Tanner. 'Lots of grub. I'm hungry.' He looked at Johnson and sniggered. 'Mr Flinders?'

***

My green coat and bonnet on, I checked that I had my room key and a few shillings in my purse for incidentals and opened my door just as two men passed by.

Those carpetbags!

No! It couldn't be!

I abruptly shut the door just as Johnson turned his head to see who had opened it. Hands shaking and fumbling nervously, I forced the key back into the lock and twisted hard. The bolt clicked. I turned and leaned petrified against it, my chest heaving. I waited for the dreaded moment Johnson would pound his fists against it, cursing me and demanding to be let in. My heart thundered violently. My mouth was dry. I could hardly breathe.

The silence seemed to stretch to infinity.

No pounding on the door. No knock. No whisper of anyone on the other side of that thin layer of timber that separated me from eternity.

Think, Rebecca, think!

I pulled myself together and scrambled to the chest of drawers, tore it open and grabbed my canvas satchel. With Pitt's gun clutched in both trembling hands, I dropped into my chair facing the door and waited for the inevitable.

How had they found me? Who told them? Hobson? No—he didn't know I was Robert.

Were they looking for Robert … or for Rebecca?

Think, think …

Johnson did not come to my door so Hobson didn't tell him. Then how did he know I was here?

Think …

The missing luggage tag! But it only had 'R.D. Melbourne Terminus' written on it. And only the Wangaratta desk clerk knew I'd be staying here. As Rebecca.

Had Johnson connected me to Robert?

No … he'd be breaking down my door. And he'd been looking for Robert on the train.

But why would the desk clerk in Wangaratta give me up to these murderers? Did they threaten him?

It made little difference who they were looking for. They were here now and they had come for the money. And I was an inconsequence that they would readily destroy.

I needed to leave immediately and the money had to come with me.

I flung the valise onto the bed and threw the lid open. Inside were the wads of stolen banknotes and bags of gold sovereigns. I grabbed a handful of sovereigns and shoved them into my canvas satchel along with Pitt's gun and cartridge pouch and slung it over my shoulder. I relocked the valise with the remaining sovereigns and banknotes. It was heavy. I lugged it to the door and listened.

No movement in the passageway.

Carefully unlocking the door, I cracked it open to see a waiter wheeling a trolley laden with covered dishes past my door and stopping two doors down.

'Room service,' he announced as he knocked.

The door opened and I heard Johnson's distinctive gruffness. 'Bring it in.'

My knees gave way. I pressed myself against the wall for support. They were right there. Two rooms away!

A few moments later, the waiter returned sans his trolley and I heard the door to Johnson's room close and the key turn in the lock.

My heart in my throat, I took a deep breath and dashed towards the stairs. The valise was heavy but I managed to get it downstairs and to the front desk where Hobson, thankfully, was still on duty and not attending to any guests.

'Mr Hobson,' I said in a breathless whisper. 'I need to keep this valise safe and out of sight. It has some valuable … family heirlooms in it,' I lied, 'and I know you are careful about whom you—'

'Miss, I do apologise for lodging "Mr Flinders" and his associate on your floor but we had no other rooms available. I do understand your concern and I promise to keep your heirlooms safe and out of sight.'

Mr Flinders? I thought as Hobson came from his position behind the desk and relieved me of my red valise with a slight grunt.

'My, Miss Davies,' he commented. 'You are stronger than you look.'

I hid my unease with courtesy. 'Thank you, Mr Hobson. I am indebted to you.' I wanted to tell him of my anxiety over the reason these two murderers were here, but I thought the better of it; it would raise those awful unanswerable questions again.

'Is there anything else, Miss?' he asked upon seeing my vacillation.

'Um, no, thank you, Mr Hobson. I, um, have an appointment I need to keep and may not be back until quite late. I would like to keep my key with me if you are in agreement.'

'Of course, Miss.'

With one final look towards the stairs, I thanked Hobson and made my way through the bustle of the foyer and the afternoon throng and on to eighty-seven Collins Street—to Madeleine—and hoped she wouldn't be cross with me for arriving unannounced.

***

I ran up the stairs and reached the landing just as Madeleine was locking the door behind her.

'Rebecca! What are you doing here? I was about to leave.'

'Madeleine,' I said, catching my breath. 'I'm sorry. I had to see you.'

'Goodness me! You look as though you've been chased by the devil.'

'I … I have. I need your help. I don't know what to do. I don't know who to turn to.'

Madeleine put her arm around my shoulder to comfort me. 'My sweet child, tell me what has happened.'

I could not tell her everything; I did not want to involve her in my criminal acts. I just needed a safe place to think things through. My reluctance was obvious.

'They've found you, haven't they? Your parents?' she asked quietly.

'Yes … yes, they've found me.'

Madeleine looked at me, seeming to search my eyes for the truth. I could not hold her gaze. 'Rebecca, I cannot help you if you don't tell me the truth. Who has found you?'

I looked around. We were standing at the top of the stairs; hers was the only apartment here, but I needed complete privacy if I were to divulge all. 'Can we go inside?'

She seemed agitated but acquiesced and unlocked her door. As we stepped inside, she glanced at her mantle clock then showed me to the sofa. I removed my bonnet and we sat next to each other.

'Now tell me all. The truth,' she said, taking my hand.

'I am running away,' I began, 'but not from a marriage—from two men who believe I stole from them. I haven't. The money is mine. I earned it. They want it back. They arrived at the hotel this afternoon. But they don't know it's me they're looking for.'

'Don't know it's you?' Madeleine queried.

'No. They're looking for Robert.'

'You're a boy?' The surprise in her voice was almost comical.

'No. I'm a girl but I was dressed as—'

'That explains the short hair. Just who are those men? Private detectives?'

'Madeleine, please don't ask questions. I don't want to involve you. All I need is a place to stay while I work out what to do next.'

Madeleine glanced around the room. 'My sweet, I sometimes conduct my business here—'

'Anywhere. I don't know where to go.'

'Obviously, going to the police is out of the question,' she said perceptively. 'Rebecca, I need to meet someone and I am quite late already,' she said, furrowing her brow. 'You're very welcome to stay here until I return, then we can work out what to do next.'

Just as she finished her sentence, the door flew open, startling us both. The alarm that flashed across Madeleine's face as she shot to her feet frightened me; she was always so calm and self-possessed.

It was him. The same flesh-monger who had menaced us in the laneway after the theatre now burst in. His weedy shadow, the Flesh-monger's Dog, lurked in the doorway, silent, hands twitching in his coat pockets, his stony expression a mask of menace.

'Harry …' Madeleine's words were filled with fear. 'I was on my way to see you, I swear—'

'Yes, I can see that,' Harry snapped, a sneer twisting his coarse features. 'You,' he barked over his shoulder to his Dog. 'Outside. Close the door.'

The protector did as he was told but not without locking eyes with me, his glare an unmistakable warning.

'Canoodling, were we?' His smirk fractured into a snarl. 'Where's my money?'

'Here,' she said rummaging through her purse. 'I have it here. I was on my way—'

Harry grabbed the folded bank notes from her grasp, gave them a quick glance then grabbed her by the arm. 'You've got more. I know you've got more. Here somewhere.'

'No, Harry, please, there's no more. You have your cut. Please leave.'

'Oh, you owe me more than this,' he threatened with a lecherous grin that showed his tobacco-stained teeth.

'I know. I'll give you what you want but not here. Not now. Please.'

This beautiful woman was begging the ruffian. I stood up beside her, very aware of the weight of the revolver in my satchel; I watched the play between them, fearing what was to come.

Harry pulled her closer. 'You missed our appointment.' He dragged her by the arm towards her bedroom.

A jolt of fear shot through me. I understood what he was about to do.

Madeleine struggled. 'Harry, please, not in front of the child.'

He swung around to me. 'Your new recruit? Do you want to watch? Learn a thing or two?' He then snapped his attention back to Madeleine. 'You know the cost when you're late.' And he pushed her further along to the bedroom.

Madeleine saw me remove the revolver from my satchel.

'No!' she screamed.

Harry must have assumed she meant for him to stop and sneered. He didn't know how close he had come to meeting Satan—I reluctantly replaced the gun in my satchel. The bedroom door slammed shut behind them. I stood there, transfixed and angered, knowing what he was doing to her. This was my fault. I had delayed her. This wouldn't have happened if I hadn't come.

It didn't take long. The brute emerged from the bedroom with an expression of self-satisfied contempt, doing up the buttons to his trouser front. He shot me a glance then snatched up Madeleine's purse and removed the few remaining bank notes from it. I met his gaze with a glare. As he passed, he shouldered me almost off my feet.

He left, giving me one last loathsome grin before slamming the door behind him.

I went to the bedroom, fearful of what I would find. Madeleine was standing with her back to me adjusting her skirts. She glanced over her shoulder when she heard me approach. All her mirth had drained from her being.

'I'm so sorry, Madeleine,' I started. 'I didn't know—'

'It makes him feel powerful, to have control of my body. But he will never own me,' she said in tones both resolute and vengeful. 'It's not your fault, my sweet child. Come,' she continued, her voice laced with irony. 'I have time now.'

She led me back to the sofa but stopped by a cabinet and found two glasses. After pouring brandy from a flask into each, she joined me on the sofa and, handing me one, she asked, 'Have you tasted brandy before?'

Taking the glass, I confessed, 'I worked as a barmaid since I could remember. There is nothing I haven't tasted. To the Queen.'

'To the king of Dudley Mansions,' Madeleine added derisively. Seeing my puzzled look, she explained, 'Mr Harry Kepple grew up in a shanty on the Dudley Moors and rose to riches on the backs of whores, larcenists and burglars, and by fencing stolen goods. He now lives in Carlton, in a new, fancy pile on Grattan Street. His taste in clothes extends to his taste in architecture. His is the gaudiest, most repulsive townhouse on the street. Long live the king.'

We sipped the fine brandy in reflective silence.

'Did he hurt you?' I asked.

Madeleine laughed. 'He has a very small appendage and even when it is fully functional, it is hardly anything to crow about. No, the only thing he hurt was my pride. This is the only aspect of my profession that I detest but one which I can do nothing about.'

'Why can't you?'

'He is my protector.'

'Protector?' I was confused. 'But he … he raped you.'

'Rebecca, my sweet child, this is a means to an end. I won't be doing this for the rest of my life. I will leave Melbourne and Australia as soon as I have enough saved for my passage and enough to start a new life in the Mother Country.'

'How much more do you need?'

Madeleine regained her good humour. 'Do you intend financing me?' she teased, then became quite serious. 'I would have had enough by now if it were not for that limp-cock demanding his exorbitant protection money.'

'Can't you leave him?'

'Nobody leaves Harry Kepple. I knew a young Irish girl, Aoibhin, who took to this trade, under Harry's protection. After a few months, she wanted to leave …'

'And?'

'She was found floating in the Yarra. Strangled.'

I gasped. 'The constables? Did they not pursue it?'

Madeleine gave a dry, bitter laugh. 'My dear, the constables care not a fig for what becomes women of our profession. That's why we have bullies and bludgers—to protect us. It's little more than ownership in disguise.'

She paused; her eyes glistened. 'She was such a beautiful young girl, Aoibhin.'

She composed herself and reiterated, 'Nobody leaves Harry Kepple.'

'How will you, then?'

'By keeping my plans secret. By not telling Harry everything I earn. By keeping my savings hidden here and not in a bank. It won't be long now.'

'Why are you telling me this? Aren't you afraid I'll tell someone?'

'My darling Rebecca, I think you are holding greater secrets than I. I know of no other young lady who carries such a large weapon in her canvas bag, nor who confesses to have masqueraded as a boy, nor who can afford the most expensive hotel in Melbourne yet has not a change of clothes to her name. If, in fact, your name is Rebecca Davies.'

'It is.' Now was the time for truth. 'I have done things, Madeleine. Unspeakable things. Two men are after me. They are cold-blooded killers. And they will stop at nothing to get what they believe is theirs.

I too intend to leave Australia, but I don't have a plan. That's why I came here. I need to sort my head out. I'm so sorry I caused you this grief. I will find somewhere to stay—'

'Nonsense!' she insisted. 'You'll stay here tonight and we'll work something out together.' Madeleine downed the last of her brandy and stood up. 'Now, I must get ready for my paying appointment this evening. But first, I must wash the fetid discharge from that disgusting limp-cock mongrel bastard off my body ...' Madeleine saw my expression. 'Oh my, I do hope I haven't shocked you with my vulgar language.'

I was beyond being shocked.

***

I removed my bonnet, coat and satchel and hooked them on the rack close to the door and settled into the warmth of the settee, grateful for its comfort after the frayed tensions of that awful day.

An hour or so later, Madeleine emerged from her bedroom, resplendent in a magnificent crimson silk gown studded with brilliant rhinestones and an almost immodest décolletage. Her face, beautiful as it was before, was now powdered and enhanced with rouge to her lips and cheeks. At that moment, and the only time in my life, I wished I'd been born of the other gender, for my desire for her made me forget my tribulations.

'Don't look at me like that, Rebecca,' she said seductively as she floated towards me, 'or I may change my mind and stay.' She tapped my nose with her gloved finger. 'And I believe that's yet another of your secrets.'

I flushed with embarrassment; was I so readable?

'Lock the door behind me,' she advised, taking a fur-trimmed stole from the closet near the door. 'Make yourself at home. I won't be back until the small hours of the morning. We'll make plans then.'

I did as she asked and locked the door after her. Her apartment certainly was full of treasures, new and old, but what I appreciated the most was the painting of her as Andromeda. I could not help but stare at it in admiration and, perhaps, a little lustfulness.

My attention was drawn by the sound of a key twisting in the front door's lock. Expecting Madeleine had forgotten something, I went to meet her—only for my blood to run cold when Harry Kepple opened the door. He strolled in followed by his ever-present Dog who closed it behind him.

They didn't rush. They took their time to eye me with perverse disdain.

My satchel and the gun within it were hanging by the door beside him—just out of reach.

'What more do you want? You got what you came for.' I was afraid. Were they going to do to me what Kepple had just done to Madeleine? *If I could just reach that bag …*

'Ah, the new recruit,' he rasped, his voice dripping with malevolence. Each step he took towards me intensified my fear. 'Sit down, stay there and you won't get hurt,' he snarled.

Fear screamed louder than reason. I made a dash for my satchel but he caught me by my arm. He swung me around and threw me onto the sofa. 'I told you to sit!'

I sprung up. I shoved past him. But the Dog was ready.

He grabbed me mid-stride and overwhelmed me with unexpected brute strength. He rammed his fist into my stomach.

I gasped for breath.

Then a backhand exploded across my face. I reeled, stumbled and my head struck the wall. Blood trickled down my temple. I slid to the floor, gasping, retching, darkness threatening to engulf me. My world spun and tilted. The pain was intense.

'Get up from there and I'll beat you senseless,' Kepple growled.

They set about ransacking the place—emptying drawers, upturning vases, upsetting tables and chairs in a frenzy of destruction. They invaded Madeleine's bedroom.

My world throbbed in and out of consciousness. A million cicadas were screeching in my ears, my eyes could not focus and my lungs fought for each breath. Pain rolled through me in waves.

The floor creaked.

A vice grabbed my neck and dragged me upright.

'Where is it?' the whoremonger shouted in my face. Spittle sprayed me. His breath tasted like rot. 'Where does she keep her stash?'

I managed a ragged groan—words would not form. Even if I had known, I would have choked on them before telling him.

He flung me aside. I dropped like a deadweight.

He scanned the room. The only piece of furniture he hadn't despoiled was the sofa. With a rage borne of wanton greed, he upturned the sofa and stopped.

He snarled in victory; he'd found Madeleine's hiding place. Cleverly stitched into the canvas covering the base of the sofa was a deep pocket. He savagely ripped it open and bundles of neatly folded and tied bank notes fell out and lay strewn about the floor.

'Ah, Maddie, you lied to me,' he sneered as he looked upon the destruction of Madeleine's life. 'You will pay dearly for this. No one leaves Harry Kepple.'

The Dog stooped to collect all the packets of notes and stuffed them into his coat pockets.

Not satisfied with ruining Madeleine's dreams, Kepple loomed over me and jabbed me with his boot.

'You. Recruit. You tell Maddie to come and see me tomorrow, you understand? Do you hear me? If she doesn't show, I'll come after her. And I'll find her. She can't hide from me. You understand? You tell her.'

Through the fog in my brain, I understood.

He was going kill her.

***

I slumped on the floor, propped up against the wall next to the door. I was shattered both physically and emotionally.

Any sense of time escaped me; it raced past, yet flowed like honey on a cold winter's day. Buzzing in my ears persisted, but my eyes, at last, could focus. Dried blood encrusted my face. My head and body screamed in pain—but I was not powerless. My satchel lay beside me and I gripped Pitt's revolver.

I sat there motionless, wavering between reality and peace, exhausted, defiant.

The door opening roused me.

I raised my gun; my senses teetering between fear and fury. If it was that mongrel again, he wasn't going to leave this place alive.

'No, no, no!'

Madeleine saw the utter destruction of her apartment.

She then saw me behind the door.

'Rebecca!' she screamed and dropped to her knees beside me. 'My dear God! Rebecca—'

'I'm all right,' I uttered, my breath ragged. It wasn't true, not even remotely. My body sagged with relief. I dropped the gun onto my satchel. 'Kepple came back.'

'Look at you.' Her voice quivered. Her pity made me fear my injuries were worse than I'd felt them to be. 'My God, my sweet Rebecca. We must get you to an infirmary.'

'No.' I reached for her wrist. 'You've got to go. He knows you were going to leave. He wants to kill you.'

Madeleine slung one of my arms over her shoulder and gripped my waist. 'Let me help you to a chair,' she murmured, lifting me upright. We hobbled over the wreckage-strewn floor to an upturned armchair, each step wringing a whimper from my lips. With great dexterity, she righted the chair and sat me in it.

She leaned over me and examined the gash to my head. 'Thank goodness it's only a small cut. Sit still.'

She vanished into her bedroom and returned with a basin of water, a blue bottle of carbolic acid and what appeared to be a clean folded menstrual cloth. Carefully washing the congealed blood from my face and hair, she assured me, 'He won't return—'

'He found your money, Madeleine,' I interrupted. 'He knows you were going to leave. He wants to see you—'

'First we'll fix you. Then we'll fix Harry.' She daubed some carbolic acid on my wound. I flinched. The sharp sting, the sickly-sweet smell brought back memories—bad memories. 'I'm sorry,' she continued, carefully blotting the edge of my wound. 'You must be in dreadful pain.'

'I've survived worse.'

She cupped my chin and lifted my gaze to hers. 'You are an enigma, Rebecca Davies,' she whispered. 'Another secret?'

She wasn't listening. 'Madeleine, he wants to kill you!'

'He won't. I'm his best asset. He may roughen me up a little and insist on more frequent coital access, but he won't kill me.'

'How can you be so complacent? How can you give yourself to that animal? Look what he's done to your place! And he's stolen every last pound of your savings!'

Madeleine stopped pampering me and took in the utter destruction of her beloved apartment. 'This isn't the first time,' she finally confessed. 'And it won't be the last, I'm sure. I will pick myself up again. I will leave this place and I will make a new life for myself in England.'

She was a contradiction: a pessimist and optimist, a fatalist and dreamer all rolled into one. And she called *me* an enigma.

'How much did he take?' I asked quietly.

'Three hundred and twenty pounds.'

I was astounded. 'That's a small fortune. Why ever didn't you keep it in a bank?'

Madeleine gave a joyless chuckle. 'Harry has spies and informers everywhere, even in a bank. I did have my savings in a bank once and, when he found out, he forced me to withdraw it all. "Nobody cheats Harry Kepple," he reminded me. Then he had me beaten. And, do you know what the upshot of all this is? He does the same.'

'What do you mean?'

'All his money—and now all of mine—is hidden at his place. He doesn't trust the banks. "Who needs the piddling interest when I've got my little whores and footpads," he says. Come, let's get you something to eat and into bed.'

'I could do with a measure of your fine brandy ...'

'Of course.' Madeleine went to her cabinet and found two unbroken glasses amongst the debris and poured a good quantity in each.

'You're not going to see him?' I asked desperately, hoping she would say no.

'I'm not going to run, Rebecca,' she said, handing me a glass. 'To the Queen.'

It pained me to watch Madeleine survey her broken treasures lying strewn around her apartment along with her dreams of a new life. I was determined that this time another person would not pay for my stupidity.

I would make this right.

27

Sunday, 10th May, 1874

Melbourne, Victoria

The hotel foyer was almost deserted and the large longcase clock chimed the half hour after three when I returned shrouded by the darkness of night.

The cabbie had been most obliging, ensuring my safe passage after I had impressed upon him the urgency of my circumstance—a false circumstance but urgent none the less. I had borrowed some clean clothing from Madeleine's wardrobe, slipping away as she had prepared for bed. My bonnet that had protected me from discovery by Johnson earlier now concealed the bruising that was beginning to bloom on my head.

My plan was to retrieve my belongings without being discovered by Johnson and Tanner, then find Harry Kepple and recover Madeleine's money—somehow.

I would work out the details, but first I needed the freedom of Robert's clothing.

By this late hour, all the hotel's guests and visitors had either departed or retired to their rooms.

A solitary porter sat beside his trolley, dozily reading the previous day's newspaper. I slipped past him unnoticed. At the reception, the desk clerk, his back turned to the room, rearranged his stock of stationery in the cabinets along the back wall. Otherwise, the large foyer was empty save for one dishevelled individual sprawled on the richly upholstered Borne settee in the centre of the lobby, snoring.

With a jolt of horror, I recognised the incongruous pile of mismatched attire: Tanner!

I rushed by him and the preoccupied clerk, my head lowered and my face concealed by my bonnet. I silently ran up the stairs, without interrupting the rhythm of Tanner's wheezing.

At that very moment, Johnson sauntered down the stairs, muttering sibilant curses under his breath at Tanner for sleeping. He was too absorbed by his anger to notice me.

We passed each other on the first-floor landing. My heart stuttered.

We exchanged a fleeting glance.

He caught the edge of my eye. His step faltered.

What was he thinking? Did the blueness of my eye stir something in his memory? Had he ever noticed that my eyes were blue?

I quickened my pace.

He resumed his descent.

On the top floor, breathless and trembling, I reached my door. My hand shook so violently, I could hardly insert the key.

***

Unaware of just how close he had come to finding his quarry, Johnson reached the dozing Tanner and kicked his boots. 'Is this the way you keep a lookout for the boy?' he hissed.

Tanner jerked upright. 'It was only for a second, Boss,' he stammered.

Johnson was not long on patience and now it was all but depleted—*still* no sign of his prey.

Scanning the empty room, his eyes landed on the young man behind the desk—a new clerk. And an opportunity to wring out the information he wanted.

He strode over. 'Where's the other fellow, Hobson?' he asked curtly.

'Mr Hobson doesn't work Sundays, Sir. May I assist you?'

'Yeah. He was going to tell me if you had a Robert Davies staying here. From Wangaratta. The Royal Victoria.'

The young man hesitated. 'Sir … I do apologise … but I am not permitted to divulge that sort of information.'

Johnson nodded towards the box of cards. 'You got the cards right there in front of you. Take a look.'

'Sir … I can't …'

Johnson withdrew the revolver from his belt and placed it on the desk. 'Yeah, you can.'

The message was unmistakeable. The desk clerk looked around nervously, catching the eye of the porter who abandoned his paper and straightened from his chair. Johnson noticed this and nodded to Tanner, who understood and rose to block the porter.

'Look!' Johnson demanded of the clerk.

The clerk fretfully fumbled through the file of cards. 'Sir, there is no Robert Davies here.'

'Give me that!' Johnson demanded and snatched the box from the clerk. He rummaged through and found no Mr Robert Davies. He went through the cards again and, this time, stopped at Miss Rebecca Davies and pulled the card out. Further down, the clerk had written, 'Referred by the Royal Victoria, Wangaratta'.

'Found you!' crowed Johnson. 'Room two thirty-two.' He turned to Tanner. 'This way,' and loped up the two flights like a man possessed by the thrill of violence.

'Fetch the constables!' the desk clerk called to the porter.

***

Inside my room, with the door bolted securely behind me, I stood frozen against it, my frantic breathing echoing through the darkness.

I had no time. He'd recognised me. I could feel it.

No options. I had to run.

I tore off my clothing and bonnet, and fumbled through my valise, frantically donning my trousers and shirt. I flung the satchel across my shoulder. It slapped against my battered chest.

I looked for a way to escape.

The way in was not the way out.

The window!

I pushed it open. The night's chill hit like an icy blast against my fevered skin.

I climbed out onto the narrow stone ledge that skirted the building's façade, fingers grasping any protrusion for purchase.

I inched along sideways, my satchel hitting against my side and my heart thundering against my ribs like a beast desperate to escape. Below me the city slept, oblivious.

My objective drew closer: the hotel's open balcony.

I hastened to it.

My foot slipped.

I lurched forward—caught the balustrade. A heartbeat—a tremble. I hauled myself over the stone capping—safe—for now.

The glass doors were unlocked. I thanked God.

I slipped inside the short passageway and edged towards the corridor.

To the right, the staircase and my room. To the left, the service door and the only exit for me.

I listened and held my breath.

They were at my door!

'This ain't our room, Boss,' I heard Tanner gripe.

They'd found me out!

'Shut up, you idiot. The molly boy's here.'

'Two rooms away?'

The door knob rattled.

I had locked it.

Johnson reared back and with a violence born of hatred, he kicked the door in, splinters flying.

They burst into my room.

I seized my chance and scrambled towards the service door.

It was my only chance.

Down the stairs I fled, stumbling, tripping and righting myself.

Pain flared—a reminder of the beating I'd taken. My head pounded. My ribs burned. My legs threatened collapse.

Three flights down and I was in the service rooms that fed the kitchens.

Empty. Silent. No sounds bar the hum of the cold room.

I found the door to the street.

Bolted.

Damn!

My hands clawed at the sliding bolt. It held tight.

If it didn't give? If Johnson found the back stairs?

Pull!

At last, the bolt gave and I wrenched it free.

The door moaned open. The cold night air seeped in.

I was out.

***

Johnson and Tanner stormed into the room.

They invaded every possible hiding place—under the bed, inside the wardrobe, inside the bathroom—their prey was gone.

A red valise was on the bed. Johnson flung the lid open. The whelp's clothes! He *was* here!

Johnson yanked open the chest of drawers. Underwear. Grooming things. Nothing else. No gold. No banknotes.

Tanner picked up the pile of discarded clothes from the floor—skirt, bodice, bonnet and a green overcoat.

'Wrong room, Boss, this is sheila's clobber.'

'He dressed as a slattern, you moron. That's why we couldn't find him.' He let out a growl of frustration—the kind that meant someone, somewhere, would pay for this.

And dearly.

Johnson stormed to the window and peered out into the still, predawn darkness.

'That sawney foot-scamp has to be somewhere,' he snarled.

A movement caught his eye.

'There!' he yelled. 'He's on the street.'

***

I ran for my life eastward along Bourke Street. My footsteps struck a desperate rhythm, muffled by newly-lain asphalt. I clutched the satchel to my chest. Every breath shredded my lungs. My legs cramped and wanted to surrender. That was not an option. That would never be an option.

Somewhere to hide. Somewhere to think.

I veered off into Queen Street, heart hammering. The river—maybe the church.

My plan to help Madeleine had fallen apart. My only quest now was to survive.

The gun in the satchel was heavy and weighing me down. It was my only defence. Should I discard it?

I tore through the deserted, gaslit streets. Dark, unlit alleyways beckoned me but they could have been dead ends—my end. A night soil cart went about its business.

In just a few hours, worshippers would fill the streets—but I didn't have hours—maybe only minutes.

I shot down Elizabeth Street and onto Flinders. The church was only a block away.

Refuge. Sanctury.

I glanced back.

My step faltered; my breath stopped.

They were behind me! Less than two blocks away. Johnson and Tanner—and gaining!

At Swanston Street, I hesitated. Which way? Which way?

Not the church—the bridge.

I veered towards the Prince's Bridge. No time to cross it—too open, too dangerous. Hide beneath it.

I jumped the railway lines and dashed towards the river's edge.

My boots sloshed in the river's swampy verge, sucking me in. Bogging me down. An easy target.

I struggled back up to the grassy verge and fumbled for Pitt's revolver in my satchel. My hand shook violently, barely able to clutch it.

Crack!

A shot shattered the air—something whizzed by my head.

I stumbled and fell. The gun flew from my grip.

'Don't shoot, you idiot!' Johnson yelled. 'We need him to get the money back! Get him!'

I scrambled in the long grass, groping in the dark for the gun—my only hope for life.

Tanner stormed closer. Johnson not far behind.

I struggled to my feet and willed my legs to move, to run.

Tanner crashed into me from behind.

I hit the ground hard. The world spun. My body gave in. *Get up! Get up!* It no longer obeyed me.

Johnson ambled over, deliberate, cruel. He plucked Pitt's gun from the grass and slipped it into his belt.

He stood over me. 'Get up.'

I couldn't move—I didn't want to move—I knew what was coming.

'Get up, I said!' he shouted, kicking me.

Turner grabbed me and hoisted me to my feet and pushed me in front of Johnson.

I swayed, barely able to keep my balance. I was exhausted. Every muscle, every nerve no longer cared. I felt no pain. I was beyond physical torment.

'Keep calm, you little prick, and you won't get hurt.'

The idea that Johnson wouldn't hurt me made me sneer. 'Yeah,' I spluttered, 'I'm sure I can trust you.'

Tanner cackled behind me, his foul-smelling breath hot on my neck.

'You killed my boy Pitt,' Johnson snarled.

'He was going to kill me,' I threw back defiantly.

'Then you killed Perce.'

'Pitt killed Perce. But you know that. You told him to.'

Johnson laughed—short and vicious. 'Where's the money?'

'If I give it to you, I'm dead.'

'You're dead either way, boyo. The question is whether you want to die quick or slow? Where's the money?'

Facing Johnson, I faced my death. My options? None. I gave in. 'In my valise.'

His face lit up in triumph. I detested that sneer.

'In the police station,' I added with defiant contempt and with no regard of the consequences.

The smirk vanished. 'You're bluffing. You're a defiant little prick, aren't you?' He punched me in the ribs to accentuate the point he was making.

I doubled over and slumped to the ground. I'd thought I was inured to the pain but now it reached a new intensity.

'Pick him up,' Johnson ordered. Tanner gleefully obeyed, like a child with a new toy to break.

He hauled me upright to face Johnson. I hung between them like meat in a sandwich of putrid bread.

'Let me have a go at him, Boss,' Tanner pleaded. 'I'll make him talk. Then I can shoot him, yeah?'

Through the fog of pain, Madeleine and Sarah flashed through my mind; these were violent times but why were the submissive and weak sought, humiliated and hurt? If the meek were to inherit the earth, then it would be only when the strong were done with it.

Why?

Not this time.

I had only one chance.

I took it.

I summoned every atom of will left in my body and drove my elbow into Tanner's stomach and pushed Johnson backwards.

I ran.

Desperation propelled me. They wouldn't shoot.

Four strides. As far as I got before Tanner tackled me. I hit the ground hard. I rolled over. He was on top of me, grabbing my flailing arms as I thrashed beneath him, striking him with the little strength that remained.

He overpowered me. His stinking body smothered mine.

I stopped struggling and relinquished myself to my fate.

His expressions changed—from victory to befuddlement … to lechery.

His filthy hand groped my chest.

'Hey, Boss, the boy's got paps.'

His debauched grin curdled my blood. He ground his pelvis into mine.

I struggled to free myself—he wasn't going to have me! Flashes of Gerhardt invaded.

'Is that so?' Johnson muttered through clenched teeth. He pulled Tanner off me and dragged me up to face him once more.

He tore open my shirt. My camisole, my breasts, exposed.

'Well, well, well,' he sneered, eyes crawling over me. 'That explains much.'

The glint of Sarah's silver locket caught his interest. 'A nice little keepsake,' he sneered. 'I'll have that when we're through with you.'

Tanner got himself to his feet. 'Let me have some fun, Boss.'

'Maybe we'll both have some fun. Then you'll tell me where you hid the money, you little trollop.'

Johnson ripped open the rest of my shirt and grabbed me around the waist.

I closed my fist and hit out, catching his jaw.

He let go and grabbed my throat and squeezed hard. His other hand struck across my face. Scintillas of white light burst behind my eyes.

He raised his hand again …

No more!

I squeezed.

The report was muffled by his flesh.

His face twisted from disbelief to horror.

I had shot him. I had grabbed my gun from his belt and fired at point-blank range into his stomach.

Tanner stood transfixed. 'Boss?'

Johnson staggered back, his knees buckled and he fell to the ground, blood gushing from the gaping wound.

Tanner raced to his side and skidded to his knees. 'Boss? Boss, what happened? You all right?' He reminded me of a wretched dog whimpering for its fallen master.

Johnson's body twitched once. The savagery drained from his eyes.

Pitt's gun burned in my grip.

Tanner's confusion vanished when he touched Johnson's warm blood. He swivelled on his haunches and grabbed at the revolver in the pouch on his belt.

'Don't!' I warned. 'You don't have to die. Just let me go—'

'You bitch!' he roared, pulling out his gun.

I fired.

The bullet penetrated his skull and exploded from the back of his head sending shards of bone and brain onto Johnson's corpse. Tanner's body convulsed, his gun discharged twice into the blackness, then he slumped, dead.

Silence.

Had anyone seen? Heard? No, all was silence.

The silence swallowed everything—any guilt, any pity, any remorse, any grief. I didn't even feel relief.

My breathing steadied, my heart slowed. Nothing around me moved except the flow of the river and the intermittent tremor of my hand.

With renewed purpose, I rifled through Johnson's and Tanner's pockets and found some coins, a pocket watch and useless scrap. I removed all the cash and stashed it in my own pocket. I took anything of value—pocket knives, watches, pistols, cartridges—and tossed them into the river. In Johnson's waistcoat pocket I found their hotel key and paper. In the faint amber light of the street's gas-lamps, these revealed themselves to be a receipt from the Left-luggage Office at the Melbourne Terminus and my missing valise tag. Also there, and smeared with dried blood, was a business card for the Menzies Hotel.

The Wangaratta desk clerk hadn't given me up easily.

***

The Yarra River breathed a soft mist that caressed the embankment and curled around the lifeless remains of my pursuers. Without looking back, I crested the bank as the faintest glint of first light became discernible in the east.

Something in me had changed; something had taken hold of my conscience and shaken out all empathy and remorse. Nothing mattered anymore—not what I had just done, not what I had done to Pitt or Harper, not what I was about to do. My soul would burn in hell when my time came, but for now, it was my heart that burned—seared with hatred, retribution and a primal rage for justice. *I* was justice— the court, the sentence, the bloody executioner. It was my mission to right the injustices of the world. Injustices against Sarah and now Madeleine.

I reloaded my gun, secured it in my satchel and did up the few buttons that remained on my shirt. I ran my hands through my hair in an attempt to make myself presentable to the first person I met. Droplets of blood on my shirt and trousers betrayed the carnage on the riverbank. These were citations of survival, of a war won.

Crossing back over the railway track that ran through the station, I breathed in the crisp morning air filled with the aromas of freshly stoked coal fires and freshly-baked bread. The eastern sky blossomed mauves and pinks, pushing the depth of night westward.

I needed directions.

Across the road, a young newspaper boy shuffled past the Princes Bridge Hotel carrying a bundle of broadsheets, barefoot and yawning.

He'd know. I crossed Flinders Street.

'You. Boy,' I called. My soiled, dishevelled clothing and dour expression gave him a start.

'Yeah?' he asked warily, backing away a few steps.

'Carlton. How do I get there?'

'Up there,' he said, flinging an arm at Swanston Street. 'Right up the end.' He hurried off before I could ask anything else of him.

The pre-dawn street lay ahead of me, unawakened, silent. Gas lamps lined the footpaths like a guard of honour showing the road to retribution. Soon church bells would call the sleepy faithful to prayer. The haberdashers, confectioners and booksellers of the beginning of the street made way to the sombre learning of the university and proceeded through the tangle of the tradesmen's shops, pawn brokers and billiard rooms of the upper end—all closed in deference to the Sabbath and the laws that controlled the exchange of money on that sacred day.

Grattan Street emerged ahead, standing on higher ground east of Elizabeth Street. Nearby were the new Carlton Gardens—a grassy forest only thirty years ago. Somewhere here, among the dignified houses of the wealthy, was the gaudy mansion built on the earnings of high-prized pin-boxes, such as Madeleine.

It didn't take long to find. The 'Kepple eyesore' stood brazenly among the more elegant piles of stone and brick. What it lacked in taste, it more than made up for in sheer size, sprawling across two allotments and three storeys of vulgar opulence. A six-foot high wrought-iron fence, topped with spearpoints, ringed the perimeter like a warning.

I gazed at the garish monolith from across the street in the dim, early morning light. A stray dog trotted by, nose skimming the ground. Napoleon. My chest seized at the memory. Nothing else on the street moved.

Resolve anchored me: Kepple would restore to Madeleine what was hers and he would release her from his hold—there would be no negotiation.

The thick silence was broken by a tolling bell—distant, hollow, unanswered. Perhaps the wealthy attended the later mass. I doubted that Harry Kepple was a man of faith. But belief didn't matter now—I had made my choice.

The single-minded determination that had brought me this far, pushed me through the front gates. They rasped a brittle warning to anyone who listened. I flinched. The path was littered with dead forgotten leaves, moist with the morning dew. I tested the door. As expected—locked. I made my way around the building, each footstep crunching loose gravel and betraying my approach.

At the back, I came to the kitchen door. The door yielded.

I paused.

Godfrey Saunders' words came to mind: Your path is predetermined by God. There's no choice. Whatever you do, God has chosen for you. You can't go against God's will.

If God has predetermined my life, I thought, *and my destiny is to die here, so be it.*

I withdrew the revolver from my satchel and nudged the door aside.

All was quiet. There were no servants scurrying about, no fire had been rekindled in the stove, no aromas of cooked food—only stale air and the echo of my breath. Perhaps Sundays were the servants' free day.

I stole through the kitchen, along the passage and eased open the green baize-lined door. The foyer yawned ahead of me. Not a soul to be seen nor a whisper to be heard. Nothing disturbed the unnatural stillness of the place—a mausoleum.

I ascended the staircase to the first floor, my footsteps baffled by the plush Persian runner. No movement from any of the closed rooms. No whispers from behind the doors. I took the stairs to the next floor. The deathly silence was pulling at each nerve.

Where was everybody?

Where was Kepple? The Dog? Servants? No one. Nothing but a smothering void.

At the second-floor landing, I halted.

There. A sound.

A whimper. A dog? I strained to hear. No, not a dog. Something else. It drifted from the last room down the short corridor. Its door was slightly ajar. Another whimper.

I crept towards the sound; each step taken with foreboding. I checked behind me: nothing. I reached the door. My hand tightened around the revolver's grip.

I slowly pressed the door open with the revolver's barrel. The door creaked.

What I saw made my chest tighten and loathing rise like bile.

In the shadowy depth of the far corner, a bundle of dirty clothing trembled and exhaled a sob. Not discarded rags but a girl huddled in fear, arms tightly wrapped around her knees. Her straggly soiled hair clung to her tear-streaked face. Her eyes flicked towards me—desperate, pleading, filled with dread.

I was here for Kepple and to retrieve Madeleine's money—nothing more. But I couldn't leave a distressed child. Not with a man like Kepple.

I peered into the windowless room and moved in carefully, gun raised, every sense alerted.

Behind me—movement.

I spun, gun raised, backing away.

The shadows released them. Kepple. The Dog.

'Ah, the new recruit,' Kepple's abrasive voice was now as unctuous as the oil-slick on his thinning hair.

He stepped towards me.

Something glinted in the Dog's hand—a knife.

'What brings you here?' Kepple's face was a study in lechery—obscene and unabashed.

I didn't blink.

'Think carefully,' I warned, voice calm, breath measured. 'I have nothing to lose.'

His step faltered.

'Drop the knife,' I ordered.

The Dog growled, glancing to Kepple for direction.

'Drop it now,' I repeated, calmly, and thumbed the hammer back. The blade clattered to the floor. The Dog slinked behind Kepple.

'Have you come for a position?' Kepple's scorn dripped from every word he uttered. 'As you can see, I am interviewing right now but I'm afraid you're far too old to be of any interest to my "special" clients.'

'I'm here for Madeleine's money,' I sneered training my revolver on Kepple's chest. 'The money you stole from her.'

'My money, you mean. Madeleine was dishonest. She withheld. *She* stole from *me*.'

'Just give me the money you took,' I said coldly, 'and I won't kill you.'

The words came too easily. Johnson's words. False promises soaked in blood. They horrified me because they were true. I had nothing to lose.

Kepple's arrogance didn't change. 'My dear recruit, I will give you some money but I will also tell you this: you have made the worst mistake of your life. You won't leave this place alive. You are already dead. Your dead, bloated body will be found floating down the river.'

'Just like Aoibhin's?' I tilted my head towards the girl in the corner. 'While I'm at it, the girl's coming with me.'

'The guttersnipe? She shows promise. And profit.' He sneered. 'She's a virgin.'

My stomach twisted.

How would he have discovered that?

The answer came with a sickening thud.

The girl had been examined. Her worth measured like livestock. But not yet ruined, I hoped—not yet.

Rage licked at the edges of my composure. I was losing self-control and tiring of this game. Sleep-starved, battered by the Dog and those two thugs, Johnson and Tanner, every bruise throbbed, every bone ached. So tired. But I was still breathing.

And I was armed.

They were not.

'The money!' I rasped, every syllable edged with violence.

Overwhelming silence filled the room, thick with promised bloodshed and unyielding resolve. A silence that would only be broken by Kepple's next words—or a gunshot.

Then a word, soft, barely audible and hesitant. 'Kitchen …' the girl whispered.

'Argh!' The Dog roared, primaeval and unhinged. He lunged towards her, his intent clear. She shrank. I fired twice. The shots exploded in the airless room.

He screamed and fell mid-stride, hitting the floor with a sickening thud.

Kepple moved instantly.

The knife was in his grasp. He rushed me.

I fired again. Missed.

His speed was unexpected.

We collided. The gun flew from my grip. It clattered somewhere beyond my reach.

He slammed me against the wall, the weight of his body smothering mine, his hot breath on my face.

'You filthy bitch!' he snarled, teeth bared. 'You think you can come here and make demands? When I'm through with you, you're going to wish you had never been born.'

I twisted and slipped free just as he struck out with the knife, missing me and piercing the wall.

The gun. Where was the gun?

He slashed again. I caught his wrist mid-swing. He was too strong for me—I could barely hold the blade away.

We grappled—breaths ragged, bodies locked.

He swung me around like a ragdoll but I still held onto his wrist.

He had the knife but I had the advantage: desperation.

With a surge of fury, I drove my knee into his groin.

He doubled over with a choked wheeze, and crashed to the floor.

I found my gun and staggered to the girl.

'Come with me,' I panted, reaching for her.

She hesitated—doubt and questioning in her eyes.

'You're not safe here. Come.' I pulled her up. Her eyes widened. Behind me.

Kepple.

Knife in hand. Arm raised. Charging.

I fired twice at point-blank range. Each found its mark.

He dropped.

Lifeless. I nudged his still form with the toe of my shoe. Blood slowly seeped into the floorboards. Dead.

Damn! The money.

The girl withered, crying out in fear, and shrank back into her corner.

I hadn't meant to frighten her further.

Strewn on the floor was a soiled and ragged coat—too large for her—a man's coat. Hers, I guessed. She must have been a street urchin lured by this mongrel with a promise of food and shelter, then delivered to hell.

'Everything will be all right,' I reassured her, handing her the coat. 'Put this on.'

She hesitantly took it, looking up at me with pleading eyes. Her sobbing abated.

'What's your name?'

'D … Daphne,' she choked.

'Daphne, put on the coat. You're coming with me as soon as I find what I came for.'

As she pulled on the coat, I saw the extent of the brutality she had suffered. Her small, emaciated body was covered in welts and bruises, mostly to her inner thighs. I forced my fury down—justice had already been served.

'They can't hurt you any more,' I promised. 'I need to look for something,' I explained. 'Something they took from a friend of mine …'

'The money's in the kitchen.' Daphne's voice was quiet, almost apologetic.

I raised an eyebrow.

'I saw them hide it.'

'Show me.'

Daphne led me though the abandoned house, now haunted with ghosts of its own, and down the two flights of stairs. The pain to her small frame was obvious as she gingerly took each step. She led me into the kitchen and pointed to the wide, square flue that connected the kitchen stove to the chimney stack.

'There.'

That explained the lack of fire in the stove. I removed the access cover that was about a foot up along the flue and felt down inside it. My hand connected with a metal handle, which, in turn, was connected to the lid of a metal strong box that fit neatly inside the venting shaft.

I pulled it out and was dismayed when I saw it was locked.

'He put the key there,' Daphne proffered, now a little more composed.

I pulled out the drawer she pointed to and found a small cluster of keys tied together with string, nestled amongst the knives. A new snub-nosed revolver was also stashed at the back of the drawer. Had he brought me to the money, Kepple would have used this.

It took me only two tries to find the correct key. The box was filled to capacity with bank notes and gold sovereigns. I recognised the wads of notes on top as being Madeleine's and, without hesitation, I emptied the entire contents of the strong box into my satchel, filling it to overflowing.

Replacing the box in its original cavity and securing the cover to the flue, I turned to the youngster who stood, statue-like, watching my every move. 'Daphne, where are your parents?'

Her eyes lowered to the floor. 'I don't have any,' she whispered.

'Do you want to come with me?'

She looked up at me, confused and scared. Her eyes darted from my face to my trousers, back and forth, until it dawned on me how I presented to her.

'Daphne, I'm a girl. Like you. I'm not like the men up there.'

I could see the storm behind her eyes—doubt, fear, turmoil. 'I won't hurt you, I promise. Will you come with me?'

Even though her face was crinkled with doubt, she gave an almost indiscernible nod, then returned her gaze to the floor.

'Will you stay here and wait for me? I have to do something.'

She looked up at me again and gave another slight nod.

'Promise?' I asked.

'Promise,' she whispered.

I clasped her shoulders to reassure her. Going to the knife drawer, I tossed the keys back in and removed the small pistol and a knife. 'I'll be right back.'

When I returned a few minutes later, Daphne was exactly where I had left her; she had kept her promise.

***

There was an ample number of hansom cabs running along Grattan Street, ferrying worshippers from midmorning mass back home or to the numerous entertainments around town, but I had trouble hiring one. We didn't offer a picture of the normal Sunday recreationalists, Daphne and I. She was wearing oversized shoes and a man's coat, and I was dirty, dishevelled and spattered with dried blood, carrying a canvas bag heavy with secreted gold, bank notes and firearms.

However, once I showed the next cabbie the gold sovereign I would pay him, he begrudgingly took us to our destination.

At eighty-seven Collins Street, I knocked on Madeleine's door—I needed her assistance once more and to explain why I had left without notice or warning.

There was no answer. Perhaps she was sleeping. I knocked again, harder, pushed by desperation.

Finally, the door opened to a cautious crack but, once she saw it was me, Madeleine flung it open. 'Where did you go? Why did you dis—' She stopped mid-sentence when she took in my appearance. 'Why—? Are you hurt?' She saw Daphne. 'Who is this?'

'May we come in, please?' I asked quietly, trying to allay her alarm.

Our intrusion had clearly roused her from her sleep. Hastily swathed in a dressing gown and boudoir cap, Madeleine stepped aside, bewilderment creasing her brow. I ushered Daphne inside and closed the door behind us.

The room was as I'd left it only a few hours before—a shambles from Kepple and the Dog's frenzied search for her money.

'This is Daphne,' I said. 'She needs our help.'

Madeleine's gaze darted between the two of us. 'Where have you been? What happened to you?' Her sharp questioning felt more like a mother hen's panic than that of concern for a new friend.

I ignored her very obvious consternation. I didn't want to tell her everything: it was important that she not know of the deaths at the Prince's Bridge.

'I went to Kepple's and retrieved your money.' I stated simply and without emotion.

'You did what?' Her alarm surged again. She blanched, shook her head, and steadied herself against an upturned armchair. I could see it in her eyes—the fear of the reckoning that was sure to follow. The reach, the retaliation, of a man like Kepple were inescapable. 'What have you done? Do you know what he's capable of?'

'He won't do anything,' I said quietly, taking Daphne's hand in mine. 'Daphne's been hurt. She needs someone to help her. Where's the nearest infirmary?'

Madeleine's demeanour softened. 'Oh, child, I am so sorry.' She glanced to me. 'What happened?'

I was reluctant to go into specifics for Daphne's sake, but I owed Madeleine an explanation. 'Do you know the little windowless room on the second floor?'

'The Chamber ...' Madeleine's mouth fell open. She knew what transpired in that room.

'That's where I found her,' I continued. 'He was there ...'

Madeleine's eyes filled with unspoken questions.

'I don't think they … But they did hurt her.'

'Come with me, Daphne,' Madeleine said, her voice tender. 'We'll try to make the pain go away,' and led the young girl to the bedroom.

The satchel was heavy on my shoulder. Opening one of the drawers to the display cabinet, I emptied the notes and sovereigns quietly into it, retaining both firearms, then sat down on the sofa.

I was all in—spent. All I wanted was sleep.

From the bedroom, I could hear Madeleine talking kindly to Daphne, reassuring her that she would mend and everything would be all right. She asked questions but Daphne remained quiet and withdrawn. It was too soon to speak of what had happened.

I was numb, devoid of any feeling. My entire body ached where it had been punched and pummelled by three of God's most despicable creations.

The soft murmuring from the bedroom faded in and out of my consciousness, lulling me into the warm, safe nest that cradled me. My breath slowed. Sounds distanced themselves … peace …

A sharp, frantic rapping on the door shattered the silence.

I jolted awake, heart pounding, the fog of sleep evaporated with each insistent crash against the door.

Madeleine flew into the room from the kitchen, her face drawn tight with foreboding.

I leapt to my feet, pulled out Pitt's revolver and aimed it at the door—no one was going to harm any of us anymore.

The pounding on the door became louder, persistent.

'Maddie!' called a female voice. 'Maddie, are you in there? Open up!'

'That's Christine,' Madeleine said as she ran to the door and unlocked it.

The second it was opened, an hysterical young woman pushed her way in. 'Have you heard? Have you heard?' she blared. 'Someone's done Harry in! Harry's dead!'

'What are you talking about? Harry? Dead?' Madeleine glanced at me with a look of panic.

'Yes! Georgiana went this morning to pay her dues and found him in the Chamber … shot to pieces. Blood everywhere!'

Madeleine gasped. I slipped the gun back into my satchel and sat down, unmoved by the telling.

'Him and that mongrel cur that follows him around. Followed him straight to hell and good riddance to the both of them! And,' continued Christine, with a certain amount of glee coating her shock, 'his cock-a-doodle was cut off—'

'Oh, God,' Madeleine whispered. She stared at me in wide-eyed disbelief.

I didn't flinch.

'—and shoved in his mouth!'

This was too much for Madeleine; her legs gave way and she sank to the floor, her back to me. She buried her head in her hands and her shoulders convulsed. Christine was immediately on her knees beside her, consoling.

I couldn't believe that news of the demise of that extorting mongrel would bring Madeleine any sort of grief.

Madeleine looked up at Christine, her hands still covering her mouth. 'Do the police know who did it?'

'No, and quite frankly, I don't think they give a damn. I reckon they're as glad to be rid of him as we are.'

'What about his hoard? Has anyone found it?'

'Georgiana said she was going to get some of the girls to tear the place apart as soon as the coppers leave.'

I watched them both as they sat there, looking at each other and digesting the news and its ramifications. Finally, Madeleine whispered, 'My God, Christine, do you know what this means?'

Christine nodded.

'We're free of that bastard.'

Madeleine turned to me. Her initial look of shock slowly turned to one of realisation. I watched her as fear was replaced with hope. She turned back to Christine. 'Who else knows?'

'Apart from Georgiana and the coppers, you're the first I've told,' she said, rising to her feet. 'He treated you the worst, even though you were the best.' She made her way to the door. 'I'm off to tell the rest of the girls.' With a big smile she added, 'And to look for that money!' She disappeared through the doorway as quickly as she had appeared, closing the door behind her.

Madeleine rose to her feet and approached me. 'Rebecca—'

'Please, don't ask me anything,' I said.

'Another secret?'

I didn't answer. I was exhausted. My body desperately needed rest, a bath and sustenance.

'Daphne's settled and I've given her a draught to help her sleep,' Madeleine said quietly, sitting close beside me. 'Let's tend to you.'

With much gentleness, she took care of my bruises and helped me wash. Her ministrations were loving but borne of gratitude, not of desire.

She prepared a simple meal for us both. I ate in silence and slept through the rest of Sunday. I didn't go to Mass and didn't seek confession; God didn't abandon me—I abandoned God.

28

Monday, 11ᵗʰ May, 1874

Melbourne, Victoria

'There are things I have to do,' I said to Madeleine as we finished our late breakfast. 'May I borrow an outfit, please?'

My last task, before I left Melbourne for good, was to finalise my dealings with the Menzies Hotel and the occupants of room two thirty-four.

Madeleine provided me with a fresh outfit from her 'day dresses' armoire and, in the early afternoon, I made my way to the Left-luggage Office of the Melbourne Terminus. There, I produced the receipt I had taken from Johnson's vest pocket and was shown the two carpetbags he had left there only two days prior—it seemed like a lifetime ago.

They were heavy and, opening them in a private room, I was not too surprised to find they contained the proceeds from the gold escort: wads of bank notes, a few bags of newly minted gold sovereigns in one bag, and twenty pounds of pure gold ingots in the other. I later learned the value of those ingots alone, was about one and a half thousand pounds, or about ten years' wages. Once again, my conscience was in turmoil. Once again, my need won out over rectitude. *They would have been insured*, I told myself, attempting to ameliorate my guilt.

With Johnson's heavy carpetbags in hand, I struggled to the cab rank and lifted them into it, requesting the driver to take me to the Menzies Hotel. 'And, driver,' I added, 'I need to make several stops. Will you attend me at these stops, please? It will be worth your waiting.'

'Certainly, Miss.'

It was only a short ride to the Menzies. As I alighted, I handed the driver sixpence—the full fare. 'I shan't be too long. I need to collect the rest of my luggage. Thank you, driver, for waiting.'

'My pleasure, Miss. I'll be right here.'

I hurried inside where I was met by some commotion. The foyer was abuzz with porters and many of the guests still discussing the events of early Sunday morning: a door was kicked in and a guest was kidnapped! Or, at least, that was the gossip.

Mr Romsford, the hotel's manager, was frantically busy behind the desk when I approached.

'Miss Davies!' he exclaimed, apparently confounded. 'We thought you were lost to us.' This brought the unwanted attention of all those around.

'Ah, no, Mr Romsford, I am safe,' I reassured the manager, adding with as much feigned surprise as I could muster. 'Whatever made you think otherwise?'

'A dreadful incident, Miss,' he announced with much drama. 'Two ruffians, unknown to us, barged into the lobby early Sunday morning and bailed up our desk clerk and night porter, threatening to do them in if they didn't give you up. They gained access to your room by breaking down the door and, when you didn't return yesterday, we all assumed that you had been taken by force, dragged down the servants' stairs and out the kitchen door to be held for ransom.'

I laughed, not only to quell his fears but at the absurd theatrics of his proclamation—and his adjustment of the events in order to soften the hotel's culpability. 'As you see, Mr Romsford, I am well. But I do confess that, if what you say is true, I am quite shaken by the fact that this could have taken place here. I did notice that you admitted two rather … shall we say … odd persons to take up residence on my floor. A Mr Flinders and friend?'

'Hmm, ah, yes,' he blustered. 'They said they were friends of Mr Menzies himself. I've spoken to Hobson with regard to that. However, they have been very quiet and reclusive and of no trouble at all.'

'Ah …' I replied, relieved that their true identities had not yet been discovered. I hoped that their bodies had been found and were now lying unidentified in a cold morgue somewhere.

'Miss,' Romsford hesitated. 'Detective John Stevens would like a word with you. Only so he knows you are safe.'

'Of course,' I said, inwardly cringing at any contact with the police. 'Is he here?' I hoped not.

'Not at present, but I can summon him.'

'Please, do not trouble him. I will drop by the police station on my way out.'

'You are leaving us?'

'Yes. My cousin has offered me a room—in Toorak—until I can find other suitable accommodation. May I retrieve my belongings from my room?'

'Of course.'

'And Mr Hobson stored a red valise of mine for safe keeping. I will take that when I leave.'

'Of course, Miss. We are sorry to see you go.'

With that, I hurriedly climbed the stairs to room two thirty-two, my legs quivering under the weight of the carpetbags and at the thought of my litany of lies being found out.

The door to my room had been expeditiously and expertly repaired and, once behind my locked door, I separated the banknotes from the ingots and coins into one carpetbag and distributed the weight of the gold between the remaining carpetbag and my valise, into which I also placed all my belongings, few as they were.

Taking up the bag of banknotes, I opened the door a little and made sure there was no one around in the passageway. Finding it empty, I slipped out and hurriedly made my way to room two thirty-four. I inserted Johnson's key into the lock and entered their room.

Rummaging through Johnson's and Tanner's bed rolls and carpet bags turned up very little of value, except a few gold sovereigns, which I pocketed. I left all their other possessions in place, including two rifles. I opened the carpetbag and left it and the numbered banknotes on the bed. With a final survey of the room, I was content all was in place and, as discreetly as I entered, I left and locked the door behind me.

One last act was to dispose of Johnson's room key.

Back in my room, I opened the window and, making sure no one could see me, I threw it as far as I could across the road. If anyone should find it, they would surely return it to the hotel.

With these tasks completed, I believed that the constables would conclude that Johnson and Turner had met their end on the Yarra bank as the result of a bungled robbery and that they remained unidentified corpses in the morgue. I hoped that the disappearance of the two hotel guests in room two thirty-four would be attributed to the Beechworth gold robbery and that they had fled the colony with the gold, leaving everything behind including a modest fortune in traceable notes.

I trusted that no connection would be found between my visit to the Left-luggage Office at the terminus and my lodgings at the Menzies.

I collected my valise and the carpetbag and headed downstairs, where Mr Romsford had retrieved my stored valise. With a few more pleasantries exchanged, the porter took the three pieces of luggage and loaded them into the waiting cab. My last words to Mr Romsford were my promise to see Detective John Stevens on my way to Toorak—another broken vow to be added to the deficit side of the Eternal Reckoning Account.

***

I stayed with Madeleine and Daphne for another few weeks, deliberately keeping out of sight until the departure of the Nubia, a steamship of the Peninsular and Orient Steam Navigation Company destined for Europe, Egypt, India, China and Japan.

After I had settled my account and took my leave of the Menzies, I directed Madeleine to the drawer full of Kepple's ill-gotten gains—an immense sum of money that had been dishonestly wrung from all his working girls—and left it to her discretion to distribute. She would share it fairly and equitably with all the mistreated women who had been under his cruel and merciless control.

Daphne recovered from her injuries and, in time—God willing—would recover from the traumatic abuse by those monsters. She grew stronger day by day and was soon able to tell us of her abduction and defilement. She confessed she was glad they were dead.

Daphne told how late on Saturday night—the night of the ransacking of Madeleine's apartment—Kepple had spotted Daphne on the streets and enticed her to accompany him to his house with the offer of a meal and a warm bed. Once inside the house, he dragged her to the 'Chamber'. She was terrified but there was no one about, no one to help her, only the man that followed him everywhere—the Flesh-monger's Dog.

She struggled. They hurt her when they held her down and forced her legs apart. At this, she fell silent, her eyes fixed on the table, the memory too raw to recount. They spoke of money. She knew what was going to happen to her.

'Then you came,' she said softly, 'and saved me.'

We sat in silence as Daphne relived the horror. Madeleine stared into space, eyes distant, her expression unreadable.

Then, with a catch in her voice, she said, 'Daphne's story,' she paused, 'is my story, except nobody saved me.'

***

Madeleine and Daphne formed a strong bond that saw them travel to England together to start a new life as adoptive mother and daughter away from brothels and whoremongers.

The steamer Nubia would take me to India and to my adventures in the subcontinent and the East. It would be some twenty-five years before I set foot in Mother England for the first time.

How different my life would have been had I gone with them. Then again, I would never have met Wills.

29

Tuesday afternoon, 5th September, 1905

Abbottsford Hall, Suffolk, England

My thoughts were brought back to the present by the sound of a motor car's engine idling and the chattering of a man and boy.

I found myself at the vast mews of Abbottsford Hall where, in the courtyard of the stables and carriage houses, the countess' chauffeur, Jimmy Isham, was demonstrating the workings of the internal combustion engine to young Henry, the stable boy. They were on the near side peering into the engine under the opened bonnet.

'What?' exclaimed the stable boy with faux incredulity. 'It's got thirty horses in there?'

'No, lad,' explained Jimmy patiently. 'It has the strength of thirty horses.'

'Stronger than thirty Shires? All pulling together?'

'Aye, and you don't have to clean up the muck after them.'

'You're pulling my leg, Mr Isham,' Henry said with a good-natured laugh, then he caught sight of my approach. 'Miss Davies! Come look! Mr Isham reckons there's thirty horses in here! He's daft.'

'Henry,' I greeted, standing beside him and looking in. 'Thirty of them?'

'Yes! Shires!' he laughed.

The chauffeur rolled his eyes, apparently a little exasperated with Henry's mocking. He introduced himself: 'Jimmy Isham, Ma'am, Lady Chestermere's chauffeur.'

'Rebecca Davies, secretary to the duchess.' I extended my hand, which somewhat perplexed Jimmy but he shook it anyway.

'She's got the awfullest scar, Mr Isham,' Henry offered.

'Ah … yes, I see it, Henry,' Jimmy acknowledged, visibly embarrassed. 'It hurt lots, didn't it, Miss?'

'Lots, Henry.'

A harsh call of 'Boy!' from the stables caught Henry's attention and he flew off without a parting word or syllable, leaving Jimmy and me in the wake of his candour.

I broke the silence. 'Thirty Shires, eh?' Jimmy shook his head. 'How fast does she go?'

'Top speed of fifty-five,' he replied proudly. 'But we only made fifty … under the direction of the countess, of course.'

'Of course,' I repeated, impressed firstly by the speed of the motor car and secondly by the derring-do of the countess, knowing that she could have been fined for exceeding the speed limit … had she been caught.

'Have you been in Her Ladyship's employ long?' I asked. This was not idle chitchat. I wanted to know more of the countess' servants as well as the countess herself.

'No, Miss. Only five or so months. I came with the car,' he added conspiratorially.

I raised an eyebrow.

'When Lady Chestermere purchased the car, she needed someone to drive it,' he explained. 'And look after it. A mechanic. I'm a mechanic. I worked in Mr Royce's factory in Hulme and I was charged with delivering the completed car to Her Ladyship.'

'Is that when you met her maid and were smitten?' I asked nonchalantly.

His eyes widened. 'Erm, actually—'

'Seems to me the maid's affections lie elsewhere,' I interrupted.

He gave up the pretence. 'She'll come around. There's no future for her with good old George McPherson. He may be the housekeeper's son but he won't be looking to marry a lady's maid.'

'Why is that? Or do I hear jealousy talking?'

'Not jealousy, Miss. Lady Chestermere's grooming him personally in her business affairs. Put him through varsity. He'll be looking to marrying a banker's daughter or even a 'Lady Someone'. And poor Jessie will be left in the lurch.'

'From what I've seen of Jessie, she doesn't seem like one to put up with nonsense.'

'Fiery of hair; fiery of temperament. One thing's for certain with Miss Turner, you won't be spared the truth.'

The sharp sound of Jessica Turner's voice made him jump.

'Jimmy Isham! Where have ye been hiding? I've been looking for ye everywhere!'

Jimmy turned, ready for battle. 'Not hiding from you, Jessica.'

'Miss Turner to ye!'

'And Mr Isham to you!'

Jessica cast me a withering glance as she continued her onslaught. 'Lady Katherine needs some provisions from the village. Ye will take me there at once,' she ordered and clambered into the passenger's side of the car, almost pushing me aside. Once inside, she turned to me. 'And the duchess said to tell ye she's finished lunch. And ye're to attend her immediately.'

I presumed that last remark was added to exert her imagined authority over me—the duchess had made it clear she would rather not have me follow her every move. This young woman's air of superiority amused me. No doubt, it was strengthened by the knowledge that she served one of the wealthiest noblewomen in England.

Jimmy started the motor and I reached up to retrieve my notebook from the car's roof.

Jessica caught sight of the gun nestled in its holster underneath my short jacket. She glanced up at me with a look of alarm and I returned her gaze with one of warning.

I watched the motor car depart and then took myself off to the morning room where the duchess sat alone waiting for me.

'Ah, Davies,' she began spiritedly. 'We have an exciting afternoon of perusing the menus Mrs Plummer and Cook have devised for the weekend. Are you up to it?'

***

The Duke of Bramwell and his niece, Katherine, the Countess of Chestermere, sat by the large oaken desk that occupied one end of the duke's study. Seated nearby were George McPherson, the countess' business secretary, and Mr Angus Hollingsworth, their solicitor and banker, both perusing a thick folder of documents. Mr Hollingsworth was in his mid-fifties and had made his way up to this position through honesty, hard work and strict Christian scruples—qualities which the duke and countess admired more than inherited titles.

'Hm, this seems to be in order,' Mr Hollingsworth said, putting that document aside. 'Balance sheet,' he requested.

George duly handed him the item.

'Yes … yes … Directors' statements?' He read through the papers diligently amid the silence and anticipation of the other three in attendance. Finally, he set those papers aside and, squaring them up neatly, announced, 'Your Grace, my lady, Mr McPherson, all seems to be in good order and ready for your signatures.'

He handed the title deed to the duke who took up his black onyx fountain pen and signed the document with a flourish. The duke passed it and the pen to his niece who added her signature.

'I didn't realise Your Ladyship was left-handed,' Hollingsworth said, taking the document offered by the countess.

'Believe me, old chap,' the duke interceded, 'her priest, her parents and her teachers all tried and failed to have her use the appropriate hand.'

Lady Katherine's expression held a hint of victory as she screwed the lid back on the pen.

'Thank you, my lady, and congratulations. Once the title deeds are registered, you will be the new owners of Clydebank Shipbuilders of Scotland Limited.'

'A small company now,' added the duke, 'but with excellent potential for growth. And all thanks to Mr McPherson's comprehensive investigations and to my niece's tenacious negotiating skills.'

Hollingsworth beamed at George. 'You are a very lucky young man, George. Would that I had, in my formative years, the sponsorship of such a fine lady as the Countess of Chestermere.'

'I thank you, Sir. I am very fortunate, I know.'

Hollingsworth picked up the paperwork on the desk and placed it, together with the newly signed deeds, in his leather briefcase. He stood.

'Not staying for a celebratory dram, Angus?' the duke asked, clearly a little disappointed.

'Sir, I thank you but the sooner I return to London, the sooner I can register the deeds and release the funds.'

The duke graciously acquiesced. 'Katherine, perhaps your driver can see Angus back to the railway station?'

'I'm sorry, but I sent Jessica on an errand,' she apologised.

'No matter,' said the duke rising and pulling the servant's bell cord. 'I will have Thomson arrange a carriage for you.'

'No motor car, Sir?' was Hollingsworth's surprised query.

'We are still in fervent negotiation, the duchess and I,' the duke replied.

'Ah!' Hollingsworth acknowledged. 'Understood, Sir. A good day to you all.'

Once the solicitor left the study, George gathered his papers and briefcase. 'Your Grace, my lady, if you no longer require me?'

'Of course, George, and thank you,' Lady Katherine replied.

George bowed and he, too, left the room, closing the door behind him.

The duke watched George leave then addressed his niece 'He's an able young man.'

'Quite.'

'He has a good future and a good marriage will only enhance that. A poor marriage …'

Lady Katherine hesitated. 'Uncle, I am loath to interfere with the workings of the heart.'

'Hm. Pity. I have nothing against the Scots—your father was one and I had nothing but admiration for him. However, a prudent marital alliance will see that young man achieve great things. As it would for you, my darling Katherine.'

Lady Katherine rose and, with mock exasperation, said, 'You're beginning to sound like dear Aunt Mary.' She kissed him on the cheek before leaving him standing there ruing his last comment.

***

It was midafternoon at New Scotland Yard and the large office that accommodated the eight desks of Sir Giles Hawthorne's handpicked Department of Special Operations officers were unoccupied save the one being used by Scott.

Though the bullet he had taken in the pursuit of Lady Warburton's murderers had passed cleanly though his calf muscle, Robert Scott could still manage the stairs with the aid of crutches. He was as committed to finding these butchers as any of his fellow officers and he'd be damned if he was going to lay himself off while the killers remained at large.

Piles of papers littered his desk as he flicked from one to another, laboriously pencilling notes. He was immersed in his assignment.

One floor above, Sir Giles' outer office was enjoying the peace of an unoccupied room when the tranquillity was broken by a sharp, strident bark from the speaking tube on the wall: 'Fawkner! Fawkner!'

A few moments later, a flushed and angry Sir Giles burst into the room from his office. 'Where the dickens are you?' he bellowed.

He stormed out of the office and down the stairs to the DSO facility. Bursting through that door, he was evidently annoyed to see only one agent there, Scott, who looked up from his work.

The sight of a red-faced Sir Giles bearing down on him made the detective constable involuntarily rub his injured calf, as though massaging one pain would make another go away.

'Where the dickens is Fawkner?' Sir Giles demanded.

Scott casually moved a file to cover his notes and rested his arm on it. 'Sir Giles ... I don't ... There's only myself here, Sir.'

Sir Giles looked about. 'And who are you?'

Scott stiffened in his chair. 'Scott, Sir Giles. Robert Scott, Detective Constable,' he replied with the controlled exactness of having introduced himself one time too many.

'Yes, yes, of course.' Sir Giles approached Scott's desk. 'And the others, Yabsley, Dolby ... and er—'

'Hewitt and Byrne, Ramsay and Hathaway, Sir?'

'Yes, yes.'

'On assignment, Sir.'

Sir Giles' expression wavered between confusion and ignorance.

'Investigating those trade unions as per your orders,' Scott elucidated. 'You felt they had a hand in the abductions and murders and you wanted us to find links to them.'

'Quite. Quite. And you?'

'Consolidating the evidence, Sir,' Scott warily answered.

At this, Sir Giles' hand darted to the papers Scott was holding down with his forearm but Scott's arm did not yield.

'Sir! Ah, these are just my scribbled notes. I will have them properly typewritten and presented in due course, when complete. If it pleases you, Sir.'

Sir Giles clearly was not pleased. He bristled—first at being fobbed off and, second, with not being able to find his missing, ne'er-do-well of a secretary.

'Tell Fawkner to present himself to me immediately or he can find himself another position,' he ordered and turned on his heels and left.

'Yes, Sir,' Scott replied. 'If he happens by, I will tell him.'

Once Sir Giles had left the room, Scott penned a lengthy note. He put it together with various papers and reports and retrieved a large manila envelope from his drawer. He carefully placed the twenty or so folios inside and sealed it. On the outside he wrote, 'For the Attention of Mjr R Williams, Abbottsford Hall, Sf. Strictly Private and Confidential'. He slid that into his briefcase and, with great effort, lifted himself from the chair, steadied himself on his crutches and, gripping the briefcase, hobbled off for the post room.

It didn't take long for that envelope to reach Abbottsford Hall, the special messenger taking the same route Wills and I had taken a few days before.

***

After her meeting with the duke, Lady Katherine and her aunt enjoyed the warm autumn afternoon in the gazebo, surrounded by the fragrant rose beds and lush lawns while Thomson and Florence served afternoon tea. I stood by at a distance of ten yards in the shade of a large oak tree, discreetly observing the goings-on of the various gardeners in the distance.

Every now and then, a wave of refined laughter wafted across to me on the scented breeze, drawing my attention to the Countess of Chestermere. I could not help but notice that, from where she sat, I was in her line of vision and wondered if that had been deliberate.

Her beautiful countenance enthralled me—and I fought assiduously against being so enslaved again.

It wasn't long before the duchess gave instruction to Thomson and he approached me. 'Miss Davies, Her Grace wishes you to join Her Grace and Her Ladyship.'

I was puzzled by this request but acceded. I was further surprised when Thomson showed me to a chair at the table. I stood there until the duchess invited me to be seated.

'Your Grace,' I wavered. 'I really must not—'

'Oh, pish, Rebecca … if I may call you that. Sit.'

With much reluctance I did sit and felt terribly out of place. Doing my best to ignore the countess, I concentrated on the duchess.

I could feel Lady Katherine's gaze upon my disfigured face and wondered to what depth of revulsion she reached.

'Rebecca,' continued the duchess, 'you haven't been properly introduced to my niece. After all, you will be spending quite some time in our company until her departure Friday.'

I glanced at the countess but could not see any sign that she was repulsed—a true aristocrat.

'Katherine, may I present to you Miss Rebecca Davies, Assisting Clerk to Major Reginald Williams of the Metropolitan Police Special Branch,' the duchess continued. 'Rebecca, my niece, the Right Honourable, the Countess of Chestermere, Lady Katherine Delaney.'

'Miss Davies,' Lady Katherine intoned in a voice as soft as velvet.

'My lady,' I replied, meeting her eyes until the duchess interrupted with her usual candour.

'Rebecca is my day shadow,' explained the duchess to her niece, 'and the major is my shadow of the night. Rebecca will be riding with us tomorrow morning and she assures me she won't fall off.'

A breath of laughter escaped me and Lady Katherine's expression warmed with subtle amusement.

The duchess continued in a far more serious tone. 'I read your dossier, Rebecca, and I understand your mother was Welsh. Your father?'

'My father?' What was the duchess contriving? In truth, it fazed me not—I was well resigned to being known as a bastard. 'I don't know who my father was, Your Grace. I'm a bastard.'

This didn't appear to be of any concern to the countess whose calm expression still did not falter.

The duchess continued with a persistence I couldn't fathom. 'And it doesn't state your religion. Are you an atheist?'

I then understood where the duchess was heading with the interrogation; I would happily condemn myself in the eyes of her niece.

'God and I don't see eye to eye, Your Grace. He believes justice and retribution are His domain alone. I believe in not waiting for Him but to expedite the repayment of criminals' debts to humanity. I also drink to excess, but not in public, swear like a sailor, but not in front of ladies, and enjoy other improper pleasures in my leisure time. I am a liar when it suits me and I break my promises more often than I keep them. And I cheat at cards. I am certainly no saint. I am a woman who has survived adversity through persistence and foolhardiness, and I don't shrink from my duties. And it is these attributes and convictions, Your Grace, that see me here in this place and moment in time.' I rose from my seat. 'With your permission, Your Grace, I will resume my obligation.' I turned to Lady Katherine. 'Your Ladyship.'

I left Mary, the Duchess of Bramwell, lost for words and perhaps a little miffed, but I was damned if I allowed anyone to take my history and make me feel less worthy than they because of it. I was sure that it was nothing personal against me but, rather, an effort by the duchess to protect her niece. For this, I forgave her; she was not to know that I did not intend to seduce the Lady Katherine—tempting as it was.

'Rather well put, don't you think, Aunt?' I heard Lady Katherine playfully chide the duchess.

I believed that I may have found a friend.

It wasn't long after that the two peeresses retired to their respective boudoirs to prepare for dinner, which was my cue to hand over to Wills. I accompanied the duchess to her suite, making sure her rooms were secure. As I was about to leave, the duchess addressed me somewhat apologetically. 'Davies … this afternoon … I would like to explain my actions—'

'No need, Your Grace,' I said.

'No. Please listen. My niece … Katherine is more like a daughter to me … to us. She's been in our care since my sister and her husband passed away suddenly. Katherine was only fourteen. The last thing I want for her is to be hurt … in any way. She holds a very important place in society and her good reputation is paramount. You do understand.'

'Your Grace, I understand your concerns. I know my place and I know my worth. Once this assignment is brought to an end, you won't see nor hear from me again.'

Emma, the duchess' maid presented at the door, drawing our discussion to a close.

'Good night, Your Grace,' I said with a slight bow and left to confer with Wills.

In his suite on the same floor as the duchess, Wills was up and ready for the night's work. He had received a large envelope from Scott and was flipping through the pages when I knocked on his door.

'Come in,' he called. He glanced up at me. 'Close the door. Scott's reports. Interesting. And disturbing.'

I sat next to him at the desk. 'How so?'

'Interesting because the Croft we're seeking is most likely Norman Croft, imprisoned at Newgate until its closure and then removed to Pentonville until a year ago when he was released on licence.

'"Mean Man" is most likely to be Harry Hogan, Croft's partner in crime since they were both nine years of age. He fits the description Timmy gave. Look.'

Wills handed me a prison photograph of Hogan and he certainly fit Timmy's description of being ugly. His wrinkled, wart-covered face was further disfigured by a nose that had been broken and reset and was now lying almost flat against his face.

Wills continued, 'They both have arrests and convictions stretching back thirty-odd years. House breaking, stealing, all with acts of violence. And depravity. They certainly are not new to crime. And they certainly don't have the intellect required to be the puppeteer behind these abductions. Hogan was released at the same time as Croft.'

'Have they been picked up for questioning?'

'No known address. They absconded after being released.'

We sat for a moment in contemplation. 'And the disturbing news?' I hesitated to ask.

'Scott informs me that Hawthorne has taken all the investigating agents away from seeking the whereabouts of Croft and Hogan and set them looking for links between the abductions … and trade unions.'

'Trade unions? That doesn't make sense. Some of the bank notes from the Richardson abduction turned up at the Russian Embassy. How is that connected with the trade unions? Surely, it's more likely that these abductions are for the Russian revolutionists' cause, not the trade unions'.' I was exasperated by Hawthorne's stupidity.

'I agree, but that's what Hawthorne has directed.'

'Did Scott find any connection between the abductions and sudden deaths of locals?'

'He's still investigating.' Wills rose from his chair and handed me the file. 'Go through these and tell me what you find. Put your report on my desk.'

He donned his suit jacket, straightened his tie and left me in his room.

I sat there pondering the events of the day. Croft and Hogan most certainly were the perpetrators of these abductions but not the instigators. Hawthorne changed focus from foreign revolutionists to internal trade unions—why? Were Wills and I on the right track— or completely wrong? Timmy was killed—what more could he have told us and who could have ordered his death? Everything seemed to point to Hawthorne. Was he the mastermind of a grand scheme or simply incompetent? And what influence did this mysterious Colonel Humphries have on the old bugger?

My thoughts veered to the duchess: why was she warning me off? I had made no overtures towards her niece. Yet she perceived some sort of subterfuge on my part. She knew nothing of me nor my preferences … but she did know her niece. And her niece's history. In warning me off, the duchess had inadvertently confirmed my hitherto unformed suspicions: The Most Honourable the Countess of Chestermere was … The thought amused and intrigued me.

So, the duchess was most concerned with protecting her niece's reputation and, in doing that, protecting the vast investments her husband had made with their niece. This certainly shone a different light on the hitherto frivolous and playful duchess.

***

I left Wills' suite moments before the dinner gong sounded. It signalled the meal would be served in half an hour, at eight o'clock.

As I ascended the stairs to my room on the floor above, I heard the duchess and countess emerging from their suites. From the landing,

I caught sight of them proceeding down the main staircase to the formal dining room, chatting amiably. Both peeresses were splendidly dressed in the haute couture of leading fashion houses and sparkled with tasteful ostentation. Wills, waiting at the far end of the long corridor, followed them down at a discreet distance. I caught his eye but he continued after them without acknowledgement.

Jessica Turner, Lady Katherine's maid, emerged from her mistress' boudoir with an armful of clothing and, instead of heading for the servant's stairs, she turned to the duchess' suite and stopped at the partially open door.

Intrigued, I descended the stairs unseen and listened.

'Emma,' Turner called softly.

Within a second, the door opened wide and Emma greeted her with a bright expression. 'Jessie. Does Her Ladyship need something?'

'No,' Turner replied. 'What's going on? The duchess has a secretary now? She didnae remind me of any secretary I've seen. She wears a gun!'

Emma glanced up and down the corridor—missing me entirely— then pulled Turner inside the duchess' room and closed the door.

The carpeted floor muffled my footfalls to the door where I listened.

'You're not to tell a soul, Jessie. Promise,' she demanded in a conspiratorial whisper.

'Promise? Promise what?'

'I can't tell you anything unless you swear to God that you won't say anything to anyone.'

'I swear. What's going on?'

'Swear to God.'

'I swear tae God.'

'Swear on your mother's grave.'

Turner's voice sharpened. 'I swear on my mother's grave. And on my father's grave. And on all my ancestors' graves. What's going on?'

'Mr Thomson said that the man and the woman, Mr Williams and Miss Davies, are from the government and here to take care of Their Graces and that we're not to interfere with them or talk to them or ask them anything but that we are to answer any of their questions and do as they say.'

There was a pause as Turner processed what Emma had blurted. 'Take care of them? Are Their Graces in trouble with the king?'

'Well, I don't know, but I *do* know the duke always makes excuses when hunting season comes around and always goes abroad or closes the house for renovation or declares some sort of ailment. I swear, the last time King Edward was here was when he was Prince of Wales and Prince George was a lad of twelve. Well before I was born and well before my mother was born.'

'That's a secret? Not much of one.'

'That's all I know and that's what Mr Thomson made me swear to.' As an apparent afterthought Emma added, 'And I believe Miss Davies to be a tribade.'

'A trivet?' Turner said, voice rising in confusion. 'You're a daft wee lass, Emma.'

'No, a tribade. A man-woman. A woman who … you know … with women. Not men,' she said.

'I have not got the time tae waste. Talk tae me when you're ready tae talk the King's English.'

I was away and up the stairs before Turner made it to the door.

***

Wills regretted not having brought along his overcoat as the night air was sharp and seeped through the weave of his jacket right to his bones. For an hour or so, he trod the grounds in the darkness, cold but vigilant of anything untoward. Finally, his icy fingers retrieved his pocket watch—dinner would be almost complete.

He made his way back into the Hall, grateful for the warmth it offered and waited by the open doorway to the dining room. There, the duke and duchess, their niece and George McPherson were in pleasant conversation after enjoying the last course.

Lady Katherine folded her napkin and placed it on the table. 'My compliments to Mrs Russell, Aunt,' she said appreciatively. 'That was a superb dessert. I must take the recipe to Cook.'

'Care for a cigar and port, George?' the duke asked the young man.

'I don't smoke, Your Grace, but a port would be most welcome.'

The duchess rose from her chair with the help of Thomson, prompting the duke and George also to rise. 'Katherine,' she said, 'shall we repair to the drawing room?'

'Aunt, if you don't mind,' Katherine replied standing, 'I'd like to take some air.'

'Of course, dear. Then I'll bid you all a good night. I'm rather weary and we have an early start tomorrow.'

***

That same night I had read all the intelligence from Scott, written up my daily report for Wills—not mentioning my discourse with the duchess—and shed my boots, jacket and holstered Webley. Tired from standing all day vigilant and observant, and with very little physical activity, I was ready for bed. My body missed its usual routine of attending the gymnasium and performing sets of calisthenics. These, together with honing my skills in fencing and jiu-jitsu with my sparring partner, Wills, helped alleviate the monotony of my occupation when we weren't active in the field. Alternatively, when I *had* participated in dangerous fieldwork and bloodlust had overwhelmed me, the only relief from the nightmares was absinthe and hashish, which were especially effective in Miss Sophie's company.

Many conflicting thoughts raced through my mind; sleep was going to be difficult. My bottle of absinthe would have greatly assisted in summoning Hypnos, but I had left that at home to appease Wills. Perhaps tomorrow I would secure a bottle and keep it at hand.

A glance at the mantle clock confirmed the time as quarter of ten, so I went to the window to close the shutters. A movement in the grounds below caught my eye. It was Lady Katherine strolling in the garden alone. I wondered what was going through her mind. Business? Pleasure? She was truly a beautiful creature.

My hand went to the silver locket about my neck and thoughts drifted to my own beautiful Sarah who would have been fifty-two had she survived her murderous husband. I wondered where we would have been today? Where I would be?

I pushed these useless thoughts out of my head, closed the shutters and retired to bed.

30

Wednesday, 6th September, 1905

Abbottsford Hall, Suffolk, England

The early morning air was crisp and refreshing, and the activities of the stableboys and grooms were in full swing when I accompanied the duchess down to the mews.

At the servants' entrance to the Hall, delivery wagons, dog carts and bicycles were busily coming and going, providing the household with their daily newspapers, post and provisions from the nearby village and railway station, as well as the extra provisions required for the coming weekend.

Lady Katherine had not yet arrived but I could see the three mounts that had been prepared for us. They were being attended to by the young stableboy, Henry, an older man, Pitman, who I discovered was not only the stablemaster but Henry's father, and Reynolds, a stable hand. I recognised the magnificent bay thoroughbred, Peleus, standing tall among them, flanked by Tommy, Peleus' stable companion, and another beautiful black mare. Peleus and the black mare were fully tacked up with side saddles but Tommy had only a bridle and saddle blanket.

'Good morning Mr Pitman, Reynolds, Henry,' the duchess said greeting each with a cordial nod.

And each in turn gave a slight bow and returned her greeting. ''Morning, Your Grace.'

Young Henry was holding onto Tommy's reins.

'Davies, this is your mount,' the duchess informed me. 'I do hope he meets with your approval.'

'He's a fine animal, Your Grace,' I said rubbing the horse's nose. 'A good sort.'

I had noticed a change in the duchess' attitude towards me—subtle but unmistakeable. She seemed cooler, more measured. Perhaps I spoke out of turn the day before and perhaps she hadn't realised that as much as I was not her equal, nor was I her servant.

'What saddle would you like, Miss?' Henry interjected. 'Side or general?'

'General, thanks, Henry.'

'Yeah, I thought you would,' he replied. 'Told you, dad,' he threw to his father as he led Tommy back to the stables.

The senior Pitman moved the black mare away from Peleus and a mounting block was positioned on her near side for the duchess to use. By process of elimination, this meant that the countess would ride the towering Peleus, being settled by Reynolds. I was impressed.

A commotion caught everyone's attention and we turned to the hall to see the driver of a heavily laden delivery cart taking his whip to the horse and yelling profanities at the unfortunate animal. One of the cart's wheels had become lodged in the loose gravel on the verge of the driveway. The horse was very obviously old and not in very good condition, nor was it of a size that should have been pulling such a heavy load.

'Oh, dear!' cried the duchess. 'That awful Mr Graves! Mr Pitman, see what you can do.'

'Yes, Your Grace.'

The stable master loped to the wagon. 'Hold there, Graves!' he called. 'Stop whipping that animal! We'll help you out.'

'Mind your own business, Pitman,' the recalcitrant driver yelled back, flogging the horse once more, 'or I'll settle some of these on you!'

Pitman clambered onto the driver's seat and attempted to take hold of the whip. Graves pushed him off then took the whip to the fallen man.

A jolt of anger erupted in me and with a few rapid strides, I was upon Graves. I caught the airborne whip's tail and wrapped it around my wrist. He yanked it back hard but a solid jerk from me saw Graves pulled out of his seat and fall out of the wagon and onto the ground on top of Pitman.

I pulled the whip from his hand and tossed it aside. My other hand grabbed Graves' collar and tie and I dragged him off Pitman, pushing him back onto the ground. My knee dug into his soft belly and my hand gripped his throat. I squeezed and he gasped for air.

Graves sputtered expletives as his feet scrabbled to find purchase on the gravelly surface. 'You fucking bitch! Get off me! Let me go! Let me go!! I'll—'

He stopped spewing his foul language and ceased his violent struggle immediately when he felt the cold muzzle of my Webley pressed against his cheek.

I released my grip on his throat and stepped aside, my gun trained unwaveringly on his face. 'Get up,' I ordered quietly. 'Get out.'

Graves scrambled to his feet and turned to his wagon.

'No,' I said. 'Walk.'

Graves' scowl threatened all sorts of things—things he didn't have the courage to vocalise. But he did manage a cold and hateful, 'Them's my goods. My horse. You can't take them.'

'If Her Grace allows,' Pitman offered, having righted himself. 'I can get the wagon back to the village once we've unloaded it.'

'But not the horse,' I insisted.

Graves became agitated again.

I levelled my gun at him. 'The horse needs to be put out of its misery. I don't know which would be better: to shoot it … or to shoot you. Get out of my sight before I make that decision.'

We were deadlocked—tension crackled between us.

Graves backed down and, with a grotesque sneer, leaned in towards me. 'You'll die regretting this, bitch. And the duchess will get hers.' He smirked knowingly and shot the duchess a menacing glance. Then he spat on the ground and stalked away, watched in disbelief by all present.

My eyes followed his retreating figure as I holstered my gun. It was of great concern to me that this vile individual had threatened the duchess. I needed to find out more about this obnoxious man and his relationship with Her Grace.

Behind me, the sounds of normality were returning and I turned away from the object of my musings, only to see Lady Katherine regarding me with mild horror. I wondered which point of my dealing with Graves had earned such an expression. Turner stood behind the countess, clearly struggling to contain an invective she wished to hurl at me.

"Morning, my lady,' I said with an almost indiscernible nod. 'Turner. You're looking rather flushed.'

Behind me, Pitman called upon several stable hands to unharness the old overworked plug and hitch a more suitable draught horse to pull the wagon out of the rut.

By this time, Reynolds had assisted the duchess onto her mount and she approached me. I did not regret my actions but thought it best to offer some sort of explanation.

'Your Grace, I apologise for putting you in this position but the maltreatment of work animals appals me. I will arrange to compensate Graves for his horse but I ask that you keep the animal here until I can make suitable arrangements.'

The duchess took a moment to consider my request. 'That poor animal is on its last legs. I think we can accommodate its final days here and I will speak to Mr Graves about restitution.' She looked down at me, literally from her high horse. 'I cannot tolerate violence in any form, Davies, but I thank you for going to the aid of my stablemaster.' She swung her horse towards Peleus.

I watched as Lady Katherine patted Peleus and rubbed his nose, actions that were well received by the thoroughbred. With the assistance of Reynolds, she took her seat and Turner handed her a crop.

Henry returned with Tommy, all saddled up. 'You showed that basket what for, eh, Miss?' he said with some enthusiasm while I checked the straps. 'My dad's getting old, you know,' he added humbly.

I quietly asked if he knew that Graves fellow.

'Oh, yes,' Henry confirmed. 'Everyone knows that bluster ball.'

'I want to talk to you about him when I get back, all right?'

'All right,' he echoed with a wide grin.

'Oh, and Henry,' I murmured, taking two sovereigns from my pocket. 'Can you buy me a bottle of absinthe, please?'

'Ab-what?' he asked.

'Let's make that whisky. The best, all right?'

Henry was a most accommodating young boy and at times like this reminded me of Patrick at the same age.

'All right, Miss,' he said, pocketing the coins. He turned to go then looked back at me. 'You're not a real secretary, are you?'

I ignored his naïve impudence, took to the saddle and settled into it. I had made a friend of Henry, but had most likely alienated both the duchess and the countess.

The day had barely begun and already I was weary of it.

***

Sir Giles Hawthorne had summoned the remaining active officers of the Department of Special Operations—all seven of them—for an early briefing: Yabsley had uncovered some vitally important information regarding the link between the trade unions and the abductors, which would change the course of their investigations.

Hawthorne sat imperiously at the desk normally occupied by Yabsley, who as detective sergeant, was the most senior officer in the room, after himself, of course. Grouped around him and seated on the edges of several other desks were Hewitt, Ramsay, Byrne, Dolby and Hathaway. Scott sat apart from them at his own desk, listening intently but not voicing his disagreement. His crutches stood propped up against his desk.

Yabsley addressed the assembled group from his position standing in front of his desk. 'Gentlemen,' he expounded in a superior tone, 'yesterday, Detective Constable Byrne and I questioned John McGregor, the leader of the Amalgamated Plasterers and Renderers Union of Greater London at his home in Bromley. While I conducted the interview, Byrne here made a search of the premises and found these hidden in a drawer.' With a flourish, Yabsley withdrew a wad of bank notes from his coat pocket and slapped it onto the desk. 'These, gentlemen, are bank notes from the Richardson ransom.'

The declaration caused a ripple of murmured comments.

Scott, sitting quietly, nudged Hewitt who was standing near him and whispered something to him. Hewitt leaned across and picked up the bundle of notes and handed it back to Scott.

'Of course,' continued Yabsley, unaware that the notes had been removed, 'McGregor vehemently denied any knowledge of the money. We then conducted a more extensive search of his lodgings and uncovered these handwritten plans for the next abduction, of one Lady Felicity Penworth, the eighteen-year-old, third daughter of Viscount Bonningwick.' He held up several sheets of folded paper scribbled over with notes and drawings.

A new round of mutterings filled the room.

'We brought in McGregor for further interrogation and he is now being held in the cells. Today, with Sir Giles' approval and authorisation, you will conduct extensive searches of the residences and work places of McGregor's known friends and accomplices while Byrne, Dolby and I interrogate McGregor further.'

'Well done, Yabsley,' enthused Hawthorne as his protégé retreated to stand behind Sir Giles like a subservient valet. Hawthorne addressed the meeting: 'By the evidence Yabsley here now has presented, it appears that the line of enquiry Major Williams had been pursuing was completely wrong. I say it was a good job that I urged Mr Quinn to insist the major go on enforced leave, thus allowing the rest of us to carry out our duty unimpeded by false leads and misinformation. This afternoon, I will inform Mr Quinn of our success—that we have broken this vile and vicious criminal ring.' Turning to Yabsley, he added, 'There will be a citation in this for you and Byrne both.'

The collection of special officers broke out in spontaneous applause—except for Scott who had shuffled through a file and the bank notes, and now sat quietly with a perplexed look. He was clearly not convinced.

Hawthorne noticed. 'You there … er … Scott, you don't agree?'

Scott hesitated. 'Sir, I'm confused. What affiliation does the Amalgamated Plasterers and Renderers Union of Greater London have with the Russian embassy?'

'The ransom money, man. The ransom money!'

'But, Sir, please forgive me. The three lists I have at hand indicate that the notes Byrne found in McGregor's residence were from Lord Meagher, not Mr Richardson.'

Hawthorne glared at Scott then looked up at Yabsley over his shoulder. 'You checked the serial numbers. Who did they come from?'

'Richardson, Sir, both. My list categorically confirms that the notes from the Russian Embassy and those in McGregor's possession were from the ransom Richardson paid the abductors. No doubt.'

'Sir,' countered Scott, 'the three lists of bank notes I have were issued to me as and when each lot of notes was withdrawn from the bank—weeks apart. The Russian Embassy received notes from those on the Richardson list. The notes from the McGregor house are on Lord Meagher's list. Not Richardson's, Sir, as Detective Sergeant Yabsley indicated.'

'Your lists are wrong!' insisted Hawthorne. 'Notwithstanding your assertion, Scott, doesn't it give strong credence to the fact that the Russians are in league with the trade unions to bring this mighty empire to its knees?'

'Perhaps so, Sir, but it also gives rise to the question of why Yabsley's list differs to mine. It appears that we have discrepancies within this office and that should be of some concern to us all.'

This statement, although phrased quite meekly, raised some debate between the officers.

Hawthorne's face bloomed red. 'Quiet! Quiet!' The mutterings died away. 'Scott, the facts are these: the Russian embassy is in a state of flux under the upheaval of the social revolutionists in that country. Our trade unions are full of communists and socialists wanting to destroy our constitutional monarchy and, with it, the capitalists that have made it great. The unions are feeding off our aristocracy and wealth.' Hawthorne took a deep breath. 'And, apart from these facts, Scott, what you have there, in your so-called lists, is another monumental foul up by Major Williams and that immoral, reprehensible excuse of a woman he calls his Assisting Clerk. Just like they bungled the coordinates last week, they botched the lists. The matter is finished, Scott. We have our man.'

Scott withered under the unwarranted verbal onslaught and said no more.

Hawthorne, satisfied with Scott's withdrawal, turned to Yabsley. 'Yabsley, I want to know everything that traitor, McGregor, says. I want him and everyone involved with him charged with these heinous crimes, sent to trial and to suffer the capital punishment they deserve.'

***

As the duchess had promised her patient and uncomplaining husband, we didn't take the bridlepath that led into the woods but another leading to the river.

The three of us left the mews at a walk, then, once past the tended lawns and gardens and onto the open field, we urged our horses into a trot and then into a comfortable canter. The duchess and the countess preceded me; a position I was happy to hold as I could scan the countryside for anything suspicious.

The two peeresses were certainly in their element and were excellent horsewomen, easily told by the way they held their seats. They were enjoying the brisk fresh air and the pale sunlight, chatting with ease, their measured laughter carried along in the breeze.

The incident at the mews still concerned me: why had Graves threatened the duchess? I was determined to find the reason. My thoughts returned to the job at hand when I noticed Lady Katherine glance back at me and then to her aunt. Without warning and with a gentle slap of her crop on Peleus' rump, she urged him into a full gallop, which her Aunt Mary emulated enthusiastically on the black mare.

Tommy was no slouch and, without much prompting from me, launched himself forward to heroically keep up with the two in front. I own that I was enjoying this as much as anyone there—woman or beast.

We rollicked along the grassy bridlepath at a scorching pace and finally came to the banks of the river that cut through the duke's estates. The duchess and Lady Katherine slowed their pace to a walk allowing their mounts to cool down and catch their breaths. Lady Katherine cast another glance over her shoulder, eyes full of mischief. I had been tested it seemed and, while I had enjoyed the flight immensely, I did not enjoy being scrutinised so.

I drew up beside the duchess as we walked along the pathway that ran upstream along the riverbank. The other side of the bridlepath was flanked with low bushes and dotted with old-growth trees. Very rustic and pleasant, but not as safe as I had imagined.

The duchess was the first to speak. 'You did well, Davies. What do you think of Tommy?'

'A courageous animal, Your Grace.' I took my chance and changed the subject. 'I understand that you recently had poachers in one of the cottages along the river.'

'Yes. Nothing extraordinary. They come along every now and then. Our estate manager, Mr Truscott, reported that Catfish Cottage had been left fouled and disarrayed. He's had it returned to its proper condition.'

'This river cuts through the estate?'

'Yes. Quite beautiful, don't you agree?'

'What lies upstream?'

'Woodland. Quite wild and with excellent hunting, should His Grace ever decide to partake of the blood sport.'

'Downstream?'

'Our village, Abbottsford.'

'And the railway station?'

'Yes, as well as the post office and our main provisioners and other businesses that supply the farmers of the area.'

'How far is it?'

'Oh, about five or six miles. Why do ask these questions, Davies?' The duchess was becoming annoyed by my incessant questioning. 'We've had poachers in the past and I am certain we'll have poachers in the future. As much as we do try to provide for our tenants, they must eat and are sometimes too proud to ask for assistance.'

My suspicious nature wouldn't allow the simplicity of the explanation. 'How many cottages are there along the river?' I persisted.

'Goodness me, Davies. So many questions!'

This drew a concerned look from Lady Katherine.

'Forgive me, Your Grace, but I must know. How many?'

'Three. Carp, Catfish and Pike, spaced at two-mile intervals. The seventh duke built them for the fishing competitions he held annually, a hundred years ago. Now they stand mostly disused but kept in good repair.'

'And they each have a boat ramp or jetty?'

The duchess looked at me with confused annoyance. 'Why do you ask all these questions? Are you planning to holiday here?'

'No, Your Grace. Does each have access from the river?'

'Yes. Now, if you please, I would like to converse with my niece.' That was her courteous but unmistakeable invitation for me to drop back and leave them alone.

I was uneasy with what the duchess had told me. The river provided a route to and from the village, and the train station provided a way into and out of the area, albeit under the scrutiny of a station master. My concern was heightened to the point of alarm when I took in the surrounds: the bushes and dense forest beyond could certainly conceal anyone with evil intent—or a body.

It was only another ten minutes of riding at a leisurely pace when we came to the first of the fishermen's cottages, the so-called 'Carp Cottage'—a simple, single-storey structure of stone with a tiled roof. A short track led off the bridlepath to the wooden front door, a sash window set in the wall on one side.

'Your Grace,' I called from my position behind her. 'I would like to inspect the cottage.' I diverted Tommy to the front door and dismounted. I could see the duchess was displeased with my curiosity, but both she and the countess stopped and watched me as I looked through the window and checked the doorhandle.

'It's kept locked,' the duchess informed me.

Through the window, I could see that the cottage was a simple, one-room affair. The opposite wall was a mirror of the front with one window beside the door. I strode around to the back and checked that door—also locked. A short pier jutted into the river. Five yards extending around the cottage was cleared of all vegetation except for a carpet of lush grass. Dense forest encroached the opposite side of the bridlepath.

I walked back to the front and remounted Tommy.

'Are the other two cottages like this one, Your Grace?' I enquired as I approached the duchess.

'Yes. More or less. May we proceed?'

I nodded but felt quite put out that the duchess' attitude indicated I was wasting her time. Lady Katherine's warm expression of gratitude showed she was far more appreciative of my concern for her aunt's safety and well-being.

The rest of the ride was at a leisurely canter and took us past the two other fishermen's cottages and through beautiful countryside, looping back to Abbottsford Hall along a wagon road that circumvented the dense woodland. I was anxious to interview Henry and find out more about Graves.

Once we had arrived at the mews, we dismounted and three stable hands took charge of our mounts and returned them to the stables for hosing and feeding. Before leaving, I called Henry over and told him to go to the servants' entrance and wait for me there until the duchess was at lunch.

***

When the duchess was safe in the presence of her husband and Thomson, I made my way to the servants' entrance and found Henry there, sitting on a step and rolling a pair of dice. Next to him was a small hessian sack. As soon as he saw me, he pocketed the spotted cubes and shot to his feet.

'Miss Davies!' he cried enthusiastically. 'Can I see your gun?'

'No, Henry. It's not a toy. Come with me.'

He picked up the sack and followed me to the bench under the large oak, away from the household's activities.

'Tell me about yourself,' I began, wanting to know more about this little dynamo.

'Me?'

'Yes. Were you born on the estate?'

'Nah, but the duke let me stay here and help my dad when my nanna died. Didn't know my mum.'

'And you want to be a jockey when you grow up. And ride Peleus.'

'Yeah.' His face lit up. 'Or a detective! Are you a lady detective?' he queried with such conspiratorial earnestness, it nearly drew a laugh from me.

'No, I'm just a secretary.'

'Yeah, who carries a gun and can dustup a bluster ball!' He chuckled.

'Tell me about Graves,' I requested, ignoring his disbelief.

Henry calmed down and relayed what he knew. 'Nobody much likes him. Not here, anyways. He's a real windbag and uses bad language all the time, even in front of Her Grace.'

'Did the duchess have words with him? Angry words?'

'Not what I heard. But I know that Mrs Plummer did. She went real crook with him when he cheated her and Her Grace.'

'How did he cheat Her Grace?'

'Dunno. Something about he was short.'

'Short? As in short delivery? Short supply? Cheating by not delivering everything he billed the duchess for?'

'Yeah. I heard Mrs Plummer tell Mr Graves that unless he brung the stuff over, she would call the constable. And he swore oaths that I ain't never heard no one here ever say before.'

'Has Mr Graves always lived in the village?'

'No. I think only a couple of years.'

'Is he married?'

'Who'd want to marry that gasbag?' Henry laughed.

'Quite so,' I replied, attempting to keep him on track and in good spirits. 'Do you know his Christian name and where he came from?'

'I think it's Stewart 'cause my dad calls him Stupid.' Henry laughed again.

I smiled and pulled his attention back to my query. 'And where did he come from?'

'Dunno. But I wish he'd go back there!' Henry laughed so hard he almost toppled off the bench.

I fished a coin from my pocket and gave it to him. 'Thanks, Henry, you've been very informative.'

Henry looked at the shiny coin. 'A crown! Thank you, Miss.' He took off for the stables.

'Don't gamble, Henry!' I called to his disappearing back.

'I won't, Miss!' he called back.

I sat there in the shade of the oak trying to delve into the minds of the abductors. Much depended on what Scott was able to uncover.

The so-called poachers reported by the estate manager could have been Croft and Hogan surveying the best place to take the duchess. The river and bridle trail offered access and the dense forest a place to leave the duchess once … I hesitated to think of what they would do to her before they killed her.

If all this conjecture were true, then we needed to discover when the planned abduction would take place. Two things were certain: Wills and I had to be extremely vigilant and we needed immediate assistance to capture the criminals and prevent her capture by these foul murderers.

But now I had to return to the Hall.

Standing up, I realised Henry had left behind his hessian bag. I looked inside and discovered a sealed bottle of Old Highland Whisky, one of the best Scotches money could buy. The change from the two sovereigns I'd given him clinked against the bottle in the bottom of the bag. An honest young man; yes, Henry was proving to be more and more like Patrick.

***

Afternoon tea was served in the drawing room—a private affair with only the duchess and countess in attendance—and me hovering discreetly at the periphery. Even this modest interlude between luncheon and dinner was a splendid production with silver service and a selection of dainty sandwiches, warm scones and delicate petit fours and tea, of course, served with sombre ceremony.

While the duchess had prepared for the occasion, I had penned my concerns and slipped the note under Wills' door.

Exactly as scheduled, the last post of the day was delivered to the Hall in the late afternoon. I was eager to see what information Scott had uncovered regarding any sudden deaths of the locals and I hoped that Wills had time to digest the notes I'd left under his door before our shift change.

After accompanying the duchess to her suite to dress for dinner, I went to Wills' rooms. I found his door ajar and him pacing the floor with a wad of paper crushed in his fist. He was furious.

'Come in. Sit down,' he commanded and handed me some of the creased paper. 'Read.'

I read through the crumpled pages.

'The trade unions are the culprits,' he put forth. 'Unequivocally. Indubitably, according to Hawthorne's report.'

'The trade unions?'

'The Amalgamated Plasterers and Renderers Union of Greater London to be precise. And Lady Felicity Penworth, third daughter of Viscount Bonningwick, is to be the next abductee.'

'How? Why?' I was becoming equally vexed. 'None of the demands has ever been for better working conditions or wages, only for money. The unions might be aggressive but they haven't taken up arms. And how are they connected with the Russian embassy?'

He shook his head. 'I would have been more convinced if they had discovered the ransom money with any of the Irish nationalist groups. But the trade unions …'

'Quinn bought this?'

'I will telephone him tonight as soon as the opportunity arises. I hope that Hawthorne—and Yabsley—haven't convinced him of this farcical situation.' Defeated, he sat down next to me. 'I've read your report and your theory, Rebecca, and I agree with you. This,' he said flicking the papers in my hand, 'is total claptrap.'

'Do you think this is a diversion? To draw us away from Abbottsford Hall?'

'If that's the case, then the informer is here.'

'Wills, there has to be a spy within the DSO as well.'

He considered my assertion. 'Yes. But who? Every man in the DSO has been vetted and handpicked by Quinn personally. Even Hawthorne.'

'His pet,' I added with derision.

We sat for a moment in perplexed contemplation until Wills remembered the last report still in his clutches.

'This is also from Scott,' he said handing it to me. 'Untimely and unexpected deaths occurred in the vicinity of the Warburton and Richardson abductions, just as you suspected. The first was a woman who had been a chambermaid at the viscount's estates and had been sacked for theft. And the other a gardener of the Richardson household who had been badly beaten by Richardson himself after he had attempted to seduce Mrs Richardson.'

'Both with grievances against their respective families—'

'And both suffering an untimely death,' Wills concluded.

'And the first?'

'The only death remotely connected to twelve-year-old Lady Cecilia D'Arcy was that of a journeyman whose decomposing body was discovered two weeks after the abduction. He had carried out some work at Lord Meagher's estates a few days prior to the girl's disappearance.'

The dinner gong sounded.

Wills rose to his feet with a most dejected look and headed for the door. 'Get some sleep,' he advised. 'We're going to have a fight on our hands and not just from without.'

***

I climbed the stairs to my second-floor room reading and re-reading the reports Wills had given me. Little in them rang true. Once inside my room, I paced and attempted to make sense of every conflicting detail until my head was a jumble of misinformation and suppositions. I needed fresh air and I needed the contents of that hessian bag.

Grabbing it, a corkscrew and a glass from the table, I turned for the door then paused. I collected a second glass and departed.

Making my way through the green baize door and down the servants' stairs, I encountered no one, all being otherwise engaged with preparing or serving dinner.

Once outside, I returned to the old oak tree and the bench Henry and I had occupied earlier that day and made myself comfortable. The night was dark and the only light came from the Hall's many windows, but here beneath the oak's shadowy canopy, I was unseen. I uncorked the bottle and poured myself a generous measure, sipping it slowly and reflecting upon the day's events.

***

From the first night of Sir Giles Hawthorne's marriage twenty-something years ago—he didn't care to remember the exact date or to recall the event—his wife had insisted on his being home by half six every evening without fail, or woe betide him! She asserted that a family must partake of the evening meal together else it fall apart. The so-called 'family' comprised himself, his domineering wife and her even more domineering mother.

After their 'family' meal together, he was released from his bonded duties and free to do as he pleased, so that his wife could enjoy the rest of the evening in the company of her mother without the intrusive, boorish company of a male.

This pleased him immensely, as the endurance of dining in either icy silence or nonsensical gossip would be more than recompensed by an enjoyable evening of male companionship at his club.

This London night was foggy and chilly but that didn't prevent him escaping to his exclusive refuge—the Marlborough Club; at least here he was his own man.

He'd had a bastard of a day, getting nowhere in his hunt for the perpetrators of the abductions and murders. The interrogation of John McGregor had led absolutely nowhere despite the intensive questioning by Yabsley, Byrne and Dolby, and the last thing he wanted was to be harassed by a wife who was more interested in the balanced display of her best china than the stresses he was currently and barely enduring.

Settling into his favourite armchair with a cigar, a port and the Evening News, he felt respected and appreciated in this selective environment, where he was left to enjoy his free time in peace and quiet and as he pleased. He had barely read the weather forecast on the front page when a familiar voice broke into his much-needed solitude.

'Sir Giles, old boy,' exclaimed Neville Humphries cheerfully. 'I didn't expect to see you here tonight.'

Sir Giles looked up over his shoulder and was somewhat disconcerted to see Humphries.

'May I join you?'

'Actually …' Sir Giles hesitated. 'I was—'

'Thank you, old boy.' Humphries folded himself into the opposing armchair. 'I hear you've had a most successful day.'

'Oh?'

'Yes. The confession. And may I be the first to offer you my heartiest congratulations.'

'Confession?' He was unaware of any such development. He had left the Yard at the usual time and had received no news.

'Yes. McGregor's confession. The kidnap ring. You've broken it.'

Sir Giles released an exasperated sigh. 'Not quite, old boy. I don't know where you got your information but as of this afternoon, McGregor maintains his innocence and refuses to confess.'

'Oh. My mistake,' Humphries admitted, shrugging off his apparent faux pas.

Sir Giles peered at Humphries. 'How *did* you hear of it?'

'Of what, Sir Giles?'

'The confession, man.'

'Why, from Quinn himself, dear boy,' Humphries supplied. 'Rather, Quinn's wife told my wife who told me. Why do you ask?'

Sir Giles settled back into his chair, apparently satisfied with the answer. 'Hmm. Right.'

'I suppose you'll be needing all hands on deck, so to speak, to round up the rest of his trade union gang?' Humphries nonchalantly took out a cigarette and lit it with his newfangled lighter.

Sir Giles' expression tightened, his eyes narrowing as he tried to decipher what Humphries was suggesting.

'I mean to say, old boy, you must be stretched, what with one man dead, one man incapacitated and two on enforced leave. That would leave you with only, er … how many active in the field? You may need to call in reinforcements … or rescind the enforced leave.'

'Hmm …' was Sir Giles' exasperated, noncommittal reply as he resumed reading his newspaper.

Humphries paused, appearing to assess the situation then continued in a jocular manner. 'Perhaps I could ask my wife to speak to Quinn's wife about getting Quinn to rescind the enforced leave of those two … ?'

Sir Giles' scowl deepened.

'I'm joking, old man. You look as though you could use a little levity.'

'I don't know where you're getting your information, Humphries, but the situation is well in hand. You may tell that to your wife and she can pass it on to Mrs Quinn.'

***

The first glass of Old Highland had fulfilled its purpose commendably. I was in a calm and mellow mood, my mind almost freed of its previous encumbrances. A little more libation would see them gone altogether, so I poured myself another measure. There was a chill in the air but I felt a warmth radiating from inside. I leaned back against the bench and stretched my now-relaxed legs. A barn owl screeched in the distance and every now and then a whinny drifted across from the mews, but otherwise all was quiet. I felt at peace in the dark as I always had; the blackness of the night absorbing the blackness of my sins and absolving me.

The rustle of a skirt and the redolence of a floral perfume alerted me to an approaching presence. I turned to see Lady Katherine strolling in the garden, peering unseeingly ahead, deep in thought. Over her gown, she wore only a light shawl wrapped tight about her otherwise bare, graceful neck and shoulders; she must have felt the chill. I watched her as she came closer, oblivious to all around her. I marvelled at the exquisiteness of her features even in the sallowness of the artificial lights from the Hall.

Uncorking the bottle of whisky, I poured a measure into the spare tumbler. The clink of glass and the gurgle of the liquid startled the countess, eliciting a gasp. I held up the offering. 'A wee dram, Your Ladyship?'

Lady Katherine settled at the sound of the familiar voice and approached me. 'Miss Davies. I didn't expect anyone to be out.'

I proffered the glass once more. I suppose I ought to have stood in deference to her rank, but the whisky dulled my sense of obligation.

The countess took the glass and noticed the bottle on the bench. 'Old Highland Whisky. My favourite.' She indicated the bench. 'May I?'

I nodded, very pleased she had come along and wanted to join me.

She sat, rigid and formal, next to me, the square whisky bottle between us acting as chaperone. Raising her glass, she toasted, '*Slàinte.*'

'*Do dheagh shlàinte,*' I replied, clinking her glass.

'Your Gaelic is impressive.'

We sat back and peered out into the infinite darkness of the gardens, sipping the amber liquid and quietly retreating into our own thoughts. Out of the corner of my eye, I caught the furtive glances she sent my way. Something was on her mind.

After what seemed to be an eternity of silence, Lady Katherine enquired, 'Are you married, Miss Davies?' Then, realising what she had said, gave a stifled embarrassed laugh. 'Of course not, otherwise you'd be *Mrs* Davies, wouldn't you?' She took another sip of her drink. 'Have you ever been married?'

'No.'

'Why not?'

I languidly turned my head to her. 'I suspect for the same reason you're not,' I said, my voice low but with unmistakable intent.

She sat motionless, save for the rhythmic heaving of her chest, and stared into the depth of the night.

I studied her in silence. 'Were you flirting with me today?' I asked softly but with deliberate provocation.

Her look of mild horror and the colour that rose in her cheeks amused me—I had discovered her secret. But she didn't leave in a huff or chastise me for my impertinence. Rather, she looked at the glass in her hand and composed herself.

'Jessica, my maid, said that my aunt's maid, Emma, told her that you were a trivet.'

This revelation made me chortle out loud. 'A trivet? I've been called many things in my life but never that.'

Lady Katherine's face beamed with quiet delight. 'Of course, I knew what she meant …' she said, then added more seriously, 'Are you?'

I considered my reply carefully before answering. 'If I were, would that make a difference … to you?'

Lady Katherine stared into the shadowy expanse beyond the rose gardens but said nothing; what thoughts were turning in her mind?

'My lady,' I said facing her. 'I earnestly own that you are a most desirable woman. In another world, another time, I would have made my desires clear.'

Her eyes searched mine, silently begging *why*.

'I can offer nothing. And you have much to lose.'

Our universes had overlapped—briefly—but they were set on divergent paths.

I regretted my words the moment they left my lips and a sadness overcame me for I truly wanted to know this woman better. But many reasons not to take this path flashed through my mind: the duchess' warning, the wide social gap between us and, above all, my own reluctance to fall in love again.

'You are an extraordinary woman, Rebecca. I have never known anyone like you,' she said, her voice a mere whisper.

Her loneliness was tangible and her eyes spoke of need. I would have fulfilled that need, freely and unencumbered, but it would mean certain heartbreak for one of us and I was not prepared to suffer that anguish again.

Long moments passed until I put down my glass and stood. I offered her my hand. 'I think we should go inside, my lady.'

She placed her glass on the bench, took my hand and stood in front of me.

I marvelled at the softness of her hand and how cold it was.

'You're cold, my lady.'

She gazed at me—her eyes held the loneliness of solitude. 'For many years.'

I felt her breath on my face, the warm closeness of her body. She searched my eyes. 'I want you,' she uttered in a barely audible whisper.

This was not a command but a plea borne of isolation and desire. And I wanted her.

No matter how I had tried to deny my feelings, in that moment I realised I had fallen in love with her the instant I had seen her. I'd tried to fight the need—the same need I had felt for Sarah, which I had long since buried with my beloved. Now, it was resurrected against my will.

I searched Lady Katherine's eyes and saw nothing but desire, her mouth inviting me. The next moment came unbidden. Her soft lips met mine and I tasted a faint hint of whisky. The kiss was light and tender and yet conveyed undeniable yearning. She leaned into me, her hands hesitantly resting on my shoulders.

I was lost and helpless; my arms involuntarily wrapped around her and pulled her in close.

It felt so comfortable, so right, to have her in my arms. She gently pulled away and regarded me, surprisingly shy and demure. This was not a voracious New Woman for the new century, but an innocent girl who had found passion and desire and pleaded for more.

'Will you stay with me tonight?' she asked with a tremor of uncertainty.

I wanted to … my God, how I wanted to.

'I can't,' was my pathetic reply. 'Your aunt. If anything were to happen to her on my watch …'

She lingered for a moment before averting her gaze. Her hands slipped from my shoulders and trembled as she drew her shawl tightly around her.

'I understand,' she whispered. 'I'd best go inside. It's become much colder out here.'

I watched her retreat into the warmth of the Hall.

***

It was one in the morning and the Hall was devoid of any movement— by man, maid or mouse—as I stole my way down to Lady Katherine's bedroom, unseen and unheard. Even Wills on duty didn't hear me. I knew he would be working away in his rooms opposite the duchess' suite. His door was open and he would be able to see the duchess' door, but not the countess' further along the corridor.

Dressed in my regulation field blacks and black, rubber-soled shoes, I quietly slipped into the countess' darkened boudoir through her unlocked door and closed it just as silently behind me.

Shadows cast by the glowing embers in the fireplace filled the room and the warm air hinted at the fragrant scent of the woman sleeping peacefully in the large bed.

I gazed longingly at her delicate features and recalled the gentle touch of her lips and the warmth of her body.

I had gone to my room and tried to sleep, thoughts of my duty to the duchess combatting my desires for the countess.

My desires had finally won out.

Leaning over the sleeping woman, I touched her hair, brushing it away from her face. Her eyes fluttered open and, upon seeing me hovering over her, did not show any sign of alarm or displeasure. Instead, she raised her hand and caressed my face. 'Miss Davies …' she whispered.

I sat on the edge of her bed and drifted helplessly into her touch. Her desire overwhelmed me and I kissed her.

She replied with equal fervour. Somehow, the kiss conveyed our mutual craving, our longing for love and our consent to each other.

We were breathless when we broke away. I searched her eyes for any hesitation or regret; there was only hunger.

I kicked off my shoes, shucked my pullover and trousers and exposed not only my scarred body but the painful past it carried. Sarah's silver locket dangled from my neck, shining dimly in the half light.

Her hands began a journey of discovery, along my arms to my shoulders and down my chest, cupping each breast. She explored the most intimate parts of me with her hands and eyes. A faint gasp escaped her when her fingers encountered the long raised scar that crossed my belly; one of many scars that marred my skin. At that moment, I felt accepted, not in spite of the scars but because of them.

Without a word spoken between us, she lifted aside her coverlet in invitation. I gratefully cupped her face and kissed her. The neck of her nightdress was drawn closed by a ribbon. I slowly undid it and revealed those glorious shoulders I had admired earlier. I was wonderstruck by this woman—and that she wanted me.

I kissed her neck, her shoulders, each glance of my lips on her skin eliciting a delectable gasp, affirming our connection. With great care, I drew down her nightdress to reveal her breasts and then lowered it past her hips and to the end of the bed.

She was magnificent. Her pale skin was as silken as the petals of the roses she so admired. She watched me intently as my rough hands explored her every curve, crest and valley. I kissed each breast with equal fervour, caressing each nipple with my tongue. My hand moved down, pausing on the velvet warmth between her legs. She surrendered, eliciting an involuntary spasm. Her body arched and her eyes flickered closed.

Without warning, she pulled me in and crushed her lips to mine with unbridled urgency. Her tongue invaded my mouth and I responded. My thumb found her clitoris and the touch extorted another gasp from her; the wetness beyond told me she was ready. My first exploratory incursion caused Katherine to expel a cry of surprise and to grip my arm tightly. It almost seemed like this was an entirely new sensation for her …

I sought her consent before proceeding, and she released her grip on my arm. I kissed her again—controlled desire roaring through me. I pressed further and further inside her, increasing the depth and intensity of my ministrations. As my rhythm increased, her grip on my arm tightened again. She squeezed her eyes shut and threw her head back, her breathing erratic, each exhalation accompanied by a muted moan.

It didn't take long for my efforts to bring her to the edge. Her body stiffened and her breathing stopped. I felt her muscles clamp around my fingers like a velvet trap. I stopped so she could ride the crest of pleasure, her body surging in slow rolling waves before ebbing and fading. With a long expulsion of air, she groaned and her body relaxed.

She was covered in a fine sheen of perspiration and her face and neck bloomed with a rosy flush. I withdrew with care and gazed at her; she was beautiful. When she opened her eyes, they told me everything I needed to know. This encounter was something that I cannot express in words even now. It was a spiritual union, the culmination of intimacy, of trust … of love.

I drew the coverlet over us and wrapped my arms around her, pressing my naked body against hers, her soft breasts against mine. Once again, we kissed and, once again, we made love.

<h1 style="text-align:center">31</h1>

<h2 style="text-align:center">Thursday, 7th September, 1905</h2>

Abbottsford Hall, Suffolk, England

At quarter of seven, I was up and ready for duty after having left Katherine asleep only a few hours before and returning to my own room to prepare for the new day. I was tired, yet uplifted and looking forward to the morning ride.

Turning into the corridor, I encountered Wills near the duchess' rooms. He appeared agitated and summoned me close. Had I been caught out with the countess? His next words belied that possibility.

'I had a long telephone conversation with Alexander Quinn last night while the duchess was at dinner.'

'And?'

'Yabsley and Byrne have arrested the leader of the Amalgamated Plasterers and Renderers Union of Greater London, a John McGregor, for the abductions and murders,' he said with an expression of controlled fury.

'What! Why? On what evidence?'

'Written plans for another abduction and bank notes from the Richardson ransom were found in his house.'

'How? How did they know to go there?'

'Hawthorne got a tip-off … from that Colonel Humphries.'

Wills registered my look of astonishment and disbelief.

'Yes, stroke of luck, eh?'

I was completely flummoxed. 'And Croft and Hogan? Is there a connection?'

'McGregor didn't mention them in his confession.'

'He's confessed? McGregor confessed?' My incredulity multiplied exponentially.

'Yes. And strange he should not mention his henchmen—those who carried out the murders, don't you think?'

'Because only you, Scott and I know of their existence.'

'Mm-hm,' Wills concurred. 'The poor bastard will hang alone.'

'You don't believe his confession, do you?'

'It's all too pat,' he said with disdain. 'None of this makes any sense. Why would anyone keep such incriminating evidence lying about in a drawer? Where's the rest of the money? Quinn told me that Byrne delivered him the signed confession a few minutes before my telephone call. And that it had been read and initialled by Hawthorne. I telephoned him at nine.'

I laughed derisively. 'Hawthorne never stays later than six! His wife won't let him.'

'Exactly.'

It took a few more moments of mental gymnastics before I realised the ploy. 'It's a forgery, obviously. Someone wants us gone from here.'

'Precisely. And it has achieved its goal.' Wills' anger returned. 'Quinn has ordered us to return immediately to take charge of the investigation and to round up all the trade unionists involved.'

'Surely not! That's madness. Can't he see this for what it is? And if the Duchess of Bramwell is taken? What then? Notwithstanding what they'll do to her—God forbid—we will have lost the only opportunity to capture these bastard villains. What did you tell Quinn?'

'I argued that the information young Timmy Saddler gave us is proving correct and that it corresponds with what we've uncovered so far. I pointed out that the three previous abductions aligned with the coincidental deaths of dismissed servants and that it was very possible that one Stewart Graves here is the link to the planned abduction of the Duchess of Bramwell.'

'And?'

'He was sympathetic to our assertions but he said they were just that—assertions. He said he had a signed confession in his hand and that he needed every available man to investigate the trade unionists. He reiterated that we are to leave immediately.'

I stood before Wills in dumbfounded disbelief. Our departure would mean the certain death of the duchess.

Wills, too, was as concerned as I and knew what I was thinking. 'I spoke to the duke after the duchess retired and explained the developments—'

'We must move the duchess to a safe place,' I said, voicing the only option left to us.

'Yes. And there's the difficulty.'

'She believes all this to be piffle—'

'And she has her fifteen weekend guests arriving tomorrow, Friday.'

'It appears that we must abduct the duchess ourselves for her own safety,' I said, half-jokingly.

Wills gave me a sheepish grin. 'I thought of that. But the duke was not impressed. The best he could offer, without upsetting the duchess and her plans, was to employ a number of private detectives to keep watch over her at all times.'

'They won't get here before we have to leave.'

Wills took in a deep breath, demonstrating both his exasperation and weariness; he had been up all night and needed recuperative sleep. 'Rebecca,' he said, expelling his breath and rubbing his eyes. 'The train to London leaves the village at three. Go ahead with whatever the duchess has planned for the day then pack up ready to go while Her Grace is at lunch. And then pray to the merciful God that nothing happens to her before the detectives arrive. Not a word to Her Grace, though. We'll leave it to the duke to explain.'

He turned to go but paused to inspect me. 'You look tired. Didn't you sleep well?'

The door to the duchess' rooms opened and Mary, the Duchess of Bramwell, elegantly outfitted in her riding costume, strode out with the ever-attentive Emma following closely behind.

'Major Williams,' the duchess cheerily acknowledged, 'good morning to you. And to you, Davies.'

''Morning, Your Grace,' we both returned with a slight nod.

Lady Katherine emerged at the same obviously predetermined time and was greeted warmly by her aunt.

'Sweetling, good morning. Sleep well?'

'Exceptionally well, Aunt,' Lady Katherine replied and nodded to Wills and me. 'Good morning,' she greeted, slipping on her gloves. Although she acknowledged both me and Wills, there was something in the greeting she sent my way that prickled her aunt's suspicions. The duchess regarded both her niece and me with silent accusation.

I did not react yet I did notice the change in Lady Katherine and I wondered if it was evident to all present. She appeared more wistful and serene; her cheeks flushed with a rosiness that contrasted her pallid complexion. Did the duchess miss this subtle transformation? Her piercing gaze suggested not.

'Well, enjoy your ride, ladies. Davies,' Wills, in his innocence, interrupted our silent war.

'Thank you, Major Williams. Come along, Katherine, we have much to discuss.'

I followed the two peeresses with a growing unease. The duchess' obstinacy was going to be the death of her. It was now up to the duke to keep her safe between the time we left and when outside assistance could arrive to take our place.

My other regret was that I would not see the countess again after we returned from our ride, nor could I tell her of my imminent departure for fear of alerting Stewart Graves. Our paths would never cross again and I felt a stab of loss.

I shook myself free of it. We belonged to entirely different worlds and her reputation was paramount. I would never fit into her world— nor be accepted by those who inhabited it.

***

It was not quite a slum but far from the prestige of Mayfair. The building did, however, boast one luxury: a telephone set in the parlour. It was here that the retired Colonel Neville Humphries had made his home … and headquarters.

I learned from others that his neighbours found him pleasant enough but rather secretive. He never had any visitors, possibly due to his being away most of the time. They knew him to be a member of the most exclusive—and expensive—Marlborough Club and couldn't fathom why he couldn't, therefore, afford more luxurious accommodation and in a better part of town. The building wasn't dirty or rundown, just small and economical.

What they also didn't know—as did no one in his circle—was that he was newly estranged from his indulgent wife. She could no longer cope with her husband's mood swings and irrational rages. Better for all concerned, she had said, that he finds himself accommodation elsewhere until he had sorted out his problem.

That morning, Humphries had consumed his breakfast of a cup of tea and buttered bread and now stood before the telephone set in the tiny parlour on the ground floor of the building. Most of the other residents were either breakfasting or had already gone off to work so he was sure he would have a few moments to himself.

'Seven one five, London Wall, please,' he said, speaking quietly into the telephone mouthpiece.

A few edgy moments passed before his face became animated once more. 'Gregory. Where were you last night? You must stay close … Never mind that. Listen. Everything is set. The cargo will be ready for collection at four, just before tea. Have the chaps ready to move at half past three. The train leaves for London at three. Have you got that? Not before half three. And, Gregory, I want you there to supervise. I don't want a replay of that fiasco.'

He replaced the receiver and no doubt believed his scheme was airtight.

***

Just like the previous day, our three mounts were waiting for us, saddled up and animated in anticipation of their early morning run. The duchess and countess were assisted onto their side saddles by Pitman and Reynolds, while, a short distance away, I easily climbed on board and sat comfortably astride Peleus' stablemate, Tommy.

Henry ran out from the stables. 'Miss Davies! Miss Davies!'

Tommy snorted and stamped in agitation at the boy's alarm.

'Henry, what is it?' I quietly asked, trying to calm both him and Tommy.

'Me and Dad went into the village yesterday and, guess what?' he said, looking up at me wide-eyed. 'Stewart Graves has got himself a new horse!'

'Well, let's hope he treats this one better than the last,' I said.

'And he's been telling everyone that he's going to leave the village. That he's got lots of money coming to him.'

'Wouldn't that be the money that the duchess owes him for the provisions he's supplied?'

'Yes but no. Dad says that he owes everyone. Lots of money. And that he gambles. Lots.'

'Hmm,' I mused, trying not to sound too interested. 'Is that so? Did he say when he was going to leave, exactly?'

'Maybe today. That's why he's got a new horse. But his wagon wasn't loaded yet.'

That information further increased my disquietude over Wills' and my impending departure.

I offered Henry a grateful nod. 'Thank you.' As an afterthought, I added, 'Henry, you'll look after the duchess, won't you? Make sure Her Grace is not troubled by the likes of this *Stupid* Graves?'

He laughed. '*Stupid* Graves! Right, Miss.'

'You've been an excellent information gatherer, Henry. Thank you.'

'Does that mean I'd make a good *secretary* just like you?' he asked impudently.

'Yes, Henry. Just like me, perhaps even better.'

It was now imperative—critical, in fact—that neither Wills nor I leave before the private detectives arrived. Every instinct urged me to speak to Wills at once yet I could not abandon the peeresses to ride without me. It would have to wait. There would be time when we returned, I allowed, to set all to right with Wills.

Something was shifting and I hoped it would wait until my return.

***

That morning, Sir Giles Hawthorne ambled to his third-floor office with a heaviness that had little to do with age. The prospect of recommencing the interrogation of the trade union leader, John McGregor, wearied him more that he cared to admit. He had an irritating feeling that they had the wrong man, but he couldn't let his subordinates know of his doubt.

He also felt a little rattled by Neville Humphries' pre-emptive congratulations over obtaining a confession from the fellow. He wasn't about to act on second-hand information—he was determined to interview the suspect personally and read the confession before approaching Quinn.

It was also of great concern to him that wives were privy to secret information and bandied it about like so much gossip over afternoon tea. Another thought then struck him as odd: wasn't Colonel Humphries estranged from his wife? Something about his uncontrollable rages? Certainly, during his time in the army with Humphries, the colonel was prone to overwhelming anger and furies, but those were battle responses and he had calmed down appreciably since he'd retired from the service. Hawthorne conceded that he was certainly now a new man in full control of his temper, so much so that he was considered by some to be flippant. Or perhaps the mask fitted better now.

All these thoughts were pushed to the back of his consciousness when he entered the office of his DSO team and found it empty except for the incapacitated Scott, seated at his desk, poring over reports.

'Where is everyone?' Hawthorne barked, startling Scott.

'Sir Giles! Er … They're searching the premises of John McGregor's associates … as you ordered last night.'

'What? Last night?' Hawthorne's brow creased with confusion; he hadn't ordered any such search. 'What in Hades is going on?'

Scott was clearly thrown by the question; he was only following orders—*Hawthorne's* orders. 'Sir? As I understand it, after you left, Yabsley and Byrne interrogated McGregor once more. Yabsley returned about an hour later and said there was no more information to be had and we packed up and went home. When we came in this morning, Yabsley had a note from you instructing us to continue the raids.'

Hawthorne stared at the young man, completely bewildered. Was he going mad? He could not remember doing such a thing. Taking control of his anger, he took a new tack. 'I understand McGregor confessed.'

'I am not aware of any confession, Sir,' Scott replied.

'You are here day and night and you don't know what's going on?'

'Sir …'

'Come with me. I want to speak with this John McGregor myself.'

'But, Sir—' Scott's entreaty fell on unavailable ears as they and Hawthorne had already left the room. He struggled to his feet, propped the crutches under his arms and hobbled along trying to catch up to his superior.

Hawthorne reached the underground cells in good time—perhaps a little puffed—but in good time. Waiting for the police guard to come along and unlock the outer door didn't assuage his anger—but it did give Scott time to catch up.

The police guard finally showed up and unlocked the door. 'Good morning, Sir Giles. Apologies for the wait.'

'Yes, yes. Where's McGregor? I want to speak to him. Now.'

'Follow me, Sir, I'll bring him to you in the interview room.' The guard led Hawthorne and Scott into a bare-walled room that offered a table and several chairs. Hawthorne and Scott accommodated themselves and, moments later, two brawny constables bundled in a large, dishevelled, unshaven man of about forty years, a pair of manacles attached to his wrists, and pushed him into a chair opposite them. They clamped the restraints to each side of the chair. McGregor, his face red with rage, surged to his feet, his whole frame taut. The manacles bit into his wrists and immediately the constables shoved him back onto the chair.

They hovered close, ready to pounce on any further sign of defiance.

Hawthorne could see the loathing in the man's eyes.

This was John McGregor, a fierce Scot, who was enraged by being accused of such crimes and even more furious that he was not allowed to speak to his family or solicitor. He had vehemently protested his innocence and had demanded to be released but had been denied at every turn. For the DSO, this was a matter of national security and they had powers to keep any suspect for as long as was deemed necessary.

Locked away overnight on spurious charges, interrogated late into the night and deprived of sleep, his temper had finally snapped.

'Whit's the meanin' o' this!' McGregor roared. 'I demand ye release me at once! And who the bloody hell are ye two?'

'Calm down, Mr McGregor—' Scott said politely.

'I am calm!' McGregor stormed. 'Ye dinnae want tae see me riled, laddie!'

Hawthorne took over. 'Pipe down, McGregor!' he shouted, his face flushed, 'A little restraint, if you please—or these constables will be forced to gag you!'

McGregor held still but every muscle seethed with anger.

'Right,' continued Hawthorne, tugging at his collar to release the heat from his body, 'I am Sir Giles Hawthorne, the Chief Administrator of the Special Branch DSO and I want to talk to you about your confession.'

'I've done nowt tae confess! I've been cooked up! I want ma solicitor!'

'Soon, Mr McGregor. As soon as you tell me about the confession you've already given.'

'Yer talkin' oot yer arse, man! Ah've no' given nae bloody confession! Yer lot are barkin' up the wrang tree! An' ye'd best let me oot o' here sharpish—or I'll tear this whole bloody place tae bits!'

Hawthorne glanced at Scott, puzzled. 'No confession?'

***

Hawthorne and Scott left the two constables to deal with the implacable John McGregor and made their way back up to the general office. Sir Giles didn't say a word—he was mentally regurgitating all the contradictory information he'd received that morning. Something was very wrong.

They reached the door to Scott's room and Scott limped in while Hawthorne absentmindedly carried on.

Scott realised that Sir Giles had not followed him. He turned and hesitantly called after him, 'Sir Giles … Sir … ?'

Hawthorne's brain was awash with unrelenting questions: What was he to do with McGregor's information? Were his dogs barking up the wrong tree? Why would his friend Neville Humphries give him misleading material? Perhaps Humphries was being misled by his Irish manservant. Or was he, himself, the dupe? Should he call off the raids? But he had no other leads. Was he inept? It was not his fault! Everything was of someone else's doing. Should he go to Alexander Quinn and admit he was lost? Would Quinn bring back Major Williams and that detestable man-woman affront to humankind? The last was not an option he entertained—he would not allow it.

He had done everything within his power: Viscount Bonningwick's daughter, Felicity, would shortly be whisked out of the country and all his available men were now bringing in and interrogating the trade unionists associated with John McGregor. That should sort it out.

For now, he determined, it was best that he did nothing but wait.

***

The three of us rode the same route we had the day before and in the same manner: a frantic gallop to the riverbank then a walk along the road connecting the fishermen's cottages and finally a canter back to the mews, skirting the woods. We also held the same formation: the duchess and the countess rode abreast in front and I took up the rear.

Every now and then Lady Katherine would glance back at me with a tenderness that opened the door to a life of promise—and yet I knew it was a life we would never live.

During the more sedate part of our ride, the two ladies chatted between themselves, excluding me from all conversation. This suited me, as I did not want to unwittingly give my feelings away. I already felt dispossessed of Lady Katherine's love, but that was the condition I had accepted when I allowed myself to be consumed by my desire for her. More than this, I was fearful for the duchess if the duke did not convince her that she was, indeed, in a dire situation and that they take appropriate precautions immediately.

With my departure so close and with increasing foreboding, my senses were primed—every rustle in the undergrowth, every unfamiliar sound had me tense up in my saddle. The darting of a squirrel, the flight of a crow, the flash of a deer's flank all felt like omens. An attempt could be made at any moment, and I had to keep alert—and silent.

When we returned to the Hall, I would insist that Wills and I remain until the private detectives arrived. No compromise. The duchess' life depended on it.

***

It was now one o'clock—scarcely twelve hours since our clandestine encounter—and Lady Katherine had joined her aunt and uncle for luncheon, accompanied by her business secretary, George McPherson.

Satisfied the duchess was safe in the presence of her trusted servants, I ascended the staircase to Wills' suite.

'Wills,' I said intruding, 'I have grave concerns.'

Wills had had scant sleep and his disposition bore its mark: he was haggard and irritable. His valise lay open on the bed.

'Are you packed?' His question was unusually impatient.

'We can't leave. Something is amiss here. This entire situation doesn't sit right. We must stay.'

'That may be, but what if you're mistaken and Quinn is not? What then? Will you gamble a young woman's life on intuition? You're not infallible, Rebecca.' That last remark stung but I knew it was exhaustion speaking.

'Wills, there are the others in place should that situation arise. We must remain here.'

'We have our orders, Rebecca.'

'*You* have *your* orders.'

Wills paused; weariness etched in every line of his otherwise handsome face.

'Don't do this, Rebecca. Bramwell has assured me that the duchess will be kept safe until the detectives arrive. They are en route by motor car and expected by nightfall. Now go and pack and stop wasting time.'

'No. I will stay here until they do arrive.'

Wills was not a man to give himself over to petulance, but my obstinacy, coupled with his fatigue, drove him over the edge.

'For God's sake, Davies,' he exploded, 'just do as you're told for once! The duchess is safe! She is not the target! Know your place and follow orders!'

His outburst caught me by surprise; he had never spoken to me in that tone before. I took a moment to collect my thoughts. Perhaps he was right. Perhaps I was overreaching my station.

His shoulders sagged. He tossed his shaving kit into the bag and sank into the nearest chair.

'Rebecca,' he said, his voice repentant, 'just do as you're told and pack. The train leaves at three. And we'll be on it. We've done all we can here.'

The weariness in every word was absolute. Wills had spoken with finality—and he was right, the duchess was safe if she remained within the Hall. Yet something inside, stubborn and unresolved, still nagged at me.

With an uneasiness that refused to be quieted, I left Will to his task and I returned to begin mine. The corridor to the stairs stretched long and abandoned. I lingered at Lady Katherine's door and my memories of the night before washed over me. Her scent filled my senses and I tasted her lips once more.

No! I rebuked myself, shaking free of my indulgent reverie—this was nothing more than a fleeting entanglement, a mere dalliance, an indulgence like all the others: desired, savoured, then to be cast aside like a spent match.

With cold resolve, I ascended the staircase to my room and began packing, determined to follow orders.

***

My Gladstone lay open on a chair. I checked that my kit was all present and correct. The valise with my personal items was packed and closed and awaiting me at the door. My Webley, as always, was strapped to my chest, cleaned, loaded and ready for use. Its weight was a constant reassurance.

With my two bags in hand, I trudged down the stairs back to Wills' rooms—I hoped he had found some measure of calm during my absence. It was difficult to see him so out of control of his emotions.

'Rebecca,' Wills' now-steady voice echoed along the empty corridor. 'Ready?'

'All packed,' I replied meeting him at his door.

'I've had another word to the duke and he has reassured me he will keep the duchess indoors and watched by Thomson and Mrs Plummer at all times until the detectives arrive.' He consulted his watch. 'Have you had something to eat?'

I nodded.

'Look …' he began with a tinge of regret in his voice, 'about before—'

'Forget it, Wills. I understand.'

'Good. A Surrey cart and driver are ready to take us to the village railway station.'

That was it—no farewells, no whispered promises, no secret rendezvous. I buried the ache of it, but I knew it was for the best.

Slouched back into my seat next to Wills aboard the cart, I peered into the distant countryside as it trundled along the road that skirted the woods. Reynolds, our driver, was taking the same road we had ridden back to the Hall that morning.

'Not still thinking of quitting, are you?' Wills asked. He must have seen something was gnawing at me.

'No,' I answered without thinking, then immediately recanted. 'Yes.'

'The duchess will be protected,' he assured me. Of course, he assumed that she was the cause of my detachment. 'Once we're back at the Yard, I will convince Quinn that Hawthorne was mistaken and that we are on the right track. Scott will be there to back us up. We'll catch those bastards, Rebecca.'

32

Thursday afternoon, 7th September, 1905

Abbottsford Village, Suffolk, England

The railway station at the village was a simple raised concreted platform with several wooden benches along its short length. A small, neat and clean wooden structure provided the services of a ticket office, goods shed, waiting room, cloakroom and telegraph office all in one. A single pair of steel tracks touched the periphery of the village of Abbottsford, which was one of quite a number this line serviced. The train would arrive from London in the morning and, having reached its destination fifty miles along, return to London passing through the village in the afternoon. It reminded me of the train I took from Wangaratta so many lifetimes ago.

Reynolds, our driver, assisted us with our luggage then departed for Abbottsford Hall leaving Wills and me waiting for the train alone on the platform. I could see someone in the telegraph office whom I assumed to be the station master. Other than him, there was no one around.

Wills and I took our places on one of the wooden benches and waited for the train. Outwardly, we sat in our usual silence but inwardly my mind refused to be calmed. The train was due at three and we anticipated a wait of only five or so minutes, yet each second seemed to stretch for minutes.

Wills sat taut, glancing from his pocket watch to the track and back again more often than necessary.

It was obvious that the duchess caused his uneasiness as she had mine. Was she safe? Had we done enough? Could the duke protect her if they chose to strike now?

I told myself she was safe. I repeated it like a mantra. But they were just words and they meant nothing.

***

It was ten minutes after three and the train was quite obviously late when the station master emerged from the telegraph office and approached us.

'Sir, Madam,' he began reluctantly, 'I've just received a telegraph message from two stations up the line. The train's been delayed due to an obstruction on the track. Workers are clearing the debris as we speak. It should not be too long in coming.'

'How long?' Wills asked; he was anxious to get back to Scotland Yard as soon as possible to speak to Alexander Quinn.

'Perhaps an hour, Sir. I do apologise for the inconvenience.'

Wills looked at his pocket watch. 'Thank you,' he said then turned to me. 'We may still be in London before dark.'

Across the tracks, along the village high street, a familiar wagon and its driver emerged. It was Stewart Graves and he had, indeed, acquired a new horse. The wagon was empty save for a weathered tarpaulin opened out across the tray and draped over its low sides.

'That's Stewart Graves,' I said to Wills, alarmed by his appearance. We both watched intently as the wagon rattled on, not towards Abbottsford Hall as I would have feared, but away from the railway crossing. 'I wonder where he's going?'

Wills didn't answer but we were both relieved that it was heading away and watched the wagon until it disappeared around the curve of the street.

'The duke assured me that his wife would be well protected,' Wills replied with evident unease.

I nodded, though the reassurance did not sit well. What if we had misjudged everything?

'She will be safe,' he reiterated, softly this time, perhaps trying to convince himself.

***

Time felt lethargic. Nothing was stirring; the station master was in his little room reading a newspaper; Wills, seated on the bench, was severely fatigued by this sudden change of plans. His posture slackened and there was a vacant stillness about him.

I paced the length of the platform so many times that I knew exactly how many paces there were from one crack in the concrete to the next.

The monotony of the wait was broken when a small pony trap pulled onto the platform. The driver got out and went to the station master's office. I presumed it was the village post master expecting to collect the Royal Mail from the now-delayed train.

A glance at my wrist watch confirmed it was now twenty-six minutes past four. I looked up and, in the distance, billowing through the canopy of trees, I could see the telltale pall of grey smoke and steam of our approaching train.

From the other direction, on the road from Abbottsford Hall, a frantic scream pierced the air. 'Miss Davies! Miss Davies!'

The desperate cries startled us. Bearing down on us at alarming speed was Henry on Peleus. The mighty thoroughbred jumped onto the platform. Henry, wide-eyed and wild with panic, pulled the horse up with all the might his small frame could summon. The horse skidded to a stop, the friction from its shoes sending sparks into the air.

Wills and I grabbed the horse's reins; Peleus was skittish and trembling with excitement. We pulled his head down and managed to calm him.

'Miss Davies! Miss Davies!' Henry cried. 'They've taken her!' Tears streamed down his face.

'What!'

'When, boy? Who took her?' Wills demanded.

Poor Henry was so breathless from the flight, he couldn't utter a word.

'Boy—!'

'Henry, breathe, breathe,' I urged more calmly. 'Listen to me. Who took her? When?'

'Dunno,' Henry sobbed, his breath catching with every intake of air. 'Dunno. She was in the garden ... went for a walk in the garden and never came back ... There was blood ...'

'Goddammit!' Wills cursed. 'He was supposed to keep her inside! Bloody hell!!'

My mind tumbled, processing the events of the last few days …

'Wills,' I said, trying to control my panic. 'I know where they've taken her. The cottage.'

I ran to the bench and picked up my Gladstone.

'The fisherman's cottage?'

'Yes,' I replied as I lifted the distressed Henry off the saddle and onto the ground. 'The poachers. Must have been Croft and Hogan scouting the place.' I turned back to the boy. 'It will be all right, Henry. We'll find the duchess and we'll get her back safe and sound.'

'Not the duchess!' he cried. 'Lady Katherine. They took Lady Katherine!'

The words struck me like a physical blow; I staggered under the force of them, my breath strangled by the tightness in my chest. A flood of images surged through my mind—Katherine alone and terrified, at their mercy. I felt her fear as though it were my own and it suffocated me. I knew what they would do to her. Then she would die.

I jumped onto Peleus, laid the bag across my lap and grabbed hold of the reins. I swung Peleus around and kicked him hard into a full gallop. He flew.

I looked back only once before I rounded a bend to see Wills and Henry clambering into the postmaster's pony trap.

They would follow.

***

A few hours before …

Stewart Graves had had enough of playing the part of a respectable and diligent tradesman. He had done his best and given his all but everyone was against him and gave him nothing in return.

In the five years since he had come to the village, he'd watched his thriving, newly acquired grocery store fail and, with it, his eighteen-year marriage. His wife had walked out on him. *A blessing*, he thought, *one less to feed and clothe*.

He owed money to nearly everyone in the village and beyond, and his luck at cards only pushed him further into debt.

When the opportunity came to assist a couple of transients who needed local knowledge, he grabbed it. They were willing to pay and he liked to think he drove a hard bargain—they had accepted his terms with very little haggling.

He didn't know why they'd wanted the information, but what he didn't know wouldn't hurt him. These funds would be the means to escape this village, his woes … and his debts.

Step-by-step, the two townies revealed their requirements. With each step his concern escalated, but, rather than decline to help them further, he demanded—and, to his surprise, received—the promise of higher recompense. They assured him they would deliver payment as soon as he delivered the 'goods'.

When he finally realised that these 'goods' were to be the Duchess of Bramwell, he dismissed any thought of compassion. It was she, after all, who had accused him of short supply of goods and then withheld payment until he had made up the shortfall. And if that were not bad enough, she'd told him she would pull all the estate's business from him and give it to the new village grocer.

It could have been an easy fix if only that confounded Mrs Plummer had not delved into her records and found a few more anomalies. Trust between parties was paramount. And the duchess hadn't trusted him. *She* had caused his business to fail.

While it was of considerable concern to Graves that abduction was a capital offence, these two fellows had not only assured him that he would not be implicated, but he would have plenty of money and be long gone before anyone knew what had transpired. Besides, they said the old lady would come to no harm.

These were the thoughts and justifications that ran through Graves' mind as he drove his horse and wagon out of the village at three o'clock that afternoon as instructed, and headed for Abbottsford Hall via a circuitous route. He had draped the wagon's tray with a tarpaulin and lying beneath it was one of the two men who had contracted him— one Harry Hogan.

It wasn't long before he reached the fork in the road that led to the riverside. He carried on towards the Hall.

The wagon rolled down the road and through the impressive gates of the estate and along the lengthy drive to the mansion. The few gardeners scattered about the grounds paid him little heed and, at the mews, the stable hands were too occupied by their duties to notice him as he carefully manoeuvred the wagon to the servants' and service entrance at the back of the Hall. Even there, there was little activity; Graves presumed the servants were at afternoon tea.

He pulled the horse up near a wall that was devoid of windows and got down from his bench. He crunched his way on the gravel to the back of the wagon and discreetly lifted the tail end of the tarpaulin to see Hogan looking up at him.

A voice startled him. 'Mr Graves!' Florence said. 'I thought you'd delivered everything we ordered for the weekend.' She had emerged from the back door with a basketful of bed linen and was heading for the wash house.

'I want to see Her Grace,' Graves demanded curtly, lowering the flap of the tarp.

'Well, come inside, then, have a cuppa,' Florence said, making for the door again.

'No, out here. Tell her to come out here.'

Florence stopped and peered at him, clearly taken aback by his impertinence. 'Her Grace ain't at your beck and call, Mr Graves. Besides, she's otherwise engaged. I'll get Mrs Plummer.'

'No. I want to see the duchess,' Graves insisted, becoming more agitated.

'Tell me for why and I'll take her the message, Mr Graves,' she insisted.

Graves became visibly flustered. He needed the money and he needed the duchess outside. 'Look, you pumped-up little slattern. Tell her to come out—'

A cultured voice interrupted the escalating discussion. 'Mr Graves, is it?' Lady Katherine's enquiry came from behind Graves, startling him. 'Thank you, Florence, I'll see what Mr Graves wants.'

Florence curtsied. 'He wants a good thumping, my lady, if you ask me.'

Before he could spit out a reply, she escaped towards the laundry.

Lady Katherine approached the wagon and faced Graves. 'Now, Mr Graves, what is it that you need from the duchess?'

Graves was aware that this was a lady of some standing but didn't know what her relationship was with the duchess. 'And who are you?' he enquired rather coarsely.

She raised an eyebrow. 'Lady Katherine Delaney, the duchess' niece,' she replied icily.

Graves' expression changed almost indiscernibly—irritation gave way to opportunity. He stepped away from the back of the wagon and circled around Lady Katherine. 'The duchess' niece, eh?' he echoed, stepping in closer to her.

She stepped back.

He closed in. 'She'd be quite fond of you, right?'

She edged back again, moving closer to the back of the wagon. 'Mr Graves!' Lady Katherine protested. 'You forget yourself.'

'Perhaps, my lady. So long as she don't forget you.'

Her face flushed with indignation. 'Explain yourself, man,' she demanded.

Graves looked around. No one in sight. No one to raise the alarm.

'Now's a good time,' Graves said coolly.

'Good t—' she started saying.

The tarpaulin flew up.

Without warning, Hogan grabbed Lady Katherine from behind, his coarse hand clamped over her mouth before her involuntary yelp could escape. His other arm clenched around her waist. He dragged her backwards to the cart.

She thrashed with her arms and kicked out in desperate resistance.

Graves was useless in his feeble attempt to assist Hogan.

Hogan roughly twisted her around to face him. She struck him repeatedly with both fists—wild blows born of terror. The suddenness of the assault and sheer disbelief rendered her voiceless and unable to call for help.

Graves lunged and grabbed her waist.

Hogan leaned back and slammed his fist into her face.

She reeled, dazed, and fell against Graves. Blood spilled from the cut to her brow, streaming down her cheek and onto her delicate pastel-pink linen shirtwaist. Yet she did not yield. Through the fog of pain and confusion, she renewed her desperate struggle.

Hogan grappled her arms again. She twisted her arms and pulled away. Part of her bloodied sleeve ripped away in his grip. He discarded the scrap and struck her another savage blow.

Her legs buckled. She lost consciousness.

Before she could collapse to the ground, Hogan and Graves picked her up and threw her into the back of the wagon. Hogan quickly slid in under the tarpaulin with her. Graves covered them and jumped onto the driver's seat.

Every instinct urged Graves to flee at speed, but caution prevailed. He cracked the reins and urged the horse into a hurried walk.

They slipped away unseen, unheard and unnoticed.

The only evidence of the violent episode was the remnant of bloodied sleeve lying discarded in the gravel.

The wagon turned up the driveway and vanished through the gates.

From his perch upon the driver's seat, Graves felt a measure of recompense. He imagined the old duchess sitting at her escritoire, writing letters in her insufferably haughty tone. Perhaps she may have seen him drive away and idly wondered what business had brought him back—after all, she had settled the accounts and sorted the kerfuffle over his old nag. Perhaps she thought he had forgotten some trifling matter. She would have dismissed these thoughts— just as she had dismissed him—and would have returned to her correspondence—blissfully unaware of the humiliation she was about to suffer. Humiliation she had put him through, testing his honesty, undermining his integrity and destroying his livelihood.

Well, the scales were now even. The estate that had ruined him would now pay dearly—and he would be long gone before the reckoning came.

Graves allowed himself a sense of triumph.

He urged the horse towards the riverside but veered it onto the woodland road that cut through the dense forest. Under the tarpaulin, Lady Katherine lay insensible, the wound to her brow still weeping blood. Her carefully coiffed hair was now tangled in disarray and her fine clothing was torn and untidy, soiled by the grime of the tray's floor and her own blood.

It was not long before the dense forest and twilight shadows swallowed up the wagon and its occupants.

***

Jessica Turner, Lady Katherine's attentive maid, had prepared her mistress' tea gown for afternoon tea with the duchess and George McPherson, but her mistress was unusually late. This was most unlike the very punctual countess.

She went to the duchess' suite and knocked.

Emma opened the door.

'Emma, is Lady Katherine here?' she asked with quiet concern.

'No, Jessie. Have you asked Mr Thomson?'

'Who is that, Emma?' the duchess called from within her room.

'Turner, Your Grace, enquiring after Lady Katherine,' Emma replied.

The duchess came to the door. 'My niece may be with the duke. Have you enquired there?'

'No, Your Grace, I'll do that now. Thank ye.' Jessica curtsied, and rushed to the duke's study. Her countess *always* told her what she'd be doing and where she was going. This was most unusual. She'd said she'd be back from her walk in time to prepare for afternoon tea.

Jessica had to interrupt the duke and George McPherson's conversation, but they, too, had not seen Lady Katherine since luncheon.

In the servants' hall, neither Mr Thomson, Mrs Plummer nor anybody else had set eyes upon the countess since lunch. Jessica's unease was steadily growing into alarm. She glanced from face to face, heart quickening, unsure where to turn. Her brow furrowed and her breath shallowed in mild panic.

Florence ambled back into the servants' hall with her empty linen basket. 'What's all the to-do about?' she asked depositing her basket on a sideboard.

'Florrie, have ye seen Lady Katherine?' Jessica jumped in.

'Oh yes,' Florence replied with an offhand air. 'I left Her Ladyship confabulating at the back with that awful Mr Graves, the grocer.'

'When?'

'Oh, about half hour ago. Why? What's up?'

Had the moment been less serious, Mrs Plummer would have chastised Florence up for using another of those awful Americanisms. *'What's up', indeed!*

Outside, Henry jogged towards the servants' hall door, just in time for his usual midafternoon treat from Mrs Plummer—a piece of pie or cake. He had long suspected that Mrs Plummer was sweet on his dad and so treated Henry with little favours like these, which he gladly accepted.

But something caught his eye.

A scrap of bloodied rag lay upon the gravel. Curious, he ran to it and picked it up, puzzled as to who had left it there and why. Mrs Plummer was a fussbudget when it came to cleanliness and tidiness—or so Florence insisted.

Hurrying into the servants' hall, he found that he had stumbled into a commotion.

'What's happened?' he asked one of the kitchen hands.

'The countess has gone and lost herself!' the young woman replied.

Henry stared at the bloodied cloth in his hand—puzzled.

Jessica saw him.

'What have ye got there?' she demanded, her voice raised in alarm and recognising the colour of the fabric.

'I found it outside, Miss Turner,' he replied, holding it out, his smooth forehead crinkled with confusion.

She snatched it from his hand.

'Blood! This is hers! This is from her shirtwaist!' she exclaimed. 'Someone's taken Lady Katherine!'

The pronouncement caused gasps of disbelief and raised unanswerable questions. The distress that filled the room was manifest.

Henry stood amidst the growing chaos, wide-eyed and stricken.

He had to act. The countess had been kidnapped!

He ran to the stables, saddled and bridled Peleus and took off at sped for the station, leaving his father calling out to him in vain. 'Henry! Henry—stop!'

It didn't occur to Henry that the train should have long since departed by this time.

It was most fortuitous that there had been a delay …

***

At about half past four, the Graves' wagon broke out of the woodland and approached a stone cottage.

The moon would rise soon as the last rays of the western sun sparkled on the river that ran behind the lodge. All was quiet save the swish of the water racing past the four-oared rowboat tied to the little pier.

Graves had taken the shorter route through the forest as it afforded cover for his covert activity. Even though there was still enough light outside, the kerosene lamp inside the cottage was lit and the warm glow of the flame softly radiated from the windows.

Upon hearing the cautious approach of the wagon, Norman Croft skulked from the cottage carrying a shotgun.

'About bloody time,' he called as Graves pulled the wagon up near the doorway. 'Did you get her?'

Graves jumped down and went to the back and pulled away the tarpaulin. 'No.'

Hogan pushed himself up and clambered down from the tray, unceremoniously dragging the still-unconscious countess to the edge. 'Got something better, Norm,' he sneered.

'The duchess' niece. Some Lady Katherine Delaney,' added Graves.

Hogan reached over and with his dirty hand fondled her breast. 'There'll be some fun to be had here, boys,' he snarled.

'Bring her inside,' Croft ordered.

Hogan and Graves picked her up and carried her into the cottage.

The disused stone cottage was always kept clean and tidy by the duke's groundsmen, as were its sparse furnishings of a table, chairs, campaign cots and cupboard. Croft had readied the fire and a kettle of boiling water hung over it.

'Put her there,' commanded Croft, pointing to one of the campaign cots that had been opened out.

Graves stood back. He was not entirely happy with doing any more harm to her. He had been appalled when Hogan had punched her so ferociously, but he dared say anything lest they take their wrath out on him or, worse still, withhold payment.

He just stood there, convincing himself that he was not a wicked man. He only wanted to get back at the duchess for discovering his flimflammery. That other woman, however, the one who'd shoved a gun in his face, she was a different matter. She was not a normal woman and he would get back at her, somehow, for humiliating him. But that was for another time.

He plucked up his waning courage. 'I done my bit. Erm … my payment?'

This drew the attention of both thugs away from the countess.

'Payment's when we get paid,' Croft snarled. 'I told you that.'

'I just want my money and I'll go.'

'Why?' Croft replied with a mocking sneer. 'You got somewhere else to be? You'll go when I say it's time to go. Besides,' Croft added with unmistakable menace, 'you got one more job to do.'

This surprised Graves. 'That wasn't the deal. I done what you said. You got your goods.'

'The deal is whatever I say it is.'

Taking a creased note from his pocket, he held it out.

Graves reluctantly took it.

'That,' Croft said, punctuating the rhythm of his instruction with a deliberate prod of his finger in Graves' shoulder, 'you take to the duke and make sure he gets it. And then you return here and your payment will be waiting for you.'

Graves' composure began to unravel, his voice echoing with panic. 'They'll take me if I go back. They saw me, one of the servants—'

'Well, you'd better make sure they don't see you this time.'

Graves imagined being captured and hanged. 'I won't go—'

Croft's reaction was swift: he swung the barrel of his shotgun up and pushed it under Graves' chin, forcing his head backwards.

Graves' body stiffened, his breath caught, he stared wide-eyed down his nose at Croft.

'Now listen here, you mongrel clodhopper,' Croft calmly intoned, practically nose to nose with Graves. 'Take the note or I'll blow your fucking brains out. The choice is yours.'

Large beads of perspiration formed on Graves' brow and upper lip.

'Well?' Croft asked. 'What's it to be?'

Graves was barely able to breathe let alone speak. 'The … the note,' he rasped.

'What? I didn't hear you.'

'I'll take the note.'

'Good.' Croft removed the steel from under Graves' chin and pushed him roughly towards the door. 'Go! And if you come back with anything other than yourself, you're dead meat.'

Graves scrambled out of the door to the sound of Hogan's mocking laughter.

***

It was nearing home time when the speaking tube on the wall squawked. 'Sir Giles,' came Fawkner's voice. 'Mr Quinn on the telephone for you, Sir.'

Hawthorne's thoughts were elsewhere and he hadn't heard the telephone ring. 'What the dickens does he want now?' he mumbled to himself.

It had been a long, unproductive day and the cells were full of angry, uncooperative unionists. All he wanted to do was go home and sit in silence while his wife and mother-in-law prattled on over trivialities—an unusually welcome respite from the office turmoil.

With an exhausted sigh, he lifted the handset to his ear. 'Mr Quinn.'

'I've just had a most alarming telephone call from the Duke of Bramwell.' There was something in Alexander Quinn's voice that Hawthorne hadn't heard before: controlled anger.

'The Duke of Bramwell?' Hawthorne was confused: who the dickens was the Duke of Bramwell?

'His Grace was most distressed. His niece, the Countess of Chestermere, has been abducted.'

'Ab … abducted?' Hawthorne stammered, 'Countess of Ch … ? Not Bonningwick's daughter? Who … ? Why … ?'

'The anarchists, man!' boomed Quinn.

'Can't be! We have them all in the cells!'

'But it is! And you have a confession. Or so you claim.'

Hawthorne scrambled to straighten his thoughts. 'It must be someone else. Another miscreant pretending … No … No … ' he stuttered. 'You've made a mistake—'

'Yes, Hawthorne, it *was* I who made a mistake—in listening to you! I should have gone with my instincts and assigned more officers where they were needed rather than your damned wild goose chase!'

Hawthorne's face turned scarlet; he reeled as though the words had physically struck him. He had never been spoken to in such as manner as this—not by his superior and certainly not by his subordinates. 'Mr Quinn! Really! I must object to your tone. I have done everything in my—'

'Get a squad of men together,' Quinn interrupted. 'The train leaves for Abbottsford Village at six fifteen tomorrow morning. I want you and six officers to be on it.'

'Me?'

'You. And six officers. Leave Scott here. He seems to know more of what's going on than the lot of you put together.'

'Tomorrow is Friday—'

'And?'

'My wife …' Hawthorne was most reluctant to share this. 'Er … my wife requires that I assist her in our church's fete on Saturd—'

'Are you requesting time off? Because, if you are, Sir Giles, I can easily arrange as much time off as you need. Permanently.'

'Perm—?'

'What is it to be?'

'Of course. I understand, Mr Quinn,' Hawthorne conceded reluctantly. 'You need a captain in the field and I—'

'No. Major Williams will head the squad—'

'Major Williams?' This threw him completely. 'He is on enforced leave—'

'You will go there,' insisted Quinn, deliberately, slowly, 'under his direction and see how it's done. If I had listened to him, Lady Chestermere would not be in danger now.'

Hawthorne scoffed in indignation.

'Do you see any difficulty with that, Sir Giles?'

'You expect me—'

'Do you see any difficulty, Sir Giles?' insisted Quinn.

Sir Giles managed his reply through gritted teeth. 'No, Mr Quinn. No difficulty. No difficulty at all.'

'Good.'

And, with that, a loud crash in Hawthorne's ear ended the telephone call.

A fine sheen of perspiration formed on Hawthorne's flushed face. This was not the way an organisation should be run. *He* was in charge, damn it! *He* called the play, goddammit!

He shot to his feet and paced the floor.

How dare they do this to me! I am knighted! Major Williams? That pumped-up piece of nothing! Without Quinn's support, he would have been out on his ear years ago. And that … that … insult to womanhood. How dare they! Of course, without a confederate in the office to do their dirty work … Scott! I'll see to him! He wants a squad of six, eh? I'll give him six.

He surged to the speaking tube and yanked it off the wall. 'Fawkner! Get Yabsley in here. And, Fawkner, get the Marlborough Club on the telephone. Now!'

***

Yabsley had come and gone with his orders within a matter of minutes. He was to assemble Dolby, Hewitt, Ramsay, Hathaway and Byrne at the railway station early the following morning. Sir Giles gave no other explanation or chance of reply, and bluntly dismissed his second-in-charge.

Fawkner hailed Hawthorne via the speaking tube. 'Sir Giles, the Marlborough Club is connected, Sir.'

Without any further niceties, Hawthorne put the handpiece to his ear. 'Sir Giles Hawthorne here. Let me speak to Colonel Humphries.'

***

Peleus responded well to my urgings.

We thundered back down the road towards Abbottsford Hall. He was a true thoroughbred with a mighty heart. He understood the urgency.

I had no idea of what I'd do when I reached her—only where she'd be. And I knew with appalling clarity what they'd do to her if I didn't reach her in time.

The sun was setting and would be gone in an hour. Long shadows already fell along the road. The air was cooling and prickling my face but the heat of my resolve burned through it.

The moon would be rising soon—a waxing gibbous moon—and the sky was clear. That could betray me. Darkness was my ally; moonlight my undoing.

If the ransom note had been delivered, it would give the duke a day. It would not be a trifling amount. Then they would kill her. But not before—God help her …

I would not let that happen. Not again.

I'd failed once, thirty years ago; I would not fail again.

Abbottsford Hall loomed in the distance. This road would soon branch off—one road to the Hall—the other to the riverbank and the three fishermen's cottages.

It was time to change my approach.

I pulled Peleus into a shallow clearing and jumped off. Jacket and skirt shed. From the Gladstone, I pulled on my blacks: turtleneck over my white shirt and holstered gun, trousers on over my underwear. Jacket on. Checked the pockets: gloves, balaclava, twelve rounds, manacles and garrotte. I rethought the manacles—for a prisoner. I discarded it. My stiletto was in place—in my right boot.

I mounted Peleus again, leaving the discards in the undergrowth, and spurred him on.

Twilight, and I reached the fork in the road. The Hall stood silent.

No movement. Wills would arrive soon. The private detectives? Where were they?

No time to ponder.

I turned and raced towards the riverbank. No sign of Graves' wagon. The rutted road was too compacted to show new tracks. He was complicit. He would pay the same price as the others.

Now—caution. These monsters would kill without qualms. Lady Katherine's life was in jeopardy.

Peleus was tiring. He'd been pushed hard: this morning by Lady Katherine, then Henry, and now by me. His gleaming brown coat was white with clammy froth. But he pressed on without faltering.

We approached the first of the cottages—the Carp.

Was Lady Katherine here?

I pulled Peleus into the wooded side of the road and dismounted. I tethered him, hidden from the path.

I slipped through the shadows across the track and into the scrub that bordered the cottage.

No light. No movement. I had to be sure.

I circled through the undergrowth to the back.

I peered through the window.

Deserted.

Damn!

I ran back across the bridlepath and swung onto Peleus. He surged forward on to the next cottage, the Catfish—the one the so-called poachers had sullied.

The last light of day was fading rapidly.

***

It was well past his home time and his wife and mother-in-law would be most upset that he had not shown up for dinner. The note he'd sent along would not appease them at all. He would make suitable amends later; this was far more important. His reputation was at stake.

Sir Giles Hawthorne strode purposefully and resolutely through the long, wood-panelled corridor and into the reading room of the Marlborough Club where he expected Colonel Humphries to be waiting for him.

Colonel Humphries was, indeed, waiting for Sir Giles and stood to shake his hand when he approached.

'Sir Giles, old boy, what on earth is so urgent that you miss dinner with your esteemed wife and mother-in-law?' Humphries crowed, clearly intending his remark to rankle his old friend.

'Indeed,' Hawthorne replied, taking a seat opposite. 'It appears your valet was misinformed about the unions and I've been "leading a damned wild goose chase" according to the ingenious Mr Alexander Quinn.'

'What are you saying, dear boy? The unions are not involved? Wild geese?'

'Precisely. Where did your valet get his information? He has caused me no small embarrassment and a significant loss of credibility. I must speak to him immediately so I can put this ridiculous situation to right. Where is he?'

Hawthorne noticed a change in Humphries' humour as he dithered with his reply.

'Still in Ireland, I'm afraid. Some little croft in the hills. Quite unreachable, I'm afraid.'

'That won't do! His information was wrong. Entirely wrong! And I'm paying the price. I trusted you, Neville.'

'Steady on, old chap. All in good faith. I only passed on to you what was passed on to me. I will do my best to contact him and have him return immediately to face you and explain himself.'

'Not only has Quinn shut down my investigation of the trade unions, he has also directed me to another part of the country! The nerve of the pup!'

'What do you mean?' Humphries' words were urgent.

'What do I mean?' Hawthorne looked about. 'Where's the waiter? I could use a stiff brandy …'

'Sir Giles—' Humphries stopped himself short. 'Sir Giles,' he continued after suppressing his insistency, 'tell me what has you so upset. Perhaps we can work something out together. As we always have.'

Sir Giles took a deep breath then expelled it with self-pitying resignation. 'I'm to head a squad of six of my men to someplace in the country, a small village in Suffolk, somewhere.'

Humphries' smugness dropped from his face.

'I say, Neville, you've gone as white as my wife's tablecloths.'

Humphries forced a chuckle. 'Er … just had a bit of a spasm. The old war wound playing up. So, you're off to this country village, you say. When might that be?'

'First light tomorrow. Are you sure you're all right, old boy?'

'Yes … yes … Perhaps you're right, Sir Giles. Perhaps I should take myself home and rest. I'm feeling a little ragged.'

'Right, right.'

Humphries stood to take his leave.

'I'm feeling much the same, old boy. Not looking forward to confronting Williams and that abomination.'

Hawthorne stopped. 'Pardon?'

'Hmm?'

'You're saying Major Williams and that Davies woman will be travelling with you tomorrow?'

'No, old boy. Apparently, they're already there. And have been since—'

'At the village?'

'Yes. And I'm not happy to have them under me. A bit of a conspiracy, I say. That Quinn has a lot to learn about leadership—'

'Yes … Please excuse me, Sir Giles, I must go.'

'Of course, of course. You do look ill. Look after yourself, old boy. Waiter! There you are …'

***

A large flagon of rum stood on the table in the fishermen's cottage, opened and the contents partially consumed. Croft sat with Hogan at the table, cups in hand. But they were not drunk. It would take a lot more to make them so. They drank and waited and Hogan watched.

He watched *her*.

The countess.

Hogan, salacious and callous, was already imagining what was to come. His face betrayed every vile intention as he leered at the unconscious woman lying on the cot. His hand cupped his crotch. Croft saw it—and the lechery in his eyes. Hogan was waiting for the moment she'd scream. He enjoyed that. He enjoyed the power he had over them. He enjoyed watching them suffer. He enjoyed watching them die.

Norman Croft was no angel himself. He had known no other life than one involving thievery, housebreaking, thuggery and all shades of malefaction up to and including rape and murder.

He enjoyed taking the same carnal advantages as Hogan—and would do so again. But not yet. Not until all was done. That was the difference between them. Hogan was ruled by his prick; Croft was ruled by his brain. He was more concerned with avoiding the noose. That meant leaving no one to testify.

A soft moan broke the silence.

Lady Katherine was regaining consciousness.

Where she had suffered the blows, the side of her face was swollen and her eye partially closed. The blood from the gash to her brow had congealed and dried blood encrusted her temple, cheek and neck. Her once-immaculate pastel-pink shirtwaist, now torn and sullied, was also spattered with her blood.

She slowly stirred, groaned and winced. The touch of her hand to her damaged face caused her to cry out in pain.

'Jessie …' she feebly cried as she turned her head. She dry retched and coughed.

'Ah, the lady awakes,' Croft snarled, moving to stand over her.

She opened her eyes at the sound of his voice and all colour seeped from her face. 'Who are you? What do you want?' she managed to utter, panting with terror.

Hogan loomed beside him. 'No need to fear, m' lady,' he sneered. 'I'll take care o' you good and proper.'

His malicious cackle would have done nothing to assuage her fear.

Croft didn't bother stopping him—she'd learn soon enough what he intended. He leaned down, his rum-soaked breath making her gag once more. 'You just lie there and don't move. It'll be over soon enough.'

'Why? Why are you doing this?' she murmured.

Croft didn't answer. He owed her nothing.

***

I kept Peleus to the edge of the bridlepath, ready to veer into the woods at the slightest sign of danger.

We covered the two miles to the second cottage at a punishing pace. The ride was treacherous now—the night darkening, the ground uneven. One misstep and we'd tumble.

In the east, the moon was ascending.

I saw the cottage ahead. I slowed, heart pounding, eyes straining.

No light. No activity.

Deserted? I had to make sure.

I leapt down, left the horse in the roadside scrub and ran, fast, silent, to the back of the cottage.

Nothing. No sound. No sign. No Lady Katherine!

Dread shook my bones.

Was I mistaken?

Could they have taken her somewhere else? Where?

Oh, God, please, no.

It was the first time in years I had prayed. I was desperate, beginning to panic. My heart felt like it was about to burst. My breath was ragged.

I had one chance left.

Please God, keep her safe.

***

It was sunset when Wills and Henry reached the Hall. Along the way, Henry rattled off the information he had told Miss Davies about Stewart Graves—confused and frantic—but Wills already knew most of it through Rebecca's reports. Wills was impressed by the boy's courage and responsibility.

The lights and torches of Abbottsford Hall were ablaze. Frenzied activity filled the forecourt. Saddled horses champed at the bit, kept in check by armed stable hands. The duke waited readied, shotgun in hand, flanked by Thomson and Pitman, peering into the twilight towards the entrance gates.

Lady Katherine's Rolls-Royce stood idling, doors to the body flung open. Jimmy and George checked their rifles. Jessica looked on, pale, tense and jittery.

Emma, Mrs Plummer and Florence hovered around the duchess. She was fraught with worry—her hands trembled as her fingers twisted the edge of her handkerchief; she stood rigid, bracing herself against the worst of news. The rest of the staff stood by at the ready, waiting, watching, simmering with anger at the grocer's audacity.

Pitman spotted the pony trap. 'Your Grace! There!' He ran to it. 'Henry!' he called when he saw his son. 'Thank the heavens you're safe! Where's Peleus?'

'Miss Davies has him.'

The duke hurried to the pony trap. 'Major Williams! Thank God! My niece has been taken!'

Wills handed off the reins and jumped down. 'So Henry said. What have you got here?' He scrutinised the crowd—armed, angry.

'I'm waiting for the constable from the village,' the duke snapped. 'I telephoned to him to come immediately. Also Akers-Douglas and Quinn to send help right away. He's sending six.' His breath came fast, his hands clenching and unclenching the shotgun he held. 'We're going after her the moment the constable arrives.'

'The private detectives. I don't see them.'

'There's been a delay. Not until tomorrow.'

'Too late. All too late.' Wills said plainly. 'We believe that Lady Katherine is at one of the fishermen's cottages. She'll be removed from there.'

'Then we must go at once! We are ready!'

Wills shook his head and held up both hands in protest. 'No. The men we pursue are killers. They will shoot it out if they are cornered. They've killed one of my officers and wounded another. I won't risk more lives—'

'She's my niece!'

The crowd shouted their support, brandishing their weapons.

'Quiet!' Wills barked. 'Listen to me!'

The shouting ebbed into an uneasy quiet.

'If we descend like this, they will kill her! And make their escape. Don't be foolish. Let Davies and me handle it.'

The duke huffed out a heavy breath, his face tight with suppressed rage.

'The car is the fastest,' Wills continued. 'And it has lights. I need the driver.'

'Aye!' Jimmy called. 'I'm willing and I'm a bloody good shot!'

'Good. You know the way?'

'I do,' piped Henry, elbowing himself between Thomson and his father.

'No. You stay here,'

'I know the way,' Pitman volunteered.

'I'm coming with you, Major,' insisted the duke.

'Me, too,' called George and Jessica in unison.

'No,' Wills insisted. 'No women. No children. It's too dangerous.'

Jessica protested but Wills cut her off. 'No,' he said definitively; they were frittering away precious seconds.

'All right,' he said. 'You men—follow my orders. No exceptions, no questions. Understood?'

Every man agreed and hurried to the car. George, the duke and Pitman clambered into the car's enclosed body, Jimmy and Wills filled the two front seats of the doorless driver's compartment.

'Summon a doctor,' Wills called to Thomson. Wills knew these bastards and knew there would be blood. 'Tell the constable to hold.'

'Thomson,' the duke called out, 'keep the duchess inside and, for God's sake, keep her safe!'

Jimmy thrust the car into gear and began to move off. Without warning, Henry bolted forward, hurling himself into the front seat and across Wills' lap. He scrambled upright and wedged himself between Wills and Jimmy just as the car increased speed.

'I'm coming, too!' he insisted. 'I got to look after Peleus!'

Jimmy looked to Wills for instruction. Wills gave up. 'Go! Just go!' The last thing he needed was to have a child underfoot, but he'd sort that out when the time came.

The car's wheels churned the gravel and sped off.

***

'Where the bloody hell is Dickie?' Croft muttered peering out the front window. 'We could have had all this sorted by now.' The delay irritated him—Dickie was always late. His jaw clenched as he scanned the darkened track by the forest for any sign of movement.

Hogan was far more relaxed, sprawled on a chair, legs akimbo, and an arm hooked on the chair's back. His eyes never left the countess. Croft didn't know what Hogan was thinking but he was predictable. He would soon act on his base impulses. Dickie's delay only forestalled the inevitable.

The countess lay on the cot, curled up on her side. Her face was swollen and blood-encrusted. Her breath was shallow but controlled. Her gaze met Hogan's—defiant. Was she aware of her fate? She didn't show it; she didn't show fear only defiance. This woman wouldn't beg for mercy. Hogan liked them to beg. He liked to break them.

Croft returned his gaze to the track.

***

The Rolls-Royce arrived at the junction where one path led to the riverside and the other led through the heavily wooded forest.

'Through there!' called Pitman from the seat inside the car. 'Through the woods. It's faster and you can turn back out to the first cottage.'

Jimmy veered as instructed, the bright headlights carving the way through the semi-darkness.

***

I was some distance away but, as I cautiously approached the last of the three fishermen's cottages, I could just make out a faint light from the windows. My hopes swelled. Lady Katherine was here. She had to be. I clung to the belief that she was still alive.

At least two men would be inside—most likely three: Croft, Hogan and Graves. Timmy told of only two. But were there others? I had to proceed with utmost caution.

At the back of my mind, I was certain that Wills would be raising assistance and on his way. But I couldn't wait. Time was as much my enemy as those who had taken Lady Katherine.

I was on the edge of the bridlepath within fifty yards of the cottage when I paused. There was no movement outside. No sounds, just ominous silence.

Dismounting, I led Peleus into the woods. He needed to be protected—he was our only means of rapid escape. I tethered his reins to a low-hanging branch then pulled the balaclava over my head. My white hair and pale skin would be like a beacon in the night.

Scanning the terrain, I committed each detail to memory. The trees were mostly birch but one gnarled hornbeam stood apart—its low-hanging branch, like a crooked finger, pointed the way back to Peleus.

I whispered a silent prayer to the god I had forsaken then slipped through the darkening night towards the bridlepath and cottage.

***

Wills sat on the edge of his seat, peering into the narrow gloomy path winding through the forest, sliced open by the car's bright lamps. His hands clenched the vehicle's windshield frame, knuckles white.

Jimmy navigated the large motor car with precision, concentration creasing his face.

Between him and Jimmy, Henry sat stiff and upright, speechless—for once.

In the car's body, the duke, George and Pitman scanned the forest for any movement; each cradled a loaded firearm and each would have no hesitation in employing it.

***

Stewart Graves was regretting everything he had done in his life up to this minute. He was sure he was heading towards his execution. He hadn't really wanted to hurt anyone. Why couldn't they all have treated him with respect? If they had, he wouldn't have taken this course.

With the foreboding of a condemned man, he unwillingly drove his wagon back to the mansion with the letter of demand weighing heavily in his pocket.

Then lights.

Rounding the bend, he saw a pair of bright lanterns coming towards him at speed.

Panic shuddered through him.

There was no way off the road—the trees encroached too tightly. He pulled back on the hand brake and reined in the horse.

He sat there trembling, his mind racing through implausible reasons why he was on the track here, on the duke's estate, at this time of night.

No time for excuses.

He jumped off.

***

'There!' Jimmy called as they rounded a bend. He could just barely make out the horse and unlit wagon approaching from the opposite direction.

'That's him!' shouted Henry. 'That's Stewart Graves!'

'Pull up, man!' Wills commanded.

Jimmy stood on the brake pedal and pulled the handbrake lever simultaneously bringing the heavy vehicle to a juddering halt just feet from the horse. It whinnied and shied away in fear.

Graves had jumped off the driver's bench and was scrambling towards the dense woodland.

Wills was at his heels in an instant. He grabbed Graves by the neck of his jacket and pulled him back onto the road and into the motor car's lights.

He threw Garves to the ground. The man landed hard.

'What are you doing here?' Wills barked.

The others crowded around him.

Graves didn't utter a sound—he couldn't—fear dumbed him. He lay in the dirt, cringing, trembling.

Wills yanked him up and thrust him against the radiator of the motor car.

'Where is she!' he demanded.

'I don't … I …' was all Graves could utter before Wills slapped him hard on the side of his face.

'Where!'

Graves buckled.

Wills raised his arm—his fist ready to strike.

Graves surrendered, defeated. 'Pike. The Pike Cottage.'

'That's the last along the line,' Pitman confirmed.

Wills threw Graves to the ground and withdrew his manacles, throwing it and the key to Pitman. 'Secure him to a tree!'

Jimmy and George descended on Graves. They wrenched him up and dragged him to the nearest tree.

Jimmy landed the first punch. 'That's for Lady Katherine, you piece of shit.'

George pushed him aside and pummelled Graves—once, twice, three times.

Graves slumped, bleeding, groaning.

'That's enough!' Wills called.

It wasn't.

'If Lady Katherine is hurt,' George snarled through bared teeth, 'I will kill you.'

Jimmy kicked him for good measure before Pitman handcuffed him.

'Pitman, unharness the horse, and you two,' Wills directed Jimmy and George, 'help me push the wagon onto its side so we can pass. Quickly, now!'

Without being asked, the duke and Henry assisted and the wagon was easily tipped onto its side and they were back on their way.

***

The pier was illuminated by the soft glow of the kerosene lamp through the open back door. The moon had risen and cast a pallid glow on the rippling waterway. Croft wandered about the back of the cottage, shotgun resting on his shoulder, and peered up and down the river. He made sure the rowboat was secure then ambled back into the cottage and muttered a grunt of annoyance.

'He should be here by now. Where the bloody hell is Dickie?' he said to no one in particular. He walked to the front window and squinted through it, searching for any sign of movement. The fellow who was supposed to be in charge was nowhere to be found. And that aggravating joskin, Graves, should have returned by now.

No witnesses.

Once he returned, Graves would be sorted.

And the woman? Her breeding would not save her. Not from what they planned for her.

Not tonight.

But waiting around made him nervous. With growing irritability, he opened the front door.

'Wait here,' he commanded Hogan. 'I'm going to wait outside for that snotty bastard and the clodhopper.'

'Right, Norm,' Hogan replied with a malicious smirk.

'And, Harry, don't touch her,' Croft growled. 'I don't want none of your poxy gush on me. She's mine first.'

'Right, Norm,' Hogan echoed, his voice dripping with obscenity.

With a last warning glare at his lifelong accomplice and a sideways glance at the damaged countess, Croft stalked out the front door and closed it behind him.

Outside, he trudged up the short track to the bridlepath and scanned it both ways. With another grunt of annoyance, he settled himself against the trunk of a tree to wait for his supposed commander-in-chief, cradling his gun like a babe in arms.

***

Lady Katherine gingerly sat up on the side of the cot. Her badly bruised body ached. She was still faint and giddy from the blows to her head but her refined upbringing demanded she not falter. Not outwardly. To display hysteria, anger, rage or fear was not the way of her kind. Only calmness and reason were accepted traits.

She looked up at the despicable man in front of her and addressed him with as much composure as she could rally. 'Why are you doing this … Harry, is it?'

His mouth twisted into a contemptuous sneer. 'Harry is it?' he mimicked. 'Doing what? Thinking up ways to kill you? Or to fuck you before I kill you?'

Lady Katherine gasped at his crudity. She closed her eyes and regained her composure. Opening them, she asked, 'Why do you wish to harm me?'

He crowed a hateful laugh. 'Because I can, m' lady. Because I can.'

There was a perverse gleam in his eyes that betrayed how greatly he relished her fear.

The dread she had stifled rose again and engulfed her.

Before she could react, Hogan was upon her.

He grabbed her by the shoulders and dragged her to her feet, pulling her around to face him.

She emitted a stifled cry. His grip crushed her arms. Pain tore through her shoulders. She winced in agony. She struggled, twisting, trying to break free but it was all in vain—he was far too strong.

He pushed her against the table and ground his groin into her. Lady Katherine whimpered and turned her head away from the stench of his breath.

'Feel that, m' lady?' he sneered into her ear as he pounded his engorged phallus against her. 'That's for you.'

He let go of her arms and turned her, bending her over the table, pushing her down. His rough hand clamped around her neck and immobilised her.

Her arms were free but useless—she couldn't reach him standing behind her, thrusting against her.

She found it difficult to draw breath.

Her energy flagged.

'Don't give up just yet, m' lady,' he jeered. 'The best is yet to come.'

His free hand went to his trousers and he unbuttoned his fly with manic frenzy, releasing his phallus.

She regained her resolve and desperately tried everything she could to push him off—to push herself off the table, fight him, free herself. It was useless; he was far too powerful.

She clenched her eyes shut and felt his hand pull up her skirts and fumble with her drawers. His feet pushed her legs apart. She was pinned to the table, unable to move. She could not bear to think of this loathsome animal taking hateful pleasure in violating her.

To her utter disgust, she felt his hand fondle her pubis, then his penis touch her skin. Repulsion and fear overwhelmed her, filled every part of her being.

Then everything stopped.

His arm fell away from her neck and she no longer felt the pressure of his body against hers. His licentious panting changed to a string of stifled gasps.

Terrified, she opened her eyes and lifted her head to take in the horrific sight of the man gasping for air. His eyes bulged, his mouth gaped and his head was forced backwards by a wire tightly looped around his neck and cutting into his flesh. His hands were at once wildly flailing about and desperately grabbing at the wire. He twisted and turned his body, frantically fighting his unseen assassin, desperate to free himself, desperate to keep on living, until his body finally gave in to unconsciousness. His fight now over, he slumped to the floor on his belly and into his own ejaculated semen.

***

I followed him down, my knee pushed hard into his back, relentlessly pulling back on the garrotte with all the strength I could summon, strength magnified by rage.

Another twenty seconds.

I didn't have the luxury of time. The blood to his brain had stopped flowing and he had stopped breathing but it would take another minute to ensure he was dead. This had to be enough. He was no longer a threat—to anyone, ever again.

It was only then that I looked up to Lady Katherine and saw the panic and terror in her face as she slid slowly to the floor.

I must have appeared to be a demon from the underworld, clad in black from head to toe. I unravelled the wire from around the bastard's neck, stood and took a step towards Lady Katherine. She shrank away. I extended my hand to help her up.

'Katherine,' I whispered. 'We must leave. Now.'

'Rebecca … ?' she replied hoarsely, looking into my eyes, bewildered. She recognised me. 'I …'

She was pale, bloodied and trembling, unable to move.

'Come,' I softly urged, carefully helping her to her feet. 'Come with me. You're safe,' I lied.

It broke my heart to see this beautiful, strong creature so fearful, hurt and abused. Croft and Hogan's vile offences filled me with such fury that I wanted to empty the cylinder of my Webley into that murderous Norman Croft who stood outside waiting. I was unsure of how many more there may have been.

But Lady Katherine was my first concern. Every second's delay was perilous. I had to remove her to a safe place immediately—that certainty was all I needed to control my rage.

'Come,' I urged; I would deal with Croft and 'Dickie'—and Graves—later. And anybody else who dared.

Lady Katherine's clothing was completely unsuitable for the task ahead but thankfully her dark green skirt would blend into the forest. Her pale blouse, however, even in its dirtied, bloodied and torn state would stand out in the night. I promptly removed my jacket and helped her put it on. She was unable to move; her gaze fixed on Hogan's lifeless form.

'Katherine, we must go ...'

We had to get back to Peleus who was on the other side of the bridlepath some twenty yards in the forest. Crossing the path would be fraught with danger. Croft was watching the path for 'Dickie's' imminent arrival, or so I had overheard him say to Hogan.

I wrapped my arm around Lady Katherine's waist and drew her away from the corpse and out the back door. She became more compliant as we left the scene of her abuse behind, and we pressed ahead to the thicket beside the cottage. I had already discounted using the rowboat—it would have left us open to being fired upon and I didn't know if Lady Katherine was able to swim.

Leading the way as stealthily as possible through the trees and thick undergrowth, we made our way towards the bridlepath and readied to rush across it as soon as opportunity allowed.

'Listen,' I said pulling the countess down to a crouch.

I could hear the approach of a motor. Was it Wills coming to our assistance? I looked at Lady Katherine. 'Your motor car?'

She shook her head. She was right. This motor was not as refined nor smooth as the Rolls-Royce. And it was approaching from the direction of the village rather than the more direct route through the forest from the Hall.

'Stay here. Don't move.'

She gripped my arm—trembling, imploring me not to abandon her.

'I'll be right back,' I assured her.

Hidden by the waist-high bracken, I crept closer to the cottage. A motorcycle drew up to Croft.

'About bloody time! What took you so long?'

'Flat tyre. These bloody country roads!' the man said, dismounting. 'Never mind that. Has the note been delivered?'

This must have been 'Dickie'. In the wan moonlight, he appeared to be about forty-five, lean, tall and straight; military bearing, I thought. His speech was not that of a vulgar common reprobate. This man had some education. Was this the 'Dickie' of whom both Hawthorne and Humphries had spoken? Were Hawthorne and Humphries complicit in these atrocities? Sir Giles Hawthorne was most certainly a fool and clearly inept, but I never could have imagined him a traitor, or worse, a murderer.

'Yeah,' replied Croft. 'That country bumpkin, Graves, took it. He should be on his way back by now.'

'You know what to do with him.'

'Yeah.'

'Is she alive?'

'Yeah, but we got a countess, not a duchess.'

'What?'

'The duchess' niece. As good as the duchess. And half her age,' he added, his lewd smirk caught by the pale glimmer from the cottage lamp.

'I don't care what you do with her once we have the money,' Dickie said dismissively as he strode towards the cottage. Croft followed, shouldering his shotgun.

I watched them until they reached the threshold, then hurried back to Lady Katherine.

'Quick,' I whispered, 'Dickie's arrived and they're going into the cottage.'

Lady Katherine's breath quickened. I met her gaze with unequivocal reassurance and pulled her up. We rushed across the bridlepath then disappeared into the thick, shaggy undergrowth covering the forest floor.

Her long skirts were a hindrance, snagging on every branch and bramble, making our progress through the thick brush hard going.

I knew the horse wasn't far off. Still, uncertainty gnawed at me. Dickie and Croft would have discovered Hogan's corpse and the countess gone. My senses strained to every sound and movement.

'Where are we going?' Lady Katherine whispered clutching my hand. 'The Hall is in the other direction.'

'Peleus,' I replied in a low voice. 'We're close.'

Then—Dickie's voice broke the silence. 'You go that way! Find the bitch!'

I pulled the countess down to a crouch and signalled her to remain silent.

I held my breath—listening, looking.

A thrashing of bushes!

'Countess, oh, countess! Come out, come out wherever you are!' Croft's strident voice rang through the forest, gleeful, menacing.

Every muscle in my body tensed, trying to gauge his distance.

'Countess, I *will* find you.' His voice was amplified in the darkness. 'You can't hide. Come out now and I'll be nice to you!'

He hadn't seen us but by the sound of his voice, he was not far off.

There was no movement through the scrub. He was still on the path.

Closer.

He was so close I thought I could make him out through the moonlit gloom.

'Last chance, countess!' he taunted.

The crunch of bracken. He had left the path. Had he seen our tracks?

'Stay here,' I whispered. 'Keep down and don't move.'

I crouched as low to the forest floor as possible and moved away, at times crawling on my belly.

Croft's taunts grew ever louder. 'Give up, Lady Muck, and I promise not to hurt you!' His cruel laughter, promised the opposite. 'I know you're in here, countess.'

He was now only a few yards away from her.

He took a step closer. 'I forgive you for killing Harry. He could be a bit of a prick. I would've done the same, if I was you. Come out, now!' he roared.

Croft was upon her.

She looked up at him, eyes wide with terror.

'There you are!' he snarled.

He grabbed her arm and pulled her up.

But I was already at his back.

In one swift motion, I pulled his head back over my shoulder and drew my stiletto blade deep across his throat. He dropped his weapon and emitted a low gurgling from his severed windpipe. Blood spurted from his gashed arteries. His knees gave way. His life pulsed out of him.

I let his body drop to the ground and wiped my blade on his jacket.

Lady Katherine looked on in utter horror.

I wanted to reach out and hold her, to comfort her …

We had no time to lose. One more to deal with. But right now, Lady Katherine's safety was paramount.

I took the countess' hand and found the hornbeam tree that pointed the way to the horse.

It only took us a few heartbeats to reach the place. I was reassured to hear his whinny as we approached.

'Peleus,' Lady Katherine cried, dashing the final steps to the steed. She grasped the bridle and stroked his neck, her features softening with relief.

He flinched—ears back, nostrils flaring. He tossed his head.

Something was amiss.

A sudden movement from the forest caught our attention.

Lady Katherine's posture stiffened.

Dickie emerged, revolver in hand, its barrel catching the filtered moonlight. He was barely four yards away.

I moved and placed myself in front of the countess. She grabbed my arm tight, trembling, her breath shallow and rapid.

He levelled his revolver at me, calmly, almost with amusement. Every word he uttered dripped with mockery.

'I was tempted to put a bullet through his skull, but he's such a beautiful animal. It would be a shame. Probably worth a quid or two as well, eh?'

I studied him carefully—his stance, the way he held the gun, the way he waved it about. Why hadn't he simply shot me and retaken his prize? He was playing with us, like a cat with a wretched mouse, relishing in the dread he presumed we felt, gloating over the control he thought he had. This was a madman.

My gun was in its holster under my sweater. The safety was on. Could I possibly retrieve it, flick the safety catch and get a shot off before he fired at me? I needed to be clear of the countess.

He turned his oily attention to Lady Katherine. 'And you there, you must be the countess. The niece. The Countess of Chestermere.'

She recoiled almost imperceptibly but didn't answer, instead raised her chin in defiance. She released my arm.

I carefully edged sideways away from her. I had to draw his attention away from her to me.

'You look rather bedraggled, my lady,' he continued with feigned concern, 'I do apologise for any heavy-handed enthusiasm.' He addressed me, 'I take it Croft won't be joining us?'

I took another step to the side.

His gun followed me.

In the corner of my vision, I saw Lady Katherine sway slightly and steady herself against Peleus.

'Take off the balaclava,' he ordered.

I did as he told but kept the balaclava in my hand, close to my chest. I concentrated on his gun hand—was it single- or double-action? I couldn't tell. If it were double, I had no chance—a pull of the trigger was all it would take. If it were single, he would have to cock the hammer before firing. A millisecond was all I needed—a twitch, a blink. I willed it to be single.

'Ah, I thought as much. A woman,' he said in a tone thick with condescension. 'No, not just *a* woman. *The* woman.'

I moved another small step sideways. His gun moved with me. I was now a yard clear of the countess. I slid my free hand under my sweater and, my movements obscured by the balaclava, I slipped the safety on my gun.

He continued his soliloquy, 'You must be that *abomination* I keep hearing so much about.'

'Let Lady Katherine go and I won't kill you,' I said in low deliberate tones. He was to be brought in alive. 'Put down the gun.'

His laughter was loud and cheerless. 'It seems you've misinterpreted the situation, my Sapphist friend. *I* give the orders!'

'You're just a puppet, Dickie. You don't give orders, you follow them like a trained dog. Now put down the gun.'

'Don't call me Dickie.' His face twisted, the words squeezed out through gritted teeth.

'You're just like those two dead bastards, *Dickie*. You're a dog and a puppet.'

His arm stiffened; the revolver locked on me. His mouth tightened into a snarl. My eyes fixed on his thumb, waiting for the twitch that would cock the hammer.

'Who's the puppeteer?' I persisted. 'Who's pulling your strings, *Dickie*?' I needed to know before I despatched him—to hell with bringing him in alive.

'You're a persistent slut, aren't you, Davies?'

He knew my name. How?

He regained his icy composure. 'It's of no consequence who I work for,' he scoffed. 'You'll be dead in the next minute.'

'If it's of no consequence, then tell me.'

'You *are* a conniving bitch. He is right.'

'Who's right?' I pushed; I was getting to him. I was getting close. 'Sir Giles?'

He sneered.

'Colonel Humphries?'

His body stiffened.

That was it!

His thumb shifted.

Time thickened and slowed.

I withdrew my Webley.

He fired.

I fired.

His bullet struck my left hip—a brutal jolt—pain roared through me.

Mine missed.

'No!' Lady Katherine screamed.

My legs folded.

He fired again.

The bullet exploded through my left arm—searing, unbearable—I fell backwards.

I fired blindly.

He staggered and fell.

Lady Katherine was at my side, breathless, frantic.

'Rebecca!' she cried, hunched beside me.

I tried to get up. I could not move. My limbs failed me.

The pain was intense. I bit back a scream with every shred of strength I had left.

'Dickie …' I gasped. 'The gun …'

She understood instantly and stumbled to the prone figure. She rushed back and fell to her knees beside me. 'He's dead.'

I expelled a long breath and succumbed to the pain. I could feel the warmth of my blood soaking into my clothing.

'Your arm! You're haemorrhaging!'

I could just make out the pulsing flow of blood from my arm. 'Tourniquet … my belt …' I was feeling faint and beginning to shiver. I had to stay conscious.

Lady Katherine, her hands slick with my blood, unclasped my belt and strapped it on my upper arm.

'Tight … tighter …' I panted, shivering violently.

She pulled it as tight as she could.

I could just make out her face. Darkness. Her face again, creased with panic, tears streaming—but she uttered not a word.

She pulled away the blood-soaked trousers from my hip and gasped. Without a second's hesitation, she tore her own petticoat in two. She padded one piece and pressed it hard against my hip.

I squirmed and choked down a yelp.

'I'm sorry!' she pleaded, stricken.

I wanted to reach out to touch her face, but my arms betrayed me—neither would move.

She wrapped another piece of cloth as firmly as she could around my damaged arm to help stem the flow.

'Go …' I urged. 'Find Wills …' I gave up to spasms of shivers.

'No. I won't leave you,' she insisted. She removed the jacket I'd given her and spread it over my chest. She cradled my head in her lap and looked down at me.

I willed my eyes to stay open. If this was to be my end, then I wanted her beautiful countenance to be the last sight I beheld.

The night held its breath.

No sound. No light. No fear.

Only her.

Finally, peace.

33

Thursday night, 7th September, 1905

Abbottsford Village, Suffolk, England

Rebecca Davies lay motionless on the forest floor, her head cradled in Lady Katherine's lap. The countess didn't feel the chill of the advancing night—her tearful gaze was fixed upon the woman she loved. Both women were drenched in blood, their bodies bruised, their clothing rent by violent acts.

Only ten feet away lay a grotesquely sprawled corpse with a single gunshot wound to the head—a wild, lucky shot that had somehow found its mark.

Peleus, the champion thoroughbred stood only a short distance away, his noble bearing dulled with exhaustion. The horse, like the countess, had endured far too much that day.

Lady Katherine wept freely, her tears failing to expunge the fear and utter desperation she felt.

'Don't die, my love. Please don't die,' she sobbed.

She had to get help but didn't want to leave Rebecca.

She prayed. A silent entreaty to God that they would be found and that danger had passed; but more, she prayed that Rebecca would live.

A distant sound caught her attention.

A deep rumble …

She held her breath … a motor car … Was that a motor car approaching? Her Rolls-Royce?

Her heart surged. But they were away from the path and the motor could easily drive past. She fumbled around in the trampled bracken for Rebecca's dropped Webley.

She found it.

She prayed again that it was her car and not that of another savage brute.

She listened. The sound grew louder.

The drone of the motor approached—she fired a shot into the air.

She listened again.

Still moving—the motor car was still moving.

She fired again and listened again. Had she made the right decision?

The motor car seemed to have stopped.

She fired again and waited.

From the same direction came the thrashing of undergrowth—someone was approaching!

She fired once more.

She didn't know if the gun was empty but she raised it towards the rustle of leaves coming closer … closer. She didn't want to consider shooting anyone but, if she had to, she would.

Branches cracked. Her breath came in short bursts. Her arm ached and the gun in her hand wavered.

Out of the gloom a figure emerged, gun in hand.

The elegantly clad figure of Major Williams broke through the forest's vegetation.

Relief struck Lady Katherine like a wave so powerful that her body felt it was deflating.

'Here!' Wills called over his shoulder, holstering his revolver and running to Lady Katherine and Davies.

'My God!' he uttered. 'Rebecca!'

He fell to his knees, his fingers at her neck, checking for a pulse. He peeled back her eyelids.

'She's alive,' Lady Katherine whispered, her soft voice trembling. 'Please help.'

Wills scanned the area. He saw the body.

'Where are the others?' His tone was sharp, urgent, apprehensive.

'Two more … and Mr Graves,' Lady Katherine replied numbly.

'We have Graves—' He stopped. 'Oh, Lady Katherine, you're hurt.'

'They're dead,' she stammered, frantic to make him understand. 'Rebecca's shot … She's lost a lot of blood … Her arm …'

Major Williams inspected the wounds and recoiled when, even in the pale glow of the moon, he saw the amount of blood soaking the ground. He inspected the bandaging and gave Lady Katherine an approving nod.

Then movement from the thicket on either side.

Jimmy and George burst through from one direction then the duke and Pitman from the other, with young Henry stumbling close behind his father.

A momentary silence fell over the natural clearing as they each took in the awful scene.

'Katherine!' The duke exclaimed and raced to his niece. 'Thank God you're safe!' He helped her to her feet and drew her tightly into his arms. 'Thank God … thank God … You're shivering.' He removed his jacket and wrapped it around her and enveloped her trembling body in his embrace once again.

Young Henry caught sight of Miss Davies lying on the ground, covered in blood. He took a few steps towards her and halted, wide-eyed.

'Miss Davies … ?' he whispered. 'Miss Davies … ?'

Pitman stood over Dickie's body and confirmed he was, indeed, dead. He picked up the pistol then noticed his son gawping at the injured woman.

'Henry!' he called, abrupt but not unkind. 'Peleus! Take charge, boy.'

Henry stumbled towards the horse, looking back at Rebecca. 'Is she dead, Pa? Is she?'

'God listens to all them that pray in earnest, Henry,' Pitman replied enigmatically.

Henry reached out to Peleus and comforted him with gentle words and petting, all the time glancing towards Miss Davies.

Safe in her uncle's arms, Lady Katherine prayed in earnest and thanked Him for delivering these men to Rebecca.

***

Wills' years of experience in the field meant he was quicky able to interpret the extent of Davies' wounds. What he saw alarmed him. She had lost a staggering amount of blood; the ground beneath her was sodden with it. Her breathing was shallow; her skin clammy. If she wasn't warmed and awake, she would slip into shock.

She needed urgent medical attention.

He took off his coat and draped it over her own. Without a word, both George and Jimmy followed his lead.

'Rebecca!' Wills urged, slapping her cheeks, carefully but insistently. 'Rebecca, wake up! Wake up! Sleeping on the job again! Wake up!'

Her eyelids fluttered; she roused. 'Katherine …' she murmured.

He exhaled with relief. 'Stay awake, Davies. No excuses! Stay awake!' He turned to Lady Katherine. 'My Lady, we must get her to a doctor immediately. The motor car?'

Lady Katherine allowed herself a whimper and a grateful nod.

'You three,' Wills commanded Pitman, Jimmy and George. 'With me. Now.'

Wills crouched beside Davies, slid his arm under her shoulders and nodded to Pitman. 'Other side. Cradle her shoulders. You two—her legs. Under her buttocks. Lift.'

A long, low groan escaped Rebecca Davies as they lifted her. Her head lolled against Wills' arm, neck limp.

'Henry! Stay close. Bring the horse,' Pitman called back to his son. The boy obeyed, trailing behind with Peleus.

They moved as one in grim procession through the forest and back towards the waiting car.

Wills didn't indulge in sentimentality; that was for later. Now, his expression was set, his jaw tight, his attention fixed, every step heavy with resolve.

The duke and his niece kept pace behind them, his arm tight around the countess' waist as though he was afraid someone else would try to steal her again. Lady Katherine, pale and silent, moved without protest, her eyes fixed on Rebecca.

***

The duke prayed for a miracle as the Rolls-Royce raced through the forest at blistering speed, the light from its acetylene lamps cleaving a sharp path through the darkness and flaring against the ghostly birch trees that lined the way. The massive automobile jostled over ruts and gravel as Jimmy pushed the machine to its limits. George, in the seat beside, hung on and urged the chauffeur to go faster.

They flew past the upturned wagon, its tethered horse and its beaten and subdued driver—he didn't spare them a glance—no one inside the car did.

Rebecca Davies, her face bloodless, her breath shallow and ragged, faded in and out of consciousness as she lay across the back seat. Her blood seeped into the fine leather. Wills crouched beside her in the footwell, tension eroding his usually-unshakeable composure.

Lady Katherine sat opposite them, encircled by the duke's protective embrace, teetering on the edge of her seat and on the edge of her sanity. Her eyes never left Rebecca's pallid face. Her hands, encrusted with blood, clenched her uncle's jacket tightly around her as she watched on in wordless anxiety.

The duke sat stiff and silent. His mind raced through the unbearable 'what-ifs': what if Henry had not found that shred of fabric … what if he had not summoned help … what if the train had not been delayed … what if Davies had not overheard … what if the 'poachers' had not been discovered … what if Peleus … Each turn tugged at him and overwhelmed him. His vision blurred with tears. He was indebted beyond measure to this valiant woman who lay before him, close to death.

Major Williams, previously strong and resolute, was now worried and despairing lest this woman succumbed to her injuries. His hand trembled as he felt Rebecca's pulse again.

Every second mattered.

***

Further back along the path, Pitman and his son rode Peleus home at a steady controlled pace. They stopped at the upturned wagon and secured the still-groggy Stewart Graves onto his borrowed horse and led them both back to the Hall. Pitman warned Graves that he should not try to escape; the rifle was loaded and he, Pitman, was only too eager to pay him back for the whipping he'd received.

***

The instant the Rolls-Royce turned into the long drive to the Hall, the forecourt filled with servants pouring out of every corner of the estate, torches flaring, lanterns swinging.

Wills looked down at Rebecca—she was slipping—he knew it—only one thing could save her now.

The crowd parted just enough for the car to roar up to the stone staircase and skid to a stop on the loose gravel. They clustered around it, jostling for a glimpse inside.

The air was thick with emotion.

At the foot of the stairs, Thomson stood rigidly behind the duchess, flanked by Jessica, Emma and Mrs Plummer. Their faces were drawn tight with anxiety for the countess. The village constable was at their side, rifle slung over his shoulder, scanning the crowd.

Wills saw them all as obstacles. They needed to be cleared—he needed space—he needed every precious second he could steal.

Jimmy and George leapt onto the running boards in unison.

'Stand back! Make room! Clear the way!' Their calls cut through the clamour.

Wills shoved open the door. 'Where's the doctor?' His voice was loud, clear, sharp.

'Here!' called a young man, pushing his way to the open door, his medical bag gripped in hand. He looked barely out of university, nervous—but present.

Mary, the duchess, had found her way through the throng to the car. 'Katherine!' she called, her voice trembling. 'Katherine …'

The duke was instantly at his wife's side. 'She's all right, Mary, she'll be fine—'

'She's hurt!'

'She'll be fine,' he repeated, though Wills heard the doubt beneath his words.

Jimmy spotted the constable. 'Constable! Clear everyone away from the motor car. We need room!'

The constable valiantly tried but failed.

'Everyone!' George shouted—he had mounted several steps of the staircase so he could be seen and heard over the commotion. 'Everyone listen! Lady Katherine is safe—'

A cheer went up.

'The perpetrators have been brought to account.'

Another cheer but this time laced with angry words and oaths.

'Please! Please … please disperse. The doctor must attend to Miss Davies. Constable, please …'

This time, the crowd heeded the call and the constable ushered them back although they all stayed—at a distance—holding their torches and lanterns aloft.

The duke pulled Thomson and Mrs Plummer aside and gave them rapid instruction. The pair hurried back into the Hall. He took Mary's hand and led her away from the motor car. Emma and Jessica followed closely behind, speechless.

Wills stood by the open door as the young doctor clambered inside. He introduced himself hastily—Dr Benjamin Werner—then fell silent as he took in the broken, bloodied form of the unconscious woman. He felt Rebecca's pulse.

'Her pulse is very week. She's cold and she's lost a tremendous amount of blood—'

'She needs a transfusion,' Wills interjected impatiently and quickly outlined her injuries.

Dr Werner stared at Wills, apparently absorbing the details but seemingly bewildered.

'Do you have the equipment?' Wills demanded.

'Yes … in my dog cart … I always carry … but it's hazardous … it's disfavoured—'

'You've not performed one before?'

'In theory … but perhaps a rectal saline solution—'

'Goddammit man! Get your equipment! Quickly!'

The doctor scrambled out of the motor car and did as ordered, almost colliding with Thomson. The butler and two footmen had returned with a stretcher.

Wills immediately recognised it as one used in the Boer conflict in South Africa. The irony did not escape him. This time their roles would be reversed—it was a debt he'd willingly repay.

With utmost care, Wills, Jimmy and George transferred Davies onto the stretcher and the two footmen carried her towards the Hall.

Wills kept pace behind them, his senses focussed on every breath Rebecca took.

***

When Lady Katherine emerged from the car to follow Rebecca, the duchess caught sight of her and cried out. Her appearance also shocked the onlookers—they saw a woman desperate to maintain her dignity, clutching the duke's coat about her, trying to conceal the torn, bloodied remnants of her blouse, her hair loose and matted with twigs and leaves, and her once-flawless face bruised, swollen and blood-encrusted.

'Katherine!' the duchess cried, her voice shattered by what she saw. She broke from her husband's grip and ran to her niece. 'Oh, my dear God! Sweetling! My darling Katherine … dear God,' she cried, unable to contain her anguish.

Lady Katherine saw guilt in the duchess' face, and the awful understanding that the degradations she had suffered had been meant for her aunt.

The duchess pulled Lady Katherine into a fierce embrace.

'I'm all right, Aunt, I'm all right,' Lady Katherine whispered, trying to console her. But in truth, she was barely holding herself together. Still, she did not slow. She clung to her aunt but kept moving, determined to keep up with the stretcher.

She was loth to leave Rebecca's side.

***

Davies was carried through the grand entrance foyer, through the green baize door and into the servants' hall. This was the only room on the ground floor that was large and private enough to accommodate so many people at once and was close to all anticipated amenities. The dining table had been cleared and the chairs pushed aside to make room for the injured woman.

The footmen carefully placed the stretcher on the table and gawped at Davies.

'Out!' Mrs Plummer snapped and drew the blinds with practised efficiency, then addressed her staff with the authority of a field marshal. Maids ran at her command—some fetching kettles of boiling water, others empty bowls. The laundry maid arrived with a stack of clean, folded linen. Once delivered, Mrs Plummer shooed them all out.

Through all this bustle, Wills and Thomson arranged the stretcher, preparing a space for the doctor. Wills pulled a chair in close then nodded towards the foot end.

'Raise that,' he ordered.

Thomson immediately propped it with biscuit tins.

A low groan escaped Davies. Her eyes fluttered open.

'Katherine …' she whispered. 'She's hurt …'

'Lady Katherine's being looked after,' Wills replied softly. 'You just stay with me, Davies. You hear?'

Her gaze drifted, unfocused. 'Shooting star … ?'

'No shooting star, Davies,' Wills reassured her. 'I'm not so lucky.'

She gave the faintest smile and let out a long, exhausted sigh and closed her eyes.

'Don't you die on me, woman, I need you …' Wills whispered, leaning in close, his words catching in his throat.

The meaning of this exchange left the butler and housekeeper puzzled. They knew nothing of Davies' history, nor her earnest belief that her life's thread would be cut by the whim of a passing meteor.

But Wills knew. And he would not let her go.

The jackets covering Rebecca's chest were discarded and her blood-soaked sweater cut away from her body. Wills removed the empty holster and, with Mrs Plummer's assistance, carefully cut away the blouse, exposing her sodden flannel undershirt.

'Cut the sleeve off at the armhole,' he instructed, as he concentrated on doing the same to the left side just below the tourniquet. He cautiously peeled away the blood-drenched bandage Lady Katherine had tightly wrapped around the wound.

With the wrap discarded, Wills pulled away the bloodied undershirt sleeve to reveal the gaping channel the bullet left when it tore through the flesh and nicked the artery on Davies' upper arm. An ugly bruise had formed around the injury.

The tourniquet had stemmed the flow of blood but it could not stay in place much longer. Gangrene was a real threat. Wills prayed the doctor, young as he was, had the competence to suture the vessel. The tear was tiny, but it had to be closed. If not, a transfusion would be futile and Rebecca would not survive.

While Wills and Mrs Plummer tended the upper wound, Thomson efficiently removed the clothing from Rebecca's hip.

'I served with His Grace in the second Afghan War,' Thomson said, examining the wound. 'We lost more good men to infection than to enemy fire.'

Wills offered no reply; he knew it to be true.

Dr Werner swept into the servants' hall followed by the footman, both laden with boxed medical apparatus. The young doctor took a deep breath. There was uncertainty in his features—but resolve as well.

Wills watched him closely. Rebecca's life was in this young man's hands.

Werner instructed the footman to set his equipment down and swiftly opened each box in readiness. He removed his coat and rolled up his sleeves, donning a clean apron with much urgency. From his medical bag he tore open a packet and used the contents to scrub his hands scrupulously clean in a bowl of hot water.

The footman lingered, mouth agape, staring in disbelief at the unconscious woman who languished upon the very table he'd used for supper only hours before.

'Out!' Thomson snapped, startling him into a hasty exit.

'Mrs Plummer,' Werner said drying his hands, 'those instruments, in boiling water if you would.'

Rebecca stirred. 'Wills …' she whispered. 'Dickie … He's … working …' She coughed, clearly overcome by pain.

'I'll need to put her under,' Werner announced. 'Mr Thomson, that box.'

With surprising competence, the young doctor unpacked a new Braun ether inhaler, filled the jar with a mixture of ether and chloroform and instructed Thomson in its use.

'Keep the mask firm on her until I tell you to remove it,' he said adjusting the taps.

Within moments, Rebecca's body slackened. Werner leaned in assessing the damage.

'The brachial artery is torn,' he said. 'Small, but I must close it before we can release the ligature. The hip wound has fragments of bone. There is an exit wound but we'll need an X-ray later for any bullet fragment or bone shard we've missed.'

Without pause, he sponged both wounds with pure carbolic acid then washed off the excess with absolute alcohol.

'Mr Thomson, the mask.' Thomson removed it.

Werner doused his hands with carbolic acid and began the delicate work of stitching the damaged artery with minute sutures.

Wills watched closely. His earlier apprehension slowly evaporated. The boy knew his business … so far.

A gentle rap sounded on the door.

Thomson opened it to the duchess and Lady Katherine.

Lady Katherine stifled a cry of despair at the sight of Rebecca.

'She's being well looked after, my lady,' Wills reassured her.

Dr Werner looked up. 'Your Grace, my lady,' he said. 'Please … Mrs Plummer, you'll find some antiseptic swabs and bandages in the bag. Take the carbolic.'

Mrs Plummer understood the direction immediately. 'Perhaps Your Grace and Lady Katherine would be more comfortable in my quarters,' she suggested, 'until the good doctor can see to my lady.'

'Of course,' the duchess agreed, wanting to protect her niece from further horror. 'Come, sweetling, Mrs Plummer will see to your injuries.' The door closed softly behind them. Wills caught the depth of compassion in the final glance Lady Katherine sent Rebecca.

Werner returned to his patient.

The suturing complete, the doctor carefully loosened the tourniquet. Blood flow resumed, slow but steady. The stitches held, but she had lost far too much blood.

'The hip wound can wait. The pressure pad has stemmed the blood flow. I'll work on that while we get some blood into her. Are you ready Major Williams?'

Wills sat in the chair beside Davies and offered his bare arm.

'Do you know your blood group?' Dr Werner asked unpacking his new and unused blood transfusion kit.

'It's compatible,' he replied tersely. 'Paraffin.'

'Sir?' The doctor looked at him puzzled.

'Use paraffin on the cannulas. It prevents the blood from coagulating.'

'Where did you—'

'In South Africa. Just do it.'

Despite his practical inexperience, Werner carried out the task with precision and swiftness. He disinfected Wills' wrist, administered a local anaesthetic, applied a ligature above the elbow and incised the artery at the wrist. He inserted the cannula, attached it to the India rubber tube and sutured the artery closed around it. He repeated the process with Rebecca's vein in her right arm at the elbow.

He slowly released the ligature. The tube gently pulsated.

A weak but present pulse retuned to Rebecca's wrist.

While monitoring the flow, Werner turned to the hip wound. He flushed it with disinfectant, probed the gash with infinite care, removed bone fragments, and stitched the tears. A sterile gauze and plaster followed.

Slowly, colour returned to Davies' lips and skin.

Wills, on the other hand, was becoming faint and pale.

'That's enough,' Dr Werner said decisively, and retightened the ligature on Wills' arm. The tube ceased pulsing.

'Mr Thomson, a bowl.'

He placed the bowl under Davies' right arm to catch the overflow, removed the canula and stitched the wound, applying a tight bandage around it.

He reverted to Wills.

Just as rapidly and expertly he removed the cannula from Wills' wrist, sutured and bandaged it as he had done with Rebecca.

Exhausted but pleased with the outcome, Dr Werner checked Davies' pulse once more then took in Wills' wan complexion.

'A cup of tea and something to eat for the major, I think,' he instructed Thomson.

'Perhaps a cup of tea all round, Sir,' Thomson suggested leaving to arrange the curative.

Dr Werner carefully spread several blankets over Rebecca and another over Major Williams.

The door to the servants' hall flew open. Much to the doctor's surprise the diminutive form of the irrepressible Henry raced to the unconscious Davies.

'Miss Davies! Miss Davies!' he cried, looking at her inanimate body. 'Is she dead?'

'No, young man,' Dr Werner quietly assured him. 'She's resting.'

'Will she die?'

'Not if you pray for her.'

'She won't die, then,' Henry assured him. His usually smooth forehead nonetheless betrayed a few worried creases.

Wills rallied himself. 'And what of Stewart Graves? Do you have him?'

Henry's demeanour changed instantly. He chuckled as he wiped an errant tear from his face. 'The doc will have to see to him, too. He fell off his horse three times coming here.'

34

Friday, 8th September, 1905

Abbottsford Village, Suffolk, England

It was well after midnight Friday morning when they entered Mrs Plummer's quarters, leaving Dr Werner to do everything possible to save Rebecca's life.

The housekeeper's sitting room was relatively spacious and offered her privacy and comfort, reflecting her position within the servant hierarchy. A fireplace, carpets, comfortable chairs and a desk fitted neatly within—not lavish, but possessed of the dignity of one who had served long and loyally.

Lady Katherine had remained stoic throughout the ordeal, suppressing the pain and turmoil that surged beneath her skin like a storm-whipped sea. Her steps were resolute, though she saw and felt little as she entered the room supported on the unwavering arm of her aunt, Mary.

Her maid, Jessica, and Emma had lingered respectfully outside the servant's hall and now followed them to the housekeeper's quarters, attending them at the open door.

'Come, my lady,' Mrs Plummer said, guiding the countess to an upholstered easy chair. 'Emma,' she called, 'fetch some hot water and, Turner, Her Ladyship's dressing gown. Quickly now.'

They sped off to complete their tasks, their steps retreating down the corridor.

Lady Katherine sat stiffly, her fingers remaining clenched on her uncle's coat, drawing it tight about her frame, attempting to keep at bay both the chill and reality. Sensation had dulled, save the subtle urgency that filled the air.

'You'll be well soon, my sweetling,' the duchess whispered, her voice hushed and gentle. 'I will have Thomson send notes to all the guests and cancel the weekend. Rest, my darling, your convalescence is paramount. It will be quiet and undisturbed …'

The countess heard the words as though through a dense fog—muffled, distant, unrelated. Her senses had retreated beyond reach, barricaded and hidden from the outside world.

Something tore at her—something indescribable, something she had never felt before. She had witnessed death, violent and merciless; and the woman she had come to love lay barely alive. She owed that woman more than her own life. What she had been given was not merely survival, but her very soul, rescued by a courage that was not her own.

Emma returned and gentle ministrations proceeded, cleansing the countess' lacerations.

The duchess spoke, earnest and well-meaning. Constant, never-ending.

'… Miss Davies will be brought up to the suite next to yours and Major Williams will have his own room back. Doctor Werner will be kept on until Miss Davies is out of danger and you have fully recovered …'

More words … gentle … practical … but they didn't reach her.

'… Uncle Charlie has let Mr Quinn know of your rescue and he expects both him and Sir Giles Hawthorne to arrive tomorrow in the forenoon, or rather, today, along with some of his constabulary …'

Incessant, irrelevant …

'… I'm sure they will want to speak to you but I will keep them away until you are ready …'

The endless flow of words washed over the countess. Her aunt was using her irrepressible proclivity for talk to do the best she could to distract, but Lady Katherine's ears had barricaded themselves against the intrusion.

The fog thickened. Something within it grew darker. The fear, pain, anger and grief continued to riot deep beneath the hatch that imprisoned them.

Jessica returned with a dressing gown.

' … You are to rest, my dear, and think no more of it. All is well. Turner, come,' Mary carefully helped Lady Katherine to her feet. 'Let us remove your soiled clothing.'

Jessica carefully unbuttoned the fastenings on the back of the countess' shirtwaist and skirt letting them fall to the floor.

Then, silence.

A gasp escaped the maid, stifled behind her hand. The bruising to her mistress' face, neck and arms was stark—purple, red, angry against the milky-white skin.

'Oh, my lady! What did they do to ye?'

The gentleness of her maid's softly spoken cry of horror brought the countess back to reality.

Lady Katherine's resolve faltered. The hatch was besieged.

Mary stepped forward. 'Come, sweetling, a bath will soothe away your pain,' Mary urged. 'You'll feel much better once you've immersed yourself in the hot water.'

Lady Katherine did not move. Her body stiffened; her eyes unseeing. *What did they do?* her inner voice questioned.

She looked at her hands; they had been washed but dried blood was still evident in the folds and creases. She looked down at the skirt that lay discarded at her feet—dark, congealed patches soiled much of it. Her shirtwaist, too, was bloodied and torn. Blood. Her blood. Rebecca's blood. Rebecca's blood was everywhere, soaking into her skin.

What did they do? repeated itself like an endless echo through her mind. Her head throbbed; her body ached. The hatch was giving way.

Visions and memories came flooding back in waves. The brutal deaths of three men, the violation of her body ... what they had threatened to do ... she would have died ... she should have died ...

The hold was breeched. It all surged in, crashing against the walls of her inner sanctum. Her knees gave way.

'Katherine!' Mary cried.

She lay curled up on the floor, sobbing and shaking.

At once, the duchess and Jessica were on their knees beside her.

'Fetch the doctor!' Mrs Plummer called to Emma.

Mary cradled her niece.

'There, there, my darling Kateling,' Mary consoled. 'You're safe now—'

'Nanny Fee ...' were the only words Lady Katherine was able to utter between her gasping sobs. 'Please ...'

Jessica met the duchess' eyes.

'Yes,' Mary said without a pause. 'Telephone her. Send the motor.'

Jessica scrambled to her feet and ran.

***

It was a quarter of two in the morning when a strident bell rang incessantly throughout Lilyfield Manor—three telephones echoing the urgent call in different rooms. The butler and the housekeeper, startled from their slumber and pulling on their dressing gowns, converged on the butler's pantry from different directions, their faces creased with alarm.

'Who could that be?' mumbled the housekeeper as the butler lifted the earpiece from the wall-mounted apparatus and spoke testily into the mouthpiece. 'Chestermere. Do you have any idea what time it is?'

His tone changed to one of surprise. 'Jessica … Yes, she's right here.'

He handed the earpiece to the woman beside him. 'Jessie?'

She stretched her small frame up to the mouthpiece. 'Jessica, is that ye? What is the matter, lassie?'

Her manner changed from curiosity to stupefaction. Colour drained from her face and her mouth parted as she listened intently. 'Aye … aye, I'll ready myself,' she said, scarcely aware she had uttered any words.

Her trembling hand replaced the earpiece into its cradle and, looking up to the butler with unseeing eyes, she hesitated. 'Lady Katherine … She's no' well … She's asked for me … Jimmy's coming tae fetch me …'

The words hung in the air between them—so many unasked questions.

The butler broke the silence. 'Fiona, what on earth's happened? Why telephone at this time of night? Her Ladyship was due to arrive today.'

'I dinnae know, Peter, I dinnae ken,' she whispered, her thoughts awhirl with possibilities. 'I must get ready.'

Mrs McPherson hurried back to her quarters. She flung open drawers and packed her valise with practised ease but, this time, with urgency. Rampant thoughts stampeded through a forest of possibilities dire enough for her to be summoned in the middle of the night. Not knowing bred its own dread.

As trembling fingers buttoned her black body-forming jacket, she sat briefly to tie on her shoes. Each tug brought a flood of memory— her thoughts drifted back, the years peeling away …

Fiona Cameron was twelve years of age when she went into service as a tweeny in the household of Donald Stuart of Glenross, in the plain of Forth and Clyde. Before long, with hard work and diligence, she had risen through the service ranks to chambermaid, parlour maid and, with the impending marriage of her laird's eldest son, Ailbeart, she was to be the intended bride's nursery maid when the time came.

Ailbeart was a handsome young man who set young Fiona's heart aflutter whenever she was in his presence but she could see that his passion was for the beautiful Lady Agnes, elder of the two daughters of the Earl of Chestermere.

Lady Agnes was only a year older than Fiona and they had immediately formed a bond the first time they were introduced.

It was just after Lady Agnes' twentieth birthday anniversary that her only child was born. Fiona doted on little Lady Kateling, the pet-name she gave baby Katherine, and the infant grew to know two mothers: the beautiful Lady Agnes who taught her the ways of the aristocracy, and Nanny Fee who took care of her education and her every need and whim.

As Lady Katherine grew beyond infancy, Nanny Fee became her governess and, when Lady Katherine entered college, it was Nanny Fee who accompanied her to London as her devoted lady's maid.

Before then, when Lady Katherine was nine years of age, Fiona married Ian McPherson and had a bonny son, George. All the while, other than during her confinement, she remained Lady Katherine's nanny and governess—something most unusual but such was the bond between the three women that it was never a question she would be let go.

Now, Nanny Fee was Mrs McPherson, the housekeeper of Lady Katherine's country house, Lilyfield Manor, and Delaney House, the London townhouse in Mayfair. And she was the only person to whom Lady Katherine turned when her needs were the greatest.

What needs would be so great as tae summon me at this time of the night?

***

The Louis XVI Directoire mantle clock in the countess' bedroom chimed the quarter hour after four and the draught of laudanum Dr Werner had administered to her was now wearing off.

Lady Katherine tossed in bed, restless. Images manifested themselves again and again, turning her much-needed sleep to fitful. She could not escape the pain and brutality being visited upon her, no matter how much she willed it. She was trapped within it. Perspiration soaked her bed clothes; her muted calls for help could not stave off the inevitable …

An anguished cry escaped her lips and she lurched upright in a sudden convulsive motion. The room spun around her as she took in her surroundings, bewildered, gasping for breath, her head throbbing.

It took her a few moments to realise it had been a nightmare and she was safe. Slumping back down, she pushed the images as far out of her mind as she could.

They were dead. They were all dead—those who wished her harm.

Her thoughts turned to her own heroine—her Rebecca. It was very early but she had a need to see her.

The suite next to the countess' was a little smaller than her own but afforded all the same comforts.

Lady Katherine, clad in her dressing gown, quietly opened the door and stepped inside the darkened room. The fireplace held a few smouldering embers but she could make out the prone form of her saviour lying on the large bed, unconscious and unaware. The rhythmic rise and fall of her chest gave Lady Katherine hope—however fragile— that all would be well.

Silently moving closer, she was startled to see the sleeping figure of Major Williams slumped in a chair next to Rebecca, his head resting on the bed and his hands clasping hers.

Lady Katherine was moved by his tenderness and devotion. She felt no jealousy towards him—only kindness and respect.

Major Williams stirred and lifted his head.

'My lady,' he said, standing unsteadily.

'Please, major, don't get up,' she replied softly. 'I just wanted to see how she is.'

'Thank you, my lady,' he said, bringing another chair closer to his. 'I had the same concern.'

Lady Katherine took the seat beside him with a gracious nod and saw the shine in his eyes. Whether through weariness or embarrassment, he rubbed his eyes.

'I came to help young Henry with his prayers,' he said, his voice cracking with emotion. He resumed his seat and took Rebecca's hand once more.

'And … how are you, my lady?' he asked softly, almost apologetically. 'I am so sorry …' he stuttered, his voice imbued with deep harrowing emotion that mirrored her own. 'So sorry to put you through that hell. It should not have happened. We should have—'

'Major,' Lady Katherine interrupted, placing a hand on his. Her voice trembled but she held his gaze. 'She will pull through this. We will pull her through this. Together.'

Wills shook his head. 'You …' He tried to reply but no words came.

'I will mend. If it weren't for Rebecca, and you …' Her voice fractured. The enormity of the alternative outcome overwhelmed her and, once again, those horrid, fleeting images came to the fore. She gasped and clasped a hand over her mouth to still the pain. 'Forgive me,' she choked.

Major Williams folded the countess into his arms and gently rocked her back and forth, murmuring soothing words she could not hear. She unashamedly wept and wrapped her arms tightly around him.

Somewhere beyond the edge of darkness, a voice whispered, 'Don't cry, my love. You're safe now.'

But she did not hear. No one did.

***

Whatever had delayed the private detectives remained a mystery but one of the first things the Duke of Bramwell did that Friday morning was to cancel their engagement. The next was to summon all the staff—maid servants, man servants, gardeners and stable hands—to assemble in the mews immediately after breakfast.

No one had had much sleep after the turmoil of the night, but it was imperative that everyone there knew what was expected of them.

The corpses of the three abductors were retrieved and taken to the village lockup, together with Stewart Graves after Doctor Werner had attended to him.

The duke stood on the mounting block, posture erect, expression solemn even though fatigue and the unspeakable events of the preceding night weighed heavily upon him. He addressed the servants crowded around him in clear, resonant tones.

'Men, women … boys and girls, we have all been through the gates of hell and, with God's benevolence, have emerged unscathed but weary. I thank you, each and every one of you, sincerely for your part in this most appalling episode.

'Lady Katherine is resting and will recover from her dreadful ordeal. Miss Davies, too, with God's mercy and Doctor Werner's invaluable ministrations, will recover but will need time and quietude for her convalescence.

'It is for this reason that I ask one more solemn request of you, each and every one.

'You have all done a splendid job preparing for the duchess' Saturday-to-Monday. Regrettably—but appropriately—the duchess has cancelled it. Some guests are already on their way and due to arrive shortly after noon. I have made arrangements for their comfort elsewhere. Thomson and Mrs Plummer have the details.

'For the privacy and well-being of my niece, no one is to know what transpired here this night. You are not to disclose any information to parties outside of ourselves. The near disaster that befell us all is to be kept strictly within these walls. Can I depend on you?'

A murmuring arose from the assembled crowd as each offered total agreement.

The duke, satisfied, continued. 'The duchess and I thank you from the most profound depths of our hearts. One last thing: the Metropolitan police will be here shortly and they may wish to speak to some of you. You will comply with their requests. Mr Thomson will arrange the interviews. The east wing of the Hall is closed off to all, *without exception*,' he warned with a purposeful look to Henry.

'Me, Your Grace?' Henry feigned surprise.

'Without exception,' the duke repeated.

***

It felt as though I had been trampled by a stampeding herd of elephants. Never, not even during the brutal beating I had suffered at John Harper's hands nor after the unspeakable acts of savagery by those Mussulmen, had I known such intense pain. Every breath was torture.

Through a muffled jumble of sounds, words jumped out and insisted on being heard.

'Doctor …'

' … Rebecca …'

' … Will she … ?'

Different tones, different pitches—the disembodied voices were familiar but I couldn't distinguish one from the other. My eyelids were impossibly heavy and refused to open. *Where was I? Why was I hurting so much?*

'Rebecca … Rebecca …' I recognised the insistent call to wakefulness. Wills.

With determined effort, I forced open a slit between my eyelids and became aware of pale sunshine invading the dimness. My vision focused on the worried face that hovered over me.

'Wills,' I rasped. 'Where am … what … ?' The words disintegrated under the intense pain that overwhelmed me. Sharp, searing pain that tore through every nerve in my left side, robbing me of air. I tried again to speak but darkness threatened to pull me under again. My limbs were too heavy to move yet I felt weightless, floating.

'I'll give her half a grain of morphine …'

'No, doctor—I need her coherent,' Wills said, his tone urgent but controlled. He leaned in closer. 'Rebecca, can you hear me?'

I could, even though his voice mingled with the shrill ringing that filled my ears. I tried to answer but the words that formed in my brain seemed to get stuck in my mouth. I needed to tell him about Humphries.

'Hum … Hum …' I panted through the ever-tightening band around my neck.

'Rebecca,' he continued, 'listen to me. Quinn and Hawthorne will be here shortly and they will want to speak to you. Are you up for it?'

I gave a slight nod when the word 'yes' stuck in my throat. I abandoned all effort to speak.

'Good for you, old girl. We'll have this sorted in a trice and you off to hospital before you know it.'

The look of compassion he gave me spoke more than his words could ever express.

'The doctor wants to examine you,' he added, then with a note of mischief. 'Make sure you're not malingering.'

I almost laughed.

Almost.

***

It was that period between breakfast and lunch that her son, George, liked to call 'brunch'—a legacy of his student days—when he and Jimmy completed their dash to bring Fiona McPherson from Lilyfield Manor to Abbottsford with all the speed the motor car could summon.

In the closed compartment of the vehicle, George had sat with his mother and recounted in grim, minute detail Lady Katherine's ordeal and the courage of the woman who had saved her. Fiona listened, her fixed gaze and clenched fists the only outward signs that she was living every moment as though her mistress' pain were her own.

The instant the Rolls-Royce entered the Hall's perimeter gates, the duchess was there, in the forecourt, as though summoned by instinct. She had known the housekeeper for all but the first eighteen years of her life and she was more to her than a servant.

They greeted each other warmly but with scant words, and hurried up the stone stairway, abandoning Jimmy and George in their wake.

The duchess rushed the housekeeper directly to Lady Katherine's suite—those same rooms in which Fiona had kept vigil a quarter-century before, where, for months, her wee Kateling at fourteen had cried herself to sleep every night after the tragic loss of her parents. It was Mary and her husband, the Duke of Bramwell, who took their grieving niece under their protective wings and raised her as one of their own. The duke was a canny businessman and had gotten along extremely well with his Scotch brother-in-law, the Laird Ailbeart Stuart of Glenross, and together they had formed a profitable business relationship.

Fiona had watched the child grow into a lass and the lass into a woman—one who had shown not only interest in her father's business dealings but also an aptitude for mathematics, law and languages. It was no surprise to anyone that after suffering such a profound and sudden loss, she applied herself with astounding vigour and determination to succeed in the masculine world of enterprise and continued in her father's footsteps.

Wherever she went—Queen's College, Girton College—Fiona was there as her chaperone, lady's maid and unshakeable pillar.

By twenty-one, Lady Katherine Agnes Stuart Delaney had claimed her birthright, her properties, and her place among England's nobility, as the Countess of Chestermere in her own right. The care, concern and regard for her staff and tenants only confirmed she was a woman who truly embodied the essence of *noblesse oblige*.

Only Fiona McPherson truly understood her mistress' nature and never tried to change any part of what made Lady Katherine who she was: not her left-handedness, not her drive to excel in a man's world, not her choice of whom she loved.

As they neared the bedchamber, Fiona's pace slowed, each step weighed down with dread. *Let it not have broken her*, she prayed. *Let it not have robbed her of her spirit.*

The duchess swept into the room followed by Mrs McPherson, startling Jessica who had settled into an easy chair beside her mistress and fallen asleep.

Jessica jumped to her feet. 'Your Grace! Mrs Mac! I … I—'

'Hush now, lassie,' Mrs McPherson reassured the young maid. 'All will be well. Off with ye and get some rest now.'

Jessica curtseyed and slipped out, casting her mistress one last worried glance.

Lying in her bed and still wearing her dressing gown, Lady Katherine seemed to be at peace.

The two older women, looked down on the bruised and sleeping form of the middle-aged peer who meant so much to both of them. The bruises to her face had deepened to a ghastly purple, but her breathing was steady and soft. It reminded Fiona of those harrowing years when she'd nursed the wee bairn through grief and adolescence alike.

'Oh, my sweet Kateling …' Fiona whispered.

'This morning, the doctor found Katherine in Miss Davies' room,' the duchess explained quietly. 'He sent her to bed and gave her another draught of laudanum to settle her.'

'Miss Davies? George explained it was she who saved her.'

'Yes.' Mary hesitated. 'I'm afraid Katherine has formed … an attachment.'

Fiona glanced up and left unsaid what they both understood.

Mary's gaze returned to Katherine; she appeared to falter—her words stumbling out over each other. 'I … she … The doctor said she will have a tiny scar on her brow, but it should fade in time … The biggest scar will be—'

Mary was unable to finish her sentence. Her knees gave way and she slumped into the chair next to the bed and buried her face in her hands. She could no longer contain the guilt that had been building and was about to explode. 'It should have been me, Fiona. Not sweet Katherine. It should have been me …'

Fiona knelt beside Mary and pulled her close and held her tightly. 'Your Grace … please … Dinnae blame yourself—'

'I should have listened … I was a fool … an old, old, silly, stupid fool.'

'Hush … All will be well, by the grace of God.'

***

The train from London arrived on time and deposited the Met's Special Branch contingent on the Abbottsford Village station platform. The two carriages that carried the seven men proceeded directly to the servants' entrance at the Hall where Major Williams waited, fatigue and gravity etched into his handsome features. He had had scant sleep over the past two days and the effects of the blood transfusion had only added to his lethargy.

The men alighted; Wills squared his shoulders and greeted them with solemn civility.

'Sir Giles …'

'Fancy seeing you here,' Sir Giles replied tersely. His mood was unmistakeably sour. 'What the dickens is going on, Williams?'

Wills had no desire to engage Hawthorne in catty behaviour; his energies were exhausted. With an acknowledging nod to the remaining policemen and a brief, 'Please follow me,' Wills ushered them inside without delay.

To avoid unwanted speculation and attention, Wills took them through the back stairs and into the duke's study where the duke awaited them. Much to the newly arrived officers' surprise, Alexander Quinn was also in attendance.

'Mr Quinn!' was Hawthorne's astonished greeting upon entering the study.

Quinn dismissed the rudeness and made the introductions. 'Your Grace, may I present to you Sir Giles Hawthorne, my Chief of the Department of Special Operations, Detective Sergeant Yabsley and Detective Constables Hewitt, Ramsay, Byrne, Dolby and Hathaway.'

'Sir Giles, gentlemen. Normally, it would be a pleasure to meet you all. However, under these most distressing circumstances—'

'We are here to find your niece—' Sir Giles interrupted.

'The countess has been found,' Quinn cut him off.

This piece of news had the seven officers exchanging glances, clearly perplexed.

'She is safe and as well as can be expected,' Quinn continued. 'And the three perpetrators have been … neutralised. They are in the village lockup.'

'How? When? When did you know this?'

'Very late last night. Well after I spoke to you, Sir Giles. His Grace telephoned to me at home and gave me the good news. I did contact you, Sir Giles, but as you do not have a telephone set in your home, I sent along a note. You obviously did not receive it.'

Hawthorne ruminated the information; there was no note on the salver; his wife had said nothing this morning. But she did have her mother's streak of vindictiveness.

'I travelled all night by motor car to arrive here before you,' Quinn continued. 'Major Williams has given me a detailed account—'

'Yes,' interrupted Hawthorne, his evident annoyance colouring his speech. 'And just how did the good major know about all this before me?'

'I will discuss that with you later, Sir Giles. Meanwhile, we still have some very important information to gather.'

'What, the major hasn't solved the case yet?'

Quinn was clearly becoming irritated by Hawthorne's petulance and tried to interject.

'I—'

'You want us to interrogate the perpetrators?' Hawthorne cut him off again. 'Do you trust us with that, Mr Quinn?'

Quinn took a deep breath to suppress his rising anger. 'They're dead.'

Wills watched the silent confusion that rippled through the room.

'Davies!' Hawthorne expelled the name as if it were a curse. 'This has the vengeful arrogance of that despicable woman stamped all over it. Tell me she didn't murder our perpetrators like she did the last lot. And where is she anyway? Have shame and guilt finally overcome her?'

Wills clenched his jaw—he could not remain silent a moment longer. 'She's been shot.'

The only response from Hawthorne was a cold, 'Dead?'

'She'll survive,' Wills replied, his voice calm but firm, his contempt for the so-called 'knight' manifesting in his tone and glower.

Hawthorne snapped his attention from Wills to Quinn. 'Why did you keep this from me? I am the Chief of the DSO.'

'This was another line of enquiry and I did not want to jeopardise your reputation, Sir Giles, if Major Williams' theory was incorrect. As it happened, it wasn't and we have, by the grace of God, managed to save one innocent woman from despicable acts and ultimate death.'

The duke, clearly uncomfortable at being present for this vitriolic discourse, pulled the bell cord.

'You should have kept me informed,' insisted Sir Giles.

Thomson appeared at the door.

'Your Grace?' Thomson asked.

'Ah. Thomson. Gentlemen,' the duke said addressing the six. 'Cook has prepared some refreshments for you. If you would follow Thomson, please. Mr Quinn, Sir Giles, Major Williams, please remain behind.'

Detective Sergeant Yabsley, eager to assist his besieged chief, stayed back and sought confirming instruction from Sir Giles.

'Have lunch. I'll be with you shortly,' Sir Giles directed.

With their departure, the study became quiet but the air hung with acrid hostility.

'Davies is a loose cannon!' Hawthorne resumed before anyone could dampen his fire. 'She does as she pleases and she can't be trusted! She is a murderess!'

'Steady on!' Quinn warned.

Hawthorne ignored him. 'She is the only one in my department who has not been vetted by you, Mr Quinn. She's a damned colonist! An opium eater and a self-gratifying abuser of women! And she is Williams' pet—'

The mention of Davies' name, the insinuations, the slurs. Colonist. Opium eater. Murderess. Wills' self-control finally shattered.

'She is worth ten of your men but you're too arrogant to see it!' The words exploded from Wills. 'Instead of vilifying her, accept her for what she is—better than you'll ever be!'

'Major! That's quite enough!' Quinn snapped, his patience gone.

'Who killed all those who could have led us to the head of this conspiracy?' Hawthorne persisted. 'Who had access to the coordinates? Who had the opportunity to change the lists of bank notes? And plant the evidence in that unionist's home—'

'Excellent questions, Hawthorne! Why don't you do a little investigating yourself and find out? It wasn't Davies! She was with me!'

'That raises another question,' Hawthorne submitted, reverting his attention to Quinn. 'Why is Williams permitted to run his own investigation? Goddammit, Quinn, you are aiding and abetting this fiasco!' Waving an accusing finger at Wills, Hawthorne spat out, 'For all we know, *he* could be the head of the cobra!'

The duke could take no more. 'Gentlemen! Please! My niece is lying upstairs with contusions and lacerations to most of her body and, if it had not been for the quick-wittedness of the so-called vengeful, arrogant, despicable woman, Rebecca Davies, *and* Major Williams, my niece would now have been brutally raped and murdered! Can you imagine how I feel? Can you imagine how she feels?'

'With respect, Sir,' offered Sir Giles firmly, 'you have no idea what sort of woman this Davies is. She is not natural—'

'I understand how you feel about women such as she,' the duke continued angrily, his irritability trouncing civility, 'but, from what I have perceived of Rebecca Davies, she is a most capable woman with an uncanny aptitude to analyse situations correctly. This, alone, should be cause for plaudits not reprehension.'

Sir Giles rebuked the assertion. 'You don't see—'

'You, Sir Giles, should be singing her praises instead of maligning her! My niece is alive because of her! Only because of her! Davies risked her life and she may yet die ...' His words petered off. His shoulders sagged and he leaned heavily against his desk. 'Forgive me ...' he uttered, regaining his decorum and straightening himself up. 'My apologies. It has been quite an exhausting day.'

'Your Grace, perhaps it's best we leave you,' Quinn offered.

'No, Alexander,' the duke returned. 'You remain here. I will see to our guests. Thomson will bring you refreshments.'

The duke, clearly weary and overcome with pent-up emotion, took his leave, abandoning Quinn, Wills and Hawthorne to resume their bitter discussions.

The three men stood in silent contemplation, frustration and anger bubbling just beneath the surface.

Quinn was the first to speak. 'What do you have to say for yourself, Sir Giles?'

Hawthorne scowled.

'Out with it, man!' Quinn insisted.

'Very well. Firstly, you have relegated me to third in command after you and Williams. How does that make me look in the eyes of my subordinates? And you, Williams, went behind my back to Quinn, instead of coming to me with your ... your theories.'

'You would have discounted them,' Wills stated firmly.

Hawthorne expelled a dry, mirthless laugh.

Wills hesitated then decided to voice his concerns. 'We have a spy in our department, Sir Giles.'

Quinn watched Hawthorne's reaction; Hawthorne's response appeared to be genuine shock and incredulity. 'What? What ... a spy?'

'Think about what you accused Davies of doing. The wrong coordinates, misleading information, incriminating money in the unionist's home, written abduction plans. It was not Davies. But it was someone in our department. Your department. There is a spy—'

'You have the wrong end of the stick,' interrupted Hawthorne. '*You* think about it! Count the bodies, Williams. The two men with the boy and his dog. Dead! These three blackguards. In the palms of our hands. Dead! It is she who needs to explain her actions!' He turned to Quinn. 'Was it not you who said that you wanted these criminals taken alive? To interrogate them? We can't do that with corpses. Can we, major? Secrets are safe with dead men.'

'The major has adequately explained the circumstances. The countess' life was in peril. There seemed to be no other choice.'

'Hmm, *seemed to be*,' was all Hawthorne would concede.

A knock on the door brought the argument to a sudden halt, scowls chiselled in their stony faces.

'Come in,' called Quinn.

The butler and two maids brought in trays laden with sandwiches and pots of hot tea and coffee.

Hawthorne approached Thomson. 'I need to get a note to my wife,' he said in subdued tones. 'I take it the house has a telephone set I may use?'

'Of course, Sir. If you will follow me.'

'Excuse me,' was the perfunctory phrase Sir Giles spat out as he left the room.

Wills slowly exhaled his exasperation and studied Quinn whose only response was the clenching of the muscles in his jaw.

***

Thomson left Sir Giles in the privacy of a small room adjacent to the cloak room off the entrance hall.

'Thank you,' he said and waited until he saw the butler leave.

'Operator, a London number, please. The Marlborough Club.'

***

Tick, tock, tick, tock…

The measured metronomic monotony of a clock somewhere on the periphery of my consciousness slowly drew me out of my enforced incoherence.

Where was I? What time was it? What day?

The vault of my memory began to open … Wills had spoken to me … Quinn … Hawthorne … they were to speak to me … Lady Katherine … was she safe? Relief surged … inexplicable … however it came, I knew: she was safe.

Pain throbbed throughout my being. I was aware that Dr Werner had administered analgesics and was grateful that, despite my physical distress, they had not dulled my senses as much as laudanum or other opioids would have done.

I was ready to give my evidence to Quinn but was not in the least eager to have Hawthorne interrogate me.

So, I lay there, eyes closed, motionless and willing the anodynes to reduce the pain.

The handle on the door clicked and the whisper of a skirt alerted me that someone—a woman—had entered my room and approached me. This was a game I liked to play: guess the intruder.

This woman's respiration was measured and calm—certainly not Jessica Turner—her normal state was one of agitation and nervous tension. It also wasn't Lady Katherine; the fragrance that hung about her was of delicate roses. This woman's scent was of perfumed soap so, it wouldn't be any of the maid servants; they would not be able to afford such luxury. And the duchess preferred violets.

I capitulated. 'Who are you?' I croaked, eyes still closed.

The woman gasped.

Opening my eyes, I saw the matronly visage of a woman peering over me. She had grizzled red hair not dissimilar to Jessica's. Kindness showed in her eyes.

'Fiona McPherson, Lady Katherine's housekeeper,' she pronounced with a thick Gaelic-Scottish inflection.

'Ah,' I exhaled. 'George's mother.'

'Aye, that too. I came tae make yer acquaintance and tae—' she broke off, took a deep breath, then continued, 'tae see if there was anything ye needed.'

'A new arm. A new hip. A new life …' I slowly breathed, for speaking was still difficult. 'Lady Katherine?' I managed to rasp out.

'Sleeping. Doctor says her hurts will mend.' She paused. 'Doctor also says ye almost didnae make it,' Mrs McPherson added with some hesitancy.

I screwed up my face—the only part of me that didn't scream with pain. 'Only the good die young …' It was painful to laugh but I managed a little chuckle that made the housekeeper's face light up.

She studied me in a most curious way. Her intense scrutiny gave way to a softening of her worn features. 'I ken now. I'll leave ye tae yer rest.'

And, without any further word, Lady Katherine's housekeeper turned and left me there wondering what she 'kenned'.

***

Sir Giles Hawthorne was not used to being kept waiting, least of all by his inferiors. It was long past the luncheon hour and his stomach was reminding him that he hadn't eaten since an early breakfast of a stale crust of buttered bread. He paced back and forth before the desk—the two steps the telephone cord allowed. The delay gnawed at him more than his hunger. The sandwiches—his sandwiches—were awaiting him, withering away just like his patience.

Finally, a voice crackled through the handpiece. 'Who is calling?' The question was posed almost threateningly.

'Humphries? Is that you? Sir Giles here.'

'Ah. Old boy,' he responded with quiet relief. 'You caught me … What, er … what news?'

'Dead, old boy.'

A pause on the other end of the line. 'Who … ? Davies?'

'The three abductors.'

'Three? I … I understood there were only two involved.'

'Four apparently. Three dead and one captured.'

'Oh? Who survived?'

'A shopkeeper. Local. Irrelevant,' Hawthorne supplied with a dismissive wave of the hand. 'That is why I'm calling. Neville, I need your counsel once more.'

Silence.

'Neville? Are you there?'

'Yes … yes … What is it you need?'

Hawthorne took a deep breath. 'It was Davies who despatched the three felons. I firmly believe that she is involved in all this—that is, in being part of the conspiracy to abduct and ransom these women. She had to kill them so they wouldn't indict her. There are too many other factors that point to her, but I don't know how I can prove it. This is where I need your guidance.'

'Yes … yes … I see the connection … and motivation … Have you presented Quinn with your theory?'

'Yes,' replied Hawthorne, his voice rising with indignation. 'But the fool is blind to the facts and deaf to my assertions. He can't make a decision to save his life.'

'Is there any evidence of her involvement?'

'I believe so, but it's all circumstantial. All hearsay.'

'Have you checked her place of residence? Perhaps there—'

'No. We haven't.'

'Perhaps you could send those two … er, Yabsley and … you know, those who found the evidence in that union fellow's place, to check things over. Tell them what you're looking for and—'

'If there's nothing?' Hawthorne demanded, frustrated at the mere thought of failing again. 'Where do I go from there, Neville? Am I to grovel at the feet of the Home Secretary?'

'I'm sure you'll find something if you tell your men what to look for.'

Hawthorne expelled his irritation with a heavy breath. 'Yes … yes … You're right …'

Another faint voice transmitted over the line. 'Colonel Humphries, your valises have been loaded. The carriage is ready for you, Sir.'

'You're going somewhere, Neville?'

'Oh, er, yes, Sir Giles. A respite. My war injuries are playing havoc with my insides and doctor insisted I take a little break.'

'I see. Where can I contact you if I need to?'

'I will telephone to you when I reach my hotel. I must go now. Good luck with Davies and everything at Abbottsford Hall.'

Without waiting for a response, Humphries put down the phone and left Sir Giles Hawthorne, receiver in hand, puzzled.

His brow furrowed.

Did I mention Abbottsford Hall? he asked himself, but immediately shrugged it off as inconsequential—luncheon awaited.

***

Sir Giles opted to take lunch in the morning room, foregoing the fine fare offered in the duke's office—and, more pointedly, the company of that insufferable Major Williams. He preferred the company of his men.

With a plateful of sandwiches, he approached Sergeant Yabsley and Detective Constable Byrne who sat together at a small linen-clothed table. Both men stood when Sir Giles pulled out a chair and settled in.

'Gentlemen, please,' he invited, indicating their chairs then taking a bite of a roast beef sandwich. 'You are aware of how I feel about this Davies woman and, no doubt you—especially you, Yabsley—both feel the same way.'

Byrne and Yabsley exchanged a brief glance before returning their attention to Sir Giles who resumed his speech. 'The difficulty in terminating her services is that we have no hard evidence to put before Quinn. This is where your expertise is required.'

Sir Giles took another mouthful, stretching the moment and leaving both officers waiting in anticipation. He wiped his mouth. 'I will arrange that you two return to London with the three deceased and, once there, I want you to search that woman's flat for evidence. Turn it upside down and inside out if you must, but I want hard evidence that she is part of the conspiracy. Do I make myself clear?'

Both officers nodded.

He withdrew a slip of paper from his waistcoat pocket and handed it to Yabsley. 'This is her address in Newington.'

Yabsley read out loud. 'Louisa Mansions, Borough Road. Er … how do we … ?'

'I don't have a key,' Sir Giles cut in dismissively. 'Use your initiative.'

Byrne had been attentive but silent throughout the discourse but now appeared apprehensive and shifted in his seat. Sir Giles narrowed his eyes and lowered his sandwich mid-bite.

'You have misgivings, Byrne? Out with it if you do. I can put another in your place.'

'Sir, no,' he said without hesitation. 'I am more than willing to go with Sergeant Yabsley and find the evidence you seek.'

'Hm,' Hawthorne replied. 'Right. I am depending on you to do so.'

'Thank you, Sir Giles.'

'Whatever it takes, gentlemen, to be rid of her once and for all.'

***

It was late afternoon when Doctor Werner paid me another visit to check his handiwork and change the dressings on my wounds. I was still in much pain but felt better than I had earlier in the day. My voice was easier to use and my head clearer.

He asked permission to loosen the neck of my nightdress so he could access my left arm and, pleased with its condition, lifted the dress up to my hip and examined that injury. Pulling up the sleeve to my right arm, I asked him why it was bound.

Doctor Werner went to great lengths to describe the complex procedure of transfusing blood from the 'gallant major' to me, sheepishly adding that he had never done one before but was clearly yet modestly well-pleased with himself.

After his thorough examination, he announced that he was satisfied that there didn't appear to be any infection at the three surgical sites.

'When can I get out of bed?' I asked impatiently.

Doctor Werner looked down at me, his eyebrows raised in mild surprise. 'Two weeks,' he said sternly and with a hint of admonishment.

I knew full well the time it would take to recuperate—I had been in this situation twice before—but I was burning to see this damned case though. A fortnight of enforced indolence—even if spent being coddled in luxury—was not something I wished to endure.

The doctor must have sensed my irritation because he immediately added, 'Maybe one week if you look after yourself and do as I say.'

Then, to underscore the gravity of my situation, he continued, 'Miss Davies, your hip won't be able to carry your weight until it mends properly. And your arm, dear lady, your arm must be kept immobile lest the stitches give way. The external sutures can be mended but the cat gut to your artery, internally, should it tear away, well, that could be disastrous—even fatal.'

He rummaged through his kit and withdrew a square of cloth. 'It's best that we keep your arm immobilised and close to your chest.' He folded and tied the cloth around my neck and threaded my injured arm into it. The sling was set.

'Doctor,' I said earnestly, 'perhaps a wee dram of Scotland's finest every now and then will assist—'

'No.' His reply was absolute. 'No alcohol. It will interfere with the analgesics and one "wee dram" too many could just kill you.'

He sensed my utter disappointment. 'I trust you will heed my advice and do as I say,' he warned.

I compliantly nodded but, inwardly, I had already planned an insurrection.

'Good,' he said. 'Now, let me help you sit up. You need sustenance.'

Before I could accept—for I was indeed very hungry—there came a knock at the door.

The doctor opened it and I was surprised to see Mrs McPherson enter with a large bed tray cluttered with silver dish covers.

With great effort and the doctor's assistance, I struggled up and propped myself against numerous pillows, barely overcoming the throbbing to my hip. 'Mrs McPherson,' I wheezed, 'this is an honour.'

She regarded me in a business-like yet warm manner and placed the tray across me. 'Just doing my duty, Miss.'

Dr Werner had packed up his medical bag and stood at the door. 'I'll leave you ladies to it. Miss Davies, I urge you to heed my advice. I've left some more pain relievers on the bedside table. Take them sparingly. Mrs McPherson, if the patient needs anything at all, please don't hesitate to call me. The duke has asked me to stay another day.' He gave a gentlemanly nod. 'Ladies,' he farewelled, and closed the door behind him.

It was then that I noticed Lady Katherine had entered the room. She was dressed in a most becoming tea gown, her hair immaculately coiffed. Had it not been for the fierce bruising marring her face, she would have appeared an apparition of grace and light. The dissonance of such beauty marred by violence unsettled me more than I cared to admit.

'Lady Katherine,' I gasped—for she truly did take my breath away.

She came to me and, reaching out her hand, stroked my disordered white hair into submission. 'It's good to see you looking so well,' she murmured, her voice barely a whisper. 'I was so afraid that …'

Her words trailed off and the air seemed to still. I could feel the weight of everything unspoken pressing between us. Her fingers lingered longer than the gesture required, long enough to speak of need, of tenderness.

In that silence, the memory of our night together rose unbidden. I felt again the heat of her body against mine, the tremble in her breath, her touch, her passion.

She did not look away. Nor did I.

The clattering of silverware jarred me back.

Mrs McPherson had uncovered the bowls and plates to reveal an array of foodstuffs: broth, sandwiches, cold meats, cheese, jellies and a large pot of steaming hot tea. Whether she was aware of the frisson between her mistress and me, I could not fathom—her manner was brisk and workwomanlike.

She brought a chair for her mistress and placed it next to me.

I could not take my eyes off the countess. My mind refused to believe that a woman like her could have feelings for a woman like me. Not *those* feelings. What we had shared a few nights ago was—I told myself—not an act of love but one of need. I had truly believed our paths would never cross again.

'Please,' Lady Katherine urged. 'Eat. You must be famished. Let me pour you a tea.'

I accepted the tea she prepared. 'How are you, my lady?' I enquired earnestly. 'Did sleep find you?'

'Morpheus certainly did. In the form of laudanum.'

Her troubled countenance almost imperceptibly spoke of the pain she carried. There was a fragility in her voice—a quiet tremor—that betrayed the effort it took to quell the horror she had suffered.

I felt a swell of compassion for her; she had seen and endured more than any woman should. This terrible episode would not pass without consequence—it would leave deep scars on her psyche for many years to come. I knew that truth intimately.

Lady Katherine seemed at ease in the company of Mrs McPherson who was busily fussing with the shutters and curtains. I glanced at the older woman and, taking another sip of the hot tea, I looked back at Lady Katherine over the rim of my cup.

It was as though she had read my thoughts.

'I've known Fiona all of my life and Fiona knows everything about me,' Lady Katherine stated, hinting at history and shared secrets.

'Aye,' interjected the housekeeper from a corner of the room, 'and I'm very protective of my lady, if ye ken my meaning.'

'I ken, Mrs McPherson, I ken,' I reassured both women.

An easy silence fell over the room.

I took another sip of the hot tea; our eyes seemed to be locked on each other's. Images of that night in the forest returned—of insurmountable agony when the bullets struck me, of Lady Katherine's unwavering commitment as she fought to preserve my life, risking her own. I owed her so much—so much more than gratitude but, for now, that was all I could offer.

'Thank you,' I said as nonchalantly as I could.

She tilted her head, puzzled.

'For preserving my life.'

A faint smile touched her lips but her glistening eyes told me more.

'It is I who owe you her life.'

I loathed to cry. I swallowed the emotion, cleared my throat and opted for levity.

'I believe I owe you some articles of clothing.'

'Oh?'

'The bandages.'

'Aye,' Mrs McPherson piped in. 'That was one of yer best Swiss cotton dickies, my lady.'

A single word jolted my attention. 'What did you say?' I demanded.

Mrs McPherson was taken aback by my sudden change in demeanour. 'Em ... I was jesting—'

'About the Swiss cotton. What did you call it?'

'The petticoat? A dickie. That's what my grandmother, God rest her soul, called it.'

Flashes of Humphries and Hawthorne at the Marlborough Club filled my head; the photograph in Hawthorne's office; the man Croft was waiting for ... It had to be ...

'Mrs McPherson, would you find Major Williams, please? I need to see him urgently.'

'Of course,' stammered the housekeeper. She withdrew without delay, clearly confused.

'What is it, Rebecca?' Lady Katherine enquired, equally mystified.

'That last man, the one with Peleus, I think I know who he is. And, if I'm right, I know who is behind all these abductions.'

It wasn't more than five minutes after Mrs McPherson had left us that the door swung open.

'I hear you're looking for Major Williams,' trumpeted Sir Giles Hawthorne, leading the charge into the room ahead of Yabsley and Byrne. 'He's gone off to the village lockup to interrogate that shopkeeper, Graves.'

Lady Katherine abruptly rose to her feet, her back rigid and her face, usually serene and composed, flashed with indignation.

'How dare you enter a lady's bedroom without invitation!' she said, standing her ground, her chin lifted in righteous fury.

'I do beg your pardon,' Sir Giles slithered. 'And, by the looks of you, you must be the Countess of Chestermere. I do apologise.'

'And you are?'

'Sir Giles Hawthorne,' he said, brazenly. 'Chief of the Special Branch, Department of Special Operations. And these are my subordinates, Detective Sergeant Yabsley and Detective Constable Byrne. I'm here to interview Davies.'

'*Miss* Davies is unwell. And she requested the attendance of Major Williams.'

'Hm. I'm here now, so let's get on with it.'

Lady Katherine strode to the bell cord and, pausing just long enough to settle a defiant glare on the interloper, pulled the cord several times. 'We'll see about that.'

Hawthorne's contempt was unmissable. He turned to me. 'What is it that has that old housekeeper all aflutter?'

I was amused that this pompous ass would consider to even attempt to lord it over me. 'I'm as well as can be expected. Thank you for asking,' I declared with the kind of politeness I reserved for pompous asses such as he.

An angry flush rose up his neck. He took two steps towards me and leaned in. 'You arrogant Sapphic jade!' he threatened through gritted teeth so only I could hear. 'You will be found out and you will pay the price!'

A deep, disembodied voice from the doorway interrupted his threat. 'You called, my lady?'

'Yes, Thomson, these gentlemen seem to have lost their way. Please show them their proper place.'

Hawthorne's face darkened. With a venomous sneer and reddened cheeks, he turned on his heel and stormed out without another word, his two cohorts trailing closely behind.

Thomson closed the bedroom door leaving me with a disgusted Lady Katherine.

She approached me. 'Does he always speak to you like that?' she asked, bewildered.

'No,' I replied honestly. 'He never speaks to me at all. He hates my kind.'

'Your *kind*?'

'Yes. Independent women. Colonists in general but more so Australians. And, of course …' I drew a slow, theatrical breath, 'trivets.'

This made Lady Katherine burst into an uninhibited chortle. She winced mid-laugh and put a hand to the side of her face. 'Don't make me laugh. The hurt hasn't mended yet.'

Sweet, endearing Katherine. I didn't want to love her but I could feel myself falling for that irresistible combination of beauty, grace and quiet courage.

And she asked nought of me.

If I had, indeed, saved her life, then she had already repaid that debt in full by tending me and preserving mine. Whatever she saw in me, I prayed it would always be there, for, at this moment, there was nothing I wanted more than to be with her.

She drew closer to me and touched my face.

The warmth of her fingers stirred something deep within me—but so too did the jolt of pain that surged suddenly from my hip, radiating through my body and into my wounded arm. A searing reminder of how close to death I had come—and how achingly fragile this moment truly was.

***

It was evening and I had dozed for most of the afternoon after taking an ample dosage of pain relievers when Mrs McPherson woke me to insist on helping me with my ablutions.

'Cleanliness is essential for a swift recovery,' she asserted and quickly conducted a well-planned attack on my hands, neck, face and arms with a hot, wet, wrung-out flannel. She also applied herself to my disordered hair with a comb and macassar oil and gave me a new toothbrush and dentifrice to freshen my mouth, which she somehow found offensive.

I own that I did feel better for the attention, even with the feeling that I was being treated like a helpless newborn. When she left me, I felt refreshed, warm and comfortable and once more fell into a light sleep.

It must have been around the servants' supper time that a very timid knock on my closed door brought me out of my light nap. Lady Katherine had promised to return so I imagined it was she.

'Come in,' I called and was very surprised to see little Henry's inquisitive face peer in. He looked about warily then sprang inside, closing the door behind him, as though he were being pursued.

'Henry,' I said. 'Come in. It's good to see you, but what brings you here?'

He approached me and appeared to be awestruck. 'You're not dead.'

'I'm sore. Very sore. But not dead,' I assured him.

His face lit up with uncontainable delight. 'It worked! My prayers worked!'

'Ahh, it was you! Thank you, Henry! You saved my life.'

'Aye, me and God.' He looked at me with such intense sincerity that a quiet laugh escaped me despite myself. 'Oh, and Peleus says to say he's glad, too, that you're not dead.'

'Well, thank you. That makes three of us.'

'I've got to go now. His Grace said no one should disturb you and Lady Katherine. But I don't think he really meant me.'

'I see,' I conciliated. 'You come and see me whenever you feel like it, Henry. Just don't get into trouble.' As an afterthought, I added, 'Henry, do you know where my valise is? The last I saw of it was at the railway station.'

'Leave it to me, Miss, I'll find it!' he assured me enthusiastically. 'I want to be just like you. A detective!'

'I'm not a det—'

Another knock on the door stopped me mid-sentence and made Henry jump. The startled look on his face confirmed he was going against orders.

'Come in,' I called and, as the door opened, Henry bolted through it, squeezing himself between the door jamb and Wills' legs.

'What … ?' Wills exclaimed as he watched the little boy streak along the corridor and out of sight.

Wills came in and closed the door behind him. 'He was there when we found you, you know. And again, when the doctor patched you up. Something a boy that age should not have seen. I tried to stop him. He's a determined little monkey.'

'He said he prayed for me.'

'We all did, old girl. Well, most of us,' he conceded as he sat next to me on the bed. 'You look much better than you did this morning.'

'Doctor said I have to stay here a week! Can't get out of bed to pee. I have to use a damned bedpan.'

'How's the pain?'

'Painful. Manageable. Meditation helps but medication's better. I need more of those pain relievers Dr Werner supplied. Where were you today? I needed to see you.'

'Interviewing Stuart Graves at the village lockup. He was quite bruised and battered and feeling quite sorry for himself.'

'He'll be feeling much worse climbing the stairs to the gallows.'

'He couldn't tell us much. In essence, it was the same story as young Timmy Saddler's family. Needed money, had a grievance with the landed gentry, saw an easy way to get out of debt. Like the Saddlers, his only dealings were with Croft and Hogan. He never met or was aware of anyone called Dickie.'

'I think I know who Dickie is. Was.'

'That third man? Lady Katherine said she heard you call him Dickie. And that it annoyed him.'

'I believe he was connected to Hawthorne.'

'Hawthorne?'

'Quite possibly. Either by coincidence or by design. Remember when we barged in on Hawthorne and that Colonel Humphries at his lunch meeting at the Marlborough?'

'Yes. Quinn hasn't found anything more regarding their connection.'

'They were talking about one of their acquaintances, a certain Smithy who was cashiered. They referred to him as captain of the dickies.'

'Yes ...' Wills leaned closer, his attention fully focussed on my next words.

'A dickie is an old-fashioned term for a petticoat. And he was given the epithet because he wore a frock to escape the Boers.'

'And ... ?'

'On Hawthorne's "trophy wall", there is a photograph of Hawthorne in South Africa surrounded by his troopers. Only one of them had the rank of captain. And his name was "G. Smith".'

'Smithy. Captain of the dickies.'

'Yes. I didn't get a good look at all of the men in that photograph but it shouldn't be too difficult to compare our dead Dickie to this G. Smith. And it should be easy to find out if Captain G Smith was cashiered and if there is any connection with Colonel Humphries. From what Hawthorne said, he hadn't heard from Smithy since he was discharged.'

'I'll set Scott onto that first thing tomorrow. If you're right, then this Colonel Humphries may be involved. And, if he is involved, we need to get to him without delay, before he discovers his henchmen are dead. He's sure to take flight if he is complicit.'

'Hawthorne may be complicit, or may be a dupe, but he's involved whichever way it goes.'

Wills slumped into his usual thinking pose, head bent, staring straight ahead, then shot me a look I hadn't seen before.

'What's wrong?' I asked. 'You look as though you're about to go to a funeral.'

'Hawthorne has accused you of being embroiled in this conspiracy.'

I was utterly astonished. 'What? What are you saying? What is he saying?'

'He was in quite a fury this morning and made some very wild accusations about you to Quinn. He asserted that you tampered with all the evidence. After Hawthorne stormed out, Quinn asked me if there was any possibility that his allegations were correct. He's planted a seed of doubt in Quinn's mind.'

'For Christ's sake! Why would I abduct someone then rescue them? Hawthorne's a desperate crackbrain. And you? Did he plant one in yours?'

Wills scoffed. 'Of course not. But make a false assertion often enough and it inevitably mutates into truth in the minds of those who ought to know better.'

'That bastard,' I exclaimed, recalling Hawthorne's intrusion that morning.

'We must be very careful, Rebecca. Hawthorne has ordered Yabsley and Byrne to accompany the bodies to London for the autopsies.'

'His best men to watch over corpses? Is he afraid they'll get up and run away?'

'Something's afoot, Rebecca. Just be careful.'

'The three of them—Hawthorne, Yabsley and Byrne—paid me a visit this morning.'

'What? He had the nerve to question you?'

'No, not to question me—to threaten me. He said I would be found out and I would pay.' I gave Wills a dry look. 'I thought everybody knew I was a deviant.'

'This is no time for levity, Rebecca. He means you harm. And there's no love lost between you and Yabsley. Both he and Byrne have been sent to London for more than watching over three cadavers. But what?'

35

Sunday, 10th September, 1905

Abbottsford Village, Suffolk, England

Over the following two days, Wills directed the investigation effectively and, with a generous helping of undeserved deference, yielded some authority to Sir Giles. It was quite clear to me that this was deference not so much due to Hawthorne's superior investigative skills, but more to keep an eye on him.

The four remaining detective constables, Hewitt, Ramsay, Dolby and Hathaway, were directed to interview everyone who knew Stewart Graves and his wife, or who had seen any strangers lurking about. They came up with very little we didn't already know.

Meanwhile, Major Williams kept our suspicions about the Hawthorne–Humphries connection under wraps, even from Quinn. He directed Detective Constable Robert Scott, who had remained at New Scotland Yard, to uncover information about one cashiered Captain G Smith who served in South Africa with the then Major Giles Hawthorne and who was at the siege of Ladysmith.

Young Henry found my valise, as well as my abandoned Gladstone, and brought both to me. I told him he would make a very clever detective, as I directed him to withdraw the partially consumed bottle of whisky and place it in the top drawer of my bedside table. He was chuffed that I was well pleased with his efforts and left my room with an enormous self-satisfied grin.

Of course, during those two days, Lady Katherine spent more time with me than her aunt Mary deemed proper. But, after allocating whatever business she could to her secretary, George McPherson, what else was there for her to do? She was determined to stay with me until Dr Werner saw fit to discharge me.

We played cards—I restrained myself from cheating (mostly)—and we talked about our lives. Of mine, I spoke only of the good times of my childhood in Paddington, the Far East, the archaeological adventure in India and the expedition in Africa.

She spoke of her childhood in Scotland, of her parents, of her country retreat, Lilyfield Manor and its quaint, ancient village of Rusby. 'You must come and stay with me when this business is over.'

My look of surprise amused her.

'No, I insist.'

'But, Katherine, what would the duchess say?'

Her eyes sparkled with impish defiance. 'I can only imagine. But you will come, won't you? A train from London to Rusby village and I'll send the motor for you. Promise you'll come.'

How could I possibly have refused?

Despite the pain, those two days were most enjoyable and I found myself thinking of Lady Katherine whenever she wasn't with me.

36

Monday Afternoon, 11th September, 1905

New Scotland Yard, London, England

Detective Constable Robert Scott had worked tirelessly at his desk for two whole days after receiving that early morning telephone call from Major Williams. The major had given Scott permission to kip on the sofa in Wills' office to save time and the effort of climbing three flights of stairs. Besides, he was unmarried and lived alone so he had no one to go home to.

And with no one in the office to disturb him, he was able to work uninterrupted and unobserved. He had uncovered some very alarming facts during those two days and was putting together his report for the major when he was startled by the unexpected arrival of Detective Sergeant Yabsley and Detective Constable Byrne.

'Sergeant! I wasn't expecting you,' he stuttered, trying to conceal some of the reports and papers scattered about his desk.

'What are you working on, Scott?' Yabsley questioned as he and Byrne flanked the seated detective.

'Nothing much, Sergeant,' Scott excused. 'Catching up on reports.'

'Get on with it, then.'

Byrne persisted in scanning the contents of Scott's desk.

'Problem there, Byrne?' Yabsley spat out.

'Em, no, Sergeant!'

'Then get your notebook and we'll be on our way,' Yabsley ordered.

Byrne gave Scott a threatening look then made straight to his own desk and unlocked a drawer. Scott watched as Byrne turned his back but noticed his furtive movements: one hand dipped into the drawer, the other shielded whatever he retrieved. A shift of the elbow, the quick flattening of fabric as something slid out of sight into his jacket. With the other hand, he collected a notebook. Scott had seen enough covert handovers in his time to know when a gesture carried more than it claimed.

'What are you doing back so soon?' Scott asked Yabsley. 'Have the investigations been completed?'

'No. Still open,' Yabsley replied.

'I see. And, Sergeant. Where can you be reached … if Sir Giles asks?'

'He knows,' was all Yabsley divulged as he led Byrne out of the office, leaving Scott troubled.

He looked down at his paperwork strewn untidily on the desk and admonished himself for his disorderliness. What had Byrne seen? He winced with self-castigation when he realised that, partially visible, was his handwritten note that read 'Kieran Byrne?'.

***

It was easy enough getting into the foyer of the Louisa Mansions flats; the front door was surprisingly enough unlocked, and the old custodian, Grayson, was nowhere to be seen.

Yabsley led Byrne up the stairs, checking the door number at each landing until they reached the third floor. There, they found Rebecca Davies' flat.

'Keep watch,' Yabsley ordered, removing a wallet from his pocket and retrieving his well-worn lockpicking tools. Within moments, they were inside and closed the door behind them.

Yabsley detested the woman Major Williams insisted on calling his Assisting Clerk. She involved herself in everything the DSO touched as though she belonged. She didn't. In Yabsley's mind, she was a self-appointed judge, jury and executioner and the bodies of those she left in her wake proved it. She was just a callous murderess with a warrant card.

As though that were not bad enough, she was also unwomanly. His opposite gender should be just that: opposite. Women should be feminine and ladylike and she was neither. On top of all that, she was arrogant, always giving men the impression that they were beneath contempt and irrelevant—at least, that's how she made *him* feel. And, for that, he despised her even more.

He did reluctantly concede—only to himself—that Rebecca Davies was somewhat capable both in physical and mental attributes, but she was still a woman and women had no place besting men. They were inferior—that was a proven medical and scientific fact—and that was that. He would be pleased, very pleased indeed, to be rid of the abomination. If there were evidence to prove her guilt in this distasteful matter, he would find it.

'I'll check the bedroom,' Byrne offered and immediately strode towards it as Yabsley took in the rest of the residence. It was sparsely furnished and neatly maintained, so it wouldn't take long to find incriminating evidence should there be any.

The little dining nook held nothing but a couple of chairs and a table and it was bare save for a few unopened letters. They all appeared to be invoices or account statements, bar one from Australia.

The letters held very little interest, so with renewed vigour, Yabsley took to the cabinets and then the drawers in the kitchen nook, opening, carefully rummaging, and turning out the contents. From the bedroom, he could hear Byrne doing the same but with less subtlety; he was quite heavy-handed in fact, much like when they had conducted the search at John McGregor's.

Yabsley reached the bottom of the four stacked drawers in the cabinet and pulled it out. Peering into the darkened void the drawer left, he spotted a small, black wooden container about the size of a cigar box.

Retrieving it, he carefully opened the hinged lid and was astonished to see, nestled in soft layers of silken cloth, polished gemstones of various shapes, sizes and colours. The afternoon sun caught each and reflected a dazzling show of light; he had never seen such an array of brilliance.

'Sergeant!'

The call from the bedroom brought Yabsley back to the task at hand. He instantly closed the box and slid it into his jacket pocket. 'Byrne. Found something?'

Byrne emerged from the bedroom with a triumphant sneer, holding his discovery aloft. 'Bank notes! I would wager that these come from the victims' families.'

Yabsley was both elated and sceptical of the discovery. Byrne had found the same evidence in McGregor's home—evidence that was later disputed. Surely Davies was smarter than that; would she keep such incriminating evidence where it could so easily be found? Then again, he argued, he did find a hoard worth thousands behind a drawer. How could she be in possession of such a valuable cache? And why was it hidden here and not in a bank vault?

Whatever the reason, it seemed he now had the evidence to rid himself of someone he despised and who should never have been in the DSO in the first place.

Byrne approached him and handed the notes over.

'Where did you find these?' Yabsley asked.

'In one of the drawers, stuffed in a stocking.'

'Show me.'

***

Doctor Werner's treatment was expert and effective. Four days after being wounded and repaired, and against doctor's advice, I was determined to take my first steps from the bed—mainly to avoid using that repugnant bedpan.

The good doctor's pain relief medication was proving remarkably effective and I was able to sit up with relative ease—relative, that is, to my previous total incapacitation. After a fair amount of persistent cajoling, Wills had managed to find me a walking stick and pair of crutches and Lady Katherine offered to secure me a wheelchair commode from London, which, grateful as I was for the offer, I politely refused; it would have been one degree up from the bedpan.

Of course, a little surreptitious sip of my medicinal scotch every now and then helped to relax whatever muscles were paining.

With the investigation both at the village and at the Hall now near completion, Wills was awaiting further orders from Quinn who had returned to London the day before, on Sunday. He never did bother to speak to me. Nor did Sir Giles Hawthorne after that first intrusion with his two attendants. Wills was as mystified as I as to why neither of these men were interested in what I had to offer.

The duke and duchess insisted I stay for the full two weeks of recuperation that Doctor Werner had prescribed, and that Dr Werner himself also stay to ensure I was fully recovered before I made the long journey back to London. The doctor was confident that I did not require X-rays on my hip but did insist that I seek further medical attention once home.

Notwithstanding all these generous offers, I decided that when his orders came through, I would leave with Wills.

Lady Katherine also made plans to leave for her country manor very soon—she had pressing business at her estate that neither George nor her steward could resolve in her absence. It was with great reluctance that we would part company but, once I was fully recovered and after I had resigned from the service, I would be free to venture wherever my heart and head took me. And, at that moment, I knew exactly where that would be.

I now had a purpose in life.

***

The evening autumn air that Detective Constable Kieran Byrne had enjoyed in Abbottsford had been crisp and clear. In London, the air was a smoky fog—a smog.

Through this sooty pall, he strode, silhouetted against the pale yellow glow from the gas lamps, through the streets towards a tobacconist not far from Whitehall. He greeted the shopkeeper by name, then made his way to the back corner of the premises where a silence cabinet had been installed a few years earlier. This call office was the best and most private way to make contact at tuppence for a three-minute telephone call and a penny a minute thereafter.

Byrne opened the half-glassed door to the wooden silence cabinet and stepped inside; it never failed to remind him of entering a large, standing casket. He withdrew a folded piece of paper from his jacket pocket, readied his coppers then lifted the earpiece from its cradle.

'Yes. Operator, Enfield 368, please,' he requested, reading from the slip of paper. As instructed, he deposited two pennies into the box and waited for the connection to be made.

After a few moments, Byrne murmured into the mouthpiece. 'It's done ... Yes, it'll be there on tomorrow's train with Yabsley. And the other one ... ? You have his address ... ? Tomorrow? I'll be there. What time? ... Oh. Bad luck about Smith.'

37

Tuesday, 12ᵗʰ September, 1905

Abbottsford Village, Suffolk, England

It had been only four days recuperating—it seemed like four years. I hated being laid up but Doctor Werner was watching me like a mother hen. From my bed, I could hear the magnificent longcase clock in the foyer on the ground floor chime the quarter hour after six.

Even with the shutters closed I knew the sun was still to rise and Mother Nature was calling me with some urgency. I decided to forsake the cumbersome tin pan and try to leave the bed and use the water closet. The walking stick was at hand and I had dosed up on pain relievers. With much effort, I wriggled off the bed and took my first tentative steps towards the privy. The good doctor would have been horrified and I certainly was in a lot of pain even with the analgesics but, once I achieved my equilibrium and with one careful step after another, I made it.

After answering the call, I decided to wash whatever I could reach. As much as I appreciated Mrs McPherson's generous attention, I hated being dependent on anyone for anything.

The effort of washing and dressing exhausted the little energy I had, but I nevertheless felt a sense of accomplishment as I stood in front of the long mirror and took in the sight. There I was, propped up by my walking stick and my damaged arm appropriately moored against my body by a white flag of truce. I had never been a pretty sight but, right now, dressed in my spare black trousers and turtleneck sweater, my complexion wan and my body bent, I own that I would have frightened a classroom full of school boys—had I come across one.

With this disconcerting thought, I hobbled to the armchair and lowered myself gingerly into it with beads of perspiration trickling from my brow. How I wished that bottle of Old Highland were not so far away.

A quick knock at my door and Wills poked his head in. 'You decent?' He saw I wasn't in my bed. 'Rebecca? Rebecca?'

'I'm here, Wills,' I replied from the snug of my armchair.

'Should you be out of bed? Why are you dressed?'

'Ready for our return to London.'

'Hm,' he voiced with disapproval. 'Quinn hasn't given the orders, yet. And I don't think Dr Werner will allow you to travel.'

'We'll see.'

'We'll see, indeed,' he said returning to the open door. 'Can I bring you breakfast? Or will you come and fetch it yourself and crawl back upstairs?'

Sometimes his drollness amused me—this was not one of those times.

***

Wills was trotting down the main staircase towards the morning room when he heard the faint tinkling of a telephone's bell.

That will be Quinn with his orders, he thought and, sure enough, upon reaching the landing on the ground floor, Thomson approached him.

'Major Williams, a telephone call for you, Sir.'

A streak of human lightning, in the shape of a young boy clutching several pairs of boots, flashed between the butler and Wills upsetting the almost unflappable Thomson.

'Henry! The back stairs!' he called after the recalcitrant lad, but to no avail. With a defeated shake of his head, he turned back to Wills. 'This way, Sir.'

'Thank you, Thomson,' Wills said and followed the butler to the ante room off the foyer.

Once inside, he picked up the telephone handpiece. 'Major Williams here.'

'Reggie!' The scream—shrill, urgent—was indisputably Cornelia's, his wife.

Wills' face fell. 'Cornelia? What's wrong? What's happened?'

'Reggie!' Her voice, wild and fractured, cried incoherently between sobs. 'Reggie! They forced their way in! They took us. Help us!'

'Cornelia! Who took you?'

The line fell silent.

'Cornelia? Cornelia!'

Then, through the crackling line, a new voice—measured, cultured, chillingly composed.

'Major Williams,' it began. 'I don't believe we've been formally introduced …'

That voice! He knew that voice.

'Permit me. Colonel Neville Humphries, retired—'

'What the hell is going on?' Wills snapped. What was this man doing with his wife? Where were they? Anger raged through his entire being. 'If you harm—'

'Steady on, Major,' Humphries soothed. 'All will be well with your wife and son if you do as I say.'

'If you harm them in any way, I swear I will find you and kill you!'

'You really are in no position to make such a threat, Major. But I promise you, as one officer and gentleman to another, they will be released unharmed once your task is completed. If you fail … well, let's not talk about that right now.'

Wills' heart pounded; his chest tightened with dread and his thoughts scattered in every direction … Quinn! He would put a call through to Quinn—

'Oh,' continued Humphries intuitively. 'It's of no use to call in the gendarmes. We have removed Mrs Williams and young Master Williams. They are under my care and they will be safe as long as you do as I ask.'

The word 'we' caught his attention; who was with him?

'And,' the colonel added in an idle tone, 'we'll be moving about somewhat so trying to locate this particular telephone through the exchanges will be a futile waste of time.'

Wills' mind reeled, but his singular concern was the safety of wife and son. 'What do you want?' he barked.

'Many things,' was the colonel's obscure reply. 'But, in essence, blood.'

The word baffled him. What in God's name did he mean by *blood?*

Humphries continued, cold, conversational, as though delivering a lecture. 'Do you know what happens to a man when his testicles are removed, Major? He becomes impotent. People ridicule him behind his back. His wife openly mocks him, belittles him. She tells her family and friends and, soon enough, he has been stripped of his dignity. His many accomplishments are nullified, negated. That alone is enough to send a proud and able man falling into the abyss of depression and self-loathing. In order to survive, those feelings of dejection and gloom soon transform into hatred and contempt for those who taunt him; for the women in his life. And for women at large. Of course, modern medicine can help allay those murderous thoughts.

'However, should this man be remiss and fail to take his abrogating medication, a man such as he could quite easily vent his rage on any woman near him. Do you understand me, Major?'

Desperately trying to keep his anger in check, Wills replied, 'Your story begs the question, "why my wife?" She has done nothing to you—'

'Simply a means to an end.'

'What end?' He was losing the little control he had. 'What game are you playing at?!'

'SHUT UP!'

The sudden violent outburst caught Wills by surprise. Over the telephone cable, he heard his wife and son's fearful cries and the frantic yapping of their newly acquired dog, Mikey.

'SHUT THEM UP!' Humphries screamed at his accomplice.

A moment later, Wills heard a loud yelp from Mikey, a few sobbing cries from his son and Cornelia comforting him with soft, quieting words.

Wills' fists were clenched tight. He strained to steady his breathing and keep his composure.

'Now, where were we?' Humphries returned to Wills with a controlled tone. 'Ah, yes, blood. You do realise, Major, that an arrest warrant has been issued for your cherished colleague?'

'What?'

'Yes, for treason, I believe. Capital offence, you know. "Off with her head" and all that,' Humphries chuckled. 'BUT THAT'S NOT GOOD ENOUGH!' he screamed. 'SHE HAS TO PAY!'

Humphries was deranged. And apparently Davies was the very catalyst of his hatred of women in general. Why? His unspoken query was answered.

'She ruined everything, that damned woman! Damn her! DAMN HER TO HELL!'

'How? How did she ruin everything? You don't even know her.'

'I know *of* her! How she's thwarted every attempted advancement. They all loathe her, you know. I am doing them a service!' His breath came fast and ragged over the line before settling back to his measured tone. 'It was all planned. This would have been the last. I would have had enough to start over.'

'You?' Wills couldn't believe what this bedlamite was admitting. 'You had those women abducted?'

'Is that so incredible, Major? I was an excellent campaign strategist in my time. Highly regarded.'

'Why? Why kill them? You had the money.'

He scoffed. 'They were just women. They'd served their purpose.'

'They were innocent women. They did you no harm.'

'They were like all wealthy women: pampered, spoilt, selfish, indolent, stupid, uncaring sycophants and adulterers and burdens to the men, husbands, fathers and brothers who looked after them. We were taught to treat them like goddesses, with respect and adoration. And what did they do? They abused that veneration—'

A chill went through Wills. 'How is Mrs Humphries?'

'Dead. Now, shall we get on with this, Major? I haven't got all day and your missus may have even less.'

All Wills could do was listen to this madman and wait for his demands.

After a moment, Humphries resumed. 'You asked me what I wanted in exchange for your wife and son. And dog. I want blood. Davies' blood. No! Her heart. Yes, I want her heart ripped out and brought to me.'

'You're a lunatic!'

'Am I?'

Without warning, a scream pierced the line—his wife's, raw with pain.

'STOP!!' Wills shouted but Cornelia's plaintive cries continued. Over them, he could just make out his son's desperate pleas for the perpetrator to stop.

'Understand, Major, only you can bring this to an end.'

'I'll do it! I'll do it … stop … please stop … stop …'

'Well done, Major!' and, with that, his wife's screams became a quiet string of sobbing cries.

'Now,' Humphries voice turned light and jovial, 'the details. Let's see. Hmm … there's a small town about twenty-five miles north from you—Wickham Upper. There's a slaughterhouse there. Perfect, don't you think, Major? Get her off her deathbed, into a cart and there after six. Tonight.

'I will have my man waiting there to collect that deviant's warm heart as soon as you've excised it from her chest.'

Wills' mind was awash with jumbled contradicting thoughts: those he cared most for in this world were under threat of death and he was driven to make an unthinkable choice. It was not a matter of life or death; it was a forced betrayal. His usually calm and controlled state had been shattered. He was unable to speak and barely able to breathe.

'Oh,' the retired colonel continued, his manner condescending, 'and do remember that the arrest warrant will be there by noon with the indomitable Sergeant Yabsley and that our esteemed Sir Giles Hawthorne will hear from said Yabsley once he's collected that warrant from Mr Quinn.'

'Wha … ? Where does Hawthorne fit in all this?'

'Sir Giles? Hah! He's a fool, an idiot. A little man with a big ego. Pity Dickie wasn't a better shot—could have saved us all a lot of bother, eh?'

Rebecca was right. But he wanted to hear the confirmation from Humphries. 'Captain Gregory Smith. Dickie.'

'Good work, Major! You're worth your salt.'

'The *deviant* worked it out.'

'Hmm … The last postulation she will make, I'm afraid. Right-o, Major, we're now off to parts unknown—to you, that is. Don't disappoint me, Major Williams, and your wife and child will live to see the morrow's sunrise.'

The disconnecting click of the telephone echoed in Wills' brain. He stood there in a trance as visions of his wife and son being cruelly mistreated jumbled together with a vision of him bloodily extracting Rebecca's heart …

There had to be a way … there had to be … But he couldn't see it.

Stupefied, he turned to go.

Right there before him was Henry, staring up at him open mouthed.

'Gaw, Major Williams, you look like you seen a ghost.'

'Henry …' Wills licked his lips; his mouth had become very dry. 'Henry, I need a horse and cart. Do you know where Wickham Upper is?'

'Wickham Upper? Aye, about twenty mile up the Middlebrook Way. Why do you need a horse and cart?'

Young Henry reminded Wills of his own son, always asking questions. 'I'll tell you later. Can you find one for me or should I ask the duke or your father first?'

'Nah, I know how to hitch a cart. And the duke said to give you whatever you want.'

'Good boy.'

'Can I come, too?'

'No.'

Henry's face fell.

'I have an errand to run and I won't be back until well after midnight.'

'I can help—'

'I said no!' Wills softened at the boy's fright. 'No, Henry. Just me. Make it ready in an hour, all right?'

'Aye.'

Wills felt bad leaving Henry there sulking but there was little else he could do.

Rather than taking breakfast in the morning room with his squad, Wills wandered into the gardens and drifted back and forth, his heart heavy. What he had to do was kill his only steadfast friend, someone who had fought alongside him for some twenty years, someone who had saved not only his life on several occasions, but his reputation as well. Someone whom he loved dearly and for whom he pledged to give up his life as she had pledged to him. And now it would be he who would take that life away.

He had to choose between the life of his compatriot and that of his wife and son.

There had to be a way …

***

I was amused and a little surprised when, at the knock on my door and my invitation to enter, Mrs McPherson swept in ushering a clearly apprehensive Florence into my room. The girl paused at the threshold, eyes flicking about, clutching the breakfast tray as though it were a shield. Mrs McPherson's nod directed her to place the laden breakfast tray on the nearby desk.

'Good morning, Miss Davies,' greeted Lady Katherine's housekeeper as she made her way to the shutters to allow the morning sun to invade the room. 'Ye shouldnae be out of bed. Did ye have a good rest?'

'Yes, thank you, Mrs McPherson, and you needn't bother with our morning ritual. As much as we both enjoy you fondling me, I took care of my lavations myself.'

My comments were meant to rattle Florence, which, by the sound of the clanking of the crockery on the tray, they did. This brought a modicum of amusement and a disapproving scowl from Mrs McPherson.

The desk was only a few feet away and I was determined to get there under my own steam.

'Och! Let me help ye,' clamoured the housekeeper, rushing to my assistance.

'I can manage, thank you.' I straightened and took a few unsteady steps towards the desk.

'Yer a stubborn woman, Miss Davies.'

'Thank you, Mrs McPherson, I appreciate your insight and candour,' I replied with unintended sarcasm.

Easing myself carefully onto the prepared chair at the desk, I noticed Lady Katherine standing in the doorway.

'Good morning, Rebecca.'

'Good morning, Katherine.' This familiarity elicited the requisite gasp from the young parlour maid. Satisfied, I continued, 'Will you join me for breakfast?'

'No. Unfortunately, I must confer with the duke on final matters of business before returning to Lilyfield this afternoon. However, I will take luncheon with you so we can discuss plans for your stay there.'

'I eagerly look forward to it.'

'Until then …' There was no mistaking the warmth in her expression. My stay at the Countess of Chestermere's estate gave me hope that my life had finally found some meaning and, as unlikely as it seemed, someone who felt the same way as I.

***

Wills lost all track of time pacing the garden. Checking his pocket watch revealed he had wandered the grounds for more than half an hour. With half-hearted resolution, he strode back into the mansion only to be met by a grinning Sir Giles Hawthorne.

'Major Williams,' he began, barely able to conceal his smirk. 'Detective Sergeant Yabsley telephoned to me and informed me that he will be on today's train from Kings Cross. You and Davies will be present when he arrives, I presume?'

Wills shot him a deadly glare as he brushed past.

Hawthorne replied with a self-satisfied, 'Checkmate!'

***

I was left to my own devices and was happily downing my last cup of tea when a little imp-faced head poked around the open door and looked about.

'Henry!' I called. 'Come in and close the door. What brings you here?'

He appeared worried and withdrawn, which concerned me as he was always so cheerful and self-assured.

'What's the matter?' I asked. 'Has Peleus taken ill?'

'Who is Cornelia?'

'Why do you ask?'

'Major Williams got real angry at someone who was with Cornelia. Does he live in Wickham Upper?'

'What are you talking about, Henry?'

'Major Williams asked about Mrs Humphries and then he got real scared. He ordered a horse and cart to go there and he won't let me go with him.'

Henry's simple unattached sentences made no sense to me at all. I was about to question him further when a sharp rap on the door was immediately followed by Wills stepping inside.

For a moment, time stopped; Wills was startled to see Henry with me; Henry equally startled to see Wills and I was mystified as to the cause of Wills' uncharacteristic disposition.

'What's he doing here?' Wills queried brusquely.

Before I could answer, Henry darted out of the room.

'I honestly don't know,' I replied. 'Are you all right? You seem agitated. Has Hawthorne—'

'Come on,' he said without ceremony. 'We've got to go.'

I didn't understand what was going on but I trusted Wills completely. I pushed myself out of the chair. 'Let me get my things—'

'No. You won't need them.'

'I won't? Where are we going?'

Wills gave an exasperated sigh and his shoulders slumped. 'Hawthorne has a warrant for your arrest and it's on its way here with Yabsley.' The way he looked at me told me he I was hearing only half the story.

'I'm not going to run, Wills. I've done nothing wrong.'

'Don't argue with me, Davies!'

His outburst caught me by surprise—not by its volume but the way he said my name. *Davies.* Not Rebecca; it was as though he wanted to distance himself from me.

'Please. Don't make this harder than it already is. Put on your jacket and let's go.'

I took a long moment to scrutinise my friend, trying to decipher what was going through his head. What had rattled him so? What had Cornelia, Mrs Humphries, the cart and Wickham Upper to do with my arrest warrant and all this?

A feeling of foreboding overcame me.

'May I leave a note for Lady Katherine? We were to have lunch together.'

Wills grimaced and looked away. I was now convinced that something more than my imminent arrest was causing him this extraordinary anxiety—something deep and personal.

I quickly penned a note and sealed it inside an envelope, marking it, 'For Lady Katherine' and leaving it on the desk.

Wills helped me on with my jacket, threading my able arm into the sleeve and draping the other side over my shoulder.

'My gun. My bag.'

'Leave them.'

I now understood.

It had come to this.

For long moments we looked at each other, unable to speak. Wills' face was drawn and ashen, stripped bare of compassion and resolve and replaced by regret, defeat and fear. It was the look of a man who had been forced to make a choice and now was broken by that choice.

I actually felt sorry for him.

However, fate was what it was for the both of us: unchangeable.

I took a deep breath and straightened up. Whatever my fate was, I would meet it head-on. Propped up by my walking stick, I made for the door.

'Let's go, then.'

The corridor was empty and I gingerly headed for the servants' stairs. Wills ducked back into my room and returned a few seconds later. He may have retrieved the note I had left for the countess but the bulge under his coat indicated otherwise; I didn't really care anymore.

We made it down the back stairs unnoticed by several servants too busy to look. The going was punishing for me. Wills offered assistance but I shrugged it off. I didn't need pity.

Just outside the back door of the kitchen stood a pony hitched to a two-wheeled dogcart. The vehicle wasn't very big but would have satisfactorily performed its original purpose of transporting a gentleman, his loader and his gundogs to the fields had the duke been so inclined. The box under the seat was big enough for three or four hounds and had side ventilation louvres for their comfort.

With some effort, I pulled myself up onto the box seat using the two mounting steps and seat rail. My hip ached, my arm throbbed, and perspiration betrayed the pain of my exertions.

But I sat quietly staring ahead. Fatalistic thoughts tumbled through my head. Had I been uninjured, I would not have been so compliant. Like this, I could hardly run or ride; hell, I could hardly walk or sit.

Wills took up his place next to me and, reins in hand, slapped them against the pony's rump. 'Walk on.'

Even now, with obvious turmoil and frustration bubbling under the surface, Wills remained outwardly composed and distant.

We headed out through the main gates at an easy trot and I marvelled that no one from the DSO had seen us or tried to stop us.

The cart bumped along the gravel road, causing me substantial discomfort. Wills gave me a furtive glance then reached under his jacket and handed me the cause of the bulge: my bottle of whisky.

I took it and gulped down a good mouthful.

Henry's scant, muddled pieces of information played through my head, trying to form themselves into a comprehensible chain of logic.

Another generous swig and the pain eased and my muscles relaxed. Contrarily, my wits sharpened; the individual links joined up. It was all beginning to make sense: Wills' behaviour, his reticence, the urgency. I decided not to say anything until we had reached our destination.

***

Two hours after the dogcart's departure from Abbottsford, the train from London arrived and disgorged the Royal Mail and Detective Sergeant Yabsley. Detective Byrne, much to Yabsley's annoyance, had once again requested leave to tend his ailing mother, an excuse he had used on several previous occasions and that was now beginning to wear thin. He would take that up with Byrne when this business was concluded.

Within minutes, Yabsley boarded the awaiting surrey that Sir Giles had sent and was on his way to Abbottsford Hall to serve the arrest warrant he carried in his pocket.

Yabsley was doing as ordered but he had a niggling doubt that this witch, this Medea, this woman he loathed so much, was the perpetrator of these heinous crimes. She was many things but a commissioner of brutal crimes against women? He could not convince himself that she could be so. Her deplorable actions had always been against men who, she asserted, had harmed women.

***

Lady Katherine entered Rebecca Davies' room after her discreet taps at the door remained unanswered.

'Rebecca? Rebecca, are you there?'

She looked around, puzzled to find the room empty.

Florence entered with a tray of covered food.

'Florence, have you seen Miss Davies?'

'She ain't back, my lady?'

'She left her room?'

'I seen her go down the back stairs with the major just after breakfast, my lady. I assumed she'd be back by now. I got her lunch here.'

'Oh.' Lady Katherine was perplexed.

'What shall I do with the vittles, my lady?'

'The what? Oh. Best put it on the desk.'

Florence did as she was bade and noticed the envelope.

'This was on the desk for you, my lady,' Florence said, handing the envelope to the countess, and, with a curtsey, disappeared out the door.

Lady Katherine opened the envelope and read the note.

> *My darling Katherine,*
> *I must leave. If it is at all within my power, and God*
> *willing, I will be with you once again. If not, I beg that*
> *you remember me with fondness.*
> *I will love you until my dying breath,*
> *R*

The countess was fixed to the spot, reading and rereading the hastily written words, trying to understand the reason for Rebecca's sudden flight.

The sound of a group of men bounding down the corridor caught her attention. The sight of Sir Giles Hawthorne entering the room ahead of a squad of five detectives pushed her to the cusp of impatience. She stiffened her back and held her ground with unyielding poise and composure.

The squad stopped in front of the countess.

Hawthorne's supercilious smirk made her detest him even more.

'My lady, if you would, we are here to see *Miss* Davies.'

Lady Katherine raised an eyebrow and, with impeccable grace, stepped aside.

'Thank you, my lady.' Even in this, his utterance of gratitude, she sensed his vitriol.

It was therefore with immense pleasure that, upon scanning Rebecca's room, he turned to her, red-faced.

'Where is she?' he demanded.

'I do not know. And, Sir Giles, I assure you, if I did have knowledge of her whereabouts, I would not impart it to you.'

'Do you know who you're speaking to, woman? I am an officer of the law!'

'Perhaps you should take this matter up with the duke. You are his guest here, after all.'

Hawthorne appeared lost for words. He snorted like an enraged bull but did not charge. Instead, his fist clenched around a piece of paper that now trembled with the force of his fury.

He stormed back out of the room followed by his cohort, the last two of whom, Hewitt and Ramsay, their expressions softened with genuine admiration for Lady Katherine acknowledged her with a quick bow as they passed. 'My lady.'

***

We had travelled at a steady pace all day, stopping only once to give the pony respite, some water and a little grain.

The hamlets we passed through along the Middlebrook Way were much smaller than Abbottsford village: sleepy little clusters of thatched cottages nestled in grazing fields dotted with sheep and cattle.

Not a word had passed between Wills and me, but I could sense he was carrying a great emotional burden. His face was set stone hard in a determined grimace; the only time I had seen him like this was when he vowed revenge on those three Mussulmen for what they had done to me, so many years ago.

The daylight was almost gone and so was the whisky. I was not drunk but I was almost pain free and certainly carefree. Wills would tell me in his own good time what I had already deduced.

The signpost along the road announced the next village would be Wickham Upper.

'Almost there,' I said without thinking.

Wills turned to me, his expression startled, as though I had uncovered his secret.

Another fifteen minutes or so and we were within sight of the village. In the twilight, I could just make out railway tracks in the distance. Wickham Upper appeared more substantial than Abbottsford and the hamlets we had passed through. It must have been some sort of central depot for the local farmers.

It didn't take us long before we came upon the town itself boasting quite a few shops and an inn along the high street. The shops were closed and darkened—only the inn and the street's newly-installed gas lamps illuminated the way forward. Apart from one or two local people making their way home or to the inn, the street was empty.

A solitary signpost stood near the town's common and pointed the way to our destination.

Wills manoeuvred the pony to the upper limits of the town, passing the railway station and crossing the tracks. There, situated amid fenced paddocks, stood a large wooden and corrugated iron building. Disordered stacks of kegs and broken crates leaned against the walls at irregular intervals. The was no activity within or without; all was quiet and dark.

As we drew closer, a foul stench filled my nostrils.

The sign on the building confirmed this was Wickham Upper Slaughterhouse.

The acrid odour of decaying flesh took my breath away, and so did the realisation that my deductions had been correct: this would be my last day on earth and Wills would be my executioner.

I knew I would die one day—that was everyone's fate—and I had always imagined it would be a violent death—such had been my life. But I had never thought that it would be at the hands of someone I trusted unreservedly and loved like a brother.

Wills pulled up the pony alongside one of the several doors along the outer walls. He climbed down and found a door bolted but not locked.

Looking up at me, he ordered, almost apologetically. 'Get down.'

I did as directed, not because I thought I was safe, not because I misunderstood what was coming but because there was no struggle left in me. There was no use resisting.

My injured leg gave way and I stumbled. He moved to assist me but I pushed him away and pulled myself upright. With the aid of my walking stick, I hobbled into the building. Wills followed.

It was dark inside but, once my eyes had adjusted, I could make out that the interior of the building was cavernous. Large, straw-covered holding pens that sectioned off the floorspace were separated by a wide corridor running down the middle. Some of the pens were empty but most held the unfortunate beasts awaiting processing the following day. Injured horses, old hacks, donkeys, mules and oxen that had outlived their usefulness, beef cattle, pigs, wethers, ewes which could no longer reproduce, all here dozing and oblivious to their fate. Or, perhaps like me, resigned to it.

'Here,' Will said softly, indicating an almost empty pen with an ample covering of straw.

I entered it and turned to Wills who had followed me in and had withdrawn his Webley. His arms hung limply by his side and his head was bowed. I detected a slight tremor in his gun hand.

'Don't feel remorse, Wills,' I said. 'Your wife and son are more important.'

Wills raised his head. Tears glistened as they ran down his cheeks into his moustache. His mouth opened as though to speak but only a shuddering breath came out.

'Do what you must to save them—if you are sure my death will free them. If you can trust a murderer.'

I saw the doubt in his eyes—doubt he couldn't blink away. Torment carved deep lines into his face. He looked tired, broken. He was fighting his conscience; he was pleading for forgiveness, absolution.

'I am ready,' I said.

I lied. I wasn't ready to die. I didn't want to die. Not now; not when I had found someone who loved me as much as I loved her. But why make it difficult for the man who meant so much to me? He had no alternative if he were to save his wife and son—two people who should not pay for my sins. And I had many to account for.

Wills raised his revolver but his movements were slow, reluctant. His hand trembled violently now, the barrel wavering, caught between duty and despair. His jaw clenched and he had difficulty holding true aim.

'I'm sorry, Rebecca,' he rasped. 'I am so sorry … Humphries … He wants your heart … He's sending someone …'

'It all makes sense,' I murmured. 'But there is still a spy amongst us. Find the spy and you'll find Humphries. And when you do, kill him. For me.'

Wills dropped his arm and, with it, his resolve collapsed. 'I can't. I can't …'

'Think of Cornelia. And young Reggie.' I took a breath to steady myself but still my voice cracked. 'I've lived my life. And I'm tired,

Wills. You know that. Look at me. Of what use am I to anyone now? I'm a cripple. Save your wife and son. Revenge my death.'

But I couldn't hold back the damned tears.

Wills' shuddering breaths abated, though his shoulders still trembled. He once again looked at me. His blue eyes scintillated with tears, his face contorted with regret. He raised his gun again.

I closed my eyes.

'Forgive me,' he uttered.

In the dark, cavernous slaughterhouse, a single shot rang out.

***

Outside, the night had turned bitter.

Major Williams stood there in the dark alone, waiting and shivering. Was he shivering from the chill of the night or from the aftershock of the dreadful act he had just committed? His bespoke Savile Row suit was soaked in blood, as were his hands and linen cuffs. In those trembling, blood-soaked hands he held the sacrificial heart wrapped in his partner's jacket—the ransom to redeem his wife and child from a vengeful madman.

For long moments he stared at the bundle in disbelief. He was numb. How had it come to this?

A distant rumble slowly brought him out of his inertia. A motorcycle was racing along the road from the town's outskirts towards him. It caught Wills in its headlight as it skidded to a stop just short of where he stood.

'There you are!' said the rider as he dismounted, leaving the motor running.

The Irish intonation of this statement was familiar. 'Who ... Co-Constable Byrne?'

'Right the first time, Major Williams,' Byrne confirmed taking a few steps towards him. 'Is that for me?'

Byrne was the pickup man! Byrne was Humphries' lackey. Byrne was the spy. It was Byrne who had planted the notes in the unionist's house. It was Byrne who had changed the coordinates. And it was Byrne who had passed information to Humphries. Rebecca had been on the right track. But it didn't make sense.

'Why, Byrne? Why?'

'Ah, Major, it's a long story. Let's just say that it was Mr Arthur Griffith who inspired me. Ireland should not be ruled by a foreign country. We ourselves should govern it. *Sinn Féin.*'

'The ransom money?'

'Preparation for the inevitable.'

Once more, Wills was puzzled. This was not what Humphries had intimated; the colonel's motives were purely selfish. Humphries wanted the money for himself.

'Now, Major, enough small talk,' Byrne continued. 'I have an errand to run. You have something for me, I believe.'

Wills handed the bundle over to Byrne. 'It was *you* who harmed my wife,' he snarled.

Byrne opened the bundle. 'Ah, 'twas but a little slap. She'll survive.' He marvelled when he saw the heart. 'So this is what an invert's heart looks like. What mysteries lie within.'

'You won't get away with this, Byrne.'

'Perhaps. Perhaps not. Now, forgive me if I doubt your word but I have orders to see for myself that our esteemed Assisting Clerk is, indeed, no longer breathing this fresh country air. Let me assure you that the old colonel is a man of his word—even if he is English—and, once I get back with this, your wife and son will be released unharmed.'

He gave Wills an unreadable look. 'You, however—' The revolver came up fast. Byrne fired point-blank.

The major staggered a step backwards, grabbing his chest. Shock twisted into agony. He collapsed to the ground. Searing pain ripped through his body.

He groaned.

Byrne shook his head.

Through a haze of pain, Wills watched Byrne approach. The man took the few, slow measured steps towards him and stood over him. Cold metal touched Wills' forehead.

'You there! Halt!!'

The shouted command startled Byrne. He jumped back to see two men sprinting towards him from behind the building. One was carrying a lantern and nightstick and the other a long firearm.

'Murder! Murder!!' yelled the other and blew his police whistle with all the air his lungs could expel.

Byrne bolted to his motorcycle, revved it up and skidded away, holding the wrapped heart securely in his lap.

'Stop! STOP!!' bellowed the watchman again while the other man with the lantern flew to Wills' side. He took one look at the bloodied, still form lying there, he called to his partner with the shotgun. 'He's done for.'

The watchman noticed the open door. 'Bring the lantern.'

A moment later, his voice rose again.

'Good Lord! What sort of lunatic would do such a thing?'

Those were the last words Wills heard before darkness claimed him.

***

Every situation, like a three-dimensional object, can be viewed from multiple perspectives with each being interpreted differently. Such was the case that night at the slaughterhouse.

Young Henry Pitman didn't lack discipline or education—he was intelligent and canny for his age—but he did have a propensity for being stubborn and getting his own way by whichever means were available. He would not accept that he could not do what made him happy and, right now, he would be happiest being a detective like Miss Davies and Major Williams.

It was that desire that had found him cramped up, hidden in the dog box under the seat of the dogcart, going to Wickham Upper with Miss Davies and Major Williams—but without their knowledge. He had been there for what seemed to be days and he was hungry and needed to piddle. He was comforted when Miss Davies said, 'Almost there'.

Through the ventilating louvres he saw the day darkening and then the glow of street lighting. A short while later, the cart left the illuminated road. He could just make out the large building that the dogcart had pulled up next to and was about to open the hatch when he heard Major Williams say, 'Get down.'

Something in the major's tone and the fact that Miss Davies wouldn't accept his assistance when she stumbled made him stay hidden; he sensed something wasn't right between them.

Henry watched them go into the building and, when all was quiet again, he carefully opened the hatch and crawled out of the box. His whole body was stiff and his legs tingled with pins and needles. Climbing off the back of the cart, he looked around. The sign on the building concerned him.

'Slaughterhouse?' he whispered.

The door had been left ajar—just wide enough for him to sidle his way through.

In the darkness, the first thing he sensed was the sharp rotten smell—not like an unclean privy—something worse. A little further down the aisleway he could just make out Miss Davies and the major in one of the pens. Something certainly wasn't right between them.

His inquisitiveness pushed him carefully onwards and, climbing through the rails of a nearby pen, he hunkered down, wide-eyed, waiting and listening. He couldn't see what they were doing but he could hear what they were saying. Miss Davies was concerned for the major and his wife and she told him she was ready. In this place, ready for what? She told him to do it. Do what? He said he was sorry. Sorry for what?

Then it happened!

A bang so loud it startled the sheep in his pen and the other dozing animals.

Henry recoiled. His heart raced. He clapped his hand over his gaping mouth and sat there on his haunches in disbelief: Major Williams had shot Miss Davies!

No! It could not be! How could he? Not Miss Davies!

Now, the only sounds he could hear were the rustling of straw and the slashing of flesh. The killer, Henry was glad to hear, was sorry for what he had done but that would not bring Miss Davies back! Henry would never forgive him this!

He had to tell someone. Major Williams had to be punished for killing Miss Davies. Henry was about to get up and run out to find a constable when the major lumbered by holding a parcel. Even in the gloom, he saw the blood. The murderer was soaked in blood— her blood! And his face was pale and ugly. Henry didn't care about him. How he hated that monster. How he wanted to avenge Miss Davies' death. Henry didn't breathe until the murderer had trudged out through the door.

As soon as Major Williams had gone, Henry stumbled to the killing pen. His legs could hardly carry him—they were as numb as his mind. And he prayed. He had prayed hard for her to live before— and it worked—maybe he could do it again.

Timorously, Henry approached the pen.

He stood there, heart pounding, mouth agape, wide-eyed and in total disbelief. 'M … Miss Davies …'

There she was, amid the straw, the butchery, blood and death … alive and well!

***

'Henry!' I gasped, standing there, propped up by my stick and startled at seeing him in this place. But I was more alarmed by what he may have witnessed.

'He didn't kill you!' he cried before I could utter another word, and ran to me and gave me such a hug that he almost knocked me off my feet, sending a bolt of pain through my hip. 'He didn't kill you!'

'No,' I said, steadying myself and regaining my composure. 'Where did you come from? Henry, what in God's name are you doing here?'

'Dunno …' Henry let go of me and hesitated. 'I just wanted to …' His words trailed off as he lowered his gaze, letting it wander along the straw-covered floor until it fell upon the carcass of a bloodied pig. Henry's look of astonishment spoke of his dawning realisation of what took place moments before.

'Yes, Henry,' I confirmed calmly, 'the major didn't kill me. He shot the sow and removed her heart.'

'I thought … I heard what he was saying … what you … you told him to kill you … I thought—'

'I thought he would, too. He had to make a choice. My life or that of his wife and child. He did a brave thing, Henry.' I put my hand on Henry's shoulder and squeezed. 'Henry, someone is coming and he must not know that I am still alive,' I warned, looking him squarely in the eyes. 'No one must. The lives of Major Williams' wife and son are in mortal danger. Do you understand?'

'I understand,' Henry repeated.

'Do you swear to tell no one, not even your father, that I am alive?'

'I swear,' he solemnly promised. At that moment, our attention was drawn to the sound of an approaching motor.

'Come,' I urged. 'We must go. There has to be another way out. Quickly, this way.'

'Quickly' was easier said than done. I limped along as fast as I could and Henry, bless him, stayed with me to help.

At the other end of the long corridor was another door but it, too, had been bolted from the outside. The nearby window offered the solution and Henry the wherewithal. Without a moment's hesitation, he twisted the lock, pushed up the sash, climbed through the opening and slipped the door's bolt on the outside.

There, we carefully picked our way around the side of the building from one untidy pile of crates to another.

We stopped when we heard voices approaching from the railway station and hid behind a pile of kegs.

'I'm sure I heard a gunshot. It came from here,' insisted one man.

'You're barmy, mate,' another scoffed.

'Shh. I hear voices,' the first said. 'There! Around the side!'

A gunshot rang out.

Wills … No!

'This way! This way!' called the first man. They ran past us towards the source of the report.

Henry took a step to follow but I pulled him back. 'No!' I whispered, sharp but muffled by caution.

We could hear the watchmen shouting, 'You there! Halt!!' and 'Murder! Murder!!' and long bursts of a police whistle but Henry and I held tight where we were. An instant later and the night was filled with the sound of a motorcycle's engine revving up and taking off, screaming away into the darkness, followed by shouts of 'Stop! STOP!!'

I was desperately fearful that Wills had been hurt and, pulling Henry along behind, made my way around to the other side of the building where, from behind a large, discarded barrel, we saw a watchman with a lantern crouch over an inert body.

'He's done for,' the watchman informed his partner with the shotgun.

No! … My scream was silent but it tore through my entire body. I shook. *No … it can't be …*

'Bring the lantern,' the second watchman called.

Leaving Wills in the dark, I watched both watchmen make their way into the slaughterhouse.

Then I heard it.

Hope.

Wills expelled a low, ragged groan.

'He ain't dead!' Henry cried; I barely managed to pull him back behind the barrel.

'Henry. Listen,' my whisper cut through his panic. 'Get the major to a doctor. Urgently. The constable will be here very soon. Get him to call Alexander Quinn of the Special Branch of the Metropolitan Police. Got that? Alexander Quinn. Special Branch. Tell the constable the major is on a secret assignment and no one must know about this. Or me. Got that? No one.'

With each specific instruction, Henry nodded and repeated the last word of it. I asked him to repeat the directives.

'Major to a doctor quick. Metropolitan Police. Special Branch. Alexander Quinn. Secret assignment,' he whispered back. 'And no one is to know you're here.'

'Good boy. Now go.'

Henry ran to Wills' side and dropped to his knees. 'Major! Major! Don't die!'

'Henry … ?' Wills gasped just before he slid into unconsciousness.

Henry jumped to his feet. 'Get a doctor!' he yelled. 'He's alive! Get a doctor!'

Both watchmen ran back out. From the high street, a portly man—a constable—puffed his way to them. 'What's this?'

'Get a doctor! Quick!' Henry yelled.

***

Hidden behind the large discarded barrel in the deep, freezing shadows of the night, I watched as Henry decisively directed the two watchmen and the town's constable to fetch a doctor and to call Mr Alexander Quinn of the Special Branch in London. When they dithered, he shouted that they would be up for murder if they let Major Williams die. The boy certainly had audacity and gumption to spare.

Townsmen filtered from their cottages and were astonished by the amount of blood on the dying man's hands and clothing. Conjecture ran wild but, true to his word, Henry gave not a hint of the truth. He told them that they were just passing through when they were set upon—he was a quick and believable yarn spinner, young Henry.

This is where I left them, hoping and praying to the God I'd abandoned that no time would be lost in getting Wills the medical assistance he so desperately needed.

The night air cut through my clothing. My hasty departure from Abbottsford Hall saw me dressed only in my blacks—trousers and turtleneck sweater. I had no jacket—Wills had taken that—and no coat. The white calico sling that strapped my injured arm close to my chest only added to my visibility. The only gear I had with me was the switchblade stiletto hidden in my boot and my walking stick. My Webley, gloves, balaclava, and the rest of my tools of trade had all been left behind in my Gladstone, as had my pocketbook with money and the keys to my flat.

But the chill got me moving.

I had to find a way back to London without anyone knowing. Only from there could I recover from my injuries and find Humphries. He would pay for what he'd done—and pay dearly—not only for what he had inflicted on Wills and his family, but also for the atrocities he perpetrated on those three young women and what he had planned for my Lady Katherine.

The confusion at the slaughterhouse gave me the opportunity to make my way to the train station. Moving about unseen, however, was difficult given my ambulatory constraints and the white sling about my arm, but I managed. I found the station master's office and broke in, the rim lock offering very little resistance to my deftly wielded stiletto.

The room was dimly lit by the faint light of the gas lamp on the platform filtering through the window. I rummaged around, found an old, tattered blanket, good enough to shut out some of the chill.

The station master's desk drawer was just as easily jemmied, and inside I found two penny dreadfuls, a box of biscuits, a few coppers and a shilling. The stale shortbread confections were enough to assuage the hunger pangs and the coins would be enough to get me onto a train and within cooee of a fat pocket to pick. I was in no mood to read hackneyed crime stories so I found a dark corner to wait for first light.

Tired as I was, I couldn't sleep for worrying over Wills.

***

The old stone farmhouse met his requirements perfectly. It was small, dilapidated and forgotten for decades. Outside, the surrounding gardens were a mass of untidy weeds threading their way through the dry branches of long-dead rose bushes. The night air was brisk and quiet save for the occasional rustling of some animal or other foraging through the tall grasses. The waning gibbous moon shone a pallid glow over the gently rolling pastures and the winding weather-damaged track that led to the small front door of the shelter.

Behind the house, a dozing horse was hitched to a cart, ready to go if needed.

Inside, a faint, flickering light escaped the old oil lamp set on the dirty, leaf-strewn floor of the empty, deserted hovel, itself barely a shell of cold stone walls permeated by damp and rot.

'I do beg pardon for the rude accommodation, Mrs Williams,' apologised Colonel Humphries, his voice calm and measured—he had not been remiss in taking his prescribed medication. 'I do hope you understand the necessity of removing you here.'

She didn't reply. Cornelia Williams sat trembling and huddled in a dingy corner on the filthy floor. Her arms were clasped tightly around her son, Reggie, who, in turn, clutched Mikey to his chest. An occasional tear would escape, which she would instantly brush away.

Humphries noted her fear with coldness but admired the way she composed herself. Fear was natural—a way of preserving one's life. He, himself, had known fear—on the battlefield—but that was not an admission one made to anyone—ever.

Byrne had struck the woman, and the boy, a little too enthusiastically—but discipline was necessary. They now knew their place, the boy and his mother, and they would be no further trouble.

'It shouldn't be long now,' Humphries conciliated. 'My man should be back very soon with the merchandise.'

'And you'll release us?' she asked, trying to suppress the tremor in her voice.

'I am a man of my word, Mrs Williams. If your husband has done as asked, no harm will come to you or your precious son. You will be free to go.'

'And if he doesn't … can't … ?'

Humphries merely looked at her but, even in that feeble light, he saw her understanding of what he was and the rigid intention supporting his threats.

That pleased him; that would keep her compliant.

'Yes,' Humphries said, heaving a sigh of grim satisfaction. 'It shouldn't be long now.' He returned to peering through the cracks in the shutters, waiting and watching the track for Byrne's return.

Cornelia watched him. He could feel her gaze upon him. He could almost hear her desire to know why. What could Rebecca Davies have done to cause him to have such hatred and lust for vengeance?

She couldn't know, of course, but he did. That self-appointed avenger was a torment to him. She'd thwarted his plans, made a fool of him, made him appear impotent. No woman who had done that to him would escape his wrath. Just ask his wife.

The cold silence dissolved with Reggie's whispered plea, 'Mamma …'

'Shh …' Cornelia said, comforting her son. 'All will be well, Reggie. Your Papa will fetch us soon.'

Humphries' mocking snort stunned Cornelia as though he had slapped her. He hadn't told her his plan for her beloved husband.

The sputtering of an advancing motorcycle drew their attention.

'Ah!' the colonel announced, 'the messenger approaches.'

Humphries strode to the door to meet the rider. Kieran Byrne strutted in carrying a blood-soaked jacket and wearing a face that bordered on apology.

'You have it?' Humphries asked, reaching for the parcel.

Byrne relinquished the item. 'I do.'

Humphries took it without ceremony and felt its weight—more than he'd expected. It was still warm. He carefully peeled away the covering and, upon seeing the bloodied, dark red muscle with stubs of severed veins and arteries, he began to laugh. Slowly, gutturally at first, then ringing out with appalling depravity filling the room with unhinged delight.

Cornelia gasped. Even in his moment of triumph, he saw her dawning realisation—this was the heart of someone she knew. She gripped at the cloth around her own heart and shuddered.

He cared not what she felt; he had his prize.

Her son became alarmed by his mother's uncontrollable shaking. 'Mamma! Mamma!' he whimpered.

She pulled him tight to her trembling body and cowered deeper into that dark corner, trying to shield him from the horrific sight. Her voice was a broken quiver. 'It's all right, Reggie, it's all right.'

Humphries could hear the panic beneath those words but he chose to ignore her.

'You saw her body?' he asked Byrne.

'That's her jacket, there,' Byrne replied evasively.

'But you saw her?'

'Well, no … em … there was—'

'And the major?'

'As you instructed.'

Cornelia rallied. 'What about Major Williams?' Her voice was shrill, soaked in fear. 'What did you instruct?'

'You're certain?'

'Well …' Byrne struggled. 'We were set upon by two watchmen—'

Humphries growled; his face contorted with rage. 'Outside!' he barked.

Byrne and Humphries took a few measured paces into the dead garden, their tread crunching the withered weeds. The sallow light of the moon and the wan lamp light seeping through missing slats of the broken shutters cast a pale glow and ominous shadows upon the two men as they faced each other.

'Tell me what happened.' The order was sharp, uncompromising.

'We were disturbed. But he's in a bad way. He won't survive the night. I couldn't finish him off. One of the watchmen had a shotgun. I had to go. You've got her heart. He's a goner,' Byrne prattled.

Humphries stared at Byrne for long moments.

'He's dead. She's dead. I've done my part!' He took a steadying breath. 'Just give me the money you promised and I'll be gone.'

'Hmm,' Humphries intoned, reaching into his coat pocket and retrieving a wad of folded bank notes. 'The promised renumeration,' he said as he handed the money over to Byrne together with the jacket and its gory contents.

Byrne's expression changed from delight to puzzlement to shock when he saw a revolver in Humphries' hand. Before he could utter another word, two rounds pierced his chest.

Humphries delighted in the man's final look of disbelief. He calmly took the notes and bloodied bundle from the Irishman's hands just as he collapsed to the ground dead.

'Money for the Irish revolution? I think not,' Humphries scoffed.

Humphries returned to the house to find Cornelia sobbing hysterically and shielding her son from the maniac.

'Don't! Please don't,' she wailed piteously.

'Pull yourself together, woman! I gave my word.' He casually tossed the bundle away.

She continued to sob.

'Stop that immediately or you'll force me to break my promise to your husband.'

Cornelia's hysteria abated to breathless spasms.

'That's better,' Humphries crooned and withdrew a coin from the sovereign case attached to his fob chain. 'I'll be leaving now. The town of Wickham Upper is five miles west when you reach the top of this road. There's a train station there. Don't get lost and be careful—there are some very dangerous men out there! I would wait until morning to leave if I were you.' He tossed the coin to her.

He smiled a smile so devoid of humanity that it drained the blood from her face. As an afterthought, he added, 'And you'll find your husband there.'

Humphries left Cornelia, Reggie and Mikey huddled in that corner of the disused cottage with the faint lamplight flickering against the cold stone walls, and climbed aboard the waiting cart at the back, awakening the dozing hack. A flick of the whip had them trotting off along the path to the highway. At the intersection where the cart track met the highway, he paused before turning left instead of right. He was going to Wickham Upper to make certain that both his adversaries were, indeed, no more.

***

The town was still abuzz with gawkers even at this late hour, standing around in little clusters, shaking their heads and tut-tutting.

Humphries pulled up close to one of these groups. 'Apologies for the interruption, gentlemen, but what's all the fuss about?'

'A stranger's been murdered up there near the slaughterhouse,' offered one solemnly.

'He ain't dead yet,' another contradicted.

'Won't be long, but. He's real bad off,' a third added.

'I see …' Humphries remarked but he needed to know about Davies. 'The slaughterhouse, you say. What on earth was he doing there?'

'Butchering a grunter,' the first replied.

'Covered in the beast's blood,' added the second.

'A … a grunter?' Humphries queried.

'Gutted,' another added.

'What do you mean "a grunter"?' Humphries asked of the first man.

'A porker, your honour, a pig. You know—oink, oink.'

His two friends laughed.

'You're not from here, are you?' the man asked.

Humphries sat there, his rage surging like a tidal wave ready to engulf everything in its path. The realisation of what had occurred cemented in his mind. He had been cheated. Duped. *A pig! A pig's heart! Nine lives! That bitch has nine lives!*

Suddenly he realised that he had relinquished his trump card. *The Williams woman!*

The poor hack copped the brunt of Humphries' fury—he whipped it into motion. He turned back the way he had come. He whipped it mercilessly into a full gallop to sprint back away from the town. They almost collided with several bystanders on the road.

'Out of the way!' Humphries yelled, forcing the clusters to scatter.

It took only half the time to return to the old farmhouse. He was heartened to see the faint glow still emanating from within.

'Good. She stayed,' he said to himself. 'Stupid woman.'

Pulling on the handbrake and jumping down from the cart, he raced inside.

Empty!

Gone!

'Damn!' Humphries screamed. *She can't have gone far*, he thought. *It's dark. There's nowhere to hide. She's here somewhere. I didn't pass her along the road …*

He hesitated.

He remembered almost running down a small dog. It had been that dog—their dog!

'Damn!' he shrieked again. He had to find her. But what if she'd found someone to aid her? What if she brought them here? And that bitch Davies was still alive! *I will find her and I will destroy her. I will find and destroy everything she has, everything she loves. How? How?*

He was pacing the floor of that old farmhouse, his face flushed and contorted with fury. 'DAMN YOU! DAMN YOU TO HELL, YOU FUCKING WHORES!'

***

Cornelia Williams hadn't waited.

The instant that insane Humphries had abandoned them, she'd gathered her son Reggie, with Mikey gripped tightly in his arms, and fled the old farmhouse, desperate to find her husband and save her son. She would not wait until morning lest that demented fiend return. She didn't know what he would do to them, but she did know what he was capable of doing.

Grasping Reggie's hand so tightly that it made him wince, she cautiously stepped out of the farmhouse and into the uncertainty of the dark night. The pale descending moon cast long diffused shadows over the neglected garden. Her eyes fell upon the corpse of that Irishman.

She baulked. His pallid face was frozen in a grimace of surprised terror. His vacant eyes stared blankly into the deep night sky and his mouth locked open in a final silent scream.

She stifled a cry of despair—not for him but for them and their plight.

Reggie stared at the corpse in awe.

'Mamma, is he dead?'

'Reggie ... come away ...' Cornelia whispered and pressed him to her, turning his face away.

It was then she saw it—the grip of Byrne's service revolver protruded from under his blood-soaked coat. With courage she didn't know she had, she reached her trembling hand out and, from under the dead man's coat, detached the gun from its holster.

It was much heavier than she'd anticipated; she had never held a gun before, let alone fired one, but she was adamant she would use it to protect her son.

'Come, quickly,' she urged, pulling Reggie behind her. 'We must run.'

Lifting her burdensome skirts and gripping the gun with one hand while clutching her son's life with the other, she scrambled up the dirt track, stumbling on the uneven, potholed surface to the top where, only minutes before, Humphries had travelled.

She was panting—gasping for air—from fear and urgency more than exertion. Cornelia wanted to be as far away as possible from the murdered Irishman and Rebecca Davies' irreverently discarded heart; she still could not accept that her husband had done that to someone he professed to respect.

As Humphries had directed, she turned westward along the road to Whickham Upper, following the descending moon. There, she prayed she would find her husband or news of what had become of him. There, she dared hope she would find safety.

The moon was low on the horizon and the night was ominously dark and bitterly cold. They had been taken in only the clothes they wore—no overcoats, no shawls, no mittens or gloves—and the icy night air pierced every pore to the bone. She had no idea of the hour; she only knew panic and every second lost could be fatal.

She frantically struggled along the roadway, dragging Reggie behind her. Mikey trotted closely behind. Even in the gloom she could see that the highway ran through open fields, sparsely scattered with trees and shrubs. Every now and then, a hedgerow or a low dry-stone wall marked a perimeter. No other farm houses or shelters to be seen.

So few places to hide, she thought, *should the unspeakable happen.*

Then, hoof beats. The rumble of a cart.

She froze mid-stride.

Her heart pounded in her ears.

In the distance, movement—a cart hurtling along the road towards them.

Humphries!

It had to be.

Cornelia's thoughts splintered into panicked shards. Stand and shoot? What if she missed? He had a gun! He had threatened to kill them. He was merciless.

There was no choice.

She dragged her son off the road and ran towards an unkempt cherry laurel, flinging him down under it and herself on top, shielding him should the worst happen.

To her horror, Mikey had not followed!

He stood like a sentinel, his eyes fixed on the cart as it thundered closer, growling.

'Mikey!' she hissed.

He ignored her.

'Mikey, here, boy! Here!'

He barked and continued to bark incessantly at the rapidly approaching vehicle. He barked ferociously, as though he were warning the man off.

Cornelia couldn't bear to watch the cart barrel towards the little dog and turned her head away.

The horse and cart hurtled past them and, when she looked up, by some miracle, Mikey had avoided being hit and stood his ground, continuing his remonstrations at the receding cart.

Had he recognised the dog? Would he come back when he realised what he'd seen?

She snapped back to her senses. Cross-country was safer, rather than along the road. They would be more difficult to find in the darkened, open fields. The shrubs were few and far between but, if she planned it carefully, she should be able to run from one to the other without being seen.

She hadn't gone far when the still night air was cleaved by the scream of an insane man.

***

Doctor Montgomery was a capable and experienced country doctor— Henry could tell that much, watching him attend Major Williams' gunshot wound.

The stableboy felt a pang of guilt having thought that the man that lay on the table would have betrayed Miss Davies. The major's clothing had been cut away and the blood sponged away exposing the neat hole where the bullet went in and the jagged gash where it came out.

'He won't die, will he, Doc?' Henry implored. 'He can't die. You mustn't let him.'

'Son, in my time, I've tended many gunshot wounds, both accidental and deliberate,' the older doctor explained patiently, 'and I will be straight with you, young man, his injury is of concern to me.'

Henry listened intently, his youthful face drawn tight with concern.

'This sort of wound can result in death,' Dr Montgomery continued. 'The bullet has passed through his body and caused him to lose a lot of blood but, by the grace of God, it did not strike any vital organ or his spine. It did shatter a rib. He is very lucky. Son, I've done everything I can for him here. He needs to be in a hospital. We'll get him there first thing in the morning.'

'Morning? That's hours away,' Henry's voice faltered, betraying his distress.

'Come, lad, it's very late and you need to rest.' Dr Montgomery spoke kindly to the little stranger and ushered him away from Wills' bedside. 'There's nothing more you can do here.'

'I can pray.'

'Of course, son. Come and lie down on the sofa in my office. You can pray there.'

'Just a minute, Horace.' The more mature male voice came from the doorway.

'Constable Calthrop. What—'

'I need to speak to the boy.'

Henry's attention was drawn to the man standing there. He recognised him as the same constable who had taken charge at the slaughterhouse after the major had been shot.

'Not now, Edwin,' the doctor said. 'The boy's been through a lot. He needs to rest.'

Henry's eyes darted from one to the other; he noted that they were of similar age and build but he silently resolved he wasn't going to tell anyone anything.

'I've just spoken to the head of the Special Branch, no less. In London, no less. And he's sending the Chief Inspector of the Department of Special Operations, no less. And guess where he's stationed at present? Abbottsford Hall. The seat of the Duke of Bramwell—'

'No less,' added the weary doctor. 'Edwin, the boy needs rest. You can talk to him in the morning.'

'The boy said they were passing through. Why? Where were they going?' Constable Calthrop persisted. 'Why was he shot? Why was that pig gutted? What's the boy got to do with all this? They're not from these parts. The boy's the only one who can tell us anything.'

'Tomorrow,' insisted Dr Montgomery, ushering the constable towards the door.

The policeman stopped. 'I was told to keep my eye on him. And the man, there.'

'The man there isn't going anywhere and you can keep your eye on the boy as he sleeps. Now go.'

'I'm expecting this fellow Sir Giles Hawthorne to arrive sometime after midnight. Make sure the boy's ready to speak to him,' the constable urged.

The thought that Sir Giles Hawthorne was going to talk to him made Henry baulk. He had had nothing to do with the man but what he had seen of him, Henry hadn't liked. The oath Henry had given Miss Davies resounded in his mind: *The major is on a secret assignment and no one must know that Miss Davies was here.*

And no one would.

***

The course she had chosen was arduous but Cornelia was sure she was heading in the right direction towards Wickham Upper. The moon had almost set and she was on the brink of collapse. Reggie's legs had given way long before and she now carried him clutched tightly to her chest. Her limbs tingled with exhaustion and each jarring step made his weight feel heavier. Mikey followed them relentlessly, like a tiny protective sentinel. They had been on the move for what felt like miles. Her fine house dress was torn to shreds by the holly, hawthorn and blackthorn bushes that so ably concealed them as they struggled from one to the other in their desperate flight.

'We're almost there, Reggie,' she encouraged her son. 'Not far now.' She really didn't know where they were or how far they still had to go. The night was bitingly cold but she was perspiring. Mikey kept up with them, alert and vigilant.

38

Wednesday, 13ᵗʰ September, 1905

Wickham Upper, Suffolk, England

It was just after midnight when the coach that bore the coat of arms of the tenth Duke of Bramwell thundered along the country road. The breakneck gallop of the two perfectly matched Yorkshire Coach Horses was faultlessly synchronised as they barrelled along Middlebrook Way at a blistering pace. The coachman was in absolute control of the vehicle and was as desperate as the men inside to get to Wickham Upper as soon as physically possible, but for his own reason: his son, Henry, had gone missing. When he overheard Sir Giles say that a ten-year-old boy was involved, he volunteered instantly.

Inside the elegantly appointed coach, Sir Giles, Yabsley, Hewitt and Ramsay grimly held on, both to their seats and to the thought that one of their own had been brought down. Quinn hadn't given very much information to Hawthorne other than to say that everything must be kept locked down and no details be given out to anyone until Quinn, himself, attended. This didn't sit well with Sir Giles—he was his own man and in charge of this squad and he would do as he saw fit. Sir Giles had never warmed to the major—he found him arrogant in the extreme—but this news rattled him more than he cared to admit.

Doctor Werner followed the landau, keeping pace in his fully equipped dogcart. He would render as much assistance as he possibly could to the major if, indeed, he had not succumbed to his wounds.

***

After a welcome meal of hot tea and biscuits, Henry settled and dozed on the sofa. Doctor Montgomery had fallen asleep at his desk in his leather-bound swivel chair, keeping Henry company.

Constable Calthrop interrupted the doctor's soft snore. 'Horace! Horace, come quick!'

The doctor roused, as did Henry.

'What … ?'

'You're needed,' was all the constable would say and led the doctor out into the small reception room. There, he found the innkeeper supporting an exhausted woman and child, helping them into chairs.

'Alfie was locking up when he saw these two coming in from one of the fields back of his place,' explained the constable. 'She's looking for her husband.'

The doctor immediately began examining the woman and boy. 'Madam, I'm Doctor Montgomery. Are you hurt?'

'My husband … I must know that my husband is safe,' she replied, appearing almost incoherent from distress and desperation.

'Madam, what happened to you?' the doctor persisted. 'Who is your husband?'

'Reginald Williams,' she rasped. 'I'm Cornelia Williams.'

Montgomery looked at Calthrop who looked at the innkeeper.

'Thanks, Alfie, you did good,' Calthrop said to the innkeeper. 'We'll take it from here.'

With the innkeeper gone, the constable was free to speak. 'Madam, what happened to you? Why were you wandering the fields?'

'Please, may we have some water?' Cornelia begged.

'Of course, of course,' the doctor obliged rushing to his infirmary to fetch the pitcher and glasses, brushing by Henry standing at the doorway, mouth agape.

The constable continued his questioning. 'Did your husband bring you here?'

Henry's voice intruded softly, 'You're Cornelia?' he said from the doorway, his face contorted by concern. '*Mrs* Williams?'

The doctor returned with the water and his medical bag and Cornelia helped her son drink his fill before taking any herself.

'Now let's see to those lacerations,' he said, preparing an antiseptic swab from his kit.

'The dog. Where's the dog?' she said with more alarm than seemed necessary.

'Outside. He's outside,' the constable confirmed.

'Please. Let him in …'

The constable vacillated between going and staying.

'Go, Edwin,' the doctor urged, seeing to Cornelia and Reggie's lacerations, carefully daubing each scratch.

Henry approached them and looked earnestly at Major William's wife and son. 'He'll live,' he said softly. 'I've prayed for him.'

'Wha—what do you mean? Where's my husband—' she panicked.

'Mrs Williams,' began the doctor tentatively. 'Your husband is in my sick bay—'

'In your—why? What has happened to him?'

'He was shot.'

'My God!—'

'Madam, please—'

'Take me to him! I want to see him!' she cried, jumping to her feet.

***

Cornelia was a broken woman. Everything she and her son had been through had been an unending nightmare—her home violated; their forced abduction; the uncertainty of not knowing if they would live or die; that man's violent death; the heart … the human heart … her indescribable horror at the sight of the heart; and now her husband's life hovered in the shadowy realm between life and death.

She sat alone by his bedside, praying that he be saved. He was a good man and didn't deserve this fate. She loved him; he was her life. How could she live without him? She needed him; their son needed him. How had it come to this?

The doctor had left her there in the sick bay to grieve and reconcile their fate. He had explained what had happened and what her husband's prognosis was, and what they intended to do in the morning. There was nothing more he alone could do but watch and wait.

***

Constable Calthrop persisted in wanting to know more about Mrs Williams and why she was wandering the fields in the middle of the night but Dr Montgomery insisted that she be left alone and barred the constable from interviewing her further.

He hovered about powerless, as even the young lad, Reggie, was taken to the doctor's office to sleep and recover. And the other boy, Henry, still obstinately refused to utter another word to him or anyone, but he did agree to join Reggie in slumber on the sofa. At young Reggie's insistence, Mikey nestled in between the two boys.

Defeated by Henry's lack of cooperation, Mrs Williams' need to be with her husband and Horace's refusal to allow him to interview her, the constable returned to his little police station.

As directed by Mr Quinn—no less—he had arranged for the slaughterhouse to be put on lockdown and charged the two nightwatchmen to guard it and keep the morbid curiosity seekers well away until the detectives arrived.

It was pointless going home; it wouldn't be long before Scotland Yard arrived. All these strange occurrences were a puzzlement to him but he needed his rest so found comfort on the cot in the only cell at the station. It seemed his head had barely touched the pillow when he was abruptly shaken from his sleep.

'You there! Constable! Wake up!'

***

Once more, Doctor Montgomery's office was intruded upon—this time by six unknown men and a tired and disgruntled Constable Calthrop.

The constable made brief introductions.

'Yes, yes,' Sir Giles Hawthorne impatiently interjected. 'Where's the major and the boy?'

'Sir Giles, Major Williams is unable to be interviewed,' Dr Montgomery patiently replied. 'He is unconscious—'

'But alive?'

'Yes. Barely.'

'And the boy?' Hawthorne was in no mood for congenialities.

'The boy is far too exhausted to be of any use right now.'

Dr Werner edged his way to the front and spoke directly to the other doctor. 'Doctor Montgomery, I'm Doctor Benjamin Werner. Major Williams was under my care recently. May I be of assistance to you?'

Dr Montgomery shook Dr Werner's hand. 'Yes, doctor, yes. We will use all the help we can get. The major is in the sick bay—alone—' the doctor said giving Constable Calthrop a meaningful look, 'through that door. Please. I'll be with you in a moment.'

Dr Montgomery could see that Hawthorne was most put out by this usurpation of his authority.

The Wickham Upper doctor addressed the constable. 'Did you not say, Constable Calthrop, that no one was to interview these persons until Mr Quinn arrived from London?'

'Oh! Yes, quite so,' said the constable. 'Mr Quinn. Yes.' He spoke to Hawthorne. 'Sir Giles, perhaps you gentlemen would care for a cup of tea and biscuits while you await his arrival. I can have a brew ready in no time.'

'Pardon me, Sir,' Pitman apologetically interrupted from the back of the room. 'My son, Henry. Is he here? Is he well?'

'Pa?' the sleepy voice came from the doorway to the doctor's office.

'Henry! Son!' Pitman cried as he approached the youngster. 'You've put me through hell, boy!' he said, his stern words belied by the tremor in his voice. 'You're going to get a good hiding when I get you home! Come here!' He dropped to his knees and caught Henry in a crushing hug.

'And deservedly so,' Sir Giles interjected. 'Now, boy! Tell me what happened! How in the dickens did you both end up here? Why was the major shot? It was that woman, Davies, who shot him wasn't it? Tell me!' Hawthorne placed a hand on Henry's shoulder to pull him away from his father, but Henry pushed the hand away.

'I ain't telling you nothing!!' he screamed.

'You little blackguard! How dare you speak to me like that!' He raised his hand to strike Henry, much to the alarm of all in the room.

'Sir Giles!' Yabsley called out.

The doctor stepped up to Hawthorne. 'Calm down, Sir. He's just a lad and he's been through much this day. It's better we all wait for Mr Quinn.' He took a moment to make sure Hawthorne had, indeed, calmed down, then continued. 'Now I must see to my patient. Constable Calthrop, if you would make that brew you offered?'

***

It was approaching four a.m. when the twenty horsepower Wolseley tonneau powered along Middlebrook Way towards the township of Wickham Upper. It had been in transit from London since evening and was maintaining an average speed of forty miles per hour. He wasn't driving—he gave that responsibility to an experienced constable—he needed to discuss matters with his fellow passenger and he needed them all to arrive at their destination in one piece, and as rapidly as humanly—and mechanically—possible.

In the back seat, bundled up in a thick overcoat and blanket each, their hats pulled down tight to keep the chill of the country air at bay, Quinn sat with Detective Constable Scott. They had gone over the events of the past few weeks at length and were now talked out, so they sat, quiet and subdued, silently reflecting on those happenings and the part each actor had played in bringing on this dire situation.

Alexander Quinn was a stern commander but a fair one. He had been extremely annoyed when, only a week before, he had discovered that Scott had been carrying out undercover enquiries for Major Williams. When Scott revealed—reluctantly—that the major harboured reservations about Hawthorne's integrity and involvement, Quinn ordered Scott to provide a carbon copy of every report he had sent to the major. And he was to tell no one of this arrangement. Quinn was determined to uncover the full truth behind the enquiry.

Consequently, Quinn was fully appraised of the criminality and involvement of Norman Croft and Harry Hogan; the histories of those who had aided them in the first three abductions and murders; the reason behind Captain Gregory Smith's dismissal from the army; and the said Captain's connection with Sir Giles Hawthorne. What still remained unresolved was the connection between Sir Giles Hawthorne and one Colonel Neville Humphries. They were acquaintances, having served in South Africa together but, other than belonging to the same gentlemen's club, the Marlborough, they had nothing in common and did not associate socially.

The question surrounding Detective Kieran Byrne was, as yet, unresolved but tentative links to the Irish Republican Brotherhood and the National Council under Arthur Griffiths were discovered. Further investigation would lay the matter bare.

Williams was an excellent investigator and Davies, had she been male, would have been his equal in both rank and pay, of this Quinn had no reservations. Nor did he ever hesitate in approving any line of investigation Williams put to him. Quinn knew from experience that positive results would soon follow.

Even so, Quinn seriously doubted that Sir Giles was involved. He had proven himself to be a loyal subject; however, he would concede— were he forced—that, perhaps, Sir Giles was not up to the task at hand.

The final act of this drama had been to acquiesce to Sir Giles' ill-founded demand and allow him to serve an arrest warrant on Rebecca Davies. This, Quinn was certain, would flush out the perpetrator of these heinous crimes—be he Sir Giles or another. Quinn wanted the case concluded.

His plan had worked in the first instance but had tragically backfired with the shooting of Williams and the disappearance of Davies.

His objective now was to take charge of this enquiry and uncover the malefactor behind these atrocious crimes.

***

The rattle and rumble of the Wolseley's engine as it hastened along the high street of Wickham Upper reverberated off the darkened cottages and shuttered shops. Detective Sergeant Yabsley sat with his arms folded in the gaol's cramped common room in quiet contemplation and enforced idleness. The other two officers dozed on a bench against the wall.

Sir Giles paced the restricted floorspace and hadn't uttered a word. To Yabsley, it was obvious that he was still fuming at the way he had been dismissed by Constable Calthrop; the man had refused point-blank to answer any questions until Mr Quinn's arrival and was, at that moment, asleep on the cot in the cell. Yabsley had seen the rancour in his superior's eyes and wouldn't have put it past him to lock the cell door and throw away the key if only to soothe his injured ego.

But Yabsley's thoughts were elsewhere. He was having serious doubts over the motivations of Williams and Davies. He no longer believed them to be the villains Sir Giles had painted them as. He, too, was anxious to get on with the job and examine the crime scene and interview the witnesses. Stymied as they had been, both by the reluctance of the only known witness to the event—the ten-year-old boy—to talk to them, and by their commander-in-chief's direction to do nothing, they did just that—nothing.

Finally, the moment arrived.

Upon hearing the exaggerated commotion of the motor's engine, Yabsley straightened himself ready to leap to the fore. Hewitt and Ramsay roused from their enforced inertia and prepared to meet their commander. Hewitt peered out the window and announced, 'He's here.' Then, surprised, added, 'The motor's gone past. It's going up the street.'

***

The Wolseley pulled up outside the two-storeyed stone cottage with a horse trough in front as had been described by Constable Calthrop. The brass plaque beneath the bell pull confirmed it was the correct house.

'Doctor Montgomery's surgery, Sir,' announced the driver.

'Thank you, constable,' replied Quinn. 'Wait here.'

The chief of the Special Branch and Detective Constable Scott, aided by his walking stick, were met at the door by both doctors, Montgomery and Werner, who ushered them into the small reception room.

'A pleasure,' Quinn said after hasty introductions—his mind was elsewhere. 'Major Williams? Will he live?'

'With the grace of God,' Dr Montgomery replied, 'yes. Having Mrs Williams here is certainly a positive—'

'Mrs Williams?' Quinn's brow furrowed. 'The major's wife is here?'

'Ah. Of course. You weren't to know,' said Montgomery. 'How would you? Poor woman. She's been through a long and frightening ordeal, I'm afraid. Come.'

Quinn followed the doctors, his thoughts troubled by this added complication. In the sick bay he saw the pale form of the unconscious detective lying on the table and his wife, head bowed and hands clasped in silent prayer, seated on a chair next to him.

'Mrs Williams,' Quinn quietly addressed the woman as he approached her.

She lifted her bruised and grazed face to him.

'What on earth—?' he uttered, unsettled by the sight.

Cornelia rose and fell into Quinn's arms, her composure eroded by a mixture of desperation and relief. 'Mr Quinn …' Her breath hitched, but there were no tears left to shed.

'There, there, my dear.' He folded her small frame into his embrace. 'What in God's name happened to you?'

She looked up into his eyes, her face contorted by anguish. 'Oh Mr Quinn, it was truly awful and then to come here to this! Reginald may die!' She buried her face in his shoulder, her small body quivering. Her grief was palpable and imbued him with pity.

Quinn eased her back onto the chair.

Dr Montgomery brought a small tumbler of brandy and coaxed her to drink.

Quinn watched and waited for her to settle then drew up a chair next to her. 'Cornelia, we will find who did this and bring them to justice,' he said firmly. 'This I promise you. But we need your help. Will you tell us what happened?'

Scott stood by the door, notebook in hand, ready to document every word.

Cornelia nodded and quietly related the dreadful events that had brought her there. She omitted no detail.

Quinn listened in silent loathing as Scott scribbled down every word.

'Do you know who these men were?' Quinn finally asked.

'I don't know who the Irishman was but the older man introduced himself as a retired colonel. Colonel Neville Humphries.'

'Humphries!' Quinn muttered to Scott. The look of anger and hatred raging in his eyes bore the promise of a storm held captive. His attention returned to Cornelia. 'My dear lady, if it's the last thing I do, these villains will be brought to account.'

He clasped both her hands and gave her a final look of quiet reassurance, then stood to confer with Scott and the two doctors.

'Gentlemen, what we have discovered here must go no further. No one is to know that Mrs Williams and her son are here—'

'Constable Calthrop and the innkeeper know,' Dr Montgomery provided, 'but the constable also knows that he is to speak only to you on this matter.'

'And the innkeeper?'

'Alfie? He'd be sound asleep and dead to the world right now.'

'Good. Scott, see to it that this Alfie fellow is made aware of certain consequences of having a loose tongue. Now, doctor, I need to see young Henry Pitman. I take it he's in your care as well?'

'Yes. I'll fetch—'

But Quinn needn't have waited for, as was his wont, Henry appeared at the doorway that very moment, wide-eyed and sombre. It was clear he had heard much that had transpired. 'Mr Quinn?'

'Yes. You're the brave young man who raised the alarm.' Quinn approached Henry and extended his hand. 'It's a pleasure to meet you, son.'

Henry shook his hand.

'Perhaps the outside office will be a better place to talk. Will you come with us?'

***

Quinn had barely begun his questioning when the door swung open and the four city detectives and one town constable invaded the reception room, putting the proceedings to a surprised stop.

Henry sat quietly, his small hands tucked beneath him, opposite Quinn, while Scott had accommodated himself at the little desk near the doorway, ready to add to his already copious notes.

Sir Giles appeared tired and worn, but so annoyed with Quinn that he forgot himself and abandoned protocol.

'Mr Quinn,' demanded Sir Giles. 'I was under the impression you would be conferring with us before interrogating the boy.'

'Yes, yes,' offered Quinn patiently, but equally annoyed by his underling's attitude. 'My apologies, Sir Giles. I was anxious to see how Major Williams was faring.'

Sir Giles' eyes narrowed in obvious disbelief. 'Hmph,' he dismissed. 'Perhaps we can get on with the interrogation?'

'Of course. But, before we do, I need Detective Constables Hewitt and Ramsay to proceed to the scene of the crime and stop anyone going in until I arrive.'

'But Sir,' interjected Constable Calthrop, 'the slaughterhouse processors will be starting their day shortly—'

'You must be Constable Calthrop,' Quinn surmised. 'You've done a fine job, man.'

'Thank you, Sir,' replied Calthrop puffing out his chest.

'But today, the beasts will have a stay of execution. Please show the detectives the way. And I need you to do one more thing for me. Detective Scott here will brief you.'

Quinn observed Sir Giles bristling with annoyance that his authority was slowly being stripped away.

The town constable conferred with Scott in hushed tones then briskly made his way out the door, followed closely by Hewitt and Ramsay.

'Sir?' Yabsley asked.

'You're to remain,' confirmed Quinn. 'Sir Giles, are these all the men with you?'

'Yes … er, no. The boy's father—the duke's stablemaster—drove us here. He's with the horses.'

'And your other three?'

'Dolby and Hathaway are at Abbottsford Hall awaiting my orders and Byrne's requested leave. His mother, I'm told.'

'Good. Scott, if you will.'

Scott readied himself to take notes but, before Quinn could pose the first question, Hawthorne interjected.

'This proves that the Davies woman is complicit in all this! Where is she? Gone! We had the arrest warrant you, yourself authorised. How did she know? *She* is the spy! *She* is the mastermind behind these abductions and killings! Yabsley here found incriminating evidence in her flat. Right, Yabsley?'

'Ah, Sir, yes, but I have reserve—'

'*She* lured Major Williams here and shot him in cold blood because he discovered the truth about her! Why, I saw him yesterday morning and he looked positively devastated. As one would when one discovers one's friend is one's enemy!'

Henry sat there on his hands listening and shaking his head, his brow darkening with every word. Quinn could see the tension in the boy's body.

But Hawthorne was on a roll. 'She had motive and opportunity and certainly the means! She's a murderess! A fact she has proven time and time again!'

Henry was becoming more and more agitated, rocking back and forth, his mouth tightened, holding back.

Sir Giles was unstoppable. 'I will find this traitress and bring her to the gallows myself! I will search every hovel and whorehouse, leave no stone unturned. She will hang!'

'NO!' Henry's cry was like an explosion. 'She didn't do it!'

The interruption to the flow of his tirade brought Sir Giles to a sudden halt. 'What's this? How dare you, you little rapscallion!'

Henry leapt to his feet. 'She didn't do those things!'

'You jumped-up little—'

'Hold, Sir Giles,' Quinn interceded. 'Let the boy speak. Son, what makes you think Miss Davies did not do these things?'

'We have evidence that says she did,' Sir Giles added almost childishly.

Henry looked from one stern face to the other. Quinn could see the boy's apprehension—his dread of betrayal and his need to protect her.

'Out with it, boy!' Sir Giles barked.

Henry flinched, hesitating. Who could he trust? He looked from one to the other again, evaluating each: Sir Giles … Scott … Yabsley …

He stopped at Quinn.

'I'll tell him,' Henry said, pointing.

'Who do you think you are?' Sir Giles blustered. 'You puffed-up little scoundrel.'

'That's quite enough. Sir Giles,' Quinn voiced calmly but with authority. 'Why won't you tell us all?' he asked Henry.

'I made a promise and I don't want to break it four times.'

'Quite right, son. Gentlemen, if you will excuse us?'

With evident reluctance and indignation, Sir Giles quit the room in a huff with Yabsley and Scott following.

As soon as the door closed behind them, Quinn settled Henry back onto the chair.

'Sit. Now son, what is it you know about Miss Davies?'

'You got to promise not to tell anyone.'

'But I may need other men to help me. And Miss Davies.'

'Promise.'

'Henry …'

'Promise!'

Quinn expelled all his exasperation with a long breath then solemnly uttered, 'On my word as a gentleman and the Head of the Special Branch, I swear that I will not divulge what you are about to tell me. But! I will act on the information you give me.'

'For as long as you live.'

'Henry …' Defeated, Quinn sighed. 'For as long as this information puts any lives at risk. All right?'

Henry searched Quinn's eyes then nodded.

He took a deep breath. 'Miss Davies was at the slaughterhouse but it was Major Williams that was going to kill her and take her heart because Mrs Williams and her son were kidnapped and would die if he didn't. I was with Miss Davies when someone else shot him. It wasn't her. She didn't try to kill Major Williams. She wanted to save him. That's why she left me there. She said it was best that no one knew she was alive or where she was. She made me swear not to tell anyone. Am I going to hell?' Henry blurted.

Quinn took a steadying breath. 'No Henry, you won't go to hell. Why did Major Williams and Miss Davies take you with them?'

'They didn't. I hid in the dog box.'

'Why did you do that?'

'Because I want to be a detective and I wanted to help. Major Williams looked real scared after the telephone call and I wanted to help is all. I wanted to help …'

'You did help, Henry. You just may have saved Major Williams' life. The telephone call, you heard what was said?'

'Only what Major Williams said. He was real angry and then he was real scared and then he shouted and then he was real scared again.'

'I see. Did he mention any places? Names?'

Henry shook his head.

Quinn was clutching at straws. 'Did he mention any names at all?'

'No. But he did ask how Mrs Humphries was. And Dickie.'

'*Mrs* Humphries? Dickie?'

'And Captain Smith or somebody …'

Quinn sat back in his chair and stared at the floor, his eyes darting back and forth in evident contemplation of all he had heard. He threw his attention back to Henry. 'Where is Miss Davies now?'

'I don't know.'

'Henry …' warned Quinn.

'True, Mr Quinn, I don't know. Will the major live?'

'The good doctors are doing everything they can for him, Henry.'

'And I've been praying for him. He'll live.'

39

Wednesday, 13ᵗʰ September, 1905

Southwark, South London, England

The coincidence wasn't lost on me that, whenever I found myself alone and in dire physical trouble, I turned to a prostitute to help me out. Such was the situation back in seventy-four as it was now. Madeleine Dubois helped me then and I was hoping Miss Sophie would help me now.

So that was where I found myself, knocking on a scarlet painted door on a narrow street in Southwark, South London. It was evening and Miss Sophie was most likely preparing herself for the night's 'patron'. I knocked again and waited.

My flight from Wickham Upper to Southwark had been successful but not without tribulation. It had taken most of the day to get here.

The stationmaster's office at Wickham Upper had provided me with shelter, a little food and a little coin, but sleep had eluded me.

So here I stood, propped up by my walking stick, in a 'borrowed' man's overcoat and cloth cap, waiting for the door to be opened. I was tall enough and battle-scarred enough to pass as a man and my short white hair furthered my bona fides.

Finally, Miss Sophie's housekeeper—I should say pimp—opened the door. Mrs Jannock was elderly, hatchet-faced, as straight in body as she was crooked in morals, forthright and uncompromising. She protected her girl, Sophie, with her life, for Sophie was not merely a gentle soul who could easily be abused by her clients, but also a very valuable asset and income producer.

Mrs Jannock and I had an understanding but that gave me no extra benefit or softened consideration.

'What are you doing here? She has an engagement. What happened to you?'

The last question was not an enquiry after my health but a statement of condescension.

'I need a place to stay. For a week or so. And nice to see you, too, Mrs Jannock.'

She looked me up and down. She knew me, and knew me very well. I had been visiting Miss Sophie for years and had always paid generously for her attentions.

'I can pay,' I added before the whoremongress could slam the door in my face. Coin was her *lingua franca*.

She stepped aside. 'Come in, then.'

Mrs Jannock installed me in the tiny, sparsely furnished garret, supposedly the third floor of this elegant but small terraced house, and told me not to leave it. The very last thing I wanted to do was climb back down those steep narrow stairs.

My entire being was a mass of unrelenting pain; my arm throbbed to distraction and my leg objected with stinging spasms at every step. I was afraid to look at the bandages on both my arms, lest I discover that the stitches had torn open. I had no medication and, worse, no whisky. And I was hungry. Those stale shortbreads and a partially eaten sandwich I'd snaffled from an unwary child were the only food I had eaten in a day and a half.

With a lot of gruff and to-do, but with my promise of extra recompense, Mrs Jannock directed Morton, her goliath of a son, to bring up some welcomed food and beverage and, with a fair amount of cajoling, half a bottle of whisky. With a full stomach and completely exhausted, I craved sleep and snuggled under the blankets, still fully clothed.

But sleep eluded me.

While my body's need for rest overwhelmed my physical being, my mind was in turmoil. I needed to know that Henry had seen to Wills and he was getting the medical care he desperately needed to survive.

Casting back to the night before and Wills lying there helpless caused me great heartache; he meant so much to me—more than a brother ever could—and I was helpless to give him aid. He had saved my life and endangered his wife and son's.

Lady Katherine crept into my concerns. How could I get word to her that I was not dead? Was she being watched? Who could I turn to? Quite obviously not Quinn, for it was he who had sanctioned the warrant for my arrest. There was no one I trusted nor anyone whom I could turn to obtain the information I needed.

40

Thursday, 14th September, 1905

Southwark, South London, England

The bed was comfortable and my body's aches had eased, even though my sleep was fitful and sporadic.

I awoke to the sounds of robins singing and wondered if there was reincarnation as the Buddhists and Hindus believed, what had these lyrical birds been in their previous lives? What would I be in my next?

I lay there with my eyes shut. The reality of this life rather than the next pressed me to process the events of the previous days and to separate the facts from the fallacies. With no watch nor calendar, I surmised it was Thursday midmorning and forty-eight hours since Wills and I embarked on our fateful journey to Wickham Upper.

So many urgencies tumbled through my thoughts: Wills' fate was of utmost concern to me; I had to get word to Lady Katherine; I had to find Humphries and make him pay. But how to find him?

'Rebecca?'

Sophie's muffled enquiry from outside my closed door took me out of my murderous design.

'Sophie,' I replied throwing off the bedclothes and carefully sitting up. 'Come in.'

She entered, carrying a small tray with a steaming pot on it. 'I brought you a cuppa,' she said, placing the tray on the little bedside table. 'Mrs Jannock told me you were here. What happened?'

'A very long and complicated story. I just need a place to recuperate.'

She stopped pouring the tea, her gaze asking an unspoken question.

'I can't go back to my place'

'Why? Are you in danger?'

'You needn't be concerned. You and your … um, Mrs Jannock are safe. I will leave as soon as I'm able. You know I will pay.'

'Of course, Rebecca, we're not worried about that. You're welcome to stay here as long as you need. And besides,' she added playfully, 'it would be nice to speak to someone who actually knows how to hold a conversation. I care for my … housekeeper very much but …'

I fully understood what she meant. Mrs Jannock had her own interpretation of how conversations should run. For her, 'verbose' meant running more than three words together and 'brevity' meant complete silence.

Taking the offered cup of tea, I ventured, 'Sophie, there is something you can do for me. If you're not otherwise engaged?'

'Free for the rest of the afternoon,' she confirmed. I liked her very much and, had I been twenty years younger, and not captivated by a certain countess, she may have found herself with a different 'housekeeper' and a different occupation.

***

The world, and everyone in it, owed Colonel Humphries for what he had endured. Certainly, he had an extraordinary amount of money from his three previous 'enterprises' but that was not nearly enough compensation for the ridicule and embarrassment to which his wife, her friends, society in general, and the army had subjected him. After everything he had done and endured for king and country, to be treated so was beyond sufferance … and forgiveness.

It was impossible for anyone to find him; he had concealed his movements like a true tactician. They were all dead: that turncoat Kieran Byrne, the disgraced Gregory Smith and those two blundering bumpkins, Croft and Hogan.

The final payment from the Duke of Bramwell would have seen him retire and live out his life most comfortably in the south of France or, perhaps, Spain or even Italy. But for that damned woman … that shameless, immoral excuse of a human being had ruined it all and snatched the biggest prize from his grasp!

Well, he'd put that to rights! And for free.

He was far away from his family home, which, by now would not be habitable. The thought gave him macabre satisfaction. He had posed her in such a way that was sure to shock the Reverend Father and make his toupée spin on his bald pate. Once too often, dear old Mrs Humphries had bemoaned the lack of intimate congress … well, she's got her fill of sausage now.

'Mad' was he? He'd show them 'mad'. It was no longer about financial redress; it was about revenge.

***

It had been a long and exhausting day and night for the detectives of the Metropolitan Police Special Branch, but there was still evidence to be collected and leads to investigate. The most important of these was the last known refuge of Colonel Humphries.

Following Cornelia Williams' directions, Detective Sergeant Yabsley and Detective Constable Ramsay found the disused stone farmhouse and, exactly where she had indicated it would be, the body of the Irishman.

They both studied slain man in disbelief.

'That's Kieran Byrne,' Ramsay confirmed. 'What is he doing here?'

Yabsley left the question hanging between them. His mind was trawling through the events of the past few months. Each suspicious incident that he had attached to Davies was coming undone and hitching itself to Byrne: the coordinates, the bank notes, the union leader, the wild goose chases. And it had been Byrne whom he had directed to check on young Timothy Saddler; Byrne had been the last person to see the boy alive. Byrne murdered the youth. Davies wasn't the traitor among them—Byrne was.

The worst revelation yet struck him: Byrne shot Williams! Why?

'What do we do, Boss?' Ramsay asked.

Yabsley took a moment to think clearly. 'Inside. Go inside and search the place. We must locate Humphries. Turn the place inside out. Anything that will lead us to that maniac.'

While Ramsay carried out his meticulous search, Yabsley knelt beside the dead man and went through Byrne's clothing, finding his notebook. He turned out every pocket and possible place of concealment, finding nothing untoward of an officer of the law. Noticing the revolver missing from its holster, Yabsley scanned the tall grass and weeds. He would arrange a more thorough search for it later. He thumbed through Byrne's notebook and found a loose piece of paper. He read the scrawled words: 'Enfield 368'—obviously, a telephone number.

'Sergeant!' Ramsay's called urgently.

Yabsley rushed inside to see the young detective peering ashen faced at a discarded pig's heart partially covered by a jacket on the floor.

***

As planned, Major Williams was carefully removed from Dr Montgomery's surgery but his destination was kept secret; some townsmen asserted he had died and was taken to the morgue in London; others that he had been whisked away by the Duke of Bramwell and 'that other doctor'; one even suggested that it was all a ruse and that Major Williams had got up and walked away in the dead of night, arm in arm with the Devil.

That was all conjecture. They had seen a hearse but it had been for some poor soul at the old farmstead. The duke's landau had returned to Abbottsford, empty save the driver. And the Devil? Every town had a religious fanatic.

Whatever the case, Alfie the innkeeper, Constable Calthrop and Dr Montgomery all kept mum and no one outside of the Special Branch ever found out that Cornelia and her son had been reunited with the major.

Young Henry Pitman, too, had been sworn to secrecy. Quinn knew that the boy could be trusted simply on the basis of his dealings with the lad.

Henry and his father returned to Abbottsford Hall each driving one of the two vehicles that had come from there. While Henry had done the wrong thing, his father was proud of the way he had conducted himself throughout this whole series of unfortunate events—but he would still have a stern word with him at home regarding the dangers of such rashness.

Henry longed to speak to Miss Davies; he had grown fond of her and prayed that she was all right.

It was then only a matter of days before the investigation at Wickham Upper was wound down. Once statements had been taken from what seemed to be the entire population of the town, Sir Giles and his five detectives returned to Scotland Yard as did Alexander Quinn and Detective Constable Scott, to continue their investigations from there.

41

Friday, 15th September, 1905

Lilyfield Manor, Essex, England

As planned, Lady Katherine returned to her country estate, Lilyfield Manor, the same day Rebecca Davies had unexpectedly departed from the Hall leaving that enigmatic note. Lady Katherine had fully expected to hear from Rebecca soon so that they could make arrangements for her visit to Chestermere.

Home once more, she fell into her usual routine, happily looking forward to the hopefully prolonged sojourn but, after the first, then the second day passed and she received no word, Lady Katherine began to worry.

She had read and reread that note so many times that the paper was beginning to come apart at the folds. With each reading, it was more apparent to her that she may never see her beloved Rebecca again.

At the end of the third day, it was time, she determined, to discover Rebecca's whereabouts. Her telephone call to Whitehall 1212 to speak to Major Williams was inexplicably transferred to Alexander Quinn.

'Lady Chestermere, good day. Alexander Quinn speaking.'

'Mr Quinn? Forgive me, I had asked to be connected to Major Williams.'

'Ah, my good lady, I'm afraid Major Williams is not available at this moment. May I be of assistance?'

Lady Katherine hesitated, not knowing how to address her concerns; she had been ready for an informal chat with the major.

'Well,' she began, 'perhaps. I … er … I was expecting to hear from Major Williams' Assisting Clerk, Miss Davies, and … er … well, er—'

'Lady Chestermere, if I may, both the major and Miss Davies are indisposed at present. I am more than happy to pass on your enquiry when next I speak to them.'

'Yes … yes, thank you, Mr Quinn, if you'd be so kind. Oh, do you know if Mrs Williams has a telephone? Perhaps—'

'Forgive me, my lady. I believe Mrs Williams and her son are holidaying in Italy.'

A feeling of dejection overcame Lady Katherine. 'Italy? I see. Thank you, Mr Quinn.'

Replacing the handset in its cradle, she was not convinced that what she had just been told was true. Never one to surrender, she made another telephone call to her uncle.

She detailed her concerns and the communications that had just transpired with Alexander Quinn and asked him to intercede on her behalf.

Of course, he would—he returned her call that very afternoon.

'I've had the same results,' he informed her gravely. 'I spoke to Quinn and Sir Giles and both reiterated that Williams and Davies are unavailable but neither would divulge where they were or when they'd return. All so very strange.'

'Indeed, Uncle. Thank you.'

'Erm …' the duke hesitated. 'Katherine, I am aware of a very … erm, unusual incident here a few days after your departure. Most of the detectives left rather hurriedly and the two remaining fellows received a telephone call shortly after. They immediately packed up the belongings of all their group—including those of Major Williams and Miss Davies—and left. And without the courtesy of a thank you. They were gone before I knew it.'

'No reason?'

'No reason whatsoever.'

'Oh.' This did not allay Lady Katherine's fears. 'Thank you, Uncle.'

She read the note again.

> *My darling Katherine,*
> *I must leave. If it is at all within my power, and God*
> *willing, I will be with you once again. If not, I beg that*
> *you remember me with fondness.*
> *I will love you until my dying breath,*
> *R*

It was Rebecca's plea that seemed so … final.

42

Thursday, 21ˢᵗ September, 1905

Southwark, South London, England

It was a little more than a week since my arrival at Miss Sophie's and I was much more mobile and even able to scale those three flights without too much pain. In my small attic room, I had pushed myself through my calisthenics regimen every day. My sleep was assisted by a bit of hashish Sophie generously provided and, of course, whisky.

It was now time.

I could afford no further delay.

Sophie, with Morton as her muscle, kindly fulfilled my few requests and bought me a revolver, a box of cartridges and some men's clothing. It would be far easier to go about as a man.

The account with Sophie was mounting, but it was within my means and I would settle it as soon as I was able to get to my bank account and passbook.

There was no telephone set in Sophie's house—something Mrs Jannock insisted was an unwarranted expense—so my priority, now that I was mobile, was to find the nearest call office and telephone to the only person I could trust to any degree.

***

The desk sergeant trotted up the stairs to the DSO office, tapped on the open door then strode to the desk Detective Constable Robert Scott occupied.

The only other person in the office was Sir Giles Hawthorne, who was consulting with Scott.

'A telephone message for you, Detective Constable Scott,' he said, handing a slip of paper to the puzzled man. 'She said it concerns Wickham Upper.'

'Wickham Upper? For me?' He read the scrawled message then looked up at the desk sergeant. 'This should go to Sir Giles.'

'She said to give it to you and only you.'

Scott glanced at Hawthorne then back to the desk sergeant. 'Thank you, sergeant.'

'And?' Sir Giles enquired when the desk sergeant had departed.

'She wants to meet me. Tomorrow. Alone.'

'You'd better go then. You know what to do.'

***

It was helter-skelter at Abbottsford Hall that morning, when the telephone rang incessantly in the anteroom off the foyer. Mr Thomson was busy sorting out a minor crisis with the footmen and Mrs Plummer likewise with the chambermaids. The duke and duchess were taking the crisp morning air in the gardens and the telephone continued ringing and ringing.

Florence, already annoyed by its persistent jangling, came down on it, and snatched up the handpiece.

'Abbottsford Hall,' she snapped. 'What d'you want?'

There was a slight pause, which only added to Florence's annoyance, followed by a smooth, mellow voice. 'Good morning, Your Grace. I am speaking to the Duchess of Bramwell?'

Florence tittered at being mistaken for her mistress. 'No,' she giggled. 'You ain't but what can I do for you, anyways?'

'Ah, I see,' the male voice continued. 'Tell me, if you would—I understand there was a little disturbance there a few weeks back.'

'Little disturbance? Good Lord! That little disturbance gave everyone a mighty conniption, myself included.'

'The dickens you say! And have you recovered, my dear?'

'Oh, yes, but the duchess is still a little discombobulated.'

'As I imagine she would be after going through that dreadful ordeal.'

'More so her niece what got took.'

'Pardon me? Her niece?'

'Yes, Sir, her niece the Lady Katherine, Countess of Chestermere. It was her what they took by mistake, the scoundrels. I seen them, I did.'

'Did you now?'

'And, y'know, I heard tell that the woman what saved her took a fancy to Her Ladyship an' all. I heard Emma say that she was a trivet, an' all.'

The line went quiet for a moment causing Florence to shake the handset.

'Do you know the name of the woman who saved her?' The male voice resumed the conversation.

'Yes. They called her Davies. Her Grace's secretary, indeed! A right proper piece of work she was, too.'

'Pray tell, where is Lady Chestermere now?'

'Oh, Her Ladyship is back at her country estate—Lilyfield Manor.'

'What is the best way of getting there, my sweet girl?'

'If you ain't got a motor, then train's the best. To Rusby village. Then it's a short ride to the estate.'

'Thank you, my dear. You have been a delight to talk to.'

'You're too kind, Sir. Can I tell Mr Thomson who called?'

The only response to that was the sound of the telephone line being disconnected.

43

Friday, 22nd September, 1905

The Victoria Embankment, South London, England

At the appointed time and place, Scott arrived alone as directed. From my vantage point, I could not see anyone lurking about, but if this were a trap and I were to be arrested, so be it. I had to know, whatever the consequences.

The café was alive with waitresses rushing about, serving a capacity houseful of patrons who were sipping their coffees and enjoying their delicate savouries and sweets, when Scott asked to be shown to my table. I felt sorry for him; the limp and walking stick would remain with him forever. I, on the other hand, had discarded my prop, determined to show no debility.

'Scott,' I said approaching him from behind.

Ever the gentleman, he rose awkwardly to greet me and showed surprise at my mannish garb.

'Davies,' he said a little timidly, extending his hand. 'It's good to see you well. I heard you had been badly injured.'

'A rumour,' I replied as we both took our seats. 'You came alone?'

'As requested.'

A waitress descended upon us. 'What can I bring you fine gentlemen?' she asked flirtatiously.

'Coffees. For two. Thank you,' I ordered dismissively. 'I'll get to the point,' I continued when she had left us. 'Major Williams. Where is he? And his wife and son? Are they all right?'

Scott visibly shrunk in his seat. 'Davies, the … um, the official response is that the major is unavailable and Mrs Williams is on holiday.'

'And the reality is?'

'I … I am not at liberty to say.'

'Is he dead? Are they dead?' I was not in the mood for playing games.

Scott squirmed. 'Come in, Davies. Talk to Quinn and Hawthorne.'

'Yeah, with an arrest warrant hanging over me.'

'It's been withdrawn.'

'Not that I don't believe you, Scott, but I don't trust Hawthorne, nor Quinn for that matter. I want to find Humphries, Colonel Neville Humphries. He's behind all of this.'

'We …' he vacillated, much to my annoyance. 'We know. We're keeping track of his movements.'

I stared hard at him. 'You know where he is? Why haven't you arrested him?'

He bowed his head and closed his eyes.

'Where is he?' I insisted. 'I'm going to find that bastard whether you help me or not. I will do whatever it takes to make him pay for killing Wills. Major Williams didn't deserve to be gunned down like a dog. And his wife and child—'

'They're not dead!' Scott interjected, then looked about sheepishly. 'I saw them. They're alive. But the major's still gravely ill. They don't want you to know. Quinn and Hawthorne. They want that bastard alive. They want to know who's behind all of this. And they know what you'll do to him if you find him first.'

While this news was what I was after and I was relieved that Wills and his family had not perished, I desperately wished to know more.

'There's no one else behind this,' I spat out, my impatience with Quinn's stupidity overtaking my reasoning. 'He is it. Only him. It's vengeance. And he's insane. Help me find him, Robert. Tell me what you know. Where is he?'

Our waitress returned with a pot of steaming hot coffee and a tray of accoutrements, which she transferred to the table, giving both Scott and me coquettish glances.

'I … I … can't—'

My composure snapped. 'Don't fuck with me, Scott. Either tell me or piss off. Humphries is the enemy, not me.'

My vulgar outburst rattled the waitress as well as the remaining cups on her tray.

Scott turned bright red with embarrassment, his eyes darting from the waitress to the other patrons and back again. 'Beg pardon, Miss,' he stammered. 'My friend is from the colonies,' he excused awkwardly.

She hurried away, her kittenish behaviour vanquished by my eruption.

'Byrne,' Scott continued hesitantly. 'Kieran Byrne was the spy—'

'Was?'

'Humphries shot him dead. It must have been Byrne who shot the major because it was Byrne who brought the pig's heart to Humphries.'

'Well, that's one less I have to deal with. Go on.'

'Yabsley went through Byrne's pockets and found a telephone number, Enfield 368. That was the telephone number Humphries used to call Major Williams at Abbottsford Hall that morning. We traced all the calls from that telephone through the exchanges. Humphries telephoned to a series of hotels and boarding houses. That's how we know where he is right now. Our DSO men are watching him around the clock. They will inform us immediately if he moves or someone makes contact with him. Hawthorne is adamant that there's a higher power in play and has convinced Quinn that Humphries will lead us to the head of this conspiracy. Quinn's sceptical but needs to be sure.'

I expelled a breath of frustration. 'There is no conspiracy! Where is he now?'

'Davies …'

I looked hard at him and said not a word. His shoulders slumped in defeat.

'He's on his way to a little village near the coast. God knows why he's going there. Yabsley thinks he's going to board a yacht and sail to France.'

'Don't make me drag every word out of you, Robert. What little village?'

'Rusby.'

A jolt of dread pierced me.

'Rusby?'

'There's nothing there, really. It's a whistle stop,' Scott explained.

'There is something there. The Countess of Chestermere.'

I left Scott in the café—with the bill to pay—and rushed out. Time was against me; Lady Katherine's life was forfeit if I delayed. I could not comprehend why Humphries was pursuing the Countess of Chestermere; she had done him no harm. I, on the other hand …

Suddenly, it all made sense.

Humphries must have discovered that Wills was not dead and that I, too, had survived. He must have realised that losing his hostages, Mrs Williams and her son, he had also lost his advantage. And, having discovered that I had feelings for the countess, he was now pursuing her to get to me. The bastard was bent on my annihilation at whatever cost. He was truly mad. His lust for vengeance overrode all rationality but, then, does a madman have any sense of logic or reason?

I raced to Piccadilly station and discovered that the next train to pass through the small village of Rusby was leaving very shortly. Providence favoured me.

The train departed on time and would take a few hours to reach Rusby—time enough to plan. My masculine attire meant that no one paid me much attention; my overcoat concealed the revolver that Sophie had purchased and my cloth cap revealed only some errant sprigs of white hair and the disfiguring scars to my face. My stiletto was in my boot and I could fashion a garrotte at a moment's notice, if necessary.

From the information Scott had divulged, all the detective constables from the Department of Special Operations were in the village waiting for the non-existent head of Humphries' criminal group to make contact with him. I had to avoid them in case the supposed lifting of my arrest warrant was a ruse to entrap me.

I sat alone in the first-class compartment and, for the first time in a very long time, earnestly prayed to the Almighty.

***

The days seemed interminable, as did her sleepless nights, since her futile conversation with Mr Alexander Quinn those six or seven days prior—she couldn't remember how many—time itself warped around her grief. Lady Katherine feared she would never see Rebecca again but, more than that, she would never know why she had left or what had become of her.

Day by day, she had become more and more withdrawn, delegating her business affairs to her secretary, George McPherson. Sealing deals and finding new ventures no longer excited her. Not even her devoted

Nanny Fee could bring her out of her profound funk. She spent those days walking aimlessly through her gardens or reading quietly by the fire. She supped alone and stayed in bed longer than usual. Her sleep, when she was able to attain it, was disrupted by nightmares of what she had endured, or dreadful imaginings of what had become of Rebecca. Her servants showed utmost concern for her wellbeing but there was nothing they could do. She kept to herself and grieved alone—a grief surpassed only by the loss of her parents all those years ago.

This day was like the one before and would be like the one to come. It was with that resignation that she once again found solace in her study, enfolded in the sanctuary of her favourite Bergère chair. The gramophone filled the room with the sounds of Tchaikovsky's *Pathétique* and made her heart heavy with regret. Here, she allowed the music to soothe what words could not.

She heard the gentle tapping on her closed door but was almost too drained to answer it. Regaining her poise, she softy replied, 'Come in.'

The door opened just enough for the butler, Peter, to step halfway in.

'My lady, please forgive the intrusion, but there's a gentleman here to see you.'

Lady Katherine's expression was one of weariness rather than annoyance. She shook her head.

Peter understood but continued. 'My lady, he would not give his name but he said it was urgent. Something to do with an assisting clerk?'

The countess immediately sat upright. 'Rebecca Davies? Did he say Rebecca Davies?'

'No, my lady, only assisting clerk.'

Lady Katherine found it difficult to breathe.

'Show him to the library, Peter. I'll be there momentarily.'

'My lady.'

A rush of possibilities jostled for attention. Who could it be? Major Williams would have announced himself, as would any of the DSO detectives. Nevertheless, this man had news of her Rebecca and she wasted no time in making herself presentable.

With the hopeful expectation that she would finally know what had become of the assisting clerk, Lady Katherine hurried into the library and faced the back of a tall elderly gentleman who was examining the multitude of books on the shelves. Upon hearing the rustle of skirts, he turned, his expression warm and appealing.

'Ah, Lady Chestermere. Thank you for taking my call. An honour and a pleasure to finally meet you.'

Lady Katherine took in the dapper older gentleman standing in front of her. She did not smile—she did not know this man—and she was a little peeved that he did not have a calling card or give his name to Peter.

'Sir, you have me at a disadvantage.'

'Of course. Please forgive me, I lost my card case. I am here with news of your … er, saviour, I believe. Miss Davies. Rebecca Davies?'

Lady Katherine's breath quickened. 'What news of her? Is she well?'

'Ah! I can assure you she is alive.'

That small piece of information almost made the countess faint with relief. The gentleman continued.

'It seems that she is indestructible.'

'Thank God. And thank you, Sir.'

'She has asked to see you.'

Lady Katherine was almost delirious with joy. 'Of course! Of course. Please bring her here.'

'Unfortunately, Your Ladyship, that is not possible. But I can take you to her.'

'Where is she?'

The gentleman appeared to vacillate. 'I cannot say. A matter of secrecy, you understand.'

The countess didn't really understand what the secret could be, but she was desperate to see Rebecca and to make certain she was safe and well. She took a few steps towards the bell cord.

'I'll have the motor car brought around. My driver can take us there.'

'No! Er, no, my lady. I have a horse and buggy and it's best we go alone.'

Lady Katherine found this curious; her hesitancy did not go unnoticed by the stranger.

'I take it you do wish to see Miss Davies? She did ask for you to come alone. Something about a warrant?'

'A warrant?' The word benumbed Lady Katherine. 'For her arrest?'

'Yes, I'm afraid so. For treason, no less. Hence the need for utmost discretion.'

'Treason?' Fear once again gripped the countess, but for Rebecca—she did not want to be the cause of any complications.

Longing overrode caution.

'Allow me to get my hat and coat,' she said almost breathlessly, as she tugged on the cord. 'I don't understand the secrecy but I will abide by her wishes.'

Peter was at the door instantly.

'Peter, I will be leaving with Mr …' Lady Katherine looked at her uninvited guest who simply bowed slightly—he was not going to say anything. She turned to Peter. 'My coat and hat, if you will.'

* * *

Peter and Jessica Turner watched the horse and cart as it disappeared along the long drive out of Lilyfield Manor.

'I dinnae like it,' Jessica intoned just as Jimmy joined them.

'Where's Lady Katherine off to?' he asked.

'With a man I dinnae like at all,' she replied. 'He's as smooth as rancid oil.'

* * *

'This road leads to Rusby village,' Lady Katherine stated as the driver turned onto the highway. 'Is that where we'll find Miss Davies?'

The gentleman turned to the countess, his expression unreadable.

'I don't know your name, Sir. I would be grateful to have it,' she requested firmly but politely.

'Colonel Neville Humphries, retired, at your service, my lady,' was his blunt reply delivered with a supercilious curl of his lip. 'You've heard of me, I trust?'

'I cannot say that I have, Colonel. Should I have?'

'Hm.'

Lady Katherine felt that something wasn't quite right but she couldn't pinpoint the cause of her growing unease. She persisted in trying to find out more of this mysterious man. 'How do you know Miss Davies?'

Colonel Humphries let a moment pass before replying. 'One could say through the Special Branch.'

'You are acquainted with Major Williams?'

'Hm, only remotely by telephone. But he has a lovely wife and son.'

'You've met them?'

'Yes, they were my guests for a short while. Lovely.' It was the sly look he gave Lady Katherine that sent a cold rush of blood through her veins. A discomforting silence befell her until she resumed her questioning. 'How came it that Miss Davies sought you out, rather than finding me directly? She knew my place of residence.'

'I believe she feared being apprehended by her former colleagues. The ways of wanton women have intrigued mankind since the dawn of time,' was the colonel's inscrutable and somewhat maddening response.

She frowned with confusion but she persisted.

'What … what news of Major Williams?'

'Missing, I'm afraid. As elusive as your Miss Davies.'

'Elusive? Are you not taking me to Miss Davies?'

'Of course, of course. A slip of the tongue, my dear. Please do not be alarmed. We are almost there and all will be settled very shortly.'

'There' was not the village of Rusby, which she knew very well, but a small cottage on the periphery of the little village.

'Why are we stopping here?' she asked as he drove the cart behind the lodging. 'This is Widow Henderson's cottage.'

'Yes, and a fine and obliging old woman she is, too. Come,' Colonel Humphries directed as he dismounted and helped Lady Katherine to alight from the cart. 'She went to great lengths to tell me what a wonderful lady you are and of your charity in allowing her to live here rent free. Please, do come in. The widow awaits the pleasure of your company.'

Humphries opened the back door for Lady Katherine, ushering her through the back rooms and into the dim parlour infiltrated only by soft daylight seeping through the shutters.

'Why are the shutters closed?' the countess asked, trying to keep her apprehension at bay.

'Perhaps the widow is sleeping,' was his flippant reply, as he stood by the front door.

As her eyes adjusted to the gloom, Lady Katherine became aware of a small figure sitting in one of the two armchairs.

'Mrs Henderson?' she enquired as she approached the elderly woman. 'Mrs Henderson,' she reiterated, placing a gentle hand on the woman's shoulder.

The widow's head lolled to the side.

Widow Henderson was dead.

Lady Katherine recoiled in horror.

'Pity,' he offered. 'I think she died of fright. She really did sing your praises, Katherine. I may call you Katherine, mayn't I? I feel we are going to become quite intimate before long.'

This announcement brought back the unprecedented fear she had experienced not long past.

'My dear,' Humphries tittered. 'Don't concern yourself. I have no interest in violating you as did those two loathsome animals. I truly deplored their actions but, as you know,' he said in a jocular manner, 'boys will be boys.'

'You?' she expelled with dreadful realisation. 'You were behind the plan to abduct my aunt?'

'Hm. Unfortunately for me, Williams and Davies thwarted that plan. Now, unfortunately for you, I have devised another.'

'What … what do you want of me?' Lady Katherine could not suppress her fear any longer.

'Bait, my dear. You are bait.'

Lady Katherine searched the room for a means of escape.

'There is no way out, Katherine. I have the key to the doors, which are locked. Why don't you make yourself comfortable while we wait?'

She did not respond, so Humphries continued. 'For whom are we waiting, I hear you ask? For your Sapphic friend—your female paramour. You know, I should be shocked and appalled by your choice of lovers, even by the fact that you have taken a lover rather than succumbing to marriage. Marriage is a disappointment, I must own, but a woman such as yourself—beautiful, wealthy, titled—could have any man on this blessed earth kissing her lovely feet. Why a woman? It's truly beyond my understanding. But I should not judge. Please, sit down.'

Lady Katherine was caught between defiance and dread; she could not move.

'SIT DOWN!'

The sudden explosion jolted the countess and she nervously found the vacant chair.

'That's better,' he said, but the mirth and mockery had evaporated from his tone. 'Now we are both more comfortable.'

'What ... what makes you think that Rebecca will come? That she will find you here?'

'She's a clever little fish,' he replied sarcastically. 'I've left her enough clues.'

'And when she comes?'

Humphries looked at the deceased widow.

Lady Katherine understood.

'Why? Why do you want to kill her? Why don't you make good your escape? Leave England?' she implored.

'Never leave unfinished business, I say. One never knows what may pop back up and haunt one. Particularly if one is dealing with the so-called 'fair sex'.'

'And I? Am I unfinished business?'

He simply pursed his lips.

***

The conductor announced that the next station would be Rusby so I pulled the cord once to alert the driver I wished to alight there and heard the resultant whistle. The conductor duly announced Rusby as the next stop.

I didn't know what to expect upon disembarking, but, if Scott's information were correct, I could at least expect to see the five DSO detectives keeping surveillance on Humphries.

Looking out from the carriage's window, I spotted Hewitt on the platform peering at the train as it clamoured to a stop.

My urgency was to get to Lady Katherine and to keep her safe from the insane Humphries, so I took hold of my gun and kept it in my outside pocket at the ready, should circumstance require it. I didn't want any confrontation, especially with my former colleagues, but Lady Katherine's life was in danger and she was my first and only concern.

Keeping an eye on Hewitt, I stepped off the train and turned towards the station's exit as the train pulled away. I stopped mid stride when I spotted Yabsley approaching me from the end of the platform. I did an about-face but my progress was thwarted by Ramsay coming towards me from the opposite end. On the other side of the tracks, Hathaway bore down on me. Surrounded and with each avenue of escape blocked, and my hip still causing me considerable impediment, I turned to face my longtime adversary. My hand tightened on the grip of the pistol in my pocket; I'd be damned if I let anyone stop me from getting to the countess.

Yabsley thrust his hand inside his jacket and approached me at a quickened pace. He stopped a short yard away.

'Don't do anything rash, Davies,' he warned as the three other detectives boxed me in.

'Don't try to stop me, Yabsley.' I looked from one stern face to the other. 'You're not taking me in. I don't care what warrant you have.'

'There's no warrant.'

I was momentarily disconcerted.

'Then get out of my way! Lady Katherine is in danger!'

'Hold, Davies, and listen,' he said firmly but in a tone I had not heard from him before—it was almost akin to compassion. 'We know. Humphries has her.'

The news punched the breath from my lungs. 'What? Why haven't you taken him down?'

'Sir Giles …' Yabsley appeared to be conflicted. 'Sir Giles wants us to keep him under surveillance only. Take no action. He wants to bring down the whole conspiracy—'

'There is no conspiracy.'

'I know that. We all know that now. Everyone except Sir Giles. He's bent on advancing his career by exposing this conspiracy and has Quinn stitched in his pocket. He's feeding Quinn facts distorted by his own ambition and greed. It's all gone to Hell.' Yabsley hesitated, then added. 'I've made a decision and these men are with me. Humphries wants revenge and he means to take that revenge out on you.'

I snorted dismissively. 'Well, my demise would certainly please one or two in the DSO, right Yabsley? Anyway, how do you know this?'

'I spoke to him. Humphries. He had the arrogance to summon me and lay out his terms and conditions and …'

'And?'

'He wants you there, unarmed, or he will kill the countess. He means to kill you, Davies, and then use Lady Chestermere as a shield to escape. She won't be safe whichever way we proceed.'

'Then I should go there as requested. Where is she?'

'In a small cottage at the edge of the village. Dolby's there now. An elderly widow lives there but we don't know what's become of her. He's mad, Davies, utterly insane.'

I was relieved that Yabsley finally saw Humphries for what he was: a conniving, homicidal lunatic and not part of some grand international conspiracy.

As we made our way to the widow's cottage, the scant conversation we shared concerned itself with locked doors and shuttered windows, and with reaffirming Lady Katherine's wellbeing as paramount.

***

Inside the cottage, Colonel Humphries peered through a partially opened shutter. 'Ah, your heroine approaches, Katherine,' he said with scornful derision. 'Pretending manliness, no less. And what do I see? Scurrying between the bushes like little mice? It appears that the valiant officers of the DSO have us surrounded. Fear not, my dear Katherine, for I need you alive. And they, I am certain, would like to keep you that way.'

***

Outside, I made a deliberate show of handing my pistol to Yabsley and removing my overcoat and cloth cap. Now, dressed only in my trousers, turtleneck sweater and jacket, my face and hands felt the nip in the air but my guts were burning hot with controlled rage. I was about to meet the depraved maniac who had plotted and allowed the abduction and slaughter of innocent women and who would do the same to Lady Katherine. I was ready to meet my fate. I hoped he was ready to meet his.

I knocked on the door and waited.

It was only a moment before it opened just wide enough to permit me to enter. As I took my first step over the threshold, I gambled that Humphries would not send me to Hades without spewing out some biased rhetoric or acerbic bile—I needed to face him and talk—buy time.

As I stepped inside, the door slammed closed behind me, shutting out all light. I heard a key turn in the lock. My eyes adjusted to the dimness and I could just make out two armchairs, each occupied.

Before I could utter a word, Lady Katherine's soft plaintive cry filled the gloom. She rose from her chair and rushed to me, her arms clutching me fiercely.

'Rebecca,' she whispered, her voice straining to keep control. 'Thank God … thank God you're alive …'

'Katherine …' was all I could manage. She was unharmed. I embraced her and breathed in her scent knowing that this might be the last time.

'How very touching,' Humphries mocked, emerging from the darkness. He stood scarcely five feet away, the madness in his eyes unmissable. 'Shall we proceed with the business at hand?'

I reluctantly eased myself out of Katherine's hold and, with a calmness honed through years of dealing with thugs and bullies, I addressed our tormentor.

'Who is she?' I asked, indicating the lifeless form in the other armchair.

'No one of consequence. She was old and widowed, anyway.'

I could not fathom what impelled anyone to end an innocent's life. I had ended more lives than I cared to remember but each had deserved his fate at my hands, for I knew that each would have escaped justice otherwise.

'You have me. Let Lady Chestermere go.'

His sudden mordant laughter filled the room and just as suddenly he snarled, spitting out each word. 'You stupid, stupid jade! Don't think yourself smarter than I. Katherine will stay and she will witness your demise.'

'No!' Lady Katherine cried.

'Shh,' I comforted and eased her away from me.

'Oh, yes, Katherine dear,' Humphries countered. 'Your colonial sweetheart owes me a great debt and today she shall pay in full with her blood.'

I remained composed. 'You do realise you will not leave this cottage alive if you harm Lady Chestermere.'

'Hm. It is not she I wish to harm,' he replied smoothly. 'Not yet, anyway.'

Reaching into his jacket he withdrew a pistol and pointed it at my head. I expected Lady Katherine's reactive gasp and, without taking my eyes off Humphries' gun, I again attempted to reassure her. 'Shhh …'

I recognised the gun as an old Smith and Wesson, made specifically for the Russian military about forty years earlier. It was single-action, so the second it would take him to cock the hammer would be enough time for me to react before he pulled the trigger. Still, I needed to stall him until all was in place.

'Impressive weapon,' I commented. 'American special, right? For the Russians.'

His eyes darted between me and the gun; his brow creased—he seemed momentarily puzzled.

I continued. 'Is that how you got those Richardson ransom notes into the Russian Embassy? By acquiring the gun from one of the staff, perhaps?'

'Yes,' he conceded with a smirk. 'Rather clever, don't you think? I get a nice weapon and they get implicated in the abductions. An international conspiracy,' he added derisively. 'I counted on the Russkies being the secretive bunch of peasants they are and not spilling the beans, so to speak.

'And that dullard, Hawthorne,' he persisted, 'how on earth he achieved a knighthood is beyond me. He came nowhere close to my ability in field strategy and tactics. You, on the other hand, my dour little she-man—and I sincerely hate to admit this—you would have excelled in your chosen field of endeavour had you been of the male gender. Is that why you try so hard? Do you believe that you will eventually grow the right equipment?'

'And you, Humphries, how are you faring without yours? Yabsley informed me that yours was blown to hell. You'll be re-acquainted with it very soon.'

His demeanour flipped—his face twisted into a snarl, his eyes wild with murderous intent; I should not have provoked him thus but his misogyny was wearing away my patience and it was already thin enough. I stood firm, staring him down and waiting for his thumb to cock the hammer.

But, just like a clock pendulum, his mood swung again back to gloating.

'Tell me, my androgynous misanthrope, how came it that you survived Captain Smith's onslaught?'

'Dickie's?'

'Hm. He hated that epithet. But he earned it, you know. Coward that he was.'

'But you used him anyway.'

'He served a purpose. And he was suitably rewarded. Had you not put him down, I would have had to eventually. Can't leave witnesses, you know. So I thank you for your service.'

I had to keep him talking, biding time. 'Why kill Major Williams?'

'Hm. I didn't want to do it, you know. But again, witnesses and all that. Nice chap. You know, he admired you. He told me all about you and your quick wits. Pity your wits are going to be plastered all over these walls momentarily. Tell me, how fares my friend?'

Calling Wills his friend stoked the fire of hatred I felt for this lunatic, but I suppressed the anger and remained calm. 'Alive. Unlike Kieran Byrne. Why kill *him?*'

'He was using the money to fund an Irish revolution. Can't have that, now, can we? For king and country and all that.'

The idea that this madman was a Royalist was contemptible.

An almost indiscernible clink drew our attention to the back rooms. Another scrabbling at the front door had Humphries turn to me.

'You bitch!' he yelled. He cocked the hammer of his gun.

I rushed him.

I grabbed his gun hand and pushed it upwards.

Crack!

The shot ripped through the ceiling.

We struggled violently. His free arm wrapped around my neck and twisted me back against him. He was taller, stronger; his grip was strangling me. I clung onto his gun hand with both of mine, unable to reach the switchblade stiletto in my boot.

The muzzle inched towards my temple.

'Die!' he screamed.

I heard the click of the hammer.

Lady Katherine descended on him with uncontained ferocity, grabbing his gun hand and wrenching it away the instant he fired. I felt the rush of the bullet fly past my forehead, missing me by a hair's breadth. The report deafened me.

'Fucking whore!' he bellowed and flung the countess off him.

His stranglehold on me loosened.

I contorted myself to the side and, before he was able to cock his revolver again, I grabbed a handful of his groin. I squeezed and twisted the flaccid flesh until he released me.

He howled, dropped the gun and doubled over clutching his crotch.

I turned on him and kneed him to the face. Bone cracked. He slumped to the floor and curled in a foetal ball, whimpering in pain. Blood oozed from his broken nose and pooled beneath him.

I rushed to Lady Katherine and helped her to her feet.

'Look out!' she screamed.

I spun—Humphries had writhed towards his gun and had reached it.

His trembling fingers cocked the hammer.

I was on him and drove my heel into his hand. He bellowed and released the weapon. I snatched it up and kicked him in the stomach for good measure.

Through sheer hatred, I thrust the barrel of the gun to his head and cocked the hammer.

At that instant, both doors crashed open.

Five DSO detectives burst in.

'Hold, Davies!' Yabsley shouted. 'We need him alive.' Yabsley strode over to me and took possession of the Smith and Wesson.

I reconsidered the alternative as I gazed at the broken, pitiless wreck of a human on the floor.

'You're right,' I sneered. 'Let him rot in the hell of a lunatic asylum, then die and burn in Hell for eternity.'

44

Saturday, 28th October, 1905

Epilogue

My world had changed.

Nothing now was as it had been scant months earlier.

Mad Colonel Humphries was the catalyst for that change in me— as he was for everyone he touched.

For me? He gave me new purpose in life.

For others? He left death and ruin in his wake.

Even now, more than a month later, the fallout of his vengeance was still being reconciled.

***

The house that Major Reginald Williams rented had lain empty for the past eight weeks. Mrs Williams' cherished gardens were overgrown. The rosebushes, which she meticulously tended at this time each year, remained unpruned and straggly, as did the bordering hedges.

None of their neighbours knew what had become of the genial major, his wife and son, or their new little dog, Mikey. But, since the rent continued to be paid, the lease stood and the house remained empty.

Those neighbours were still gossiping about that incident, weeks ago, when Mrs Williams entertained those two gentlemen at that unseemly early morning hour and then unexpectedly left with them. They, the gentlemen, seemed agreeable enough, army friends of the major, they said. Anyway, that's what the neighbours told anyone who cared to ask—and there had been a few who had come around and ventured a few probing questions.

***

The dingy little flat that Colonel Humphries rented in that less-salubrious part of London had also been hastily vacated weeks ago, leaving the landlady owed a good deal of rent. She had thought herself a good judge of character when she let that little room to the older gentleman without character references. He did say he was a retired colonel and he was a smooth talker. Well, she'd know better next time.

The general manager of the Marlborough Club, also, was feeling diddled. It was unusual for an officer and a gentleman to default on his commitment and not pay his annual fees. Consequently, this particular colonel had been summarily blacklisted and would not gain entry to the club should he have the temerity to attempt to do so. What remained undisclosed to all at the club—except Sir Giles Hawthorne—was that the court had declared the recalcitrant Colonel Neville Humphries insane and he was being held at his majesty's pleasure in Broadmoor Criminal Lunatic Asylum. It was unlikely that he would ever see the inside of the Marlborough Club—or the outside of the asylum—ever again, especially after the desecrated, decaying body of his wife was finally discovered in the cellar of their home.

***

The head of the Special Branch of the Metropolitan Police had purposely left many questions unanswered. It was in the nation's best interest, Mr Quinn determined, to keep the involvement of a murderous nationalist Irishman locked away. To admit that an Irish national had been involved in the abduction and murders of three Englishwomen would have inflamed an already flammable situation.

Once the Department of Special Operations had concluded its investigations into the abductions and murders of the three wealthy women, Quinn released his alternative 'facts' to an insatiable public, blooded by the hitherto unsolved Ripper murders.

With the cooperation and agreement of their families, the deaths of Lady Cecilia D'Arcy, Mrs Charles Richardson and the Honourable Laura Warburton were declared accidental and unrelated. The knowledge that the perpetrator of these heinous crimes, and his minions, had all been brought to justice by one means or another, had satisfied their families. None of them wished to have the brutality and degradation their daughters or wives had suffered be made public. Much of the ransom monies had been recovered and returned to their rightful owners.

Quinn directed Sir Giles to announce that Detective Constable Kieran Byrne had resigned from his position in the DSO of the Special Branch due to his mother's failing health and had returned to Ireland.

The deaths of Norman Croft and Harry Hogan were duly noted on their files and their cadavers sent to an undisclosed medical research college for anatomical studies.

The body of Captain Gregory 'Dickie' Smith, who had no known living relative, was interred in a pauper's grave at the expense of the public purse.

Stewart Graves was charged with a number of serious crimes, including kidnapping, which, if he were convicted, would result in the death penalty. The general consensus was that he would be sentenced to hang but that it would be commuted to life imprisonment with the first twenty years' hard labour.

The bodies of young Timothy Saddler, his father and his uncle were returned to their families and their deaths attributed to Croft and Hogan through misadventure.

It surprised me that Sir Giles Hawthorne remained head of the Department of Special Operations even though it was through his failings that Humphries almost succeeded with his plans. Hawthorne would not, at first, believe that his friend could be behind such atrocities. But, once Detective Sergeant Yabsley laid all the undeniable evidence before Alexander Quinn and Quinn, in turn, put that evidence in front of Hawthorne, there was no room left for rebuttal. He also conceded that he had been played for a fool but, nevertheless, he was exonerated from being involved in any part of the conspiracy and kept his position and, more importantly, his pension.

It was obvious to all who cared to witness it, in the case of Sir Giles Hawthorne, failure was not shown the door if you wore the right public school tie or professed the right religious persuasion.

I made my peace with Yabsley. Or rather, he made his peace with me.

It was immediately after we had returned to London with Humphries, and I still had not returned to my flat. I had intended to hand in my resignation once I had spoken to Wills and I was in Wills' small office clearing out my few possessions there when Yabsley approached me.

'Davies,' he said indifferently, standing in the doorway. 'I heard you're leaving.'

'Come to gloat?' I threw back at him without looking up.

'Came to return this,' he said, offering a small black box.

I immediately recognised it. 'You've been to my flat,' I said taking a few steps towards him and removing the item from his grasp.

'There's nothing missing,' he explained. 'I thought it best to hold onto it just in case—'

'I carked it, right?'

'—it got into the wrong hands.' He hesitated; there was obviously something he wanted to get off his chest.

I tossed the box into my Gladstone. His pause was eating my patience.

'Is there something you wanted?'

He took a breath and opened his mouth to speak but only stared at me.

'I haven't got all day, Yabsley.'

Finally, he spoke.

'You were right.'

His admission was like a quasi-apology, so I let him continue.

'I ... I am, ah ...'

'What, Yabsley? What are you?'

'I'm sorry to see you go,' he announced.

I nearly choked on his sudden revelation. 'Well, perhaps Quinn won't accept my resignation. Would that make you happy?'

He allowed my jibe to slide. 'That's a small fortune in gemstones you have there, Davies. They'd be safer in a bank.'

'Perhaps,' I said, continuing with my packing.

'They appear to be from the subcontinent.'

'Afghanistan.'

'How did you come by them?'

'Let's just say it was compensation for the injuries perpetrated on my body.'

'That's where that happened?' He gestured at the scar on my face.

Yabsley had never shown the slightest interest in me nor my history until this very moment and I didn't quite know how to take it. I put my sarcasm away and replied civilly. 'Yes. And it's where I met Lieutenant Williams. He saved my life.'

'I'd like to know more.'

'Maybe one day,' I said closing my Gladstone. 'Now, I'm off to Cornwall.'

***

The train pulled into St Columb Road railway station in Cornwall and I collected my valise from the overhead rack.

The previous afternoon, I had returned to my flat in Newington to find it in disarray but I had been relieved that my bank passbook had been left in place. I was particularly thankful that it had been Yabsley who found my gemstones and returned them to me. Had Byrne discovered them, I was sure they would have been in the possession of the Irish revolutionists by now.

I packed for a prolonged stay away and bathed and rested—for I truly did need to recuperate—and, the following morning, before embarking on the train, I ran a few errands. After visiting a dealer in gemstones, I went to my bank and sorted some business out there and then on to Miss Sophie and Mrs Jannock, where I settled my account. I was surprised that the gun had cost me nine pounds, but appreciative for the assistance and kindness they had shown me. I doubted that I would see Miss Sophie in her 'professional' capacity anytime soon.

Stepping from the train felt like stepping into a new me and a new existence. Everything had changed, even my outlook on life. I no longer felt jaded, but refreshed and invigorated—not by the restful night I had had but by what was to come.

The taxicab took me the two and a half miles directly to Rachel's Way, St Columb Major, and a cottage situated in the middle of a large, well-ordered country garden.

The autumn day was sunny with a fresh, wispy breeze that added a perfecting note to the day.

'Rebecca!' Wills' voice was strong and clear as he called from the front door of the cottage. 'Welcome to my humble abode!'

We met at the boundary gate, which he gallantly opened. He swept a low bow to welcome me. The gesture caused him to hold his chest and wince in pain. Nevertheless, he engulfed me in a bearhug and whispered in my ear. 'My little bastard colonist. How good it is to see you again.'

I pulled back and looked at him; was that a tear?

'Marshmallow,' was all I could muster before my voice betrayed my own feelings for him.

The yapping of an approaching dog averted our attention to the cottage where Cornelia and Reggie Junior stood watching our pathetic display. Mikey playfully jumped about our legs, yapping incessantly.

'Reginald! Are you going to stand there all day or are you going to bring our guest inside for tea?'

Wills took my valise in one hand and my arm in the other. 'The mistress has spoken. Come.'

Yes, my world had indeed changed.

Cornelia no longer saw me as a rival for her husband's affection but as what I truly was: a friend, a colleague and a brother-in-arms. She actually spoke to me, albeit reservedly, showing interest in my native country and my travels.

I stayed a few very pleasant days with them—days in which Wills and I discussed the final events of the case. He added a few salient facts that had puzzled me, the most pressing was why Quinn had issued a warrant for my arrest.

'That was to flush out the true spy,' Wills explained. 'I only found it out recently when both Quinn and Hawthorne paid me a visit. I was as confounded as you as to why he had done that.'

'I know Humphries went over the edge and killed his wife,' I said. 'What caused it?'

'Many factors. Firstly, he was already prone to rages which medication helped to inhibit. He had a suspicion that his wife was having amorous affairs while he was on campaign. When a cannon blew apart in South Africa and shrapnel tore into his abdomen and groin, he could no longer function as a husband and that only added to his rage and suspicions. Quinn said they could find no evidence that Mrs Humphries had ever been in the company of other men and concluded that Humphries was delusional.'

'Poor Mrs Humphries.'

'Scott uncovered the connection between Smith and Humphries. Captain Gregory Smith was in Major Hawthorne's company and was cashiered, as you know. But Smith wanted to get back at Hawthorne for not supporting him at his court martial and, when Humphries knew of 'Dickie' and his fate, he contacted Smith and propositioned him. Smith should have been satisfied as a printer's assistant rather than going down the path of vengeance. Like someone we know.'

Wills gave me a stern look that I avoided. 'What about Henry?'

'Henry? Ah, Henry,' Wills said fondly. 'He saved us both. If it hadn't been for him …'

'He wants to be a detective,' I said admiringly. 'He's certainly perceptive enough and quite a quick study.'

'A real-life Sherlock Holmes, eh?' He chuckled.

'I want him to have a bit of a head start. I've set up a passbook account in his name to help him when the time comes. A hundred pounds.'

'A hundred pounds! That's a hell of a lot of money—' He stopped mid-sentence, then continued. 'Is this from … ?'

I nodded. 'I sold one of the stones. Might as well put some of it to good use.'

While officially frowned upon by those in command, a blind eye was generally turned to whatever spoils were quietly 'confiscated' during wartime.

'Would you speak to his father?' I asked.

'Of course,' Wills agreed. 'I'll see to it before Christmas.'

'I've tendered my resignation.'

'Well that won't work. You're in my employ, not theirs.'

'And so?'

'You'll be back,' he said with confidence.

***

He could be right. The world was rapidly changing; there was insurrection everywhere in the British Empire. And my ghosts from the Middle East and Australia might not stay dead and buried.

But now, striding through the magnificent gardens towards Lilyfield Manor on a chilly winter's day, my heart was filled—not with dread, but with eager anticipation.

My past held secrets, my future, uncertainty. But my present held peace—and the unqualified love of a woman.

My pace quickened.

I reached the steps just as the front door opened.

Lady Katherine emerged, wrapped in a cloak against the brisk evening air, her cheeks flushed and her eyes sparkling with welcome.

We met halfway. She opened her cloak and her hands reached out for me and drew me into her warmth.

I felt as though I had come home.

'You're late,' she whispered.

Our lips met.

In that moment, my past died and my future was reborn.

Acknowledgements

My sincere thanks to the many who tirelessly helped, guided and encouraged me in getting this thing out of my brain and onto the page. Without you, this book would not exist.

To my editor, Ellen Spooner—your belief that this story was worth telling gave me the encouragement to persist. Thank you for your unrelenting guidance, your insight into character and plot and your precise counsel; holes were filled, passive voices weeded out, and superfluous adjectives and adverbs consigned to the dustbin. You helped me more than I could ever express.

To my beta readers and critics who, over the years, pushed me to write one more chapter, one more paragraph …

Sue Morey, my number one fan, whose enthusiasm kept me going when I wanted to abandon the book two-thirds of the way through. She's earned her coffee—and a million thanks besides.

Joan Fayle, whose medical knowledge, grammatical expertise and interest in what I was doing, helped me to smooth out the bumpy bits. To her, a warm and fuzzy blanket of gratitude.

Barb Cromie, screenwriter, published author, journalist and unstinting time-giver, who read, reread and re-reread every word and helped me polish my bits of rough-hewn rubble into something smoother. A 'thank you' simply is not enough. I am deeply indebted to her and her generosity of spirit.

Kathryn Gallagher, avid reader, who gave solid encouragement to continue and who introduced my words to her group—Sue Smith and Maria Power—who, in turn, affirmed this story was worth telling.

Terry O'Brien and Michelle Fröhlich (O'Brien) for their valuable input into the German dialogue between the Schwartzman family members, and for saving me from embarrassment.

Pamela Morrissey, published author, actor and fellow-writer from the Australian Writers' Guild for her positive critiques of this and other scribblings.

June Rogers, Executive PA and wordsmith, who appraised my words from the other side of the continent. My sincere thanks.

Irene di Bona, generous with her time, who read parts and chapters as I churned them out. Many thanks for her persistence and feedback.

Helen Raik, Kim Raik and Elizabeth Chan, who all read very early versions of the manuscript and who gave positive feedback.

AJ Collins and her beta reader Liz who diligently went through the very first versions of this endeavour and who were most encouraging.

I am also very grateful to my fellow-writers from the Australian Writers' Guild, who first heard my ideas about this story and helped me give it shape and substance in its early stage.

And, of course, the Internet and its myriad fabulous websites: Wikipedia, Internet Archives, Trove, Collins English Dictionary, Roget's Thesaurus et cetera, et al, where so much information was distilled to give my voice a measure of authenticity.

And finally, to Rebecca Victoria Davies, a figment of my imagination, who became the champion of the dispossessed and the voiceless and a vindicator of wrongs against women and children, born innocent and propelled into a downward spiral by the choices she made. She emerged from the pages as a hero true to herself—as I could only wish for myself to be.

For Peter A Cross, who believed in me.

About the Author

Susanna Bonaretti is a writer whose creative work has long centred on performance—short films, musical theatre, and song lyrics.

Cut on the Bias, her debut novel, began as a television mini-series concept but soon evolved into a sweeping historical narrative when its protagonist refused to be constrained by twelve episodes.

Fascinated by strong women on screen (think Salt, Xena Warrior Princess, Wonder Woman and, yes, even Calamity Jane and Lucy Ricardo—and so many more), Bonaretti set out to explore how one particular young woman might respond to brutality inflicted on the vulnerable. The more unchecked the violence, the more vengeful the justice—and the deeper the downward spiral. What began as an impossible television project, with its ambitious scope and period detail, ultimately found its true form as a novel.

Italian by heritage, Australian by choice, and an Anglophile by cultural passion, Bonaretti draws on her love of Australian colonial history and Edwardian England. Her writing blends meticulous research with emotionally resonant storytelling, revealing the frayed edges beneath the official record.

She lives in New South Wales.

susannabonaretti.com